CLOAK & DAGGER

Book II
of
The Dragon Mage Trilogy

Carey Scheppner

authorHOUSE®

AuthorHouse™
1663 Liberty Drive
Bloomington, IN 47403
www.authorhouse.com
Phone: 1-800-839-8640

Published by AuthorHouse 5/28/2014

ISBN: 978-1-4969-1465-1 (sc)
ISBN: 978-1-4969-1464-4 (hc)
ISBN: 978-1-4969-1463-7 (e)

Library of Congress Control Number: 2014909353

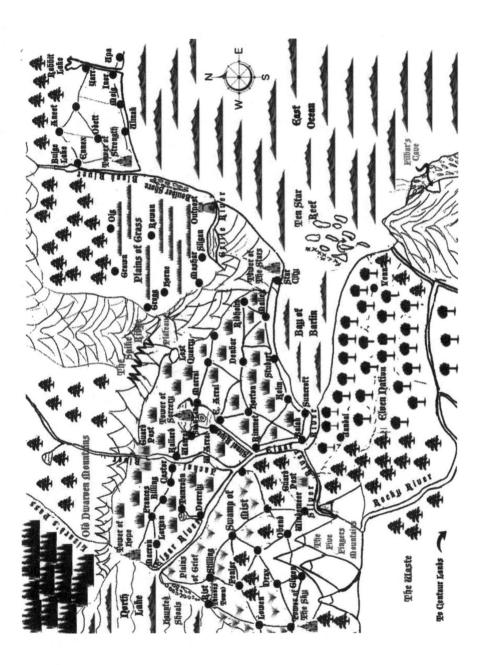

Table of Contents

Part 1

A Sinister Plan

1

Chapter 1

"A re you sure it will work?" hissed Gif.

"Of course!" hissed Garf in response. "I tested the spell this morning."

"It had better!" hissed Frag enthusiastically. "I've been itching to see what our uncle has been hiding in that study!"

"What if he finds out?" whined Gif.

"Just don't touch anything," retorted Garf. "If nothing's out of place, he'll never know we were in there."

"Besides," added Frag, "Graf's our uncle. He won't hurt us!"

"I don't know," muttered Gif.

"This is it," announced Frag as they stopped in front of a dark door set in an alcove to one side of Graf's living room.

"I still think -," began Gif.

"Shh!" interrupted Garf. He pocketed the pick he had used to gain entry into Graf's home. "I need silence for this spell to work!"

Gif and his older sister waited silently while Garf cast his spell. The door shimmered and the protecting ward on the door melted away.

"There!" whispered Garf excitedly. "I told you it would work!"

Frag reached for the door handle and turned. Silently, the door swung inward, revealing a large room adorned with a wooden table and chair and many shelves crowded with a wide variety of magical books, vials and components.

Gif's mouth dropped. "Wow!"

Garf grinned evilly. "What do we check out first?"

Frag was already by one of the book shelves. "Look at all the spell books! No wonder Graf is such a powerful spell caster!"

"I've never even seen some of these spell components before!" exclaimed Garf from the other side of the room. "I wonder what this black liquid is."

Gif, not wanting to venture too far into the room, spotted a wooden box on the nearby table and approached it slowly. Cautiously, he lifted the lid and looked inside. "Hmm. I wonder what this egg is for."

"Egg? What egg?" said Frag. She ran up to the table and shoved Gif aside to see for herself. "It's cracked!"

"What's cracked?" asked Garf. He strode up to the table and gazed into the box. "You idiots! That's not just an egg! It's a dragon orb!"

"Dragon orb?" asked Gif.

"Are you sure?" asked Frag.

"Of course!" retorted Garf.

"Well, it's broken anyhow," said Gif.

"Not necessarily," said Garf. "Remember the human necromancer Graf told us about? He activated a broken dragon orb and turned into a bone dragon!"

"He also told us it was pure luck it turned out that way," said Gif. "Graf said that the magic stored inside a broken dragon orb is unstable."

"It's only a small crack," mused Frag. "Maybe it's not completely broken." She reached for the orb.

"Let me!" interrupted Garf. He tried to reach past his younger sister's hand.

"Wait!" exclaimed Gif at the same instant. He anxiously reached out to stop them. "You told us not to touch -!"

It was too late. Frag's hand contacted the egg at the same time as Garf's, and Gif was holding Frag's wrist when it happened. A vibrating sensation traveled from the damaged orb up the trio's hands and into their bodies.

"L-let go!" stammered Gif.

"I - I can't!" cried Frag.

"S-something's happening t-to us!" hissed Garf. "My - my body is changing -!"

Suddenly, the vibrating turned violent and a bright flash engulfed the three young lizards.

"Nooo!" they shrieked together.

Then, as suddenly as it began, the light and vibration dissipated.

Frag looked from one side to the other at her brothers. "Would you guys mind giving me some space?"

Graf tried to pull away and found he could not. He looked down and his eyes opened wide in shock.

Gif gasped and drew Frag's attention. She saw her younger brother looking down as well. She looked down herself and stared when she learned what the others had already discovered. Protruding from what felt like her own body was her brother's neck and head. She spun her head and stared into the face of her other brother, whose head also protruded from the same body. Dazedly, she looked down at her grotesquely deformed body.

The body was green like a lizard's, but shaped like a dragon's, with two large, clawed hind feet, and two slightly smaller ones in front. The front claws, however, were pressed to the ground due to the massive bulk of the body, which was a thick bunch of muscles used to keep the three necks and heads in position.

"What happened?" wailed Gif.

Frag spun on her brother's head. "Shut up!" She turned to her other brother. "You're the magical genius! How do we get out of this?"

"There are some spells I could try," said Garf, "but I haven't got any hands to cast them with." He looked down with a worried expression.

Frag swore.

"At least our heads are unaltered," said Gif.

Frag turned to yell at her brother again when a high-pitched, hysterical voice cut into her thoughts.

"Free at last!" it intoned. "Not the way I expected, but it will do."

"What are you talking about?" demanded Frag, rounding on her older brother.

"I didn't say anything!" protested Garf.

The voice chuckled.

"This isn't funny!" shrieked Frag, turning to glare at Gif.

"It wasn't me!" wailed Gif, drawing back.

The voice laughed again.

"Garf!" snapped Frag, rounding on her older brother again.

The voice laughed hysterically. "This is too much! But a small modification should make things even more interesting."

Suddenly, another change began to take place. This time the three heads began to transform. The pointed lizard heads became longer and wider, and the nostrils grew in size. Teeth appeared in the mouths, growing to several inches, and jaw muscles grew and tightened around the massive jaws. The front legs also grew in size to better support the bulky body, and the claws stretched to curved, razor-sharp tips.

Frag, whose head was in the middle, panicked, and began snapping at her brothers, who retaliated in kind.

The voice laughed gleefully at the exchange. This was what it needed to maintain control of the body. As long as at least one head of the hydra was at odds, they all would be under the orb's control. Only when the three heads were in agreement could the hydra act on its own.

The voice chuckled. A hydra was a powerful creature. It was strong, intelligent, and, more importantly, magic resistant . . .

×　×　×　×　×

It was dark as Alric the elf slunk along the streets of Greenwood, avoiding lighted areas and noisy inns. He was on a mission; two missions in fact. One was on behalf of the Dark Magic Society to which he belonged; the other on behalf of the thieves' guild, of which he was also a member. He was proud of the fact that he was a member of both organizations, using one skill to aid or enhance the other. Among both guilds, he was respected and looked upon as an expert. More importantly, he was able to keep secret the fact that he was a member of both guilds. No one knew this but he, and he aimed to keep it that way.

Now, as he skirted past another inn, he concentrated on the tasks at hand. The dark magic society was an organization dedicated to the use of dark or 'offensive' magic used for the benefit of the elven nation. They had sent him to visit the lone human living in the community to see what he could learn about humans' magic. He was to do this without drawing attention to the society.

Similarly, the thieves' guild had endowed him with the task of finding a valuable magical item that could be sold to an interested merchant who was in town.

Alric figured he could do both tasks at once if he was careful. The elf decided that, instead of talking to the human mage directly, he could learn more if he studied the mage's books and scrolls. To do that, he would have to break into the mage's dwelling, a simple task for one with his abilities. But as long as the dark magic society was not exposed, they didn't care how he performed his duty. Then, while he was in the mage's house, he could easily grab something magical for the thieves' guild and be off.

The thief knew that this might not be an easy task, since it was a powerful human mage whose house he was going to break into. But he lacked any sort of excitement of late, and the challenge was welcome.

Alric lifted the hood of his green elven cloak to cover his chestnut brown hair. His face was well hidden in the hood, hiding even his dark brown eyes. Rounding the last corner of town, the elf stealthily maneuvered along a narrow path that led to a residential area where the houses were separated by thick woods. No one was about, which was fine by Alric. He continued past several houses until he sighted the mage's house. The structure was dark except for a small light in one of the windows. It was on an upper level, but Alric spotted a large tree nearby. Its branches were fairly high above the ground, but it would be an easy climb for those who could reach. Alric was slightly taller than average, with a slender build and brown hair. He was used to using his agility on a daily basis. Thus, this task was easy for him to accomplish. Deftly, he swung into the tree's lowest branches and climbed up until he could see through the window.

Seated at a desk was a female elf, whose long, golden locks of hair shone brilliantly in the firelight. The fireplace roared cheerfully, and the room was filled with shadows dancing playfully on the walls. The elf appeared to be reading one of several ancient tomes which were stacked to one side. The candles on each side of the table sputtered as they neared the end of their life span, the excess wax running into thick puddles in the trays beneath.

The female elf noticed this with a start and extinguished the flames before they drowned in the liquid wax. Then she put a marker in the book she was reading and closed it, shoving it next to the others. With a yawn, she approached the fireplace, opened a vent into another room, and departed.

Alric waited for a few moments and light suddenly appeared in an adjoining room. The thief crept along the tree's branches and stretched over to see inside. The female elf was visible carrying a lit candle she had obtained elsewhere in the house. She strode over to the wall to open the vent where the back side of the fireplace in the study was located. She rubbed her hands together for warmth and then walked over to the bed. The elf was about to climb under the covers when she paused. Suddenly, she approached a closet and withdrew a nondescript grey cloak.

What happened next nearly made Alric fall out of the tree, for, as the elf donned the cloak, she disappeared!

Alric scrambled to regain balance, and when he looked through the window again, he saw the bed covers lift of their own accord, and then lower into position around an invisible form.

The thief couldn't believe his luck. An invisibility cloak! With an item like that, the possibilities were endless! He could become the greatest thief who ever lived! Had he not seen it with his own eyes, he would never have suspected the cloak's value. Except for checking its pockets, he wouldn't have even given it a second glance!

The problem was - how could he get his hands on it? He could threaten the golden-haired elf by holding a knife to her throat, but that was not his way. His way was to steal without the owner knowing who stole from him or her. Better still, he preferred to steal without the owner knowing that something was stolen in the first place.

Alric thought about this as he crept back to the study window. He still had work to do, and the night was young. Apparently, the mage was not home. Good.

The tree's branches were solid near the window and Alric easily slid it open and lowered himself inside. Once his feet touched the floor, he immediately padded across the room to the bookshelf, his pigskin clad feet making no sound.

The books were arranged alphabetically, and, using the waning light from the fireplace, Alric scanned the bindings to search for books dealing with black magic. He soon found an entire section on magic.

The thief quickly whispered a 'spell detect' spell to indicate any wards or traps. There were none. Still, Alric was careful. Gingerly, he began to pull one book from the shelf, but stopped in horror when he noticed a light green aura behind the book in his hand. Alric swore under his breath. The crafty human mage had hidden the ward along the BACK of the books! Any book leaving the bookshelf would alert the mage to an intruder!

Sweat poured down Alric's face as he examined the aura behind the book. The spell was unbroken! Alric gently pushed the book back into position and breathed a sigh of relief. That was close!

The thief cast an antiwarding spell on the books and tried to remove the book again. This time, the green aura was gone and the book was safe to remove from the shelf. Alric flipped rapidly through its pages and sighed. There was nothing of interest here. He returned the book to the shelf and tried another one. This one was filled with complicated spells and incantations, most of which were too complex for him to understand. A third book was more informative, listing the proper spell components and incantations for simpler spells. Alric studied some of these for nearly an hour, familiarizing himself with the magical techniques used by human black mages. There was enough here to make a decent report to the dark magic society.

Alric closed the book and returned it to the shelf. Then he scratched his head. He didn't know how to restore the special ward the human mage had set around the bookshelf. He thought vaguely about trying to find the spell in one of the magic books, but decided against it. It would probably take too long to find, not to mention he likely didn't have the spell components for that particular spell anyway. The bookshelf would have to remain unwarded. There was no helping it now.

The thief scratched his chin as he thought about his next task. How could he get that cloak? Then he grinned. Of course! The thieves' guild never told him exactly what to get! Any magical item would do! As far as the cloak was concerned, he could steal it anytime for his own use!

The elf looked around the room for an alternate item to bring to the guild and spotted a dark wooden box on the mantel above the fireplace. Beside it was a portrait of the human mage standing with his elven wife. He had seen the mage before; humans were not commonly living within the elven lands; and he studied the picture for a few moments. The humans were quite ugly from an elf's standpoint, and Alric wondered vaguely why the elf was attracted to the human. Pushing the question aside, the elf checked the box for a magical signature and found one. Good. After being certain there was no warding protection, Alric slowly opened the box and peeked inside. The only thing in the box was a single gold coin. Curious, the thief picked up the coin and examined it but found nothing out of the ordinary. Then he placed the coin in his palm and closed the box, returning it to its original location. When he returned his attention to his hand, he blinked in surprise. The coin was gone!

Alric searched frantically around the floor to see where he could have dropped it when an idea occurred to him. He straightened and reopened the wooden box. As he suspected, the coin was back inside the box. He grinned. Perfect!

With the box tucked safely under his cloak, the thief left the house the way he had come, pleased with the night's work, but knowing he would soon return for one more thing.

Chapter 2

The thieves' guild master complimented Alric on his successful acquisition. "You've done well, Alric. Few could have acted so promptly and efficiently. This is a fine magical specimen. The merchant will be pleased."

"I live to serve the guild," said Alric.

"I wish more of us were like you," said the guild master. He withdrew a pouch full of gold coins and tossed it to Alric. "As you can see, we treat those well who serve well."

Alric was surprised at the large sum he was paid but didn't show it.

"You will be considered for other special tasks in the future," said the guild master.

"I look forward to the challenge," said Alric.

The guild master nodded and Alric was dismissed.

Alric hid the purse of gold beneath his cloak and pretended it was not there. The last thing he wanted was to display his newly earned wealth to a lair full of thieves.

The thief reached the gate leading from the underground lair to the outside world and stepped out onto a narrow, winding bush path. He followed the path for several minutes. The path finally led to some back streets in the city and Alric used an alternate route to reach his room in a local inn. He made sure no one had followed him and then entered the inn.

The innkeeper was not at his desk but Alric didn't care. He took the stairs two at a time to the second floor and went down the hallway to his room.

Once inside, he stashed the sack of gold coins under the floorboards. When that was done, he picked up his overnight bag containing his dark green cloak and left the inn. The dark magic society was having another meeting this evening and he had to give his report to the others.

The dark elf strode quietly from the inn, used his usual changing course, and finally reached the old blacksmith shop where the dark elf meetings took place. He entered the shop and said a secret word to the shop owner, who nodded toward the back. Alric entered a small room in the back, donned his dark cloak, and pushed a wall aside, revealing a set of stairs leading into darkness below. He descended the stairs, drawing the wall closed behind him, and stopped on a wooden platform at the base of the stairs. He spoke a word of magic and a torch on the wall lit up. The mage pulled the torch from the wall sconce and followed a narrow corridor straight ahead. The platform behind him grew dark but the corridor in front of him ended abruptly in what appeared to be solid rock.

Alric spoke another word of magic and the wall of rock began to undulate. Then the mage deposited the torch in an empty wall sconce and spoke his magic to cancel the spell that had activated it. The torch went dark and the elf simply took a step, entering a giant chamber with a stone floor, walls, and ceiling. A grey stone table was the only furnishing in the chamber. Its edges were engraved with magical symbols and diagrams.

Standing around the table and in the background were numerous mages, all hooded and cowled like Alric himself. The reason they dressed like this was to keep their identities a secret. One could be standing next to someone one knew, possibly even a relative, and not even know it. The hooded robes saw to that. As for names, everyone had a false name to identify themselves. Alric's name here was Windoor, a name given him when one of his spells had backfired in an underground study chamber during his studies as a youth. A lightning bolt had accidentally become a strong gust of wind and had blown the classroom door open. The combination of 'wind' and 'door' had given him his name.

The meeting this evening was rather boring and when his turn came, Windoor was eager to give his update on the humans' magic and the methods and components they used. When that was finished, most of the younger mages left to go to the hidden classrooms where they practiced their skills and performed tests for their teachers. The rest of the mages either went home or consulted with some of those who gave reports that evening, wishing to clarify details and facts. Windoor had only two inquiries to deal with before one of the senior black elves came up to him wishing to obtain some information.

The elf identified herself as Sawtooth. She wanted to know how Alric had obtained his human magic so handily, but he refused to give up his secrets. She wore a strange alluring scent that made him want to tell her everything, but he kept his head. After pressing for a little while longer, she left.

Alric waited a few more minutes for any other inquisitive mages and, having none, took leave himself. He left the way he had come, exiting the blacksmith shop and heading back to the inn to get some sleep. On the way, he examined the ring he had taken from Sawtooth. It was golden with a dark green gem in its center. He smiled. She probably just now realized that her ring was missing. Alric was sure she would never guess that it was he who had stolen it.

Alric was too engrossed in his new acquisition to notice a cowled figure that had followed him home from the blacksmith shop. The figure half walked, half ran to keep pace with the agile elf, and watched intently as the elf entered his inn for the night. The figure paused and then melted into the shadows. The elf's speech that night had him curious, so he had followed the elf home. What had aroused his curiosity was the amount of information the elf had gleaned in only two nights. This elf was thorough and efficient. These traits were just what the dark figure was looking for. He needed someone to do a special task for him, and this elf might be the one to do it. He decided to wait and watch awhile longer.

Alric's night was restless, the cloak of invisibility occupying his mind constantly. So he rose early, well before sunrise, and made his way to the human mage's house. There he climbed the tree and looked into the bedroom window. The hollow lump in the blankets indicated the invisible elf's sleeping form.

Alric cursed under his breath. The elf was still wearing the cloak. How was he going to get it from her? He agonized long minutes over what to do. If he entered the study and waited for her to wake up, he could sneak into the bedroom after she left and pick up the discarded cloak, then wear the cloak and sneak back out the study window.

But what if she left the bedroom and entered the study? He would be cornered! Furthermore, what if she kept the cloak on after getting out of bed? He would enter the bedroom and search in vain for the cloak!

There were too many variables. Hiding in the study was too uncertain. He would have to stay in the tree to see what she did first. Then he could decide on a course of action. But what if the sun rose before she got out of bed? Surely a passing neighbor would see him sitting in the tree. Worse still, an elven guard might spot him and he would be in deep trouble! If only he had the invisibility cloak! Alric chuckled quietly. Then he wouldn't be sitting in the tree right now, would he?

Finally the thief decided to wait. Time and darkness was on his side for the moment. He waited for an hour and was about to give up as the sky began to lighten, when the female elf began to stir. Alric tensed. This was it!

The elf stirred again and the blankets rose and then fell flat. The elf was up!

The sky lightened some more, but Alric could sense no movement in the room. Where was the elf? The bedroom door hadn't opened yet so she was still in there, but he couldn't see her! For all he knew, she was staring out the window. She could even be staring at him! Alric's heart was in his throat. To make matters worse, the rising sun was directly behind him, leaving the tree's shadow, along with his own, on the bedroom's floor!

The thief nearly cried out in fright when the elf suddenly appeared at the foot of the bed. She had removed the cloak to change into some other clothes. The cloak was thrown on the bed, visible now that it was not being used. The female elf gave no indication of having seen Alric's shadow on the floor. Alric dared not breathe for fear of moving his shadow.

Before long, the elf left the room. The thief waited to see if she was going to enter the study but she didn't. Stiff from sitting so still, Alric climbed to the study window and eased it open.

A cowled figure in the shadows watched with interest as Alric slid into the study and disappeared from sight.

"I could use such a one! Oh yes, indeed!" it whispered.

Alric peered into the hallway but everything was clear. He slid from the study into the bedroom within seconds. His hands shook with anticipation as he reached for the still warm cloak. He put it around his shoulders and looked down in surprise. He was still visible! How could that be? He quickly located a mirror on the wall and looked into it - and breathed a sigh of relief. He WAS invisible. Only he could see himself. The mirror reflection showed nothing.

The bedroom door suddenly opened and Alric froze. The elf had returned!

The female elf walked past the thief and picked up a hair brush on the mirror ledge. Then she began brushing her long, golden locks.

Alric held his breath and waited tensely as the elf finished brushing her hair. Then she put the brush down to inspect the results in the mirror. "Good enough. There's nobody here to see it anyway." She sighed. "He'd better get home soon." Then the beautiful elf departed the room once again.

Alric waited a few moments and then checked the hallway. All clear. He sprang for the study and bounded for the open window. He had spent enough time in this place! The thief climbed down the tree quickly, shaking the branches in his haste, and landed on the ground with a soft thud. Then he bolted for the nearest cover, forgetting that he was invisible anyway. He rounded a bend in the trail and sighed in relief. He had done it!

"I'm impressed!" said a voice suddenly.

Alric froze. Was someone talking to him? Was he visible?

"Don't worry," said the voice, "I can't see you but I know you're there. Don't try to run away. You'll find that you can't."

Alric tried to turn and face the source of the voice but found he could not. He was bound somehow! "Who are you?" demanded the thief.

"Why, I'm a fellow mage!" exclaimed the voice. As if to back up his words, a dark, cowled figure walked around from behind to face where he thought Alric stood.

"What do you want?" demanded Alric furiously. He was angry that a mage had discovered his secret.

"I need you to do me a little favor," said the cowled figure.

15

"Why should I?" demanded Alric.

"I'll pay you well," said the figure.

"I don't need your money!" growled Alric.

"I'll also keep your little secret," added the figure, prolonging the 's' in 'secret'.

"Forget it!" growled Alric. "The cloak's mine!" He didn't like being manipulated.

The cowled figure nodded as if confirming a suspicion. "Very well. I'll just have to turn you in. The elven guard would love to get their hands on a thief like you!"

Alric swore under his breath. He gave in. "What do you want me to do?"

The cowled figure's face was hidden but it sounded like it was smiling when it answered. "It's quite simple, really. I need you to deliver something to the Tower of Sorcery for me."

"Why can't you do it yourself?" asked Alric.

"I haven't got the - er - skills to enter the Tower of Sorcery undetected."

"What makes you think I can do it?" asked Alric.

"You can't," said the figure.

"Then why ask me to do it?" demanded Alric angrily. His patience was wearing thin.

The cowled figure held up a gloved hand. "You will be able to enter the tower while wearing the cloak, but the tower will not sense you as a human black mage. Thus, you will end up in a holding cell."

"But -," began Alric.

"Then," continued the cowled figure, "the mages will no doubt come to check on their prisoner, but the cell will appear to be empty."

"How -?" began Alric again.

"They will not see you," finished the cowled figure. "In the confusion, you can escape into the tower and deliver my package to the designated drop off point. When you are finished, simply rub the ring I give you for this task and you will be paid for your services."

"That's all?" asked the thief.

"That's all," stated the figure. "Will you do it, or are you more of a coward than I give you credit for?"

Alric thought about his options carefully. He did not want to be turned over to the authorities. That could result in a very long prison term. In the elven realm, prison life was difficult and merciless. Thieves and black mages were dealt with harshly. Black magic was frowned upon by most elves. Plus, Alric was no coward, and accepting a challenge like this would just prove it. "Yeah, I'll do it," said Alric reluctantly. "Just unfreeze me so I can get started."

The cowled figure laughed. "All in good time." He withdrew a small package and placed it on the ground in front of the thief. Then he placed a ring on top of the package. "Do you understand the instructions?" asked the figure.

"Yeah," said Alric.

"I have them written on a note inside the package just in case." The figure turned to go. "The spell will dissipate in a few minutes." He paused and turned back to Alric. "Consider it a service to your Dark Magic Society!" He turned and melted into the shadows, his laugh sounding more like a hiss than a laugh.

Alric stared after the mysterious figure with undisguised hatred and curiosity. Who was the cowled figure, and why did he want him to do this task? It must be very important for him to go to such great lengths to get a complete stranger to do this job for him.

✕ ✕ ✕ ✕ ✕

Kazin allowed the wind to whip against his face as he flew over the elven forests below. The fresh woodland scents rejuvenated his dragon body and he flapped vigorously toward his hometown of Greenwood. Greenwood was a small town just over a day's travel west of Venn, the elven capital, where the king of the elves lived. It was hidden from aerial view just like many of the elven cities because of the dense forest cover. The elves preferred to live within the forest canopy where it was safe and secure from other races. In the past, it was also beneficial to be concealed from dragons, which would occasionally attack in search of food.

But dragons were long gone, mostly disappearing from the world soon after the Dragon Wars a number of generations ago. Fortunately for Kazin, he had found a dragon orb in one of his earliest quests which allowed him to transform into a dragon. It was difficult to master, but he had now become used to it, and it was a particularly useful skill to have at his disposal. It was an extremely rare skill, and there were no other mages that he knew of who had a similar ability. Kazin didn't let this go to his head and made sure he didn't boast about the ability, using it wisely and sparingly. Indeed, it was a dangerous ability that could lead to his destruction if he were to let the freedom and power of being a dragon consume him. The dragon's essence lived within the orb, and could consume the owner of the orb by taking control of his mind and making him do what the original dragon wanted. If the original dragon won out, the human mage would lose control and become a dragon permanently. Without any form of control, the dragon would cause destruction and kill animals and people, and would undoubtedly be hunted down and killed itself. So Kazin was always on his guard when transforming into a dragon, and would change himself back into a human as soon as he could.

Now he was glad to be back home after several stressful weeks of work in the human realm to the north. Most of his work these days consisted of solving land disputes for farm territory. After the last wars over a decade ago, large tracts of land had become vacant as a result of the land owners having been killed and leaving no next of kin to take over their farms.

Kazin knew he was overworked when he nearly lost his temper trying to solve a dispute between two cousins who claimed a third cousin's land was now theirs. The cousins argued aggressively, and Kazin finally made a decision that made neither of them happy. He put the land up for sale and declared the money to be donated to the local food shelter. The final transaction was entrusted to a local farmer, whose land bordered the disputed land. Kazin allowed for a small percentage of the transaction money to go to that farmer for his trouble.

From there, Kazin sent a messenger to the Tower of Sorcery explaining his absence for the upcoming mage meeting. He was taking a much needed vacation, and he refused to wait any longer.

Now he was almost home. Soon, he spotted the town and turned west, lowering in altitude as he neared his home on the outskirts of Greenwood. The dragon came to a running stop as he landed in a clearing. Within moments, he transformed from a ferocious, lightning-breathing dragon into a much smaller, inconsequential human mage. Indeed, at first glance Kazin merely appeared to be a young man with shoulder length blonde hair and blue eyes. One would never suspect that this young man was now one of the most powerful beings alive, with the ability to transform into a dragon at will.

None of this mattered to Della as she bounded through the trees toward the clearing. She had spotted him in the clear skies above and immediately headed for his favourite landing spot. Now she broke through into the clearing and ran for his outstretched arms, her golden hair flying out behind her.

Kazin embraced his elven wife, hugging her close. When they pulled apart, Kazin ran his hand through her soft hair, exposing her pointed elven ears. He looked into her bright hazel eyes and smiled. "It's good to see you again."

Della frowned. "You took your time getting home," she pouted. Then she smiled and kissed him. "But I'm glad you're back."

"Me too," said Kazin. He took Della's arm in his and led her back to their home.

Kazin had deliberately chosen their remote house to escape the suspicious and curious stares of the townsfolk, who still weren't used to a human mage living among them. In a previous adventure, Della had been given a writ by the elven king himself, promising to pay her in some way for her part in that undertaking. She had used that offering to gain her husband entry into the elven realm so they could live together. The elven king wasn't sure that was such a good idea, but granted her wish nonetheless.

Now Kazin and Della lived a relatively peaceful life in the remote community, and only Kazin's continuing work in the north took him away from home. He was working far too much, as far as Della was concerned, but she took it all in stride, knowing that Kazin was needed by those who were less fortunate in the north, namely the humans.

"Are you going to be home for a while this time?" asked Della.

"I sure hope so," answered Kazin. "Why?"

Della hesitated. "Well, something strange has been going on lately. First of all, my invisibility cloak is missing. I know I could have misplaced it or something, but then I noticed something else was missing as well."

"What's that?" asked Kazin.

"The coin box that we store in the study over the fireplace is gone," said Della. "Only, I don't know if it was gone recently or not, because I never really paid any attention to it in the first place."

"Well, I certainly didn't move it," said Kazin. "Why don't we go inside and take a look?"

"O.K.," said Della.

Della and Kazin went upstairs and entered the study. Kazin immediately went over to the fireplace and checked the mantel where the box had originally been.

"No doubt it's been stolen," mused Kazin after a moment. "Did you notice anything else missing?"

"No," said Della, "Unless I missed something."

Kazin nodded and proceeded to check the bookshelves. The books were all there. He checked his warding spells and discovered that one of his shelves was no longer warded. He turned to the elf. "You haven't touched any of the magic books while I was gone, have you?"

Della shook her head. "No. You know I have no use for them."

Kazin nodded. "Interesting. Whoever took the coin box probably tampered with my magic books. I'm surprised they managed to disable my hidden magical warding. The fact that they didn't reactivate the ward means they were either in a hurry, didn't care, or didn't know how it was done." Kazin frowned. "My guess would be the latter. It's not an easy spell to manage."

"What would have happened if they didn't disable the magical warding?" asked Della.

"They would have been put to sleep for a couple of days," answered Kazin. "That would give you time to report the intruder to the elven guard, and hopefully give me enough time to return home to question him or her."

"Well, at least they didn't get away with much," said Della. "I really loved that cloak, though," she added sadly. "It was nice and warm at night when you weren't here."

Kazin put his arm around the elf. "I'm here now, Della. We'll get to the bottom of this."

Then an idea occurred to the mage. "Wait a minute! What if the thief who broke into the study also stole your cloak? If he was put to sleep by my warding spell, he could be lying here right now!" He quickly pulled some spell components from his robe and chanted a spell. Everything magical in the room glowed with a greenish light.

"I don't see anything unusual," said Della. She shivered. "I hate to think that the thief is still around here. It was about four days ago that the cloak went missing. If he were watching me all this time -."

"It was only a hunch," put in Kazin. "I didn't mean to alarm you. Chances are the thief is long gone."

"I hope so," said Della. She shivered again.

"There's only one way to find out," said Kazin purposefully. He withdrew his staff from his back holster and waved it around, scanning each room of the house, as well as the yard outside. He cast numerous spells until everything magical both in and out of the house glowed with a greenish light.

"There's no sign of our intruder or your cloak," said Kazin at last. "He - or she - is long gone."

"Could the intruder have evaded you?" asked Della. "They must have some magical skill if they gained access to your books."

"No," said Kazin. "Not even a mage could avoid a search like this."

Della breathed a sigh of relief. "I hope whoever it was doesn't come back."

"I'll change the enchantments on everything in case they do," said Kazin. "They won't succeed again."

Della finally smiled. She grabbed Kazin by the hand and pulled him into the house. "Let's go inside. I'll make your favorite meal!"

"Mmm!" exclaimed Kazin. "I'm famished! I have the appetite of a dragon." He followed Della into the house and closed the door behind him.

Chapter 3

lric stepped into the Square on Skull Island and for the first time since entering the human's realm was impressed. Unlike the plain, straight streets of the cities along the Simal River, Skull Island had a shifting array of winding streets and roads. All of these roads eventually led to what was known as the Square.

The Square was a busy marketplace, bordered on three sides by vendor shops and on the fourth by the well-known Tower of Sorcery. In the Square's center was a beautiful mermaid fountain. The mermaid stretched its arms out as if to greet passers-by, making all feel welcome. Branching away from the fountain were numerous avenues of carefully tended shrubs, plants, and flowers. Alternating with the vegetation were long, wooden benches where travelers of all kinds could sit and eat, chat, or simply relax.

Alric walked up to the mermaid fountain and admired the expert craftsmanship and design. Whoever had made this statue had gone to great lengths to enhance every little detail, from the scales on the tail to the sparkling blue eyes that stared back at him. The eyes seemed to penetrate deep into his very soul, as though questioning who he was and what he did. The elf shivered and started past the statue, but stopped suddenly and returned his attention to the mermaid's eyes. They still stared back at him. When he moved, the eyes continued to scrutinize him. Were the eyes following him?

Finally Alric shook his head and turned his back on the statue. Ridiculous, he thought. It must have been his imagination. He thought instead about the street value of the mermaid's eyes. Those orbs would fetch a healthy sum indeed! He would have to undertake that project another time.

Before Alric knew it, the Tower of Sorcery loomed up before him. He looked up at the multi-domed tower and was impressed with its flawless obsidian domes. A tapered pinnacle rose from the center of the structure, indicating the heart of black magic in the human realm.

Alric wished his people would accept black magic as humans had - indeed, that was the purpose of the black magic society back home. The elves in general were too peace-loving, and black magic went against their beliefs. It was also against their law. But not all elves agreed with this philosophy, so the black magic society was formed. Over the years, the society became larger and more organized. At present, nearly 7 percent of the elven population was involved in some way with the society. But there was far more work to be done before the society could come out in the open. It would be a long time before black magic was accepted among the elves as it was among the humans.

Now, Alric was anxious to see what was in the vaunted Tower of Sorcery. The mage who had sent him on this errand had told him the invisibility cloak would gain him access into the tower. It was what happened next, however, that concerned him. What kind of dungeon would he be transported to? Would he be able to escape without being discovered? Could he find the drop off point for the package?

All these things flashed through his mind as he prepared to enter the tower. His cloak was in place. Could he do this? He had never backed out of a job before. He wouldn't start now. Alric steeled himself and took one step, then another. Each step brought him closer to the tower's entrance - a narrow tunnel of pitch blackness that supposedly prevented anyone but a mage from entering. With each step he became more and more confident. By the time he reached the tunnel's entrance, he was walking almost casually. He even grinned as he took a final step and walked through the entrance. There was simply a falling sensation . . .

"Are you sure the intruder alarm went off?" asked Arch Mage Dalman. Dalman was a young but serious man with dark eyes and a rather long, pointed nose.

"I'm absolutely certain of it," answered a short, nervous-looking mage. He scratched his bulbous nose anxiously. "I double-checked the rooms but they were all empty."

"Did you go right inside?" asked Dalman. "Someone might have been hiding next to the door where you can't see them through the grate."

"I - I suppose you could be right," stammered the short man.

Dalman sighed. "Come. We will check together."

The short man followed the arch mage down the corridor and had to run to keep up with the taller man's long strides. They arrived at the first of a number of cells where intruders were teleported the instant they succeeded in entering the tower. Arch Mage Dalman removed the spell blocking the door and then unlocked it with a key. As the arch mage opened the door, he spoke a word of magic and caused the entire cell to light up as bright as day. With the exception of the two mages, the cell was empty.

"One down, several more to go," said the arch mage. He turned to the shorter mage. "Why don't you check out the even numbered cells? I'll do the odd ones. As you can see, there's nothing to fear."

"Y-Yes Sir," said the short mage.

As the short mage hurried off, Arch Mage Dalman thought he felt a slight gust of wind pass by him. Curious, he did a magical spell check in the cell but there was no magical signature. Apparently satisfied, he locked up the cell and replaced the spell to block the door. Then he hurried down the corridor to the next odd numbered cell.

Alric looked back over his shoulder and breathed a sigh of relief. He had just had enough room to squeeze by the arch mage and enter the corridor. Had he not moved when he did, he would have been discovered by the arch mage's spell. Worse still, he could have been resealed in the cell and left to die, with no one the wiser - except maybe the mysterious mage who was expecting him to do a job for him. Alric shuddered at the thought.

The thief didn't have time to dwell on this as he caught up with the short mage, who was just entering another cell. Alric waited until the mage was inside before hurrying past the room and down the corridor. He walked until he came to a set of doors barring his way. The doors were unlocked, so he opened them very slowly to see what was beyond. A corridor led up a series of stairs into the blackness. The elf nimbly ran up the stairs and arrived at another door. Beyond lay another corridor, this one considerably wider. Torches lined the walls, lighting the way for anyone who happened along.

No one was around, so Alric entered the corridor confidently. He only went a short distance before reaching an open area which bisected several other corridors almost identical to his own. He approached one corridor entrance and listened. Nothing. Another corridor had faint sounds and, judging by the occasional word he could make out, it was a magic class of some sort. A third corridor had the sound of chairs scraping amidst a murmur of voices. The next corridor was silent, and Alric chose this one to explore. He passed many rooms on both sides. Some doors were open, revealing simply furnished rooms with tables and chairs. Some rooms had their doors closed and the sounds of voices echoed from within.

Alric quickly reached the end of the corridor and was presented with another open area, identical to the one he had just left behind. The thief was beginning to despair of finding his destination when two mages exited one of the tunnels bisecting his own. Holding still, Alric waited as they passed him unknowingly. The mages were joking about the food in the tower's cafeteria. Apparently they were going to get something to eat. A grin spread across the thief's face as he followed the two mages. Perhaps this wouldn't take so long after all.

The trek through the tower had its tense moments as Alric followed his two guides. They passed numerous other mages and Alric had to press against the wall to avoid being walked into on more than one occasion. There was even one time when he thought he had been discovered. An old arch mage paused and turned around when the thief walked past. He looked straight at Alric as though he could see him. The thief held perfectly still, and patience won out as the old mage finally resumed his original course. Alric made a mental note to avoid arch mages if possible.

Finally the thief followed the two mages into the cafeteria. There were quite a few mages seated at the tables eating, studying books, or chatting quietly. Alric paid no attention to them. He looked around for the kitchen and found it across from the entrance he had come in by. Skirting the tables in the cafeteria, he headed for the kitchen.

Several cooks were at work here, and Alric had little room to maneuver to get past them. Finally he succeeded. He headed for the pantry in the back and, as luck would have it, the pantry doors were open. He examined the contents until he found the shelf devoted to the ingredients he was looking for. This was it. Alric reached into his pouch and was about to complete his task when he heard a cook coming up behind him. The thief had to shape his body to the contours of the room as an overweight cook arrived at the pantry shelf.

"It's on the top shelf," said a nearby cook.

The fat one looked up. "Got it." He reached up and picked up a jar of spice. Turning around, he called out, "You'd better order some more spice. This won't be enough for tomorrow's gathering."

"Most of the master and arch mages will be here," said the nearby cook. "We should double our usual order."

"Will do," said a third cook from up front. "I'll write it down right away."

The fat cook by the pantry chuckled. "We'll be working in crowded quarters when we're on full staff tomorrow."

"Not if you take the day off," jibed another cook.

The fat one laughed. "You can't handle the pressure without me and you know it!"

"Very funny," said the other cook.

The fat cook continued to chuckle as he finally left the pantry to continue his discussion in the kitchen, much to the relief of Alric.

Fearful the fat cook would return again soon, Alric withdrew the jar he had been given and placed it on the pantry shelf. The instructions he had been given told him to do just that. The black liquid in the jar seemed out of place amongst the lighter coloured ingredients beside it, but as Alric watched, the liquid changed colour to match its counterparts. The jar itself changed in appearance as well, shaping itself to be identical to the others on the shelf. They all looked alike. He marveled at the magic that had happened before his eyes. Only a powerful mage could create such complex magic. The mage who had sent him on this errand had him curious before. Now he was impressed.

Eager to get out of the tower, Alric rubbed his ring. He wanted to meet the mysterious mage again. He needed some answers.

The sunlight was almost blinding as Alric reappeared in the Square. He was off to one side of the tower, away from the busier areas. Across from him sat the mysterious mage. On the mage's lap was an open book. Beside him on the bench was a small leather pouch. The mage appeared to be reading the book, unaware of the thief's presence.

Alric decided to remain invisible a while longer. This way he might learn something he would otherwise not. Approaching cautiously, he examined what the mage was reading. It was a magic book. The ingredients and incantations for a lightning bolt spell were displayed, but to Alric's surprise, he couldn't read the writing. What language was the mage reading? It was not elven, and he didn't recognize any of the symbols as being common to the human's language. What was it?

The thief had his answer a moment later when the mage reached out to turn the page. Extending from the dark robe's sleeve was a scaled green, three-fingered hand. It was a lizardmage!

Alric tried unsuccessfully to stifle a gasp.

In one motion, the lizardmage snapped his book shut and rose to his feet. "So!" he hissed. "I see you have discovered my identity! No matter. Our business is almost concluded. Have you completed your task?"

"Yes," growled Alric, "but had I known who you were, I would not have done it."

"That is why I didn't tell you," sneered the lizardmage. "But all that is too late now. The task is complete. It is time for me to return to my realm in the mountains to the north. Give me back the ring I lent you and you will be paid for your efforts." He indicated the leather pouch on the bench.

Alric glanced at the pouch. "What was in the jar you had me deliver?"

The lizardmage hissed. "You'll find out eventually. Your Dark Magic Society will thank you!"

"You dirty lizard!" growled Alric. He raised his invisible arm and cast a fireball at the lizardmage. But the fireball struck an invisible barrier and deflected harmlessly aside.

The lizardmage grinned evilly and calmly stashed his spell book beneath his cloak. "You are fortunate, thief. I could kill you easily if I wanted to, but I may have need of your services in the future."

"Never!" screamed the thief in rage.

The lizardmage looked nervously toward the end of the shrubbery, then back in the thief's general direction. "We'll see."

Just as Alric made a desperate lunge at his counterpart, the lizardmage rubbed a ring on his scaly hand and disappeared. Alric landed unceremoniously in the shrubbery behind the bench. When he managed to pull himself clear, he saw two men from the island patrol nearing his location. He saw the leather pouch still on the bench and hesitated only briefly before snatching it up and making good his escape.

As the thief left the Square, he cursed himself for making such a huge mistake. To be manipulated by an elf was one thing. To be controlled by a lizardmage was something else entirely.

Unfortunately, he couldn't undo what he had done. No one would believe his story about getting in and out of the Tower of Sorcery undetected unless he mentioned the cloak, and that he wasn't prepared to do. Even if he did, the irrational humans would probably punish him for his actions and imprison him or something.

The elf could only do one thing to regain his integrity. He could use whatever means necessary to track down the lizardmage and make him pay for his treachery. That much he would be only too glad to do.

The thief headed for the port to make arrangements to sail to Warral. The mountains to the north were where the lizardmage had said he was headed. That was as good a place as any to begin his search.

Then a thought occurred to him. He still had the ring the lizardmage had given him. It was worth a shot. He rubbed the ring, and sure enough, the scene before him changed. The island and the Tower of Sorcery disappeared, to be replaced by a sheer granite cliff. The elf instinctively took a step back and nearly lost his balance. Carefully, he looked down - way down. The landscape below was swallowed up in mist. He examined the precarious ledge he was standing on and gulped. Down was not an option. He checked above and to either side for an exit but found none. His ledge was the only safe place to stand.

Alric grit his teeth. Where was he? Where could he go? He rubbed the ring again but nothing happened. Its magic was spent. Now what? He was just beginning to despair when he spotted a narrow opening in the rock face to his left. It was hard to reach but not impossible. He was still agile enough to make the jump over to the spot. What lay beyond he did not know, but he knew staying put was futile.

With a mighty lunge, the elf sprang across the gap and landed at the crevice entrance. With a short cry of victory, he pulled himself to his feet and stared into the opening. Just as he thought! The crevice was an entrance to a tunnel! Without looking back, Alric strode into the tunnel. Elves normally hated caves and tunnels, preferring open air and trees, but Alric wasn't afraid. He was equipped with an invisibility cloak, his pack still contained enough supplies for a time, and his keen eyesight quickly adapted to the darkness. Besides, he had a score to settle with a certain lizardmage. Nobody had ever gotten the better of him, and the fact that a lizardmage had used him was unsettling. It was time to turn the tables.

Chapter 4

e's right ahead of us!" hissed Lynch. He ran faster and heard the others keep pace. The light at the end of the tunnel started to dim as the seven lizardmen rounded the bend.

"There he is!" cried Lynch. He pointed at the bright orange-red figure, which was in view for only a moment before rounding another bend. "Hurry!"

Lizardmen are not known for their running ability. A short run was one thing, but these lizardmen had been running for more than five minutes, all the while losing ground to their quarry. The long run was taking its toll on Lynch, and before they reached the end of the underground passageway, his legs buckled and he crashed headlong onto the ground. His six companions tumbled unceremoniously on top of him.

A muffled oath sounded from beneath the pile. With some difficulty, the gasping lizardmen disentangled themselves and rose to their feet.

Lynch's face was savage as he looked down the passageway. The red glow of the figure ahead of them had vanished. "You idiots!" growled Lynch. "You let him get away!"

Another lizardman spoke up. "You didn't exactly help!"

Lynch spun on the speaker. "You were supposed to paralyze him! Why didn't you do that?"

"I tried," said the lizardman. "The spell didn't work."

"I told you so," said a third lizardman.

Lynch spun on the third lizardman, who continued, "Elementals are immune to magic. You're wasting your time trying to catch him using magical means."

Lynch was about to respond when he thought better of it. Instead, he said, "Shut up, Lyrr."

Lyrr leered, his unusually long snout bristling with long, pointed teeth.

Lynch frowned and shook his head. One could never tell when Lyrr was leering. His name was certainly appropriate.

"What happened to the vial?" asked Lyrr, his 'leer' vanishing.

Lynch pulled the vial from his pouch. "Right here." He looked at the clear fluid inside the vial and shook it. "There doesn't seem to be any change."

"Do you think it got hot enough?" asked another lizardman.

"You can count on it," said Lynch. "I called upon the forces of fire to heat that fire pit to its extreme limit."

"And called up the fire elemental while you were at it," smirked Lyrr.

Lynch looked at Lyrr. "That was merely a side effect."

Lyrr shrugged and then grinned. "It must have been awfully hot. Even the fire elemental couldn't stand the temperature!"

"Come on," growled Lynch savagely. He started back the way they had come. "We've got several more tests to perform. We don't have time for joking around."

The other lizardmen followed Lynch, and Lyrr looked after them for a moment in the dim tunnel. Once again, he wondered why he was the only one with a sense of humour.

✗ ✗ ✗ ✗ ✗

Tyris risked a look over his shoulder. The orange glow from his body revealed nothing. His pursuers had given up the chase. He slowed to a walk and caught his breath. He didn't know why he had been summoned from the fire pit, but knew it was for no good reason. Lizardmen were devious and foolhardy, and he wasn't about to stick around to find out what they had planned for him. It was fortunate they had tried to stop him with magic. With the exception of summoning - a skill Tyris had thought long forgotten - elementals were immune to magic.

When the lizardmage had cast a spell intending to make the lava hotter, he had inadvertently summoned Tyris himself. Appearing in the pit, Tyris had noticed that the lizardmen had a long chain with a glass vial dangling from it. They had been holding it above the surface of the lava, obviously trying to heat whatever was inside the vial. When the lizardmen had seen the fire elemental, they had cried out to each other, and one lizardman - the one casting the summoning spell – had pulled the vial up from the pit while the others tried to capture Tyris. A nearby tunnel was Tyris' only escape route and he had run as fast as his fiery legs could carry him. He felt magical spells being cast his way but had ignored them. A long chase ensued but he had managed to outrun his would-be captors.

"Now what?" mumbled Tyris. He had been summoned from his home in the fire pit. Now he was in human form somewhere inside a mountain. He looked around. It had been a long time since he had explored beyond his realm. Perhaps some things had changed. Perhaps there were new things to be seen. He smiled. Yes. It was time to go exploring.

Taking one last look back the way he had come, Tyris marched calmly down the passageway, his body throwing off heat, and more important, light to guide his way.

✗ ✗ ✗ ✗ ✗

A few days later, while Kazin was just beginning to relax at home, a knock sounded at the door. The mage answered it and received a scroll from a messenger. He thanked the messenger, went over to the fireplace, and sat down. He opened the letter and began to read. His expression became more serious as he read.

"What is it?" asked Della, who sat across from him watching his expression change. "Who is it from?"

Kazin spoke without looking up. "It's from the tower. Apparently something has gone wrong at the tower but they don't specify what it is. It happened during the latest gathering of master and arch mages. They want me to go to the nearest tower and contact them at once."

Della groaned. "Can't they let you have some time off? They're working you to death!"

"I know," said Kazin dejectedly. "But this time it must be something serious. The letter is signed by Arch Mage Fildamir."

"Why didn't Arch Mage Krendal sign the letter?" asked Della. "He's usually the one who contacts you for your assignments."

"That's what has me worried," said Kazin. "If something happens to Krendal, Fildamir is the next in line to take charge. He's older than any of the other arch mages, and next to Krendal, he's been an arch mage the longest."

"So you think the letter is about Krendal?" asked Della.

"Perhaps," said Kazin. "I'll have to go to the Tower of the Stars to find out."

"I'm coming with you," said Della firmly.

Kazin looked up at his wife sharply. "What for?"

"I'm tired of moping around at home alone for weeks on end," said Della. "I'd rather be gone with you. Besides, Krendal might seem like a sinister, bad-tempered old man to most people, but I like him. I'm coming and that's final." The elf looked directly into Kazin's eyes and defied him to argue.

Kazin grinned in spite of himself. "Well, O.K.," he conceded. "I suppose it wouldn't hurt if you came along this time."

Della nodded satisfactorily. Her expression was serious. "Fine. I'll start packing."

The next morning, Kazin cast an enchantment on their house to prevent any intruders from entering. Della informed the elven patrols to keep an eye on their house as an additional precaution. Then the dragon and his elven passenger sped across the Bay of Barlin. They arrived just east of Star City in the evening of the same day and landed in the courtyard of the Tower of the Stars.

The tower was high up on the mountainside overlooking the city to the west and the Bay of Barlin to the south. From here, one could view the islands far out on the horizon. These were the islands of Ten Star Reef, a dangerous place for most ships to navigate around.

As for the city, it was a large, bustling port, with buildings and warehouses lining the shore. Just behind them were row upon row of shops of all kinds. Residential buildings extended beyond these to give way to the fields of farmers. These tracts of land were neatly arranged and looked like giant green squares in a checker board design. Just below the tower were the houses of wealthier merchants who preferred to live above the city and away from the working class. Long gravel roads wound down the mountainside connecting the tower to the city. The setting sun bathed the city in a pleasant red hue and Della and Kazin lingered for a moment to take in the sight.

Some young mages came out of the tower and watched in awe as the elf disembarked and the dragon transformed from a giant reptile into a young, ordinary human. As Kazin approached, they quickly gave way when they saw the insignia on his cloak and realized that he was an arch mage.

"I wish I could do that," said one mage after Kazin had passed.

"Don't be silly," said another mage. "Only arch mages can transform into a dragon."

"You're wrong," said third mage. "You have to have a dragon orb to do that."

"How do you know?" asked the first mage.

"I read it in the library."

"Interesting!" said a fourth mage.

The mages watched in fascination as Kazin and Della disappeared inside the tower.

The mage and elf passed numerous paintings in the halls displaying scenes of battles that were fought generations ago. Many of them graphically portrayed close ups of dragons that fought each other and spewed their fire onto the forces on the ground. Even after all these years, their colours and images were crisp and clear.

Benjamin, a middle-aged master mage entrusted with the undertakings of the Tower of the Sky, came down a set of stairs and saw them at once. When he recognized Kazin, he smiled and opened his arms in greeting. He welcomed the two visitors enthusiastically and immediately led them to the orb room, where communication between the various towers was possible.

The orb room was simple, with a small table, an ordinary wooden chair, and a small pedestal on the table containing a clear, crystal orb. Benjamin magically activated the orb and a young, dark haired master mage appeared within its depths.

"Oh - Hi!" he stammered abruptly when he saw Benjamin and Kazin within his orb in the Tower of Sorcery.

"Good evening," said Benjamin. "Please go and fetch Arch Mage Fildamir."

"Y-Yes, Sir," said the young mage. He disappeared from view. A few minutes later Arch Mage Fildamir appeared. His expression was serious and his face was pale and drawn. When Kazin had last seen him, he was tall and proud, and he had a magical aura that one could almost sense whenever he was around. Now he looked frail and feeble.

"Fildamir!" exclaimed Kazin. "You look awful!"

"Hello, Kazin," said Fildamir. He coughed. "I'll wager I look better than I feel."

"What's wrong?" asked Kazin. "Where's Krendal?"

"He's sleeping at the moment," said Fildamir. "He's suffering from the same deadly illness that has taken the lives of nine master mages so far."

Della, who stood nearby, gasped in horror.

"So far?" pressed Kazin.

"Yes," said Fildamir. "Almost everyone who was at our latest gathering is suffering from this illness, including me. Someone has managed to poison our food, and the clerics are helplessly trying to find a cure. We tried to isolate which foods it was that caused this outbreak, but without success." Fildamir coughed again. "You're fortunate that you didn't show up, Kazin."

"Is this illness inevitably fatal?" asked Kazin with obvious concern.

Fildamir nodded. "Everyone who was affected continues to weaken, and some have even lost consciousness. No one has reported an improvement in their health. This illness is deadly, and time grows short to find a cure."

"Cure," murmured Kazin. "You say the clerics are working to find a cure?"

"Yes," said Fildamir. "But their efforts haven't paid off yet. I've even contacted Arch Mage Valdez in the north in the hopes that the clerics and druids up there can help."

North of the Old Dwarven Mountains was a land of humans and barbarians. This land was physically cut off from the rest of the human lands by the mountains. The mountains were impassable unless one could fly, and only a few magical portals connected the two realms. Kazin was the only human who was able to activate the portals, and work was being done to try to find other ways to bridge that gap. Arch Mage Valdez was an advisor to the queen of that region, and had accompanied Kazin on his previous quest in order to get to this new land. Now he was trapped there, by his own choosing. As for the queen herself, she was a druid, who had also helped Kazin on the previous quest. With magic new to the realm, the new queen, called Milena, had put in place a number of academies which determined whether any of the northern residents could cast spells related to white or grey magic. White magic was healing and defensive in nature, while grey magic was a combination of black and white magic, with black magic being offensive in nature. Grey magic was more versatile, but was considerably weaker than either white or black magic by themselves. Having skill with the different and more powerful magic of druids, the queen had also attempted to find anyone who could cast the magic of druids, but that was unsuccessful. After a decade of work, she had succeeded in finding a sizeable number of individuals who could cast white or grey magic. Most of them had the ability to cast the magic of grey mages, but amazingly, some of those people could even do some of the rudimentary druid spells as well, with limited strength, which was common to grey magic. So the training began in earnest, and Milena had made sure to have them trained in the druid magic whenever possible.

"What do you want me to do?" asked Kazin.

"You and Valdez are the only remaining arch mages that are not affected by this poison," said Fildamir. "That means that you and he must continue to run the mage guild if we fail to survive. I want you close should it come to that. However, we're not dead yet, so in the meantime I want you to go to the Tower of Hope to assist the clerics there in finding a cure. Keep in close contact with Valdez in case he comes up with anything. But whatever you do, stay away from the Tower of Sorcery. I don't want you getting sick too. As far as we know, the illness isn't contagious, but I'm not taking chances."

"I understand," said Kazin.

"I'll send word to my king to send some of our healers to the Tower of Sorcery," offered Della. "They use different herbs and techniques than your clerics do. They may be able to help."

Fildamir nodded. "We would appreciate any help we can get. Thank you."

"Then we'd better get moving," said Kazin. "Time is of the essence."

"Good luck and Godspeed," said Fildamir. "Lives hang in the balance."

Chapter 5

raf chuckled as he made his way to his favourite place - his study. Some nearby lizardmen eyed the lizardmage warily but dared not interrupt the lizardmage's thoughts. Graf was their leader, his magical prowess a symbol of his rank. The stronger the magic, the higher the rank. Graf was the strongest of the lizardmages, so he made the rules. Few openly dared to challenge Graf's decisions unless they had the knowledge or magical skill to back up their comments. With knowledge, they could make their point without recrimination. With magical skill, they were a force to be reckoned with if their idea was unacceptable - so they wouldn't be rebuked to any great degree.

Ever since his brother's death some ten years ago at the hands of the minotaurs, Graf had plotted his revenge. Not so much on the minotaurs, who were indirectly responsible for Farg's death, but rather on the meddling humans, who had created an uprising that had resulted in the minotaurs changing sides and joining them against the lizardmen. Had that not happened, the humans would have been crushed. The human dragon mage was the one determining factor in all of that, and Graf would never forget or forgive that human for foiling his plans. Humans were the only thing standing in the way of lizardmage supremacy. If they were defeated, lizardmages could take their rightful place as the dominant species in the world. No one could stand against the superior magic of the lizardmen. The elves might resist, but without allies, their numbers were not substantial enough to face the lizardmen on their own.

Many years prior to the last war, a disgruntled human, who had failed to become a black mage due to his penchant for practising necromancy, had wandered into the mountains and stumbled upon the dark magic of the lizardmages, along with a cracked dragon orb. He had taken the orb and several manuscripts on necromancy, and escaped the mountains to come out in a realm where the humans were not familiar with magic. With the orb's help, reasoned Graf, the human had been able to read and study the magic in those evil tomes he had stolen. Combining that with the black magic he already knew, the human had become a powerful necromancer with the ability to raise legions of undead. Those legions he had led against the Tower of Sorcery.

Finding a way to contact the lizardmages, the human had formed a tentative alliance, bringing them in on his devilish scheme. The lizardmen were to cause a distraction while he led his minions against the Tower of Sorcery. The lizardmen agreed to this, having no love for the humans and their magic either.

What the lizardmen hadn't counted on was the delay by the undead troops to attack the Tower of Sorcery. Everything had fallen apart because of that delay, and the rest - well, that's another story.

Graf shook his head. He shouldn't have trusted a human, even if he had the same objective. He had lost his brother because of it. From now on, he would do things his way.

The lizardmage loosened his long ebony robe as he rounded a final bend where the entrance to his quarters lay. He produced a key, entered his home, and cast a spell, lighting all the torches on the wall simultaneously. He didn't stop walking as he did so, heading directly for his study.

When he arrived at the study door, he removed the cowl of his dark robe, revealing his pointed green head and black, sunken beady eyes. His mouth opened slightly, displaying his white, pointed teeth. He half raised a hand to remove the protective ward on the door when he let out a short gasp. The ward was gone! Someone had broken into his study!

A low, guttural growl emerged from his throat, and he clenched his teeth in anger. Whoever had broken into his study was going to pay dearly! With vengeance, he barged into the study, a spell ready on the tip of his split tongue.

At first, he could see no one, but a slight movement at the corner of the room indicated someone was present. Without hesitating, Graf let loose with a fireball, flinging it in the direction of the intruder.

Several shrieks of different tones sounded at the same instant. Graf spun on his victim as soon as the fireball was cast, ready to do battle with the spell caster who had broken into his home.

In the next few moments a multitude of things happened. First, the fireball streaked toward its still-shrieking victim, making the intruder perfectly visible to Graf. On impact, the fireball, instead of doing damage, simply fizzled out and vanished in a puff of smoke. The intruder almost screamed at this point, one voice saying, "Nooo!", while another voice cried, "Don't hurt us!"

The momentary glimpse of the intruder, along with the many voices crying out at once, confused Graf enough that the next spell he was already chanting didn't come out right. At the conclusion of his chant, the intruder stopped shrieking, and a sudden silence descended upon them - along with thousands of large, white feathers.

Graf swore and chanted two quick spells, one to stop the feathers from falling, and the other to cause the wall torches to shine even more brilliantly. His eyes narrowed as he stared at the intruder, who whimpered and cowered in the corner. Each of the heads tried to hide behind the other.

"What - who are you?" hissed Graf angrily.

"Please don't hurt us!" wailed Frag's voice from the middle head. "We didn't mean to break in - I mean enter - er - it was Garf's fault!" She spun to look at the third head.

"Shut up!" snapped Garf. "It was your idea, Frag!"

"And it was your magic that got us in here!" argued Frag.

"And you touched the dragon orb when you shouldn't have!" growled Garf.

"So did you!" snapped Frag.

"Enough!" shouted Graf suddenly. He glanced at the table with the empty box on it and back at the hydra, who cowered in silence. "So! You came in here to snoop around and play with things that don't concern you, eh? Magic is a complex power that novices like yourselves should treat with great caution." He glared at the hydra. "By the way, who broke the ward on the study door?"

"Garf did," said Frag quickly.

"Garf"s head recoiled nervously in anticipation of Graf's wrath.

Surprisingly, Graf grinned. "Interesting! Not many magic wielders could manage that spell properly. I'll have to change the complexity of my warding spells in the future."

Garf breathed a sigh of relief.

Graf wandered over to his table, kicking aside feathers in the process. He examined the empty box, which had housed the damaged orb. "So, you went and touched the orb. How did it happen?"

The three heads began talking at once and Graf had to hold up a hand and command them to stop. Then he pointed at Gif's head. "You! I take it you're Gif?"

The head nodded. "Yes, uncle Graf," whimpered Gif.

Graf nodded and grinned. Gif was usually hanging around his siblings. It was not unusual that the others had dragged him into this situation. Of the three, Gif was the least likely to embellish the account of what had happened. He was the honest one. "Gif, tell me what happened."

Gif anxiously gave an account of their encounter with the orb and the transformation that had followed. "But I told them not to touch it!" concluded Gif, who regarded the others fearfully and drew as far away from them as his neck allowed.

Graf grinned as the other heads hissed at their counterpart but said nothing. He aimlessly handled the empty wooden box while thinking.

After a long, uncomfortable silence, Frag spoke up. "Are you going to change us back again, uncle Graf?"

Graf didn't look away from his box. It was a few moments before the hydra heard the hissing indicative of laughter as far as lizardmen were concerned. Graf was laughing.

Finally the lizardmage sat down and caught his breath. He turned to the hydra. "You really don't know what you've gotten yourselves into, do you?"

"What do you mean?" asked Frag.

"Can't you change us back?" asked Gif with a trembling voice.

"No," stated Graf coldly. "My magic cannot help you."

"Oh, no!" wailed Frag despairingly.

Gif whimpered.

"Can you still cast spells?" asked Graf, looking at Garf's head.

Garf shook his head sadly. "No. I tried. I haven't even got any hands to assist my spell casting."

"No matter," said Graf calmly. "It probably isn't necessary."

"Necessary for what?" asked Frag.

"It isn't necessary for my plan to work," said Graf cryptically.

"What plan?" asked Garf.

Graf stood up. "You'll see." He turned for the door and paused on his way out. "Stay put until I return."

"I'm hungry!" blurted Gif.

"I'll bring back some food," said Graf. "In the meantime, you can try to clean up all the feathers. Just don't touch anything! I shouldn't be too long." He left the study and locked the door behind him. Then he exited his quarters and headed at a brisk pace for the council hall, quietly hissing in laughter.

There was a fair bit of noise in the lizardmen's council hall as the lizardmen debated amongst themselves about recent issues and events. To the untrained ear, the sound was not much different from a snake pit full of rabid vipers.

The hall was a gigantic semicircle with elevated alcoves at the sides and end where Graf and other superior lizardmages sat or stood. Graf had the highest alcove, positioned in the middle of the others. Each of the alcoves was situated so that all of the other alcoves were visible. The only difference was that the lower-ranking lizardmen had to look up at their senior counterparts. The more common lizardmen stood in the middle of the hall, and had to turn to see each speaker above them in one of the alcoves.

Graf waited for most of the major players to arrive before rising and waving a hand for silence. A few minutes later the debating ceased and all turned their attention to Graf, waiting expectantly for him to speak.

Graf licked his lips and began. "The Tower of Sorcery has been successfully poisoned."

There were hisses of astonishment from many in the hall. Graf grinned when he saw the number of disbelievers who had once again underestimated him.

"How did you manage that?" asked a lizardmage to Graf's right, above the hiss of the crowd.

Graf lifted a scaly hand for silence and continued. "As I told you before, my magical power is superior to that of the humans. The slow-acting poison has been planted inside the tower, and it is only a matter of time before it takes effect, if it has not already done so."

"How do you know they will not detect your poison?" asked another lizardman, this time to Graf's left.

Graf sneered. "They are secure in their tower. Why would they check food coming from their own kitchens? They often check food that comes into the tower, but never the food that is already inside! No - they will not discover it until it is too late, and once they do, they will be helpless to find a cure."

There was a murmur of agreement in the crowd below.

Graf turned to a lizardmage near him and nodded. Then he sat down.

The next lizardmage, named Relg, stood up. He was taller than Graf, and his blue-green robe had a sinister sheen to it, seeming to absorb the torchlight where the flickering light should reflect the most. His wooden staff was gnarled and crooked.

"The water elemental has been contained, and my crew of mages no longer need to strain at the summoning spell to maintain control. The elemental is now entirely under our control." Relg glanced at Graf and sat down. There was nothing more for him to say.

The crowd hissed in pleasure as Graf nodded to another lizardmage.

A shorter, stockier lizardman stood up to speak. His robe was black with a red trim. The staff he bore was a chestnut brown, with a unique curve near the top. He had a blunt nose for a lizardman, and his nostrils flared as he spoke.

"The earth elemental has been summoned, but we still have no way to contain it. My mages are working night and day to control it, but our success can only be determined by a source of containment for the elemental. Fortunately, the elemental is under our control for the time being. We can maintain magical control for at least ten days before the elemental can break free. If no containment is found, we will have to regroup and start again." The lizardmage sat down.

There were hisses of disapproval from the alcoves at this unsettling news.

Suddenly Graf rose and addressed the council, looking at each of the superior officials as he spoke. "Narg has done well," began Graf, indicating the black-robed lizardmage. "He has done what he set out to do. It is not his fault that none of you could come up with a way to contain the earth elemental!"

"Neither could you!" retorted a lizardmage in a lower alcove. Sinister hisses could be heard throughout the hall at the comment.

Graf sneered. He had expected this challenge to his authority. Indeed; he had hoped for it. He turned to Relg. "Relg, you have the water elemental under your control. Can you make it create ice?"

"Of course!" hissed Relg. "What do you think?"

Graf ignored the question and turned to Narg. "Narg, can you get the earth elemental to allow itself to be exposed to the water elemental?"

Narg nodded, nostrils flaring. "Certainly."

Graf turned back to Relg. "Then you should be able to create a prison of ice to contain the earth elemental. Am I correct?"

Relg nodded in understanding. "Of course!"

Murmurs passed through the hall but one skeptical lizardmage called out, "I thought elementals weren't affected by magic - other than summoning!"

Graf nodded. "That's true. However, elementals are not immune to each other's magic."

"Are you sure?" asked another lizardman from below.

"Yes," said Graf calmly. "When pitted against one another, their magics cancel each other out. But in this case, the earth elemental will not put up resistance because we presently control it. Once it is imprisoned in ice, the containment will remove its resistance to our magic. Then it will be unable to free itself until we desire it."

Loud hisses of approval sounded in the crowd and Graf sat down, an evil grin spreading across his face. He had made everyone look like fools once again. As usual, it was he who had come up with a solution to a problem that no one else could solve.

After a few moments, another lizardman rose in a lower alcove to speak.

"The council recognizes Lynch," hissed an old lizardmage directly below Graf's alcove.

Lynch took a deep breath. "As you know, the poison Graf has devised has no antidote. Only lizardmen are immune to its effects. My task was to see if extreme heat can neutralize the poison. I took a number of lizardmages with me to a lava flow of intense heat and we increased the magnitude of the heat as far as our magic permitted. There was no effect on the poison."

Lynch paused to allow the council to absorb this information. Then he continued.

"There was, however, a strange side effect to the heat spells we were using."

A few of the senior lizardmages sat up straighter at this news.

"Go on," said Relg.

Lynch looked at Relg as he spoke. "We inadvertently called up a fire elemental from the lava pit."

Hisses drowned the remarks of several of the officials, most of whom stood up to speak at once.

Graf was surprised as well, but didn't show it. He calmly rose and held up a hand to silence the crowd. Then he nodded at Lynch, who continued.

"We hadn't expected the elemental, so we weren't prepared to capture it. It got the jump on us and ran away before we could react."

"It got away!" shrieked Relg, who was one of the officials who had risen when the strange announcement was made. He looked at Graf. "That could be a problem. If it finds out where the other elementals are, it could destroy our hold on them!"

Graf nodded calmly. He turned to Lynch. "Well, Lynch, it looks like you had better locate and capture that fire elemental."

Lynch swallowed hard. "I understand."

Graf smiled deviously. He knew Lynch needed to redeem himself, and this was the only way to do it, whether he liked it or not. Then Graf directed his attention to a lizardmage wearing a blood red robe. "Brind, your fire magic is powerful. Why don't you take on the task of summoning the fire elemental? I know it's harder to summon an elemental who is already in our plane, but that way there are two chances to capture it. We may not need a fire elemental, but we can't have one running loose in our tunnels either."

Brind nodded. "Of course."

"Besides," continued Graf, "the fire elemental could benefit our cause greatly. We could even try to get the air elemental and have all of them help us."

The crowd murmured at this suggestion.

Graf turned to a high ranking lizardmage in a nearby alcove. It was a female lizardmage. She had a bluish tinge that was common to the females of the species. "Narla, you have skill with air magic. How would you like the task of summoning the air elemental?"

Narla smiled, her fishlike lips spreading in a grin. "Certainly! I have access to the spells, and my group has the skill necessary to do it."

"Good!" exclaimed Graf. "You can begin preparations immediately."

Narla nodded.

Graf rubbed his scaly hands together. "Now! We're ready to generate more of my poison and apply it where we discussed. You all know your jobs. Let's get to it!" Graf turned to the wall at the back of his alcove, chanted a spell, and walked through the rock as though it was not even there. The other officials did a similar thing in each of their alcoves, disappearing from sight. The lizardmen in the general assembly area of the hall left via conventional tunnels, leaving the council hall in silence.

Chapter 6

yril sighed as he tended the clerical herbs known as faelora, a pink-leafed plant that thrived in the late summer and early fall. This herb grew naturally in this climate, but was rather scarce in the wild. When planted in the gardens here at the Tower of Hope, it grew in thick bunches, each leaf pressing the others aside for sunlight. Cyril was responsible for making sure weeds did not interfere with the herb's growth. He did his job well in the ten years that he had worked here, tending every form of herb and plant that grew in the tower's grounds.

"Don't forget to water the faelora," ordered the head groundskeeper behind him suddenly.

"Yes, sir," answered Cyril without looking up.

Cyril was tolerated but avoided by everyone working in or for the tower. He was a big man, some six and a half feet tall, with large arms and legs. He had no hair, and his skin had a slight green cast to it. But it was not his size or complexion that drove people away. It was his eye. For Cyril was the by-product of a human and a cyclops.

Cyril's lone eye was that of a cyclops. It was centered in his forehead, and the black pupil was centered in a yellowish background. The eye also mimicked a cyclops' in function as well as appearance. When someone looked into it, the eye had the effect of temporarily paralyzing them. Some would have considered this trait as useful, but Cyril regarded it as a curse.

Even as a boy, Cyril had few friends. Other children made fun of him, but he refused to fight back. By nature he was mild-mannered. Over the course of the years, he had paralyzed a number of people by accident, but each time they had believed he had done it on purpose, and each time he had been punished severely.

Cyril's mother, who never spoke to him about his father for obvious reasons, tired of the hardships facing her son and brought him to the

Tower of Hope at the age of ten. She had little hope of giving him a decent life, and hoped the clerics could care for him. A year later, she died of a severe illness during the winter and Cyril was alone.

Life at the tower was hard, but Cyril was treated with an aloof respect. He left others alone, and they responded in kind. Only Cyril's boss, the head groundskeeper, treated him poorly. The groundskeeper, whose name was Jake, felt that Cyril was merely a laborer, who had no special skills or abilities. The fact that Cyril was deformed only confirmed Jake's opinion of him. Whenever Cyril accidentally paralyzed someone and Jake found out about it, Cyril would have to endure another round of rude comments and remarks by his boss. Despite this harsh treatment, Cyril never once lost his temper and fought back. He simply hung his head in shame and found a quiet place in the garden to hide his embarrassment. No one who overheard Jake's remarks, be it cleric or co-worker, bothered going to comfort him.

Cyril's life was lonely in a sea of white-cloaked people until one day the previous year when he had encountered a young cleric-to-be who had just arrived from the east. She had long, black hair and an enchanting smile. Unfortunately, that smile had been frozen the moment she had looked at Cyril. The cyclops had carried the prone figure into the tower where the clerics had taken over, muttering and glaring at Cyril all the while. Cyril hung his head in shame as usual and returned to his duties outside, where his boss had done his part to make him feel even more miserable.

Surprisingly, the young cleric had come to see him later that same day. She seemed to have taken the incident all in stride, and had been understanding to his situation. She had told him it wasn't his fault and that she forgave him. Cyril had thanked her, but kept his eyes averted, afraid to paralyze her again. Despite the uncomfortable exchange, she had visited him daily, chatting about her studies and asking him about herbs. They had become good friends, and Cyril's boss had to order him to get back to work several times when the visits became too long.

"Hi!" said familiar voice behind Cyril.

Cyril half turned, remembering in time not to look at the speaker. "Hello, Vera," he responded. "How are you today?"

"Fine. You?"

"O.K."

Vera looked around. "Is the boss nearby?"

"He just went around back," said Cyril.

"Good," said Vera, relieved. "He cut our last meeting short."

"We had lots of work to do," said Cyril.

"Oh, quit defending him!" snapped Vera. "He's always working you too hard and you know it."

"Things are going to get busier," continued Cyril. "We have to harvest many of the herbs ahead of schedule because of the situation at the Tower of Sorcery."

Vera sat back. "I heard about that." She fingered the talisman around her neck. "I hope Kazin is O.K."

"Who's Kazin?" asked Cyril suddenly. He took a chance and looked over at her. Fortunately, she was looking straight ahead at the garden.

"He's only one of the most powerful mages alive," answered Vera dreamily. She looked at the talisman at her bosom. "He gave me this talisman. It provides me with fire resistance and offsets most magical fire."

"Why did he give you that?" asked Cyril.

Vera looked at Cyril, who looked away just in time. "He gave it to me when I was a little girl. My older brother, Max, who was a master mage and Kazin's closest friend, had died in a quest, and the Tower of Sorcery awarded my family with this talisman to commemorate his heroic sacrifice."

"How did he die?" asked Cyril.

"A dragon killed him," said Vera sadly. She looked down to hide her sudden tears.

Cyril nodded. "You must be proud of him."

"I am," said Vera. "From that moment on, I wanted to become a cleric so that mages like my brother wouldn't die needlessly like that."

"That's very honourable," said Cyril.

Vera blushed.

"I thought I told you to water the faelora!" said a harsh voice suddenly. It was the head groundskeeper.

Cyril started. "Yes, sir!" The cyclops looked apologetically at Vera's feet as he added, "I have to get back to work, Vera."

Vera glared at the groundskeeper. "Why don't you give Cyril a break? He works hard all day long and all you do is push him to work harder!"

"Vera, don't -," began Cyril.

"He works hard because that's all he's good for!" retorted Jake.

"That's rude!" snapped Vera.

"Vera -," repeated Cyril.

"Why don't you go and spend your time with normal people instead of wasting time with one of my workers?" demanded Jake. "I ought to report you to the high cleric himself. I'm sure he wouldn't approve of a student interfering with the work being done on the grounds. Now beat it while I'm still in a good mood!"

Vera reddened but decided not to push her luck. If the head groundskeeper reported her to the high cleric, she would be in danger of being expelled from the tower. And with the final test that afternoon, she could lose her chance to become a level one cleric. She couldn't risk a confrontation with this evil man right now. Later, perhaps, but not right now.

A bell sounded, alerting the students to return to class. Vera took her cue, said a quick goodbye to Cyril, and headed for the tower. She could feel the groundskeeper's eyes boring a hole in the back of her head as she went.

When the students had all entered the tower, Jake removed his hat and wiped a wet rag across his mostly bald head. "Stupid kids," he muttered. He turned to see if Cyril was listening but the cyclops was already over by the faelora, giving them a good dose of water.

As he left to see how his other workers were doing, Cyril glanced up at his boss' retreating form. For the first time in a long time, he was angry. Yelling at him was one thing. Yelling at Vera was something else entirely. Jake had no reason to be so mean.

Cyril was just debating whether to confront his boss when a co-worker came up to him and told him that Jake was on his way to report Vera to the high cleric.

The cyclops knew all too well what becoming a cleric meant to

Vera. He knew how hard she had worked to get this far. To lose it all now would be devastating, especially if he was partly to blame. It was conceivable that Jake would actually report her to the high cleric, but to do so at such a critical time was unforgivable.

Without responding to the co-worker, Cyril dropped his watering can and scrambled for the tower after his boss.

The co-worker chuckled as he watched the cyclops run. He wished he could be there to see the confrontation, but decided it would be safer to wait for someone to tell him what had happened afterwards. It was amazing how good one could feel after telling a little white lie, especially if it affected two people he didn't particularly care for anyway.

Chapter 7

Rebecca sauntered along the tunnel, her backpack bouncing leisurely on her back. As she went, her dwarven eyes scanned the rock walls for everything from mineral veins to traps. She was happier than she had been in a long time, despite the fact that she was far from the protection of the dwarven realm. Rebecca had worked long and hard to earn respect for her pathfinding and mapmaking skills. First, her uncle, Horst Hammarhold, needed convincing. After many successful scouting missions on behalf of the dwarves who lived outdoors near the top of the mountains, she had proven time and again that she could find and map mineral deposits with extreme accuracy. Prompted by this success, Horst, who was also the community's representative, brought Rebecca's findings before the king's council. Rebecca knew the king fairly well because he and Horst were good friends, resulting in numerous visits where she saw and spoke with the king on many occasions. She called the king 'Uncle Harran' and he didn't seem to mind. When Harran had found out about Rebecca's exceptional abilities, he had immediately appointed her the title of 'mapmaker', which was a title he had worn proudly in the past. Even to this day, everyone called him 'King Mapmaker', to pay homage to his great skill.

After that, the king had given Rebecca more and more tasks, each one more difficult than the last. There were steep rock faces to climb with unknown tunnels beyond that needed mapping, to crossing narrow ledges through lava flows that led to suspected gem deposits. Each task Rebecca had eagerly and successfully completed, with complete maps and gem deposit markings.

The king had been so pleased, that he began making preparations to send Rebecca into lizardman territory. He had his top general, General Manhar, begin training Rebecca in the art of hand-to-hand combat. Within only a few months, Rebecca had been ready to venture into dangerous and unknown territory. Her task had been relatively simple. She had to locate any lizardman lairs she could find, and return to the dwarven realm with a map leading to their exact location, along with information on the approximate number of lizardmen residing there. Then General Manhar would be summoned to take an appropriate number of soldiers to the lair to eliminate the lizardmen. Rebecca was to be extremely careful not to reveal her presence to the lizardmen because if she got caught, no one would know where to find her. She was truly on her own.

The stout female dwarf was asked if she would take on such a task and she told King Harran that she would be honoured. She was aware of the dangers involved, and would take every precaution to avoid being captured. Rebecca had survived many dangers until now. She would persevere.

Now, she walked along with those thoughts in mind. Here she was, almost two days beyond the existing map she had been given to begin her quest. She was truly alone, as the king had said. Yet there wasn't even a sign of a goblin or orc, let alone any lizardmen. She gently stroked the pendant around her neck. It was a magical item her Uncle Horst had given her to help her on her journey. It was intended to vibrate when something or someone magical was nearby. As yet, it hadn't done a thing, and Rebecca wondered if it even worked at all.

Now the dwarf paused and pulled out her large chunk of parchment revealing her new map. She scratched her head for a moment before carefully drawing an addition to it. There was a fair amount of drawing to be done to compensate for the past half hour or so, but her memory was good enough to correctly draw out details and distances. She had passed only a few tunnels branching off in different directions, and was sure to mark their locations. She could have investigated and mapped out where they led to, but chose to stay in the main tunnel. It seemed to send her deeper into the mountain and farther away from the dwarven realm, where she decided it was more likely to lead her to a potential lizardman lair.

After finishing the map, she folded it up and tucked it back into her packsack to join her crossbow pistol and other belongings. She chose to carry a crossbow pistol because it was light and handy for shooting small rodents for food. A battle axe was a little too cumbersome for traveling long distances.

The dwarf hoisted the pack over her shoulder and slipped her stout little arms through the straps. With the pack secure on her back, she reached up and ran her chubby fingers through her short jet black hair. Some faint glimmering minerals above her in the ceiling momentarily reflected off a unique strip of silver in her hair. At first glance, one would think that Rebecca had a silver brace angled from front to back to hold her hair in place. That was not so. The silver 'brace' was actually a thin strip of silver-white hair that she had sported since childhood. It grew naturally that way, and she was always proud of it.

Rebecca looked up at the glittering ceiling and sniffed. "Fools gold," she muttered. Instantly, she was on her way, bouncing along the path without further ado.

The dwarf traveled for only about ten minutes before almost stumbling past a narrow opening on her right. Another useless passageway, she thought, momentarily sticking her nose into the tight cavity. She was about to draw back into the main tunnel when a strange feeling on her chest made her gasp. She reached for her pendant and was surprised to feel it vibrating in her hand.

Rebecca stepped back into the main tunnel and the vibrating stopped. Whatever had activated the pendant was inside the narrow opening! Now Rebecca was excited. Something magical was in there!

Then a sobering thought hit her. What if there was a lizardman hiding in there? She reacted instinctively, drawing her lightweight fighting axe from the holster at the side of her backpack.

After standing perfectly still for several moments, Rebecca relaxed. If something was hiding in the opening, it would have gotten her by now. She would have to go in and see where the opening led. She had to. It contained magic, so it either led to magic wielding lizardmen, or something down there was magical. Considering it was the only thing of interest to happen in two days, it was certainly worth investigating.

Holding her axe in front of her, Rebecca squeezed herself into the opening. The going became more and more difficult, and the dwarf finally had to sheath her axe to free her hands so she could literally crawl along the tunnel floor.

First, the tunnel became nearly flat, and then it became extremely narrow and tall. All the while, her pendant vibrated more and more against her chest. Still she pressed on, determined to find the source of the magic.

It seemed like hours before the little dwarf squeezed through the final slit in the tunnel to arrive at a wider, room-sized area. The rocks in this location were almost black, and visibility was almost nonexistent, even to the dwarf. Fortunately, she had a fluorescent light stone in her pack. She rummaged around in the pack before withdrawing a fist-sized stone. It glowed with a faint greenish light. She held it aloft and peered around the room, taking a cautious step forward. A faint glimmer beneath her caused her to refrain from putting her foot down all the way. She looked down and saw what appeared to be a bone. Her forward motion forced her to step past the bone onto a safe area of footing, leaving her straddling the bone.

Cursing under her breath, Rebecca brought her other foot forward so she could stand properly. Turning carefully, she investigated the bone and saw the rest of the body as it was sprawled on the ground. Judging by its clothes, it appeared to be a dwarf. The realization that the body was that of a dead dwarf nearly made her retch. It was disgusting.

Turning some more Rebecca could make out the bones of another body adjacent to the first. It was somewhat larger, possibly that of a human. She wrinkled her nose, even though there was no odour. These bodies had been dead for a long time. Both were wrapped in tattered clothing.

Her momentary reverie was broken by the pendant, which was now vibrating quite violently. The magic seemed the strongest when Rebecca was facing the second body.

She started to step past the first body when something caught her eye. The dwarf had been carrying a bag, but the leather had dried and torn open. The items that were within were exposed to Rebecca's light and she could see them fairly clearly. There were gold pieces, a few gems, a dagger, some chunks of coal, and other personal items that one would take on a long journey. But the thing that really caught Rebecca's eye were the well-oiled parchment scraps that were rolled up tightly with a partly disintegrated string. It was a roll of maps! The dwarf was a mapmaker!

Excited, Rebecca reached down and lifted up the maps. She shuddered at the thought of stealing from the dead, but the other dwarf definitely didn't need them anymore. Carefully unrolling the maps, Rebecca was amazed at their detail. She recognized them as showing tunnels and passageways from the entire area that she had been traveling! Even some of the passageways she had skipped had already been surveyed! Some of them even led to gem deposits! Hastily but carefully, Rebecca stuffed the maps into her side pouch.

Then she glanced at the dead dwarf with respect and pity. He was a talented mapmaker. It was a shame he had come to such a sad end. "How did you die?" she wondered aloud. She helplessly looked at the bones and tattered rags and noticed that the dwarf's arm almost pointed to the second body. The rags on that arm appeared to have been burnt.

Following the pointing arm, Rebecca glanced at the second body, which was half sitting and leaning against the wall. The elbows rested on the floor with the arms outstretched ahead of them. The skeleton's lower jaw was hanging and looked as though it was laughing at her. She shuddered and looked down past the skeletal rib cage to the arms and hands. It was then that she noticed the long, serrated dagger in the skeleton's right hand. It contained a jewel-tipped haft. Curious, Rebecca leaned forward to examine it more closely in the light of her light stone. As she drew near, the pendant literally thumped against her chest. The dagger was magical!

Eagerly, Rebecca reached out for the dagger when the image of the dwarf's burned arm appeared in her mind. She looked at it again and realized that there was no hand at the end of the dwarf's arm. It had been burned off!

With a frightened yelp, Rebecca threw herself back and landed with an unceremonious thump on her behind. She shivered as she gazed at the dwarf's dead body. She had nearly ended up just like he did! That dagger was cursed! The dwarf died because he - or she - had tried to grab the dagger! Her heart pounded just as hard as the pendant at her chest. That was close!

56

After a few moments, the dwarf rose to her feet. There was nothing more for her here. The room was at the end of the tunnel. She had no choice but to retrace her steps back the way she had come.

No sooner had she risen to her feet when the strangest thing happened. The human skeleton's lower jaw fell, striking the chest on its way down. This triggered the head to roll to the side and fall on the right arm. As if spring loaded, the right elbow shot forward and the right hand flung the dagger straight at Rebecca's abdomen!

Instinctively Rebecca grabbed for the flying dagger. Miraculously, the dwarf caught the dagger in midair!

With her mouth agape, Rebecca stared at the dagger in her hand in astonishment. An instant later, she dropped the dagger and sprang away from it, landing, once again, on her behind.

For what seemed like an eternity, Rebecca stared at the dagger in fear. Then she crawled forward very slowly, never taking her eyes from the weapon. Soon she was directly above it. One thing repeated itself over and over in her mind. It had not harmed her. Was the curse broken?

Then she came to another realization. The pendant at her chest had stopped quivering! Was the dagger's magic spent? Back when Horst had given her the pendant, Rebecca had asked him about it. Horst, not being very familiar with magic, could only tell her what it was supposed to do. The only other thing the mage who had sold it to him said was that any magical items in your possession would not interfere with the magic. That meant either the dagger's magic was spent, or it now belonged to her.

Rebecca was in a quandary. Should she pick it up? According to her pendant, it no longer contained magic. That meant it didn't have cursed magic either. Conversely, if the dagger now belonged to her, it wouldn't harm her, would it?

She had to find out. Rebecca took a deep breath and grasped the dagger's handle. It quivered in her hand and she dropped it again. She examined her hand. No damage. Good. She picked it up again and felt the quivering but this time held onto it. It was definitely magical, judging by the quivering, but it didn't harm her. She smiled in relief. It was now hers!

Having had enough of this room, Rebecca quickly stashed the dagger and light stone in her side pouch to join the new collection of old maps. With that accomplished, she hustled over to the narrow tunnel and exited the strange room forever. She would discover what magic the dagger was capable of later.

Chapter 8

It would take the better part of four days for Kazin and Della to reach the Tower of Hope. During the early part of their flight, they saw many caravans on the roads below them, each carrying goods to a different destination. The ordinary bustle of activity contrasted with the suffering being endured by the mages in the Tower of Sorcery to the north. Here, people were carrying on with their lives as though nothing was wrong, secure in the knowledge that they were being protected from danger by the mage guilds and the army. They didn't know about the threat of poison that was afflicting the black mages at present. Kazin knew that once word of what had happened at the Tower of Sorcery leaked out, the people would become fearful and concerned for their lives. Their carefree way of life would be shattered.

Kazin's thoughts changed when Della suddenly drew his attention and pointed down at a narrow side road off one of the more heavily traveled roads. A caravan consisting of three wagons was stopped and there appeared to be a number of people skirmishing on both sides of the first wagon. Kazin immediately changed course and rocketed toward the battle.

Suddenly, a number of grey-cloaked people emerged from the woods to the rear of the third wagon. They snuck around the wagons and joined the fray. Della could see them raising their staves and chanting some spells.

Before Kazin got halfway to the scene, the battle had ended. Landing a short distance ahead of the caravan, Kazin and Della watched as some grey mages shackled some rough looking characters who were standing in strange poses.

"They're paralyzed!" exclaimed Della.

Kazin relaxed. "That's right, Della."

"But - what happened?" asked Della. "I don't understand."

"The grey mages are a policing force," explained Kazin. "They use 'paralyze' and 'slow' spells to trap and arrest brigands and thieves who attack caravans and unsuspecting travelers. Then they take them to the nearest town to be given a trial by the town's mayor and a jury represented by the people. Prisons are located in most of the larger communities, where guards are armed with weapons and magic. More serious offenders are imprisoned in a high security magical prison from which there is no escape. One such prison exists on Ten Star Reef."

"But isn't that the job of black mages?" asked Della.

Kazin shook his head. "There aren't enough black mages available to cover all of the roads. Grey mages are invaluable helpers."

"I see," said Della. "With the mages in the Tower of Sorcery out of commission, the grey mages will really have their work cut out for them."

"That's right," said Kazin. "Once thieves find out about the black mages, they'll come out in full force. I hope the grey mages can handle the additional pressure when that time comes."

The dragon remained at the scene to watch the grey mages round up the crooks while the caravan people prepared to continue their journey. When one of the grey mages waved at Kazin, he took to the air once again, sensing that all was well.

"The crooks are going to have to watch out for grey mages if they plan to stop caravans," commented Della, brushing her hair aside as it blew in the breeze.

"That won't be too easy," said Kazin.

"What do you mean?" asked Della.

"Not all grey mages are obvious," explained Kazin. "Many of them travel incognito."

"That's a good idea," mused Della. After a while she sighed and said, "It's a lot more peaceful among the elves."

"Maybe," admitted Kazin, "but there is crime among your people as well. Our house was broken into recently, remember?"

Della sighed again. "I know, Kazin. I know."

The rest of the journey was uneventful as Kazin and Della sped off for the Tower of Hope. Their stops at various inns along the way were short, staying only to sleep for a few hours before continuing on to their objective.

Halfway through the fourth day, the Tower of Hope appeared on the horizon. The triangular, snowy white tower glistened brightly in the sun. The tower was aptly called the white tower. It was the center of white magic in the humans' world. White magic was primarily used for healing, and white mages were more commonly called clerics. If someone needed healing, they went to see a cleric, and if the cleric was not strong enough to heal the ailment with their own magic, the injured or sick party would have to go to the Tower of Hope. There the clerics could join their power to increase healing speed and effectiveness.

Surrounding the tower were recessed battlements which enabled clerics to cast spells and archers to shoot at the attacking enemies. Tall towers at the corners made sure enemies near the wall were not safe from the defenders.

The tower itself was unique, consisting of six large, white triangles making up the main level. Three triangles somewhat smaller in size made up the next level, with a lone triangle balanced on top to create a third level. Light flowed into the tower from every angle, giving it a 'lit up' appearance. It was said that the light entering the tower assisted the clerics in their healing spells. At night, the star and moonlight were amplified, giving increased healing speed for those who recovered within the tower walls. At the peak of the tower, everyone could see the flag representing the clerics; a thin blue circle surrounding a white dot.

On this day, Kazin could clearly see both cavalry and infantry practicing their maneuvers in preparation for a potential battle. After the war that affected virtually all humans just over ten years ago, army recruitment had gone up considerably. New people were needed to replace the countless souls that were lost over a decade ago. Kazin was pleased to see the ranks swelling among General Larsen's armies. General Larsen was employed by the clerics as a guardian for the Tower of Hope. As long as the tower existed, people could come there freely to be healed. No external disputes were recognized in the tower. The clerics would try to heal anyone who came to them, even if it was a person or creature with different allegiances. Even a lizardman could come there to be healed without repercussions, provided he came in peace. (Naturally, that never happened, much to the relief of the clerics, who hated the lizardmen as much as the lizardmen hated them.) However, if there was a war going on, those who fought against the tower were on their own. Clerics would heal their own first.

Kazin landed in the tower's courtyard and Della disembarked. Then Kazin transformed into his human form amid gasps of astonishment from some of the new clerics-to-be who had never witnessed such an event before.

A cleric came out to greet the newcomers. She bowed slightly to Kazin and said, "Arch Mage Kazin. Welcome. You have been expected." She turned and led Kazin and Della into the tower.

Entering one of the main level triangles, Kazin was taken aback by the strange statue to one side of the entrance. It was a statue of a balding, middle-aged man. His face portrayed an angry demeanor. He was dressed like a gardener, with coveralls and rubber boots. A cleric sat on the floor in front of the statue, chanting softly.

"What's with the statue?" asked Kazin suddenly.

The cleric on the floor stopped chanting and looked up at Kazin. "He's paralyzed."

Kazin blinked in surprise. He had seen paralyzed people before, but this man looked just like a statue!

"How did it happen?" asked Della.

"A cyclops paralyzed him," answered the cleric calmly.

"Can't you un-paralyze him?" asked Della. "I thought that was an easy spell?"

The cleric shook her head. "The cyclops that did this is no ordinary cyclops. It - he's - half human."

Kazin and Della exchanged curious glances.

The cleric who had led the visitors inside cleared her throat and smiled. "High Cleric Malachi awaits."

Kazin waved his arm sideways. "Proceed."

The cleric led them to an inner corner of the triangle which contained several blue circles inset into the floor. The cleric, elf and mage each stood on one of the circles and were magically whisked to the second floor of the tower. A hand full of clerics sat on the floor of this level, chanting softly. Kazin knew from past experience that these clerics were chanting magic to speed recovery of all within the tower. Their concentration was deep and they were not to be disturbed.

The cleric led them past the chanting clerics to another set of circles where they were whisked to the top level. Several rooms lined the outer walls of this level, leaving only a small triangular inner chamber. Standing nearby was the high cleric.

"Ah, Kazin!" exclaimed High Cleric Malachi in delight. "It's good to see you again!" He strode forward with his hand outstretched. His pure white robe flowed out behind him. "I'm happy to see you are well!"

"Malachi," said Kazin, pumping the high cleric's hand.

"And Della!" exclaimed Malachi, turning his attention to the elf. He embraced her with a warm hug. "You're looking as radiant as ever!"

Della giggled. "It's good to see you again, Malachi. I'm glad to see you're still fit and healthy."

Malachi chuckled and patted his stomach. "I've probably put on a few pounds since we talked last."

"Nonsense!" grinned Della.

Malachi laughed heartily. "You're the only one I know who can lie and make me feel good at the same time!"

Everyone laughed.

"Now," began Malachi when the greetings were over, "we have some important things to discuss. Let's go into my study, shall we?"

Kazin and Della followed the high cleric into his office and he closed the door behind them.

"Please, be seated," said Malachi, beckoning to some chairs in front of his desk. He sat down behind the desk and looked seriously across at Kazin. "Arch Mage Fildamir gave me the latest rundown on the situation at the Tower of Sorcery. Ten more mages have died."

Kazin groaned. "Then I take it you haven't discovered a cure yet?"

Malachi shook his head. "No. But we have discovered two important things in the past few days. First of all, the disease is not contagious."

"Then why are all the mages in the tower affected?" asked Della.

"That brings me to the next point," continued Malachi. "Our clerics in the tower have discovered a suspicious bottle of spice in the tower's kitchen. It looks exactly like one of the common spice containers used in food preparation. The spice inside looks and smells like the real thing, but my clerics were doing routine tests on the kitchen's food when they discovered a magical signature around the bottle. When they applied it to some food scraps, they noticed the spice evaporate in a faint puff of smoke. It didn't look right so they studied the contents further. The spice turned out to be something entirely different."

"What was it?" asked Della.

"Poison," responded Malachi.

"Poison!" exclaimed Kazin. "So the food at the banquet in the tower was poisoned!"

"That's right," said Malachi.

"Who could have done such a thing?" queried Della. "You would think the tower would be more careful with what they let inside."

"They test all the food that enters the tower," said Kazin.

"Then you think someone may have smuggled it in?" asked Malachi.

"I guess it's possible," said Kazin.

"But don't intruders get sent to the dungeon?" asked Della. "At least, that's what you told me before."

Kazin nodded. "That's correct. The only ones who could have done this foul deed are black mages or white mages who were invited."

"Perhaps," put in Malachi. "However, there is one more unusual detail that confuses matters."

"Which is?" prodded Kazin.

"The magical spell on the spice bottle was not white, black, or grey magic as we know it. It was the magic used by lizardmages."

"What?!" exclaimed both Kazin and Della in unison.

"How is that possible?" cried Kazin. "There's no way a lizardmage could get by the tower's defenses!"

"Apparently it must have happened," said Malachi. "My clerics and the remaining black mages have investigated that possibility and it turns out that there was an uninvited guest prior to that night.

The mages in the dungeon had received an alarm and did a check of the prison cells. According to them, no one was there and they documented it as a false alarm."

"So whoever entered the tower set off the prison alarm and got out before the guards could discover them!" Kazin burst out.

"So it seems," said Malachi.

"I wonder how the lizardmen managed to sneak around the tower without being detected," commented Della.

"I wish I knew," murmured Kazin.

"At least everyone outside the tower is safe," added Della.

Malachi sighed. "I wish it were that simple."

"What do you mean?" asked Della.

"I don't mean to alarm you," said Malachi, "but two days ago, some farmers who live north of here came to the Tower of Hope suffering from some sort of illness. They claimed that some of their livestock and poultry were becoming sick and dying as well. We believe it may be related to the sickness at the Tower of Sorcery."

"Are you sure?" asked Della.

Malachi shrugged. "I can't be certain at this time, but so far we have been unable to heal the farmers. If anything, they've gotten worse."

"But I thought you said the disease at the Tower of Sorcery wasn't contagious," put in Kazin.

Malachi nodded. "It's true. Anyone who entered the Tower of Sorcery since the outbreak has not been affected."

"Then how come the farmers and their cattle got sick?" added Della.

"We believe that the same poison that affected the black mages is present to the north. By the sounds of it, the poison may be present in the water. All of the people who have come here with the symptoms live near the rivers and streams flowing from the mountains."

"If that's true," said Kazin, "then it's only a matter of time before all the water becomes contaminated. Everyone will be affected!"

"I'm afraid so," said Malachi soberly. "The tower can't heal those who are already affected. When this disease spreads, people will turn to us for help which we won't be able to give. Moreover, if too many clerics fall ill before a cure is found, the chance of recovery will be hindered further."

"How is the water on the grounds here at the tower?" asked Della. "If it becomes contaminated as well -."

Malachi raised a hand to interrupt. "No. Our water is still clean. As you know, we use it constantly for healing purposes. The source of the water is deep within the earth. It is the cleanest water in the land. Its magical properties make it more immune to exterior impurities. We expect - and hope - that it will remain pure, even if the rivers and streams around us get contaminated."

"I hope so," murmured Della.

"Did you notify your people, Della?" asked Malachi, changing the subject.

"Yes," responded the elf. "They have representatives en route as we speak to meet with you and work with your clerics toward a cure for this disease."

"Excellent," said Malachi. "We can use all the help we can get."

"Speaking of help," put in Kazin, "what can I do?"

Malachi considered. "Well - other than finding out what you can about the conditions north and east of here, I can't think of anything you can do to help at this time."

"I'll begin first thing in the morning," said Kazin.

"Very well," said Malachi, rising. "You can stay in one of the wards on the first level. We still have some room - for the time being."

"Thanks," said Kazin. He and Della got up. "Incidentally, I noticed a paralyzed man near the entrance. The cleric said he was paralyzed by a half-human, half-cyclops."

Malachi grinned sheepishly. "That's right. A number of years ago we took him in. His mother passed away and he was an orphan with nowhere to go. He was adept at tending our gardens of herbs, so we put him in the care of our head gardener. Apparently the gardener wasn't a very pleasant man to work for, and the cyclops wasn't very well treated. I guess they finally had a disagreement and Cyril - that's the cyclops - finally lost his temper. The head gardener was paralyzed and Cyril ran off." Malachi shook his head sadly. "That cyclops was always so mild-mannered. It must have been pretty serious for him to get so angry."

"Did he paralyze people often?" Della asked.

"On occasion," answered Malachi, "but always by accident."

"How long does the 'paralyze' spell usually last?" questioned Kazin. "That cleric didn't seem to be able to free the gardener."

"That's another mystery," Malachi answered. "Normally, it takes only a few minutes to cancel the 'paralyze' spell, depending on the skill level of the clerics assigned to that task. This time, however, even our best clerics were unable to cancel the spell. I even tried myself, with no effect. I suspect that it had to do with the fact that Cyril was angry and had paralyzed the gardener deliberately."

Kazin nodded. "You could be right. Frame of mind can alter magic of that nature."

Malachi suddenly snapped his fingers. "I just remembered! One of our prized pupils has left the tower in pursuit of the cyclops. She had just received her magical healing ring; a symbol of her upgrade from apprentice to a level one cleric, when news of the cyclops reached her. A strange look had come over her face and she had run out of the lecture hall. Only later were we able to discover where she had gone. Her roommate had found a note on her pillow." Malachi loosely waved his hand to the side. "Anyhow, if I recall correctly, she is the one who handed us a letter of recommendation made by you, Kazin. Her name was Vera."

Kazin's eyes widened. "Are you sure?"

"I believe so. She's from your hometown of Marral."

Kazin nodded. "That's her alright."

"Who's Vera?" asked Della, suddenly jealous.

"Frosty - I mean Max's younger sister," answered Kazin.

"Oh yeah," said Della slowly. 'Frosty' was what Kazin had called his childhood friend Max, who was adept at freezing spells. Max's younger sister was interested in healing magic from a very young age after losing her brother early on.

"I'll see if I can find out where she went when I'm scouring the countryside north of here," commented Kazin. "The cyclops most likely headed for the mountains, and Vera probably went there to look for him."

"It's possible," conceded Malachi. "Bring her back safely if you can. She has considerable talent with white magic. I'd hate to lose her, especially if things get busier around here with that new disease and all. If you see Cyril, bring him back too. Tell him I'm not angry with him. He's still welcome here."

"O.K." said Kazin.

The trio left Malachi's office and encountered a younger cleric who stood a short distance away. When he saw them exit the room, he stepped forward and gave a short bow. The cleric had short brown hair and blue eyes. His face was youthful and pleasant. He directed his attention to Kazin and spoke somewhat shakily. "Begging your pardon. Are you Arch Mage Kazin?"

"Yes," answered Kazin. He was still not used to being called 'Arch Mage', but had no choice but to put up with it.

The cleric produced a note from beneath his pure white robe. "I was instructed by a - a griffin to give this to you." He hastily handed the note to Kazin.

"A griffin?!" exclaimed Malachi in surprise. "Are you sure, Gilmar?"

"Y-yes, Sir," stammered Gilmar. "It spoke with a deep, rumbling voice."

Malachi looked at Kazin in shock. "A griffin?"

Kazin was as astounded as Malachi. Griffins were extremely rare birds. Only seafarers sailing to distant lands claimed to see griffins from time to time. Most people believed the sailors were seeing things and must have been drunk to make up such stories. Mages, on the other hand, knew they existed, and were willing to pay dearly for the feathers of a griffin. The feathers were extremely useful for a number of more complicated, high level spells.

"Griffins," said Della dreamily. She had once seen a griffin when she was a child. She had been standing on a mountaintop overlooking the ocean to the east of the elven lands. She had run excitedly to her parents who stood nearby talking. By the time she had gotten their attention, the griffin had already flown out of sight into the rising sun.

Her parents didn't believe she had seen a griffin, and told her it was probably just an eagle. Della had tried in vain to convince them it was a griffin. She stood there for long moments afterward staring at the horizon. In her mind she could still see the majestic creature. Its golden wings shimmered in the sun. The head and beak stared straight ahead, certain of its course. The fur on the underside of its body also glowed with a golden sheen. The four legs hung loosely beneath the torso, and the tail waved back and forth with each stroke of the wings. It was a sight she would never forget.

"Is it still here?" asked Kazin.

"No," answered Gilmar. "It flew away after it gave me the note."

Malachi sighed. "That's too bad. I would have loved to see it."

"Me too," echoed Kazin and Della in unison.

"What's in the note?" asked Della. She craned her neck to look at the note in Kazin's hand.

Kazin opened the note and read it aloud. "Kazin - urgent - come to the Tower of the Moon at once. Adriana & Martha."

"Who are Adriana and Martha?" asked Malachi.

"They are druids who live in the Tower of the Moon," explained Kazin.

"You know where the Tower of the Moon is?" asked Gilmar incredulously. "That tower was thought to have been lost generations ago!"

"I was there a number of years ago," said Kazin.

Gilmar gasped. "Really?" He looked at Malachi in disbelief.

Malachi grinned and patted the young cleric on the shoulder. "I'll explain that story to you someday. But right now, you'd better get ready for your next class."

"Uh - yes, Sir!" stammered Gilmar. He bowed quickly to the guests and departed.

Malachi turned to the others with an apologetic smile. "He's a good pupil. His healing skills are quite remarkable, and will likely be outstanding if he'd pay more attention to his studies instead of looking outside and daydreaming all the time."

"At least his daydreaming paid off this time," commented Kazin. "I've been told that griffins are not very patient. If no one approached it to take the note, it could very well have flown off without delivering it."

Malachi laughed. "I suppose you're right at that."

"We'd better get ready to go," interrupted Della.

Kazin looked at the elf sternly. "I didn't see your name on the note."

Della gave Kazin a glowering look. "It didn't say that you had to go alone, either."

Kazin's own serious look gave way to a fit of laughter. "Of course you can come! I was only teasing!"

Della turned red and punched Kazin in the arm. "That was mean!"

Malachi chuckled. "I'll let you two get organized. I have much work to do." He patted Kazin on the shoulder and re-entered his office.

"I only have one problem," murmured Kazin as he and Della headed for the blue circles.

"What's that?" asked Della.

"I don't know exactly where the Tower of the Moon is."

Della looked confused. "But I thought you were there?"

"I was," said Kazin. "But the druids brought me there using their magical ship. It was impossible for me to determine our speed or direction."

"Well, if they need you so badly, they'll probably use their magic again," stated Della. "You'll just have to guess where the Tower of the Moon is and fly in that general direction. At the very least they can use their magic to direct you."

"I hope so," said Kazin. "If I'm going to fly over open water with nowhere to land, I'm going to have to get a few hours rest first. Then we'll leave right away."

"You'd better not even think of leaving me behind," said Della sullenly. "If you do, don't bother coming back!"

Kazin chuckled and kissed the elf on the cheek. "I wouldn't dream of it."

Della gave him a sinister look.

"Honest!" pleaded Kazin.

Chapter 9

Captain Rubin looked across the deck of his ship 'The Griffin'. He could scarcely believe that it had already been more than five years since he had purchased the swift schooner from a merchant in Rist. His former captain, Captain Durango, had reluctantly helped his first mate with the financing. Durango was a wealthy seaman who was not thrilled about Rubin going his own way. Rubin was like a son to him. But like any good father, he could not stand in the way of his son's dream of becoming captain of his own ship.

And so it was that Rubin became the proud owner of 'The Griffin'. As captain of the new vessel, Rubin had a choice of what he could do with her. Instead of transporting goods from one port to another like Durango, he opted for the more dangerous task of finding pirates in North Lake and bringing them to justice. This was no easy task, considering pirate ships outnumbered bounty ships by at least ten to one.

Rubin had a secret, however. He had strange ties to the mythical sea-creatures known as mermaids. These mermaids were visible only to him. His eyesight was exceptionally keen, particularly in bright sunlight. As a result, he could see them far out in the distance where even someone equipped with a spyglass would have difficulty spotting them. Rubin's eyes were altered a number of years ago when he had experienced the magic of the mermaids during an adventure with the dragon mage, Kazin.

In any case, the mermaids always guided The Griffin to where pirate ships were hidden - mostly among the Haunted Shoals. These shoals were notoriously treacherous for any ship to navigate, yet Rubin had always managed to guide his ship around any obstacles both above and below the surface. This had earned the unfaltering respect of his crew. Furthermore, Rubin had always found pirates wherever he went.

Even if he aimed his ship in an unusual direction, he seemed to know exactly where the pirates were. The more experienced crew members never asked Rubin why he chose a certain direction. They knew he would lead them to some pirates eventually.

Along with unerring navigation and successful pirate hunting, Rubin's crew never lost a battle. Each time they encountered pirates, the pirates were disorganized and unprepared. Only Rubin knew why, but he would not say. Nobody bothered to ask, since they always won every battle hands down. Rubin had quickly gained a reputation for being undefeated and new recruits waited at every port in the hopes of being enlisted aboard The Griffin.

Every so often a sailor would respectfully look over at the bald, dark-skinned captain, who wore no armor, but bore a knife sheath diagonally across his chest. At his side he wore a holster with a rapier for close combat. He looked like an ordinary sailor, but his regal stance and keen dark eyes made him look like a man to be reckoned with. He was a leader who would give his all for any member of the crew and would not expect anything in return. He didn't need to. Most of the crew would gladly sacrifice their lives for this great captain. His goal was an honourable one, and with him to lead them, they would not fail.

That particular day, Rubin aimed his ship out to open water. The crew quickly adjusted the sails and the wind took care of the rest. The Griffin surged through the water with a vengeance. No one asked Rubin where they were going or why. They knew pirates would be waiting at the end of their journey. The only preparations they occupied themselves with were the readying of weapons; open seas usually meant a sea battle or a pursuit. Swords and knives were cleaned; arrows were sharpened. Rubin didn't have to give any orders. His crew knew what to do and they did it well.

Despite the state of readiness, Rubin was uneasy. The mermaids far ahead of them were beginning to outdistance even The Griffin. Within a few hours, they disappeared entirely. Rubin was perplexed. Why did the mermaids suddenly abandon him? Something was amiss. He turned and was about to shout the order to turn around when the wind suddenly died completely. The sails sagged, The Griffin slowed, and all was still.

A few of the less experienced sailors looked questioningly at their captain. What happened?

Rubin couldn't afford to show his uneasiness. He turned to his first mate. "We wait."

The first mate nodded and smiled. Rubin must have an idea of what was going to happen. He always did.

But Rubin did not.

The sea became dead calm and the noon sun came and went. Nothing happened. Now even some of the veterans looked to their captain for answers.

Rubin could give them none.

Then, when Rubin was beginning to lose his own patience, he spotted something dark in the distance. In was not in the water but in the sky. He knew the sailor in the crow's nest wouldn't see it for a few more minutes.

"Captain," murmured the first mate at the captain's side. "Your orders?"

The dark object in the distance was getting closer. Rubin smiled. This must be what he had been waiting for. "We wait."

The first mate grunted.

Then the sailor in the crow's nest cried out. There was something in the sky!

Mutters of relief surged through the crew of The Griffin. Some even fingered the swords at their sides. Veterans nudged new recruits and gave them the 'I told you so' look.

Now Rubin could make out the object nearing the ship. It was a large flying creature - a dragon! Rubin's heart leaped. He dared not hope.

Other crew members began shouting and pointing as they spotted the object in the sky.

Before long, the object flew into view and some crew members gasped as they recognized it as a dragon.

Rubin's archers stood nearby but he waved them off. He wanted to see what the dragon wanted first.

The dragon circled the ship and Rubin saw a small figure on its back.

"Permission to land?" asked the dragon in a hoarse voice.

"Permission granted!" shouted Rubin.

The sailors looked questioningly at their captain.

The dragon landed on the bow. Despite the ship's bulk and size, the ship tilted and creaked under the strain. The figure on its back climbed down onto the deck and stretched. It was an elf. Suddenly, the dragon transformed into a human, and several sailors gasped at the strange magical transfiguration. The ship righted itself again.

Rubin pushed past his men to greet the newcomers. He and the elf recognized one another at the same instant.

"Rubin!" exclaimed Della joyfully. She sprang into the captain's outstretched arms.

Rubin grunted with the impact and gently put the elf back down again. He grinned from ear to ear. "How's my little elf after all these years?"

"It wasn't that long!" pouted Della. She grinned. "You don't look that much older."

Rubin laughed. "And ye don't look any older!" He looked over at the mage who had by now come up to them, and grasped his hand firmly. "Kazin, my good friend!"

Kazin smiled. "You're a sight for sore eyes."

"What do ya mean?" asked Rubin.

"It's a long story," said Kazin weakly. "Let's just say that I'm glad I could finally land."

"Ye look exhausted," said Rubin, concerned. "Why not rest in me cabin and ye can tell me all about it?"

"Good idea," agreed Kazin.

Rubin led his friends to his cabin and gave his first mate orders to wait. The sailor nodded and sighed. He had obviously been hoping for a battle.

"So you're the captain of your own ship now, eh?" commented Della after they had entered the captain's quarters and Rubin had closed the door behind them.

"Aye," answered Rubin, beaming. "The Griffin is a good ship, and so is my crew."

Kazin collapsed on Rubin's bunk. "You earned it, Rubin."

"Thank you," said Rubin. "Captain Durango helped me get started."

"How's he doing?" asked Della politely.

"E's still carryin' cargo and fightin' with inexperienced captains as usual," Rubin answered with a twinkle in his eye.

All three companions smiled, remembering their adventures aboard Captain Durango's ship, 'The Lady of the Sea.'

"Obviously you're not carrying cargo," interjected Della, breaking the momentary silence. "It looks more like you're preparing for war."

"Aye," confirmed Rubin. "When ye're dealing with pirates, war is often what ye encounter."

"It's certainly more exciting than hauling cargo," yawned Kazin sleepily. He leaned back on the bunk and closed his eyes.

Della shook her head and said to Rubin, "He's dead tired. We've been flying for almost two days straight."

"No wonder!" Rubin exclaimed. "I'm amazed 'e lasted that long!"

"No problem," murmured Kazin. He rolled onto his side and began to breathe deeply. He was asleep.

Suddenly, the boat lurched forward and Rubin had to keep Della from landing on Kazin.

"What was that?" asked Della in alarm.

Rubin took a quick look at the mage, who still slept soundly. "I aim to find that out!" He pushed past the elf and barged out onto the deck, with Della close on his heels.

Rubin half expected to see his sails billowing in the wind. Instead, the sea was dead calm and the sails rippled only from the forward motion of the ship. Sailors everywhere staggered to their feet and regained their footing after having been thrown to the deck. They looked around, bewildered and confused.

The first mate came running up to Captain Rubin. His eyes were fearful. "Th - the ship's moving yet there is no wind!" he exclaimed.

"I see that," said Rubin slowly. Sailors were milling about uncertainly, looking to Rubin for leadership.

"Now I see what Kazin meant," interrupted Della.

Rubin turned to the elf. "What do you mean? Is this some sort of magic?"

"I think so," said Della. "Kazin told me that the druids used this sort of magic last time."

"The last time? I don't understand."

"He was headed for the Tower of the Moon," explained Della. "Kazin said last time he visited the tower, the ship he was on magically transported to Oracle's Island, where the tower is located."

"So we're headed for the Tower of the Moon?" asked Rubin.

"I assume so," said Della.

Rubin relaxed. "Then I guess we have no choice but to go there, eh?"

Della smiled. "Yup."

It was a full day before the sailor in the crow's nest reported seeing land. Rubin, Della, and Kazin came out onto the deck to see for themselves.

Kazin recognized the mountains that came into view on the western horizon. "Oracle Island," he commented aloud.

The ship cruised for only a half hour before coasting around to a lagoon situated on the southeastern side of the island. Trees and brush covered the island like a dense carpet, and songbirds could be heard above the rush of water beneath the ship's hull.

Upon entering the lagoon, the ship slowed, gliding gracefully through the clear blue water. A dock appeared on the shore ahead of them, with several green figures scurrying about in preparation for the newcomers.

"Skink warriors!" exclaimed Della in delight.

Some nearby sailors heard the comment and fingered their weapons nervously. But when they looked at Rubin, he shook his head. This was no place to do battle.

A sailor cried out and pointed to starboard. Other sailors followed his pointing hand and their eyes widened in disbelief. Swimming in the lagoon were many alluring and gorgeous ladies. Most of the women had long, beautiful hair. There were red heads, blondes, brunettes, and even a few with coal black hair.

As the ship drew nearer, the sailors discovered the most interesting feature of the women. Glistening in the sunlight beneath the water, instead of legs, were silvery tails. They were mermaids!

Rubin's entire crew jostled for position along the ship's rails to get a better look. The mermaids smiled and waved, calling to the sailors in enticing tones.

"Oh, dear! Oh, dear! Oh, dear!" cried a voice suddenly from the far end of the dock. A heavy set woman, dressed in a brilliant blue robe, huffed and puffed as she pounded along the dock toward the approaching ship. The dock bounced so heavily that several of the skink warriors lost their balance and splashed into the water.

By now, some of Rubin's sailors were getting ready to jump overboard to respond to the lure of the mermaids. Once captured by a mermaid, a human male would never return. The mermaid would use the man for mating. Then he would disappear forever.

The blue-robed woman ran right to the end of the dock, her arms flailing wildly as she narrowly avoided plunging into the water after the skink warriors. Seeing the sailors about to jump from the ship, she gasped, "Oh, no! Don't - oh never mind!" With that she rattled off a magical chant and swung her arm in the direction of the Griffin.

Up until now, Kazin had watched events unfold with an amazed detachment. Now, a sudden wave of fatigue smashed into him like a whiplash. All of the sailors aboard the ship collapsed into crumpled heaps on the deck of the Griffin. Kazin himself staggered under the blow, falling to his knees and nearly passing out. Only his mental discipline, taught to him as a mage in the Tower of Sorcery, allowed him to remain conscious. As it was, he could only watch with blurry eyes as the blue-robed figure on the dock used her magic to guide the ship into position before the dock.

"Oh, dear, oh, dear, oh, dear!" lamented the woman numerous times. She chanted another complicated spell and levitated herself from the dock up to the level of the ship's deck, floating gracefully through the air. She saw all the sailors lying there fast asleep and exclaimed, "Oh, dear!"

Kazin groggily tried to rise to his feet and the woman spotted him immediately.

"There you are!" She floated over to the mage and helped him to steady himself. "Are you all right?"

"I - I think so," said Kazin, shaking his head. "Your 'sleep' spell sure packs a wallop!"

"I'm sorry!" wailed the woman. "I saw those sailors trying to jump and - oh - it's useless!" she lamented in exasperation.

Kazin let go of the woman to stand on his own. He was O.K. now. "It's O.K. Martha. There's no harm done."

Martha started. "You remember me?"

Kazin smiled. "Of course! How's Adriana?"

Martha gestured with her hand. "Oh, as boring as ever. She's absolutely no fun at all! The treemen are more exciting."

Kazin laughed. "You sound lonely."

Martha harrumphed. "I wish we had more visitors. This reclusive lifestyle gets tiresome after a while. At least the plants and wildlife provide some amusement."

"No doubt," said Kazin.

"I'll take you to the tower," said Martha. She looked at the mermaids nearby. "If it wasn't for those treacherous mermaids, I could wake everyone, but it's better they remain asleep until the ship has left again."

"I thought you had more control of the mermaids," Kazin commented.

"We used to," admitted Martha, "but Adriana and I have been rather busy lately. We need our energies for other things, as you will soon find out."

"Is Amelia -?" began Kazin.

Martha shook her head sadly and put a hand on Kazin's shoulder. "She is at peace, Kazin."

Kazin nodded. The last time he was here, the eldest druid, Amelia, had sent him on a strange errand with his companions. Amelia had claimed to know things about Kazin and the others, and he had never had a chance to question her about her strange ability to see into the future. Now he would never know.

Kazin cast a quick glance at Della, who lay nearby fast asleep. Rubin lay a few feet to her left. "I wonder if I should wake Della and Rubin."

Martha sighed. "I'm afraid if we do that, we may alter the sleep spell I cast and some of the sailors may wake early. As it is, I know they will sleep for the duration of your visit."

Kazin grimaced at the thought of Della's wrath when she awoke, but he didn't want to interfere with Martha's magic. Druid magic was unpredictable from his standpoint. If Martha said not to interfere, he would obey. He would also tell Della the same thing when she awoke. If the elf didn't like it, it wasn't his fault.

"Let's get going," urged Martha, interrupting the mage's thoughts. Without waiting for an answer, the druid held Kazin's hand, chanted her levitation spell, and she and Kazin floated over the rails of the Griffin to land on the dock below.

By now, the skink warriors were all safely standing on the dock. Several were still shaking water droplets from their water-resistant skin.

Skink warriors were an ugly looking species to behold. Once, their ancestors were lizardmen, just like their counterparts in the mountains. But many generations ago, a dispute between magic users and non-magic users caused a rift within the lizardman population. The non-magic wielders became proficient with long range weapons to combat the long range magic of their counterparts. The magic users eventually prevailed, and banished the non-magic wielders, but not before turning them magically into skink warriors.

The non-magic lizardmen had their appearance changed drastically. Their faces were transformed from pinched, sinister snouts into wider lips and larger mouths. Their faces became more reminiscent of frogs than lizards, with eyes protruding rather than squinty and small. Their clawed hands and feet became webbed, enabling them to swim with great speed. Gills ran down the sides of their necks, allowing them to breathe under water. Spiked red fins also ran from the tops of their heads all the way down their backs.

Although not considered trustworthy, a pact with the Tower of Hope permitted their race to move somewhat more freely among the humans. Nevertheless, they still preferred to stay within their realm in North Lake, much to the dismay of the mermaids, who considered their presence an intrusion. At some point, the druids had stepped in to keep the peace between the skink warriors and mermaids. The peace was not liked by either side, but they obeyed the druids because the wrath unleashed by the druids was fearsome to behold, should the druids become angered.

Now Kazin and Martha walked past the skink warriors on the dock and entered the woods beyond. There was no trail, but where they walked, trees uprooted themselves and moved aside. When the druid and mage passed, the trees moved back into place again. Martha playfully slapped the trees as they moved stiffly around them, encouraging them and passing small bursts of magical energy through her fingertips into their trunks.

Kazin had experienced this sort of thing before, but was awed just the same. The command the druids had over nature was something to behold.

The druid and mage continued uphill, wending their way around rocky formations and through a dense jungle that didn't impede them in the least. Around a final bend, the trees stepped aside to reveal what Kazin immediately recognized to be the Tower of the Moon.

The Tower of the Moon was cylinder shaped, with slitted windows at various locations all the way up the side. Vines grew up the walls, but amazingly grew around colourful flower arrangements that lined the windows. The vines were so thick that one could hardly see the stone walls beneath. The roof, with crumbling turrets, gave one an indication of the tower's age. It was then that Kazin came to a strange realization. It was not the walls that held up the vines; it was the vines that held up the walls!

Martha led the mage to a set of enormous wooden doors that swung inward of their own accord, swinging silently on shiny brass hinges.

Kazin followed Martha down a short hallway and looked into a room on his left with an open doorway. What he saw caused him to stumble and he bumped into Martha, who was directly ahead of him. He steadied himself and looked into the room again as the druid turned around.

In the room were several cots, and each contained a mermaid. Unlike the mermaids in the lagoon, these mermaids were not smiling enticingly and beckoning. Most of them were asleep, but those who were awake were coughing and shivering and some of them were varying shades of orange or yellow. One mermaid turned to the doorway and saw Kazin. She instinctively tried to smile but a sudden pain caused her to grimace and turn away in shame.

"What -?" began Kazin. He was unable to complete the sentence.

"Oh, dear," moaned Martha. "You weren't supposed to see this yet." She put her arms around the mage and directed him to another room at the end of the hallway.

The room had comfortable chairs and a cozy fireplace. Covering the floor was a lush, lavender carpet. The walls were adorned with paintings and banners depicting scenes of dragon battles that happened a few hundred years ago. The paintings were similar to the ones hanging in the Tower of the Stars. A large painting seemed to have pre-eminence over the others, hanging by itself over the fireplace. This particular painting illustrated an old mage with a long white beard who battled a fierce looking dark object. The determined eyes and clenched jaws of the mage was a testament to the power of the spell being cast. It sent a shiver down Kazin's spine.

"I'll go and fetch Adriana," stated Martha.

"No need," said a serious voice behind them. In the doorway stood Adriana. She was taller and more slender than Martha, and her countenance was serious. Her sharp nose and shrewd gaze gave the appearance of someone to be reckoned with.

"Hello, Adriana," said Kazin lightly. "It's good to see you are well."

Adriana gave a stiff nod of her head. "Welcome. We have been waiting for your arrival. You must assist us immediately for there is a plague that has been unleashed upon us with dire consequences for all life in the world." She paused to let the words sink in, and then continued. "Amelia gave me her dying instructions to summon you when this situation should arise." With some distaste she added, "She knew it was going to happen, too."

Martha knew Adriana didn't particularly like Amelia, who was an oracle as well as a druid, but chose not to bring up the subject, knowing that Adriana was upset about the current plague situation.

"Tell me what you need me to do," said Kazin seriously. "I will do whatever is in my power to help."

"Let us hope that is enough," Adriana answered, looking distractedly above and past Kazin as she spoke. "Follow me." She turned and left the room with Martha right behind her.

Kazin was the last to leave the room, but he paused to look where he had been standing. What was Adriana looking at a moment ago? The only thing she could have been looking at was the painting of the wizened old mage.

Something about the mage's face seemed familiar. What was it? Then a realization struck the young mage. The hair on his neck stood on end. It couldn't be, could it? He shook his head and hastened after the druids. He had more important things to attend to right now.

Chapter 10

era wandered the winding trail carefully, taking care to avoid washed out areas. The path was not well used, and certainly not maintained. Indeed, there was no reason. Few people if any had traveled this route in a long time. The only reason she chose this path was its proximity to the last of the paralyzed people that Cyril had left behind. Fortunately, none of the cyclops' victims were seriously paralyzed like the gardener. Vera patiently unparalyzed each of them as she encountered them, apologizing for the cyclops' actions. Most were ungrateful and cursed the cyclops for his unprovoked assault. This saddened Vera, but not as much as the sickness and disease the villagers were experiencing. The further north she went, the worse the conditions were.

Walking along one section of the trail Vera counted as many as twenty heads of cattle which had perished. Others lived, but looked like they were near death themselves. Even farmers and their families were ill. On more than one occasion Vera was hailed by distraught people who saw her as a potential cure for their suffering families.

At first, the cleric was pleased to offer her services, confident that she could help. But one failure after another had caused her to question her clerical abilities. She had helped numerous people in the Tower of Hope, with moderate to exceptional success each time. But now on her own, she was unable to help the suffering of a single person.

Some desperate villagers, seeing her lack of success, went so far as to call her a fraud, angrily sending Vera from their houses and slamming their doors behind her.

Vera was uncharacteristically demoralized by the actions of these people. She blindly followed the trail of paralyzed people, tears blurring her vision. Despite her despair, she still stopped to un-paralyze Cyril's victims, but no longer gave an explanation, preferring to continue on her journey without communicating with anyone. She stopped only occasionally to check abandoned wells to see if the water was pure. Many wells were still free from contamination, but Vera was not one to take chances. She tried to inform villagers that their water was impure, but they chose to ignore her.

The last well Vera visited was still pure and she filled her water skins completely, not certain when she would encounter fresh water again. The cleric's other supplies were adequate for many days; she had stocked her pack thoroughly in a community near the tower.

With the Old Dwarven Mountains before her, Vera realized where Cyril had gone. The seclusion of the mountains was a logical place for him to go. There were no more paralyzed people to lead her now, since human settlements were all behind her. She had to pursue the cyclops with intuition and guesswork. The odd, freshly snapped twig on the path indicated the recent presence of a large traveler, and Vera could only hope that it had been Cyril.

Over an hour on the trail brought the cleric to an area that had recently been used as a campsite. Still smoldering ashes blew loosely in the breeze. The smell of some sort of meat still lingered in the air.

The cleric was about to continue on her way when she noticed some markings on the ground near the fire pit out of the corner of her eye. She bent closer to examine the markings. A circle had been drawn with an oval within its confines. A couple of hastily drawn lines bisected the circle and its oval. Vera scratched her head and was about to put the matter aside as nothing important when an idea occurred to her. She checked the markings again and immediately realized what the symbol was all about. The circle was a representation of a head and the oval was the eye. Cyril had probably drawn it! His anger with his disability had probably made him scribble it out, explaining the haphazard lines through the eye!

Excited, Vera stood up straight. The cyclops was not far ahead! She had to catch him before he entered the mountains. With renewed vigor, Vera half stumbled and half ran toward the mountains.

Almost immediately, the cleric reached the base of the mountains. Large boulders and rubble from high above littered the area. Looking up, Vera saw an array of sheer cliffs and rocky outcrops. She suddenly felt very small standing next to the Old Dwarven Mountains.

The cleric experienced a moment of despair as she surveyed the scene before her. Where did Cyril go? Did he climb up the mountain, or did he walk along the base to find a better location to climb up? How far ahead of her was he? It was starting to get late and the cleric had come a long way only to experience a warm trail go instantly cold.

As if in response to her thoughts, a momentary flash of setting sunlight reflected off something on the mountain face above her. Vera squinted her eyes and spotted the source of the light. It was Cyril! The sunlight had reflected off his smooth, bald head!

Vera cried out to the cyclops as loud as she could, but the cyclops continued to climb, unaware of her presence. He didn't hear her! The cleric watched helplessly as the cyclops climbed over some large boulders and sprang nimbly into a dark opening. He had just entered a cave!

"No!" cried Vera. She thought momentarily of her budding career in the Tower of Hope and then remembered her failures since leaving there. She also thought about her close friendship with Cyril and the suffering he was going through. The tower didn't need a cleric who couldn't heal people, but Cyril needed a friend. Vera was not about to abandon him.

Her fear and despair were suddenly transformed into determination and courage. She boldly climbed past the first few boulders and began her ascent, using her pure white staff for support. No mountain was going to stop her from finding Cyril. She might have failed the sick villagers, but she was not going to fail her friend. Vera vowed to find Cyril at all costs. Her sense of honour demanded it. If she let her friends down, she could not rightfully stand with her fellow clerics to help total strangers either.

x x x x x

Unaware of Vera's presence below, Cyril stepped into the tunnel, huffing and puffing from the exertion required to reach this location. He paused to catch his breath and peered into the gloomy tunnel, his lone eye quickly adjusting to the dark interior. He had half expected to enter a tunnel with sharp corners and narrow gaps, but instead was surprised to see a tall, wide passageway stretching in a straight line for quite some distance before him. The sound of the wind whipping past the entrance was amplified down the entire length of the tunnel. Eerie though it was, Cyril felt at home here.

The cyclops' stomach growled, reminding him of the tasty rabbits he had recently eaten. The rabbits were easily caught; he simply paralyzed them and captured them alive. He still had a few left in his pack, and they would keep indefinitely, since they were still alive. They would simply remain paralyzed until they were needed.

Cyril hoisted his makeshift spiked wooden club over his shoulder and began his trek down the tunnel. It was time to go exploring. His eye quickly adjusted to the gloomier surroundings as he rounded the first bend, and the tunnel's lit entrance disappeared from sight. The stony walls were cold and hard, but gave the cyclops plenty of room to maneuver. Worn cracks in the lumpy floor informed Cyril that this tunnel had been here for a long time. Many feet had undoubtedly traveled along here in the past, and many more would surely follow.

The cyclops wandered for some time and encountered a number of forks in the tunnel as he went. Each time, he chose the fork that he figured led deeper into the mountain. He was surprised he could determine his direction so easily. Somehow he sensed which way led to the outside world. Cyril wondered if perhaps his cyclops half had that instinct built in.

On the cyclops trudged, blissfully unaware of the unseen eyes that followed him. He must have been going in the wrong direction, because the owners of the watching eyes suddenly began closing in on him. They ran quickly, their short legs gaining ground rapidly. Their eyes glittered and their teeth flickered in the dim light of the tunnel. Weapons in their hands also glittered wickedly, a symbol of their evil intentions.

Cyril finally heard the panting of his pursuers and turned, surprised.

The followers were expecting Cyril to turn, and suddenly yelled a war cry, charging the hapless cyclops.

Unfortunately, a war cry was all the pursuers could manage. Too late, each of them realized what they were chasing. The war cry ended as abruptly as it had begun, as each of them tumbled to the ground like dominoes.

In the silence that followed, one could have heard a pin drop. Cyril looked at his would-be attackers with a raised eyebrow. Their large, pointed ears and greenish skin, combined with their distinct smell, identified them as goblins.

Cyril gave a half a grin at what had just happened. For once he didn't have to feel guilty about his curse. He could paralyze all types of creatures in the mountains and it wouldn't matter. Nevertheless, he knew he was still vulnerable, particularly when he slept. The cyclops shrugged. He would just have to sleep with one eye open. About to continue on his way, he paused when he realized the implications of that thought. A cyclops sleeping with one eye open! For possibly the first time in his life, the cyclops laughed. The low sound emanated from his chest and vibrated up to his mouth with a sound between a roar and a hiss. His chest heaved as he laughed. Anyone listening would never guess it was a laugh.

Shaking his head, Cyril left the paralyzed goblins behind. They would undoubtedly come to eventually, but he didn't care. He could kill them, but that was not his way.

A few hours later, he entered a cavern littered with bones. The bones were strewn about, and it took Cyril a few moments to determine that the bones mostly belonged to orcs and a few ogres. Orcs were similar to their cousins, the goblins, except they were larger, larger even than humans. They had large teeth in their lower jaws which protruded from the corners of their mouths and pointed upward. Their skin was the same green color of goblins but their ears were shorter. Their bones were more curved than that of humans, and that was the clue that told Cyril who they were.

The ogre bones, on the other hand, were very similar to the orc bones, only substantially larger. By the looks of it, a group of ogres and orcs had a battle here. Many orc skulls were smashed in, and the ogre casualties had broken legs. The orcs must have chosen to incapacitate the ogres by breaking their legs and then swarming them when they were down. The ogres, meanwhile, used their superior strength to smash the skulls of their adversaries.

Cyril did not know which side had won the battle, but it was obvious the victors had consumed the bodies of the dead. Either way, the battle had taken place a number of weeks ago. The area was picked clean of any treasures, especially with goblins living in the vicinity.

The cyclops sighed and stood up. There was nothing here for him to do. He wended his way across the cavern and entered a tunnel on the far side. It was somewhat narrower than the one he had come from, but he could still walk upright.

"Onward," Cyril stated resolutely, his curiosity aroused by what might lay around the next bend.

✗ ✗ ✗ ✗ ✗

Tyris had been on the move for several days now and he was beginning to tire of the endless tunnels. More than once he had run into roving bands of orcs and goblins. Some had run away while others had tried to capture him. But he had been faster, always managing to escape without incident. Other than that, he hadn't seen anything of interest. He had half expected to encounter some more lizardmages, but they were nowhere to be found. Not that he minded. They were only dangerous if they were near him. No one could summon an elemental who was already in physical form unless he or she was in sight and close enough to be summoned with magic.

Tyris smiled as he remembered his previous physical forms. One time he had appeared as a female, surprising his summoners. They almost lost their magical hold on her as a result. The fire elemental wondered vaguely how long it had been since his last visit. Time had no meaning to elementals. They needed no sleep, although fatigue would force them to rest from time to time. They were immortal beings, but their physical form could be commanded by summoners, and their form would be lost if a situation arose where it was 'killed'. The elemental would then be transported back to the realm from which it had come. The summoners would then have to re-summon the elemental, but it would be more difficult depending on how badly the elemental was injured. If the elemental was extremely weak, the summoning spell would fail until the elemental was stronger.

There were rare times when elementals could escape those who summoned them. If that occurred - as it had here - the elemental was free to walk; or swim or fly as the case may be; the realm where mortals lived. This would last until the elemental was either 'killed', summoned, or, if it returned to its own realm by choice. Elementals chose never to interfere in the affairs of mortals unless it was something that threatened the balance of the elements.

Elementals generally avoided one another. If a dispute arose between one or more elementals, they could wind up hurting one another and disturbing the world's balance in catastrophic ways. Earthquakes, floods, storms, and massive fires are some examples of the upheaval mortals could expect to endure should the elementals clash.

But for now Tyris was not concerned about such things. A bigger concern was the magical presence he suddenly felt in his vicinity. A magic wielder was nearby. Elementals always sensed those who wielded magic, and Tyris was no different.

A branching tunnel gave the fire elemental a quick exit from the passageway he was traveling and he ran as fast as he could. Magic wielders were a potential threat and he didn't want his freedom taken from him yet.

The elemental entered yet another crossing passageway and chose to go left. Several yards down that way he found a narrow tunnel to his right. He ducked into it and proceeded to follow it until he reached a small cavern with three adjoining tunnels.

Arriving at the cavern from the leftmost tunnel, at precisely the same moment as the elemental, was a cyclops.

Both parties stumbled to a stop and stared at one another in surprise. Then the elemental spun for the tunnel to his right and bolted into it at full speed.

"W-wait!" sputtered the cyclops finally. But the elemental was already gone.

Tyris covered a fair bit of ground before slowing. Something at the back of his mind nagged at him. The cyclops had failed to call the usual, "Look into my eye!" A cyclops always tries to paralyze its victim by forcing it to look into its eye. Then it gets to eat its prey in relative peace. This cyclops did not try to do that. But then, Tyris was a fire elemental, and the cyclops was as startled as he was. Maybe Tyris did not look edible, with his body perpetually ablaze.

The elemental looked back the way he had come and hesitated. Something else was wrong about the cyclops. It kind of looked - and sounded - human? He shook his head and decided to forget about it. He was better off not to investigate the matter. He was immune to cyclops magic, but a cyclops could be dangerous nonetheless.

Tyris started walking again. "There must be something more interesting to see than orcs, goblins, and a cyclops," he muttered. "There has to be!"

Chapter 11

ebecca sighed as she completed another section of the map she had found. So far, the map was reasonably accurate, but there were sections she had to modify and correct as well. The mapmaker who had made the map originally often missed details and got some of the distances between tunnels wrong. Rebecca made a point of visiting unexplored tunnels on her map and adding that information to the existing map.

She was interested in the fact that she was always going downward in gradual increments. The dwarf was sure she was headed in a general northwesterly direction, far from the dwarven realm. The Old Dwarven Mountains were abandoned by her forefathers after the dragon wars when mining opportunities opened up in the southeastern mountains. With the Old Dwarven Mountains all mined out, the promise of wealth was too great and the dwarves had migrated to the new area, leaving the Old Dwarven Mountains barren and devoid of life. Evidence of the dwarves' existence here was almost nonexistent. Ancient markings on the walls and the occasional mine site was all that remained of the once proud race of dwarves that lived here.

Rebecca marveled at the history she shared with these people, especially now that she was in the presence of these old tunnels. She could now be walking where her great-great-great-grandfather had once walked.

A short time later, the dwarf paused at a tunnel branch that she hadn't noticed marked on her map. Withdrawing the fragile piece of parchment, she studied it for a moment. Sure enough, it wasn't marked down. Odd, she thought. The other mapmaker wasn't all that accurate on his drawings, but he had never missed a tunnel entrance before. Rebecca jotted down the exact location where the tunnel branched off. With that complete, she put the map back into her side pouch.

Rebecca was just trying to decide if she should go down and

explore the tunnel when she heard a faint yell. Instinctively, she drew her axe from its sheath and stood there, the hair on the back of her neck standing on end. Her heart beat rapidly. For the first time in days, she would finally encounter someone. Whether that was good or bad remained to be seen.

The yell came again, echoing faintly from the new tunnel. It sounded like a cry of pain. Rebecca decided to go a short way down the tunnel to take a closer look. She wanted to find out what was down there anyway and it could turn out to be one of the lizardmen lairs she was supposed to find for the king. Resolutely holding her axe out in front of her, Rebecca stepped into the tunnel.

Not fifty yards in, the dwarf caught the unmistakable scent of orcs. She slowed and tensed, but did not stop.

The cry rang out again. The sound was definitely not the sound of an orc. Rebecca quickened her pace. Someone sounded like they were in trouble.

Soon the dwarf could hear the grunting and wheezing typical of orcs. Peeking around a corner, Rebecca saw a flickering of light in the distance. She was close. Walking as silently as she could, Rebecca moved down a short passageway and peeked around the next bend. The light that had been flickering off the walls was brighter now, its source around yet another bend. The dwarf crept as slowly as she could and peeked around the last corner.

A wide passageway appeared to the dwarf, lit brightly by a torch carried by an orc who stood only a few feet away with its back to her. Beyond the orc, Rebecca could see a large net suspended from the ceiling. The net was bulging out but appeared to be empty. That was not the case, however, when an ugly green hand holding a dagger thrust upward, jabbing at the net.

"Ow!" cried the net suddenly. There was someone in there!

The orcs laughed and slobbered. They were having fun.

Rebecca was not impressed. Someone was in the net, and though she couldn't see them, they were in trouble. Keeping her combat training foremost in her mind, Rebecca stepped forward and swung her axe at the orc holding the torch. The axe bit deeply into the orc's neck, but did not go through. The orc gurgled, dropped the torch on the floor, and fell over, the axe still imbedded in its neck. The tunnel darkened noticeably, but the torch still burned.

Alarmed, the two remaining orcs, whom Rebecca couldn't see until now because the other orc was in the way, turned around. Seeing Rebecca desperately struggling to free her axe, they charged. One carried the dagger while the other wielded a large club.

The dwarf saw them coming and let go of her useless axe. She stepped backward uncertainly and reached instinctively for her side pouch. Her hand slipped easily around the handle of her new dagger, which she had almost forgotten. With a quick motion, the dwarf brandished the dagger in a threatening manner.

The first orc had to step past its dead companion and ended up overextending itself as it swung its club. It missed Rebecca by a fair margin and staggered off balance.

With a lightning quick motion, Rebecca sliced into the orc's forearm, the dagger cutting through flesh and bone like a hot knife through butter. At the same instant, a sudden flash of light engulfed the two combatants. There was a shriek of pain followed by a sizzling sound. When the flash subsided, the orc in question lay on top of its dead partner. Its entire forearm was turned to ash and disgusting green ooze emanated from the gaping wound near the elbow. The orc lay still, staring at the remnants of its charred arm in shock.

Meanwhile, the other orc had managed to step around the pile of bodies. Fortunately for Rebecca, the blinding flash had left it somewhat dazed. It swung its dagger blindly, missing the dwarf by only a few inches.

Rebecca was tight against the wall by now and had little room to maneuver. Only one move was available to her and she used it. Lunging forward, she thrust her dagger deep into the orc's heart, blocking its flailing arm with her free hand.

Orcs are ugly creatures to begin with, but the image of the orc's grotesque face up close was unnerving. A blinding flash was followed by a gurgling noise, which turned into a rush of vile green ooze that ejected from the orc's mouth.

Rebecca gagged at the horrible stench as the ooze sprayed over her face and shoulders.

A moment later, the orc lay at Rebecca's feet with a giant hole in its chest.

Rebecca paused to brush the green slime from her face and body with revulsion as she distastefully looked at the carnage around her. Returning the dagger to her pouch, she kicked over the second orc to free her axe from the first one. In doing so, she noticed that the second orc was still alive. Using her axe, she put it out of misery with one vicious swing.

That accomplished, she climbed past the orcs and picked up the torch. The light in the tunnel brightened and she approached the net cautiously.

"Good work, dwarf!" exclaimed the net when she got closer.

Rebecca flicked a piece of left over ooze from her shoulder and suddenly noticed the now-familiar vibrating of her talisman. Magic was at work here.

"Who are you?" demanded Rebecca suspiciously. Whoever was in the net could still be a threat to her and she wanted to be certain it was safe to free that individual.

"Cut me down and I'll tell you," said the net.

"Not until you tell me who you are and what you are," said Rebecca flatly.

"This is ridiculous!" snapped the net. "I'm on your side. I hate orcs as much as you do."

"Then show yourself," demanded Rebecca. She was starting to dislike the stranger. "Undo your invisible magic."

A pause was followed by a mumble.

"What?" asked Rebecca. "I didn't catch that."

"I can't!" snapped the net irritably. "Free me and I'll show myself!"

"I thought you just said you can't!" countered Rebecca. "I think you should show yourself first. I know you have magic at your disposal. My pendant tells me so."

"A pendant -?" began the voice curiously. After another pause it continued, "I can't undo the magic because the net is too tight. I need to be freed first."

Rebecca didn't believe the voice. "Fine. I'll let you hang there until you decide otherwise." She sat down and waited.

"I'm telling you the truth, you stupid dwarf!" snapped the voice, exasperated. The net suddenly moved and Rebecca could hear the grunting of its prisoner.

"So now I'm stupid?" said Rebecca slowly. She got to her feet. "I guess a stupid dwarf like me isn't smart enough to save the likes of you!" She started to leave.

"No! Wait!" pleaded the voice helplessly. "I'm sorry! I didn't mean - oh, never mind! I should have known better. Obviously dwarves have no respect for elves anymore."

Rebecca froze in her tracks. She turned slowly. "Did you say - elves?" All her life, Rebecca had only heard stories of elves and their forests. They rarely crossed paths with dwarves, preferring to stay within their forested areas while dwarves generally stayed within the confines of the mountains. She had never seen an elf before. Here was a rare opportunity to finally see one of the original races of the land.

"Yes, I'm an elf," conceded the voice.

"Why didn't you say so in the first place?" asked Rebecca. She pulled out her dagger and started for the net.

"Noo! Don't touch me!" shrieked the stranger in the net suddenly. It squirmed and jiggled.

Rebecca paused, surprised. "But I thought you wanted me to cut you down? Now you - oh yeah!" she added, reddening. The elf was afraid of her magical dagger. And rightfully so, thought Rebecca. Even she didn't know what it would have done had she used it to cut the elf down.

"Use my dagger," said the elf.

"You have a dagger?" asked Rebecca. "Then why don't you use it?"

The elf groaned. "It's in the pile of green stew that you made over there. I dropped it when the trap was sprung. Otherwise, I would have used it long ago."

"Oh," said Rebecca, reddening again. She went and retrieved the dagger, then used it to cut some of the net's ropes.

"Careful!" warned the elf a couple of times.

"Then stop squirming!" ordered the dwarf. As it was, the net was barely within her reach.

A few cut strands later the net split open and the elf tumbled out, landing unceremoniously on the dwarf. They both landed in a tumbled heap. The torch clattered to the floor once again, but still kept burning.

"Ooof!" grunted the dwarf with the impact.

A few moments later, an elf appeared out of nowhere, flinging a plain, grey cloak over his shoulder. He stiffly bent down and offered his hand to the dwarf.

Rebecca grasped his hand and was easily pulled to her feet.

The elf smiled at her. "My name is Alric."

Rebecca stared at the beautiful face of the elf. "I'm Rebecca. Rebecca Mapmaker." She tilted her head to gawk at Alric's pointed ears.

"I take it you haven't seen an elf before," commented Alric, seeing the dwarf's stare.

The dwarf looked away quickly. "No. Elves never venture into the mountains; at least, not until now." She paused to pick up the torch.

"There's a first time for everything," said Alric.

"Why are you here?" asked the dwarf.

"I'm on a mission," said Alric vaguely.

"What kind of mission?" pressed Rebecca.

"It's nothing to concern yourself with," stated the elf. "You just go on making your maps and I'll go my way. There is much danger in my quest."

"There is in mine too," countered Rebecca.

"Just stay clear of trouble and your mapmaking will go just fine," assured Alric.

Rebecca shook her head. "Mapmaking is only a part of my quest. I'm looking for lizardman lairs."

"What for?" asked Alric, intrigued. "You must know their magic can be harmful to you."

Rebecca nodded. "Yes, but I need to know where the lizardmen are and then report their location to my king so he can send armies out to get rid of them."

"Ah, I see," said Alric slowly.

"You haven't encountered any lizardmages lately, have you?" asked Rebecca hopefully.

Alric sighed. "No. I'm starting to lose hope of ever finding them."

"You're looking for them too?" Rebecca asked.

Alric suddenly realized he had accidentally revealed his mission. He decided to tell the truth. "I'm looking for a particular lizardmage. I - owe him something."

Rebecca could tell by Alric's distasteful tone that he didn't owe something very nice. "Maybe we can help one another?" suggested the dwarf.

Alric shook his head. "I always travel alone."

Rebecca could see that the elf did not want her company. Nevertheless, she handed the elf the torch and pulled out her map. "Maybe you could give me a brief description of the tunnels you came from so I can mark them on my map?"

Alric shrugged. "Sure. It's the least I can do for someone who just saved my life."

The dwarf looked up at the elf but couldn't decide whether he was being honest or sarcastic. She un-scrolled her map so he could see and he gave a brief description of the tunnels and caverns he had encountered. He even mentioned an underground river he had crossed. At this, the dwarf became interested.

"Are there any tunnels that run parallel with the river?" asked Rebecca anxiously.

"Yeah," said Alric. "But I didn't follow them."

"Water is the source of life," lectured Rebecca. "Lizardmen often live near water. If we want to find lizardmen, any sources of water will definitely improve our odds of finding them."

"Then I'd better go back there and check out those tunnels," stated Alric.

"Me too," added Rebecca, re-rolling her map. She sensed the elf's stare but pretended not to notice. They both had roughly the same goal, and there was no reason for her to go back the way she had come anyway. Hoisting her pack over her shoulder, the dwarf trudged merrily down the tunnel, leaving the elf standing there with the torch. "You coming, Alric?" she called lightly over her shoulder.

A grumble was the only response.

Part II

A New Threat

Chapter 12

he altar at the top of the Tower of the Moon had an eerie orange glow as it reflected the setting sun. For the past two hours the druids had prepared the area for their magic. According to Martha, they were preparing to summon an air elemental. Ordinarily, they preferred to summon a water or earth elemental since they were more closely related to vegetation and life. But when they had tried to summon either one of these to help with the poison outbreak, there was no response. The only conclusion the druids could come to was that those elementals already walked the world under someone else's control. Determined to get to the bottom of this, the druids had decided to summon the air elemental in the hopes of finding some answers. The oracle, Amelia, had warned them that such a time would come, and insisted that Kazin be summoned then. She didn't say why, but the druids knew better than to question the oracle.

As the sun set, the druids began their chant. It started slowly and quietly, and built up to a rapid, undecipherable crescendo. Then the chant calmed, then became rapid again.

When the sun disappeared and was replaced by the moon, Kazin could feel the magic begin to affect him and the air around him. The chanting felt like a wave rushing over him and receding again. His breathing became strained but he held his ground, anxious to see if the druids summoned successfully. He had never seen an elemental before, and this might be his only opportunity to see one.

At last there was a rush of air and a small whirlwind appeared above the altar. It coalesced into human form, but the wind around it continued to swirl.

Seeing that the elemental was present, Adriana stopped chanting. Martha inhaled deeply and continued to chant, taking on the full brunt of the summoning magic by herself.

"Why have I been summoned?" demanded the air elemental in a deep voice.

Adriana bowed respectfully. "I beg your pardon, O elemental. We are in dire need of assistance and look to you for advice."

The elemental crossed its arms. It had a man's face and its legs and feet were hidden in a funnel of wind. "You have successfully summoned me. What do you require?"

"A plague has come upon the creatures of the land and of the sea," said Adriana.

"Then you should have summoned the earth or water elementals," stated the air elemental. "I cannot help you."

"We tried," explained Adriana calmly. "There was no response to our summoning."

"Are you certain you performed the summoning ritual correctly?" asked the air elemental. "Those spells are complicated for most mortals."

"We performed the spells properly," answered Adriana sternly. "We have performed those spells numerous times, and always successfully."

The elemental was taken aback by Adriana's confident answer. It said nothing.

Adriana chose this opportunity to go on the offensive. "Are those elementals still within their realms, or do they walk among mortals?"

The air elemental tilted its head back and seemed to withdraw into itself. A few moments later it re-formed its human form. A look of surprise registered on its face. "They walk among mortals!"

Adriana's eyes widened. "Both of them?"

"All of them," confirmed the air elemental. "Earth, water and fire!"

Adriana muttered an oath under her breath and looked at Kazin with fear in her eyes. Kazin's neck hairs stood on end when he saw her expression. Adriana was always so stern and in control. To see that fear in her face meant that something was amiss.

Adriana redirected her attention to the elemental. "Who controls them?"

The elemental withdrew into itself and reappeared a moment later.

"Many mages control the earth and water elementals. The magic I sense is the kind lizardmages use. The fire elemental is uncontrolled."

"Where are they?" demanded Adriana.

"I sense the magic emanating from the mountains east of here," answered the elemental, pointing in the direction of the Old Dwarven Mountains.

"Can you stop them?" asked Adriana.

The elemental shook its head. "I cannot."

"Are the lizardmages responsible for this plague?" pressed Adriana.

"It is possible," said the elemental. "The plague runs in many rivers. The worst spills from the water originating in the mountains."

"How can we stop them?" asked Adriana as Martha's chanting increased in intensity. She glanced briefly at the robust druid, who was sweating with the effort of the summoning spell.

"You must stop the summoners from controlling the elementals," said the air elemental. "You must go there and physically stop their magic."

Adriana looked helplessly at Kazin. She was getting nowhere.

"How do I find the lizardmages?" asked Kazin, speaking loudly.

The elemental turned to the mage. "I can guide you there with my wind. Beyond that, there is nothing I can do to help. Perhaps you can find and control the fire elemental, who is also in the mountains. The fire elemental may be better equipped to assist you."

Suddenly, the air elemental began to lose coalescence and a strange expression appeared on its face. Martha's chanting increased in pitch and intensity and she fell to her knees.

Shocked and alarmed, Adriana demanded, "What's wrong? What's happening?"

The elemental grimaced and moaned. "Someone else is trying to summon me! I - cannot maintain my form!"

Adriana immediately added her magical energy to Martha's, chanting frantically.

The elemental managed to regain its form temporarily and directed its attention to Kazin. "Do not allow the lizardmages to prevail! If they do, your destruction is assured! Follow my wind!" The elemental gave a last, painful howl and swirled into its natural form. With a sudden whoosh, the elemental's essence departed the altar and surged between Kazin and the druids on its way across North Lake. A tremendous wind blasted in its wake as Kazin staggered over to the druids.

Adriana was kneeling beside Martha, who lay unconscious on the floor.

"Is she alright?" shouted Kazin above the howling wind.

Adriana looked up and there were tears in her eyes. "She is the most powerful druid there is. Her power exceeds mine by far, yet she does not know it. If some harm has come to her because of this -." The druid broke off and her serious demeanor returned. "You must stop the lizardmages at once, Kazin! Amelia said you would do it! Go! Go at once!" She pointed after the trail of wind the elemental had left behind.

Kazin nodded and started to turn but paused. "What about Della and the sailors?"

Adriana rose to her feet and literally shook with rage. "I will take care of them, fool! Go! Go now!" She pointed again.

Kazin knew better than to argue. He took two steps toward the tower's edge and transformed himself into his dragon form. Leaping from the edge, he soared awkwardly into the wind, the gusts pushing him faster than he had ever gone before. When he was nearly beyond the view of the tower, he felt a refreshing burst of energy enter his body. Stabilizing himself, he directed his path to match that of the departing elemental.

Adriana returned her attention to Martha, satisfied that her 'refresh' spell had reached the mage. She was suddenly sorry for losing her temper. It wasn't Kazin's fault that everything had gone wrong. He was one of the few people who could save them. At least, so Amelia had said, and Amelia was always right.

Kazin flew like the wind - literally. His speed was at least five times faster than he had ever gone before. That's why he nearly had a heart attack when he heard a voice beside him.

"Hi, Kazin!"

"Wha -?" Kazin looked beside him in surprise.

"You didn't think I'd miss all the fun, did you?"

"Frosty!" exclaimed Kazin in delight. He regarded the speaker without slowing his pace. Frosty was a magical white unicorn. He was also Kazin's familiar. A familiar was a creature linked to a mage by the magical bond between them. Kazin couldn't believe his luck when the unicorn had come into his life a number of years ago, but was thankful that he had. He owed his life to Frosty on more than one occasion, and the support he had received when things got dangerous had been invaluable. Right now, his familiar was there because he sensed the danger Kazin was in and knew he needed help. Sprouting wings magically, the unicorn surged along to join him. Where the unicorn had come from Kazin couldn't even hazard a guess, and he knew better than to ask.

"It's good to see you again," said Kazin. "It's been a long time."

Frosty tilted his head so that his clear, white horn reflected in the moonlight. "More than two years since I last checked on you." His lips did not move as he spoke because he communicated telepathically.

"That's too long," stated Kazin. "We'll have to correct that."

"Agreed," answered Frosty. "So what's happening this time?"

Kazin knew the unicorn was not much for small talk and quickly filled him in on what he knew.

"Do you think you'll find the fire elemental?" asked Frosty somberly when Kazin had finished.

"I hope so," said Kazin. "If I - wait a minute!" He glanced over at the unicorn. "Aren't you going to help?"

Frosty shook his head. "My magic isn't as powerful when I'm inside the mountains. I'll be more useful to you out here."

Kazin was stunned. It wasn't like his familiar to back out of a dangerous situation. "I don't understand."

"Kazin, there is something you should know," said the unicorn sadly.

Kazin became alarmed. "What is it, Frosty?"

There was an uncomfortable pause before Frosty spoke. "My power is linked to the elementals. If they have been enslaved by the lizardmen, they will do whatever the lizardmen say. As they weaken, so will I. If they weaken too much, the magic that keeps me in this world will fail and I will be no more."

"No!" cried Kazin anxiously. "We can't let that happen!"

105

"For you to succeed," continued Frosty, "I must stay away from the mountains. I can still draw my energy from what is presently available in the world. That will last for some time. But eventually that energy will become depleted the longer the elementals are imprisoned and controlled. You will see the evidence of that in the weather and in geographical conditions. If I were to go too deep into the mountains, my source of energy would be blocked out and I would only be a hindrance to you. You must go without me, but that doesn't mean I can't help you."

Kazin clenched his dragon teeth. Things were not going well at all. Now things were getting personal. He flew in silence for a while and thought about the situation carefully. Then he remembered something.

"Frosty, I have a task for you. I don't know if it will help too much, but it's important."

"Go ahead," said Frosty.

"I need you to gather some herbs from the Tower of Hope and bring them to the Tower of the Moon. Then I need you to take some more herbs to the royal palace in Priscilla, north of the Old Dwarven Mountains. Maybe the clerics and druids there can combine the herbs you bring with their magic to create an antidote for the plague that's affecting the people at the Tower of Hope and the mages in the Tower of Sorcery."

"No problem," said Frosty. "Consider it done."

"Maybe you should bring a patient from the Tower of the Moon with you so the serum can be tested as well."

"Sure," said Frosty. He started to turn back.

"Wait!" said Kazin suddenly.

Frosty looked at him questioningly.

"Do you even know how to find the Tower of the Moon?"

Frosty laughed. "Of course!" He turned and flew off in the opposite direction.

"I should have known" muttered Kazin.

Time was not an issue for Kazin, and by morning he neared the Old Dwarven Mountains. A storm was brewing directly over the mountains and thunder rumbled ominously in the form of a thick black cloud. Lightning surged haphazardly in all directions from the cloud, bathing the mountains in a dazzling display of blue and white light. Kazin needed no urging to find the nearest cavern entrance. Despite his speed, the dragon could not outrun the torrents of rain that burst from the clouds like a massive waterfall. He finally reached a cave entrance and transformed back into his human form before lunging into the safety of the cavern. The mage shook the raindrops from his cape and glanced out of the entrance. The rain was so hard that even the light could not penetrate the cavern. It was daytime, but one would never know it from where Kazin stood. He chanted a spell to light his staff and turned to face the passageway. It would be easy to become lost in these mountains. In the past he had guides to lead him through the maze of passageways. This time he was alone. Truly alone.

× × × × ×

The river was almost deafening as it rushed through the cavern. The over-spray of water was cold but refreshing as the dwarf and elf trudged along its shoreline. Rebecca paused to fill her wineskin with water by a small spring that trickled from a cleft in the rock. The spring's water ran across their path in small rivulets to join the torrential river as it wended its way out of sight in the darkness. Alric joined the dwarf and opened his wineskin.

"The water in this spring is very cold," remarked Rebecca, moving aside so the elf could fill his wineskin in turn.

"That means it's fresh," said the elf. He eagerly took a few big gulps of the fresh water. "Ahh, that's good," he said, refilling his wineskin a second time.

While he was thus occupied, Rebecca reorganized the contents of her pack. The talisman's vibrating was becoming annoying due to the fact that Alric had magical items in his possession, so it was moved to the bottom out of the way. The dagger was repositioned in the side pouch for easier access.

Satisfied, they moved on. The footing along here was slick at times and both of them slipped and stumbled along as best they could. Finally they encountered a tunnel on their left that led up from the water's edge.

Rebecca hesitated. "Should we investigate?" She nodded in the direction of the tunnel.

Alric stopped to examine the ground. He appeared to be peering at something.

"What is it?" asked Rebecca.

Alric picked up an object and held it closer to Rebecca's torch light. He rotated it in his fingers. "It appears to be the tip of a claw. The slender shape is consistent with the claw of a lizardman."

Rebecca became excited. "Really? Then maybe this tunnel leads to a lizardman lair!"

Alric shrugged and cast the claw aside. "It's possible. I guess we'd better check it out."

Rebecca smiled and led the way, making sure to hide her grin. The elf had said 'we'. That meant that he no longer objected to her presence. Either that, or he knew she would come along anyway and there was no point arguing about it.

A good half hour of exploring revealed nothing and they were about to turn back, when Alric stopped suddenly and raised his hand. Rebecca, who had chosen to let Alric take point a little way back, almost ran into him.

"Wha-?" Rebecca started to speak out but Alric shook his hand furiously for silence.

"Shhh!" he whispered. "I heard something."

Rebecca strained her ears. After a moment, she heard a distant shuffling noise ahead of them.

"Someone's coming!" whispered Alric. He looked back at Rebecca. "Let's go back to that last intersection. We might be able to avoid a confrontation."

Rebecca nodded and turned to lead the way back. They rounded one bend in the tunnel, but that proved to be futile. Coming toward them was a group of orcs.

Alric swore and looked behind them. The shuffling noise they had heard earlier was almost upon them and the tunnel began to flicker with the reflection of torchlight. "We'll have to make a stand here," grumbled the elf. He pulled his dagger from his robe pocket.

Rebecca drew her axe and looked at Alric's dagger. "Is that all you

-?" she began. Her words trailed off as Alric chanted a spell. With a small flash of light, his dagger grew into a long sword. Rebecca's eyes widened. "That's a clever trick!"

"It's magic," said Alric.

Rebecca knew it was. She could feel her talisman vibrating right through her pack.

Alric positioned himself with his back to the dwarf and braced himself to face the creatures making the shuffling noise. He could see them now and immediately recognized them as orcs. The shuffling noise was made by an injured orc that was dragging its leg.

Rebecca was already facing her opponents as well. They had slowed and were approaching the duo cautiously. They were looking at Rebecca's waist and licked their lips anxiously.

"Water!" murmured one orc, trying to edge past his friends. He was somewhat smaller than the others and they roughly pushed him back behind them. "Hey!" he cried, obviously disappointed.

"You'll get your share," growled the orc with the torch.

Rebecca threw down her torch and it went out. With the axe in one hand and her other hand now free, she withdrew her magical dagger.

The orcs slowed but continued to advance.

Alric's opponents weren't as cautious. They drooled and pointed at him, shambling forward eagerly.

The two groups of orcs struck at roughly the same time. Alric grunted as he withstood a vicious blow from an orc's club, his sword biting into the rough wood. With a powerful thrust, he threw the orc back into his friends, freeing his sword at the same time.

Behind him, an orc swung his club at the dwarf's head. Instinctively, Rebecca ducked the blow, realizing almost too late that she was not protecting the taller elf at her back. Not a second too soon, she thrust her axe upward against the club with such vehemence that the club was redirected hard against the tunnel ceiling. The vibration of the club, along with the unorthodox battle tactic, caused the orc to drop his weapon. Another club came in low to Rebecca's right and she only had time to twist her dagger hand. The club struck the tip of the knife and a small flash occurred. Any life within the club was burned out of it and the remainder crumbled in the orc's hand.

The orcs facing Rebecca stumbled back into their buddies looking confused and helpless without their weapons.

Meanwhile, Alric had already slain two orcs with some straight thrusts and had a moment's respite to glance behind him.

"How's it goin'?" he asked.

"Everything's under control," answered Rebecca.

The sound of steel against steel told her that the battle behind her had commenced. Seizing the moment, Rebecca lunged at the orcs and swung her axe deep into one's shoulder while her dagger found the abdomen of the other. The now familiar flash of light signaled the death of one orc. A scream was its final act as it dropped to the floor. The other one winced as green blood oozed from its severed limb. It wobbled uncertainly before sagging to the floor, unconscious. The orcs behind them were preparing to step in to do battle, but the bright flash had impaired their vision. One stumbled over its dead companion and fell flat on its face. Rebecca chopped its head off with a single one-armed blow from her axe and stepped back to brace for the next assault.

Alric sliced the head off of the orc armed with a sword, his agility giving him the edge in that battle. Unfortunately, this gave another orc an opening. It struck Alric in the leg with its club and the elf went down with a yelp. Fortunately for Alric, he was already moving in the same direction as the blow so it didn't do any serious damage. Nimbly rolling to his feet, the elf made a couple of quick moves with his sword and dispatched the offender before it could cause any more harm.

Rebecca was now facing a terrifying orc armed with a meat cleaver. The orc was the largest and ugliest she had encountered thus far. With a vicious downward thrust, the orc tried to chop the dwarf like a log being prepared for kindling. Rebecca tried to block the attack with her axe but could not hinder the heavy blow. Falling to her back, she rolled out of the way as the weapons clashed to the floor beside her head. Letting go of her axe, she rolled up to the orc and stabbed it in the leg with her dagger. The orc was already off balance, and the searing pain in its leg was enough to fell the giant. In the blinding flash, Rebecca rolled out of the way, while Alric turned back to stab the creature as it fell.

When Alric saw that Rebecca was O.K., he turned to find that his remaining adversary was fleeing. It was the limping orc. Wasting no time, he sprinted after it and finished it off with a couple of quick stabs.

Rebecca rolled to her feet and faced her last opponent. It was the small orc. Somehow it had ended up with the torch. It trembled as it faced the fierce looking dwarf. Sizing up the situation properly, its voice quavered in some unknown gibberish as it dropped the torch, turned, and fled back the way it had come.

Rebecca was out of breath and knew it was pointless to try to follow. She turned and saw the elf approaching with a slight limp. His form looked somewhat eerie in the flickering light of the torch the orc had dropped.

"My side is secured," said the elf.

Rebecca nodded. "My way is clear. Only one got away."

The elf sat down and winced, rubbing his bruised leg. "I think we should rest for a few minutes."

"What happened?" asked Rebecca, indicating Alric's leg.

Alric told her, and when she offered to examine it he waved her off. "It's nothing."

Rebecca sighed but knew better than to argue. She stood up and made sure the unconscious orc was dead. Then she checked the bodies for anything useful but found nothing of interest.

"They wanted something," mused Alric as the dwarf returned to his location.

"They mentioned water," said Rebecca. "They seemed to be looking at my wineskin too."

"Maybe they thought you had dwarven ale," suggested Alric.

"That's ridiculous," retorted Rebecca. "I don't carry that kind of thing on a journey."

"Orcs like dwarven ale," stated Alric. "You're a dwarf."

"True," admitted Rebecca finally. "But they did mention water."

"That's what boggles me," said Alric. "Why would they kill for water?"

Rebecca shrugged. "If water was hard to come by, why don't they go to the river and obtain it there?"

"Maybe it's not drinkable," suggested the elf.

"But we filled our wineskins with it and even drank some of it!" said the dwarf. "It seemed like good water to me."

Alric shook his head. "We filled our skins with water from the spring that ran into the river. We didn't use the river's water. I thought I smelled a strange odour from the river. Maybe it isn't drinkable."

Rebecca had also noticed the strange odour. The elf could be right. "I guess we'd better ration our water from here on in. It could mean the difference between life and death."

"Agreed," said the elf. He rose to his feet. "Ready to go?"

The dwarf hopped to her feet and picked up their extinguished torch. She took it over to the still burning torch from the orcs and relit hers. Then she stomped out the orc's torch and kicked it aside. "Let's go."

As they left the battlefield behind, the elf commented, "You fought well."

Rebecca was surprised at the elf's comment but did not show it. "Thanks. You're pretty good with that sword." She noticed at that instant that the elf had already returned his sword into dagger form.

The elf did not respond and Rebecca respected his silence. She knew now that Alric had accepted her presence and she was not about to jeopardize that with pointless babble.

Chapter 13

any hours had passed and Vera was beginning to become fatigued. Her quest to find Cyril was more difficult than she had imagined. There were numerous tunnels that the cyclops could have gone down and it was entirely possible that she had missed the right path. Furthermore, she had to be careful not to become lost. The paths she had taken thus far were becoming difficult to remember. She made sure to mark intersections by making scratches in the walls in case she wanted to leave the mountains. The cleric narrowed down her search to the tunnels that seemed more heavily traveled because the others were too dusty and cobwebbed to have been used recently. Cyril was large in stature, so the smaller tunnels were definitely out of the question. That left the larger tunnels and main branches. Even using these tactics, Vera was beginning to lose hope. The only things that kept her hopes up were scuff marks and signs of recent disturbance in the sometimes soft soil on the tunnel floor.

But now the cleric was in need of some much needed rest. She hadn't slept for a day and a half now and her body ached from the climb up the mountain. Her lit staff indicated some low alcoves ahead where she could crawl in away from the main tunnel. It was off to the side at an odd angle and she was fairly certain it would hide her from view should any undesirable travelers come along. It was also deep, so she could crawl well out of visible range should anyone actually look in that direction. The dirt and cold of the ground was a far cry from a soft, clean bed in the Tower of Hope, but it would have to do. She laid out her blanket so her clothes could remain as clean as possible and laid down. Sorting through her pack, she withdrew some compressed rations and ate a sizeable portion. Then she took a small drink from her wineskin and put it safely into her pack. With dinner completed, she canceled her spell on her staff and her alcove became dark. Then she curled up on her blanket and fell asleep.

She didn't know how long she had been sleeping when she awoke with a start. Something furry had crawled into her blanket and was rubbing her leg. With a cry, she shook herself free of the blanket and found her staff on the ground nearby. Chanting an incantation, she lit the staff and caught sight of a furry creature as it fled from her alcove. It was a mouse.

Composing herself, Vera gathered her belongings and stuffed them in her pack. She was fully awake now and decided to move on. Hoping that she hadn't fallen too far behind the cyclops, Vera hastily crawled from her resting place and proceeded to follow the tunnel at a brisk pace. She didn't go very far before she heard a muffled sound ahead. It sounded like something large was shuffling along. Her heart jumped to her throat. Could it be Cyril? She hoped so. A side passageway appeared to her right and that's where the sound had originated. She entered and walked around a gradual corner. The shuffling sound was nearer now. Vera's heart pounded. Shakily, she attempted a loud whisper. "Cyril?"

The sound stopped. Vera braced herself, hoping that it was Cyril and not something entirely different. The shuffling continued and became louder still.

Holding her staff high, Vera fingered a small dagger at her side in a belt holster. Whatever was there was getting closer. "Cyril?" repeated Vera, louder this time. If it was Cyril, he would answer.

The shuffling sound paused but still there was no answer. Now Vera was afraid. She turned and started to run back to the main tunnel. The shuffling sound was right behind her. Whatever it was, it was now running after her.

Vera was a fast runner, yet whatever was behind her seemed to be keeping up. She began to panic. There were all manner of creatures in the mountains and she could be in grave danger. She was foolish to have entered the mountains alone. She wondered what had possessed her to go after Cyril in the first place.

Her thoughts changed when she stumbled over some uneven ground. Right now she had to get away. She looked behind her before entering the main tunnel, half expecting to see a gruesome creature in pursuit. Only flickering shadows from her staff light were visible. Breaking free of the side tunnel, Vera turned to go back the way she had come, but the way was blocked by a massive creature. Her momentum prevented her from stopping in time, and she flew headlong into the creature's arms. The creature instinctively embraced her while she instinctively let out a blood curdling scream.

Vera fought like a demon to escape the grip of the creature, and to her surprise, she succeeded. Spinning away, she turned and stopped dead in her tracks. The way was blocked by the creature that had chased her. It was an ogre. Its eyes were a pale shade of yellow, and it had a messy mat of black hair. Its head was shaped like a Neanderthal, and its arms hung like a gorilla's, with long hair under the armpits. The entire body was covered in dark brown hair, and the stench of its unclean body filled the air. Yellow teeth grinned at her and spittle drooled from its mouth. Looking up, it suddenly saw the other creature behind Vera. Its jaw started to open in surprise and it froze on the spot. Vera spun to see what it was staring at and froze herself.

Cyril was the first to recover from his look of astonishment. "V-Vera?" he stammered. "What are you doing here?"

Of course there was no answer. The others were both paralyzed. Cyril shook his head in bewilderment. He stepped forward and gently picked up the prone figure of the cleric, hoisting her over his shoulder. Deftly stepping past the ogre, he strode purposefully down the tunnel until he came to a fork. He chose the left one and walked a short distance before entering a conglomeration of bisecting caverns. Winding his way through several of these, Cyril found a smaller tunnel that appeared to have been abandoned for an extended time. Entering this tunnel, he walked for a good half hour before he deemed it safe to stop and rest near a moon-shaped alcove.

Gently putting the cleric down, the cyclops surveyed his surroundings. The walls here were wet with dew and veins of some sorts of minerals ran in all directions.

A moan signaled the awakening of the cleric from her paralysis. Cyril made sure to avoid his gaze as Vera regained consciousness.

115

"Cyril!" exclaimed Vera suddenly. The fragile cleric sprang at the cyclops and embraced him. "I've found you at last!"

"You were looking for me?" asked the cyclops. He tried to detach the cleric gently but she refused to budge.

"Yes!" said Vera. "I couldn't just let you run off like that! It wasn't your fault that you paralyzed the head groundskeeper!"

"Sure it was!" retorted Cyril. "He was my boss! I had no right to do that!"

Vera finally let go of the cyclops to look at the side of his face. "He had no right to treat you like he did! I would have done far worse to him if I were you!"

Cyril shook his head. "You don't understand. Someone like me could never be allowed to roam in the human's realm. I'm a freak!"

"No, you're not!" stated Vera resolutely. "Just because you only have one eye and accidentally paralyze people doesn't mean you should be confined to a life of exile! You have a special gift!"

"Gift? It's a curse, not a gift!" snapped Cyril.

Vera calmed her voice before continuing. "You can let it be whatever you want it to be, Cyril. If you want it to be a curse, then it's a curse. But if you want it to be a gift, it can be a very useful gift."

"How?" asked Cyril. "Tell me how it can possibly be a gift!"

"Look at what you just did," said Vera. "You used your gift to save me from an ogre, and an ugly one at that. Your gift saved my life."

Cyril tilted his head in consideration. "I could have paralyzed you and not the ogre if the ogre didn't look into my eye. You could have been hurt!"

"Nonsense!" shot back Vera. "You would have protected me by force if necessary. I know you better than that."

Cyril grinned sheepishly. "Yeah, I guess."

Vera gave the cyclops a shot in the arm. "You guess! My foot! You would have beaten the hair off his smelly armpits!"

Cyril's grin got wider. "They did smell, didn't they?"

"Something awful!" said Vera. Her serious demeanor suddenly returned. "You can use that gift of yours to save others, you know. You just have to use it wisely."

Cyril's grin vanished. "Maybe, but most people wouldn't see it that way. You might understand me, but others would think I'm up to no good. Every time I try to help, someone interprets my actions as being bad. It's been that way all my life. I doubt those attitudes would change now."

"You'd be surprised," said Vera. "If I understand you, there must be others who think the same way."

Cyril sighed. "It doesn't matter, Vera. After what I did to the head groundskeeper, they will never let me return. I ran away like the guilty creature I am. It's pointless to consider the possibility."

"I'm not so sure," said Vera. "The Tower of Hope does not discriminate."

"The groundskeeper did."

"True," admitted Vera. "But he paid the price for his actions. I don't expect he would treat you like dirt anymore."

"That's a sad way to gain respect," said Cyril.

"Some people learn the hard way," said Vera. "But most people would accept you without resorting to those measures. Just give it time. You'll see."

"I don't know," Cyril mumbled.

A dull echo halted their discussion.

"Did you hear that?" asked Vera.

"Yeah," said Cyril. "It came from over here."

The cleric followed the cyclops to the side of the alcove where a fissure in the rock became evident.

"I never spotted this earlier," said Cyril. "It's an opening into another part of the mountain."

Vera held her staff closer to the opening to shed more light on the crack. "I wonder where it leads."

The cyclops and cleric looked at each other in anticipation.

"Do you want to check it out?" asked Vera.

"Sure!" said Cyril. "I think I can just squeeze through there. I'll go first."

"I'll follow you," said Vera.

The cyclops squished through the opening and Vera followed. It was a struggle to get through the tunnel, but they doggedly continued.

A short while later, they ended up in a small cavern that was just big enough to accommodate both of them if they stood close together.

"Now what?" panted Cyril, who was glad to be able to stretch to his full height.

Another echo interrupted their thoughts.

"Something is just beyond the wall," said Vera. "I can't see any openings, but maybe if I put out my staff's light we can see light beyond through a hole or something."

"I don't know," muttered Cyril. His breath was hot against Vera's head.

Vera grinned and knew what the cyclops was thinking. Without debating the point, she put out the staff light.

A long tense pause was followed by a sudden twitch in the cyclops' arm. "Wait! I see something!"

"What is it?" asked Vera. She could see nothing but blackness.

"You were right!" exclaimed Cyril. "There is a hole!"

"Can you see through it?" asked Vera.

"I - you're in the way," said Cyril apologetically.

Vera tried to move over but couldn't. "Do you have room on your left side?"

Cyril moved and twisted. "Not really."

"Maybe I can slide over here," said Vera. A sudden movement followed some pushing and shoving and Vera's voice came from somewhere below the cyclops. "How's that? Can you look through the hole now?"

Cyril was glad it was dark in there. "Let me see." He twisted to his left and peered into the source of the light. "I see something!"

"What is it?" asked Vera. The echoes could be heard again.

Cyril did not respond. His eye widened at what he saw. A number of ogres had gathered in a large cavern. One stood on a platform speaking to the gathered throng. He wore black gloves and held a wineskin in one hand. As he spoke, he pointed repeatedly to the wineskin. His voice was faint, but as Cyril watched, he could make out the odd word that the ogre spoke. Every so often the throng would react and that's when the echo could be heard where Vera and Cyril stood.

"Well, what is it?" demanded Vera. "I'm getting cramped down here."

"It's a bunch of ogres," said Cyril. "They're talking about a wineskin. It looks like they want to fight for the wine in the wineskin. Maybe they found a stash of dwarven spirits or something. They just went to get - wait a minute! They've captured a lizardman! The lizardman is dressed in some sort of armor. He looks like a guard or something!"

"A lizardman!" exclaimed Vera. "Good for the ogres!"

"They're taking him on stage," continued Cyril. "They're jeering and throwing things at him!"

The echoes were again noticeable.

"The head ogre is drawing his short sword!" exclaimed Cyril. "He's going to - ugh!" He turned his eye away.

"What is it?" asked Vera.

"They just slit his throat," spat Cyril distastefully.

"Good for them," said Vera coldly.

Cyril was shocked by her tone. "Not for the lizardman."

"There are plenty more where they came from," said Vera.

Cyril sighed. "You have no compassion for lizardmen, do you?"

"No," answered Vera. "Lizardmen and humans have always hated one another. That's not about to change."

"How do you know that this lizardman was evil?" asked the Cyclops.

"They all are," said Vera.

"Just like all cyclops are evil?" said Cyril slyly.

There was a pause before Vera answered. "That's different. You're part human."

Cyril didn't answer.

"What's happening now?" Vera asked quickly, changing the subject. The echoes were getting louder.

Cyril looked through the hole again and focused on the proceedings once again. The ogres had hacked the lizardman into pieces and their leader had his sword raised over his head. He yelled several commands. With a roar, the entire assembly charged from the cavern into a tunnel and disappeared from sight, leaving the fragmented remains of the lizardman in a bloody pulp on the floor.

"They just left," said Cyril. "They looked like they were on the warpath. A battle is probably going to take place. It won't be a pretty sight, either."

"Battles are never pretty," said Vera.

"That's it, I guess," said Cyril. "There's no more to see here. We might as well get back to the other tunnel."

"Easier said than done," said Vera.

"What do you mean?" asked Cyril.

Vera giggled. "I'm stuck!"

✗ ✗ ✗ ✗ ✗

Graf was irritated by the noise in the council hall. Lizardmen were arguing and hissing at each other. The whole place was in an uproar at the announcement made only moments ago by one of the army generals. Graf rose and chanted a short spell. A deafening thunder clap cracked from his staff, causing the entire assembly to cease their chatter at once. All turned their attention to their leader. Graf turned to the general, known as Slong, and told him to continue before sitting down.

Slong nodded. "As I was saying, some of our remote front line garrisons have recently been attacked. My scouts have returned with reports that confirm large numbers of ogres and orcs have been responsible for these attacks. It appears we are at war."

"Why are they attacking?" demanded a lizardmage from an alcove.

"I have been informed that the orcs and ogres are blaming us for the poisoned water. They don't see us suffering from the same illnesses that affect them, and assume our water is pure. They don't realize that we are immune to the poison."

A murmur filtered through the council hall but subsided immediately when Graf rose to his feet again. "Continue, Slong."

Slong nodded. "Reinforcements have been dispatched to bolster our second line of defense, but I don't know if it will be enough to stem the tide of ogres and orcs heading our way. They are angry and unafraid of our magic."

The murmurs began again but ceased when Graf tapped his staff on the floor for silence. Relg rose and Graf nodded at him to speak.

"We were counting on the ogres and orcs to assist us in our upcoming battle. Perhaps we should convince them the humans are responsible for the poison and get them to join us using that as a source of motivation."

Murmurs of agreement rippled through the lizardmen in the hall below.

"Perhaps we should give them clean water," countered Graf suddenly.

The idea was so preposterous that the entire assembly stared dumfounded at Graf in complete silence.

"B-but how will that help this situation?" sputtered a lower-ranking lizardmage. "If we give the ogres and orcs fresh water, they might stop attacking and go away, but they might be angry enough not to join us in our cause!"

"By giving in to their demands so quickly," added another lizardmage, "they might continue their assault, thinking that we are weak and can be defeated!"

Graf's lips slid into a devious grin as the crowd began to murmur again. He chuckled evilly, just loud enough to be heard by those nearest him. As the murmurs waned, Graf's chuckle became a sinister laugh.

"I take it there is a reason for your statement," interrupted Relg irritably. He knew better than to shoot down Graf's idea out of hand.

Graf stopped laughing and nodded. "We will give the ogres and orcs fresh water - and anybody else for that matter - but only if they agree to fight for us in exchange. Those who do not fight for us do not receive clean water. It's as simple as that! Why, we could even recruit humans to fight for us, should they be in need of clean water! By the time we attack, many humans will only be too grateful to swell our ranks!"

This time the hall exploded in a roar of hissing as everyone spoke at once.

"Do we even have clean water to offer the ogres and orcs?" cried out one lizardman loudly.

"We still have access to clean mountain springs!" bellowed Graf, though he was barely audible above the raucous below. "We also control the water elemental, so good water is easily acquired!"

When the raucous died down, Graf sighed. "Is there anything else?"

A lizardmage fairly high in rank rose to her feet. Her lips were puffy, like a fish, and her navy blue cloak had purple trim at its edges.

"The council recognizes Narla," stated the lizardmage below Graf.

Graf knew who she was but the announcer below him had to get a word in from time to time. His position was virtually meaningless, but he was tolerated nonetheless.

"Proceed," stated Graf.

Narla smiled, her fish-like lips spreading grotesquely - although it was considered attractive from a lizardman's point of view. "The air elemental has been contained within a solid wall of rock created by the earth elemental. There is still resistance, but full control will be established shortly."

"Excellent!" praised Graf. "Now all we need is that fire elemental and the world will be ours!" He turned to Brind, the black-cloaked lizardmage. "Have you summoned the fire elemental yet?"

Brind shook his head. "Not yet. I need to get closer to it in order to summon it."

"Lynch!" called Graf in a serious voice.

"Present!" answered Lynch from below. He was glad he was mixed in with the crowd. He did not want to be singled out when Graf was angry. He wasn't in his alcove right now because he was close to the main hall when the meeting was called.

"I take it you still haven't been able to capture the fire elemental?" Graf had a note of sarcasm in his voice.

"No," said Lynch quietly.

"What?!" yelled Graf. "I didn't hear you!"

"No!" repeated Lynch, louder this time.

Graf scowled. "Keep trying!" He turned to the general. "Slong, lend some of your scouts to Lynch. They know the tunnels beyond our realm better than most."

"Of course," answered Slong.

"And begin sending caskets of water to the orcs and ogres," ordered Graf. "It's time to generate an army!"

"Yes, Sir!" said Slong.

The meeting was over and everyone exited the hall, eager to put Graf's plan into action.

Chapter 14

Rebecca rummaged through her pack looking for some fungus she had accumulated in the last couple of days. Alric was complaining more and more frequently about being hungry, and Rebecca decided to do something about it. She found the fungus she had wrapped to keep it fresh. "Here," she said, extending it toward the elf.

"What is it?" asked the elf, taking the package in his hands and holding it close to his face.

"Fungus."

Alric quickly held it out at arms' length when he heard what it was. "Fungus!" he exclaimed. "Are you trying to kill me?"

"Of course not!" retorted Rebecca. "That fungus is safe to eat. It's good for you, and some dwarves even use it for medicinal purposes."

"What's it taste like?" queried the elf, pulling his hand close again.

"It's O.K." said Rebecca. "It's not something you would eat on a regular basis, but it beats being hungry."

Alric looked at the dwarf uncertainly as he brought a small piece of fungus up to his mouth. He popped it in and chewed. Suddenly his face wrinkled in revulsion. "Eww! This stuff is terrible! Are you sure it's not poisonous or something?"

"It's perfectly safe," said Rebecca. "Here." She took a piece out of Alric's hand and put it in her mouth. She chewed a few times and swallowed. "See? I'm not trying to poison you."

Alric continued chewing slowly and then swallowed. He wrinkled his face again. "I wouldn't recommend this stuff to anyone unless they're starving to death. It's horrible!" He popped another piece of fungus into his mouth and chewed distastefully.

"It'll keep you from starving," said the dwarf. Sitting down with a faint 'plop', Rebecca pulled out her map and began making modifications.

Alric swallowed with a grimace. "Do you know where we're going?" Gingerly, he lifted another piece of fungus to his lips.

"We seem to be spiraling downward," commented Rebecca. "Things should be getting warmer in a day or two."

Alric stopped chewing. "Warmer?"

"Yup," answered the dwarf. She ran her fingers along the silver streak in her hair. "As we get deeper, the mountain gets warmer. The rocks in the mountain are so compressed that they become hot. We may even start encountering lava flows."

"Interesting," said Alric, swallowing the last of the fungus. "A few days ago we were in cold, damp conditions. Now we're going to be experiencing the exact opposite."

"It's a bigger world down here than you elves realize," said Rebecca. She quickly wrote a few more notations on her map and then stashed it away. "Are you ready to continue?"

"I was waiting for you," said Alric, springing to his feet.

Rebecca was about to argue the point when she saw the elf wink at her. He was only teasing. Feigning an angry tone, she jabbed him in the ribs and ordered, "Get moving!"

A few hours later, the duo ran across a fork in the tunnel.

"Which way?" asked Rebecca, looking at the elf.

"I think we should go right," said Alric.

"I was thinking the left path is better," said Rebecca. "It seems to slope downward, deeper into the mountain."

"I have a hunch there are more chances of finding lizardmen on the right path," insisted Alric. "It seems to be more heavily traveled."

Rebecca hesitated. "I don't know."

Alric brightened. "Why don't we investigate both?"

The dwarf looked up at him. "Huh?"

"I'll take the right path and you take the left," continued the elf. "We'll explore for an hour or two and then meet back here. We can compare notes and make a decision then."

"I don't know," said Rebecca slowly.

"I can even give you information to help you expand your map," insisted Alric. "We've got nothing to lose."

"And we'll meet back here in a couple of hours?" asked the dwarf. She looked searchingly into the elf's face.

Alric sensed her discomfort. "I promise."

Rebecca didn't know whether elves kept their promises or not so she didn't feel reassured. Reluctantly she agreed.

"Great," said Alric. He handed the torch to the dwarf.

"How will you be able to see?" asked Rebecca suddenly.

"Elves have keen eyesight," stated Alric. "I'll be fine." He moved a few steps away and donned his invisibility cloak. In an instant, the elf vanished.

Rebecca felt momentary wind as the elf ran past her into the right tunnel. "Good luck," she called after her companion.

"Same to you," came the response.

Rebecca sighed. She was alone again. She was just beginning to enjoy Alric's presence and wondered vaguely if he would rendezvous with her back at this spot in a few hours. She realized that the only way to find out was to fulfill her part of the bargain. Shouldering her pack, Rebecca strode resolutely into the left tunnel.

Nearly half an hour of ducking into side tunnels and alcoves turned up nothing, and the dwarf was almost ready to call it quits and return to the rendezvous point. Up ahead, she could make out a five-way intersection that had a promising look to it. As she neared the intersection, her nose picked up the faint smell of orcs.

Rebecca quickly put out her torch and waited for her eyes to adjust to the darkness. Soon, she could distinguish between the walls and the ground. The tunnels ahead looked black and forbidding. Withdrawing her light stone from her pouch, Rebecca cautiously walked forward to the middle of the intersection. She peered down each tunnel but saw nothing. There was also no sound but that of her own breathing.

Looking down, the dwarf noticed some marks in the soft ground where she stood. They were orc tracks. Almost all of them meandered between two of the tunnels. The other three tunnels were joined by only a few footprints, including her own. Rebecca was more interested in the tunnels that were heavily traveled.

Suddenly, the dwarf saw an increase of light in one of the heavily-traveled tunnels. Someone was approaching!

Hiding her light stone and springing back to the tunnel she had come from - it was the only one she knew to be safe - Rebecca ran for cover in a nearby alcove. Poking her nose around the corner, she watched and waited.

An agonizing minute later, the light increased and footsteps could be heard. The light continued to brighten and Rebecca almost had to close her eyes. It was as if whoever was coming had ten torches lit! With a hot rush of wind, a flaming figure burst into the intersection. It spun around, looking at each of the tunnels in turn. When it looked down Rebecca's tunnel, the dwarf ducked back into the alcove, hoping she hadn't been spotted. The footsteps could be heard again, and Rebecca immediately realized that the burning figure had not chosen her tunnel.

As the light began to fade, the dwarf left the refuge of the alcove only to dive back into its safety. Yells and stomping feet could be heard originating from the same tunnel as the flaming figure. Before long, Rebecca could smell the unmistakable scent of orcs. Running like a bunch of savages, the orcs piled into the intersection and milled about uncertainly.

"Where is he?" asked one orc.

Another sniffed. "I smell dwarf."

"That was no dwarf!" retorted another.

"This way!" cried another one. "Burn marks!"

"Let's go!" cried several orcs in unison. Their trampling feet indicated their departure down the tunnel the flaming figure had chosen.

One orc trailed behind the others. "I smell dwarf!" he lamented.

"Come on!" cried another orc.

The footsteps died away.

Rebecca cautiously exited the alcove. All was quiet once more. She took a moment to consider what she had seen. The orcs were chasing some sort of flaming creature. She didn't know what it was, but it was in trouble.

She thought briefly of helping the flaming creature, but remembered that she had to rendezvous with Alric. There was plenty of time, but exploring any further alone would be dangerous. She didn't need the elf to protect her, but she had made an agreement. If she didn't keep her side of the bargain, how could she expect the elf to keep his? He might even return home to his people and report that dwarves don't hold to a deal! She would be responsible for making all dwarves look dishonourable!

Rebecca couldn't let that be on her conscience. She turned to head back when some hollering and yelling echoed through the tunnels. It came from the tunnel the orcs and flaming man had gone down. Had they captured him? If so, should she try to save him? She didn't know him. The flaming man could be just as evil as the orcs were. But what if he wasn't?

Rebecca looked uncertainly back the way she had come. Go to the rendezvous or help the flaming man? Honour demanded both. Then again, if she didn't show up at the rendezvous point, would Alric come searching for her? Or would he just give up on her and go his own way, cursing her for wasting his time? What if he didn't show up either? Then he wasn't going back for her, was he? But if he got into trouble, he might be expecting her to come and rescue him.

The dwarf stamped her foot furiously. Then it occurred to her. The elf had made the promise to return to the rendezvous point. She had not. She was not obligated.

More yells emanated from the tunnel. Arming herself, Rebecca ran to the aid of the flaming man.

✗ ✗ ✗ ✗ ✗

Tyris the fire elemental searched in vain for an escape route. The passageway behind him was a dead end and he was forced to turn back. One of only a few side passages he had passed was the only other route, but unfortunately the orcs were now in the way. He had to get past them to escape.

At first, when they charged him, he increased his heat level to blind them and force them to step back. It worked, but only temporarily. They overcame the brightness and moved forward again. Then Tyris seared the closest ones with fire and the orcs yelled in pain, pulling back once again.

Unfortunately, Tyris had used much of his energy earlier, and he was in a severely weakened state. Not long ago, he had been cornered by some lizardmen who had been trying to use summoning magic to capture him. He had used a great deal of energy to try to withstand the magic. They would have succeeded, had a legion of orcs not stormed the cavern at that moment. The orcs had killed most of the surprised lizardmen before turning their attention to the fire elemental. Tyris had used the diversion to reach an unguarded tunnel and make his escape, but some of the orcs had pursued him. That led to his present predicament. Now he was cornered again. Ordinarily, he would have easily escaped by creating a firestorm and blasting a path through his pursuers, but his powers eluded him.

"Surrender!" cried one orc. "You can't escape!"

Tyris looked helplessly at the side passage just beyond the orcs. So near yet so far. If he charged the orcs, some of them would get injured or killed, but Tyris would likely die in the attempt, being returned to his element. As soon as he recovered, he was sure the lizardmen would succeed in summoning him from his realm. He would then be forced to do their bidding, something he did not want to happen. He needed to stay alive and free in the mortal plane for now, because he could elude their magic by staying out of their sight.

"Give up!" cried an orc. It stepped forward, menacingly waving a meat cleaver.

"Precisely!" called a strong female voice behind the group of orcs.

The orcs spun around to face the speaker.

"A dwarf!" growled one orc.

Tyris used the opening he was given and barged into the throng of orcs. Screams rent the air as orc flesh burned on contact with the fire elemental. Steel clashed against steel as the battle commenced between the dwarf and a few of the orcs.

Tyris dove into the side passage and ran as fast as his legs could carry him. He ran long after the sounds of the battle died away. No one pursued him. He slowed to a walk and thought about the dwarf who had created a diversion for him to escape. Was she alone? Could she hold off the orcs by herself? Not likely, he thought. The fire elemental stopped walking. The dwarf needed help and here he was, running away. Some gratitude! For the first time in his new existence, Tyris had a purpose. Resolutely, he turned and started back. The more he thought about it, the more urgent was his desire to help the dwarf. Despite his weakened state, the elemental ran. His purpose was clear.

× × × × ×

Rebecca took down three orcs and was battling a fourth one whose arm was still smoking from contact with the burning man when she heard a sound behind her. A moment later everything went black.

"I told you I smelled a dwarf!" said an orc armed with a club. He waved the weapon at the other orcs. "You didn't listen."

The other orcs simply growled.

"Let's check the pack for water!" cried one orc, grabbing Rebecca's pack and almost ripping it open while it was still around her waist. He reached inside and started to rifle through it when his hand came in contact with the dagger. The resulting flash of light and sizzling noise made all the other orcs jump back in alarm. In a matter of seconds, the orc who had his hand in the pack was turned into a pile of ashes. Only some of his clothing remained intact.

"The pack's enchanted!" cried one orc hoarsely. "Don't touch it!"

After an uncertain pause, the orc who had clobbered the dwarf said, "Let's take the dwarf to the dungeon. We'll deal with her after the lizardmen are rounded up."

Two orcs picked up the dwarf, making sure not to come into contact with Rebecca's pack, and followed their injured companions back to the dungeon. As they departed, their torchlight lessened and the tunnel became dark and quiet.

Sometime later, the tunnel began to light up again as the fire elemental returned. He paused to inspect the dead bodies, and was surprised to see one of them burned to ashes. It was not magic of his doing, he was sure.

Satisfied that the dwarf was not among the dead, he rose and started walking back to the five-way intersection. Already, he could feel his strength returning.

"You shouldn't have come after me," stated Cyril.

Vera paused and turned to look at the cyclops, who turned away his gaze.

"And quit looking at me," continued Cyril. "Do you want to become paralyzed again?"

"We've been through this already," said Vera coldly. "I came after you to tell you to come back to your friends."

"What friends?" asked Cyril. "Who on earth would want to call me their friend?"

"I would," said Vera. "I wouldn't have come after you if I wasn't your friend."

"O.K." said Cyril. "So you're my friend. I defy you to name someone else. I'll bet you can't think of anyone else, can you?"

Vera's mind raced. "Well, there's High Cleric Malachi. He's your friend."

"How so?" demanded Cyril. "I hardly ever saw him!"

"He supported you by getting you a job at the tower," argued Vera. "He thought you were good with the herb and flower gardens. He knew you preferred the solitude that comes along with a job like that. Didn't you enjoy that job?"

"Sure, I guess," conceded Cyril. He spread his hands. "But if Malachi were my friend, wouldn't he have sent someone to come and look for me?"

"How do you know he hasn't?" countered Vera.

"I don't know," said Cyril, subdued.

"Besides," continued Vera, "Malachi and the clerics have their hands full with this disease and the poisoned water."

Cyril reflected on his journey to the mountains. "It does look pretty bad, doesn't it? Even livestock were dying."

"It's the water," said Vera. "Anyone or anything that drinks the poisoned water gets sick. Only a few of the wells and springs that I encountered were still O.K. Most of them were no good."

"I hope I didn't drink any bad water," said Cyril. He withdrew his wineskin, which appeared to be mostly full.

"Let me check it," said Vera. She opened the lid and chanted a simple spell. After a moment she relaxed. "It's fine."

"I filled it at a spring not long after I entered the mountains," said Cyril.

"You were fortunate," said Vera. "You found a good spring."

"I hope the water I had before that was good," Cyril stated.

"I'm sure you would have gotten sick by now if it wasn't," said the cleric reassuringly.

Cyril relaxed. "Did you pass your test?" he asked suddenly.

"Yes!" smiled Vera. She held out her hand containing the magical healing ring. "Now I'm a level one cleric." Her smile faded. "Not that it does much good."

"What do you mean?" asked the cyclops.

"I tried healing people while I searched for you," said Vera, "but my healing magic was useless. People chased me off when I couldn't heal them. I guess I'm not much of a cleric after all."

"Don't say that!" said Cyril sternly. "Healing magic is not a skill that can be learned overnight! You may be a level one cleric, but your skills will take time to master!"

"You have more faith in my skill than I do," Vera lamented.

"You have more faith in my gift than I do," countered Cyril.

Vera could find no words to argue Cyril's point. He was right. One had to have faith in oneself. There was no middle ground. She turned and started walking again. "So what are we going to do now? Are we going back?"

Cyril sighed. He didn't really want to go back. "What do you think we should do?"

"Don't you think wandering these tunnels is a bit boring?" asked the cleric in return.

"Actually, I don't," said Cyril. "I'm starting to enjoy it."

"So you want to stay?" asked Vera.

Cyril did not answer.

"Then I'll stay too," Vera stated. "Sooner or later I'll convince you to come home."

Cyril knew what she meant. The only problem was, he already was at home, right here in these mountains. He decided to change the topic. "Vera, do you think the ogres are fighting with the lizardmen over clean water? It looks like the ogres blame the lizardmen for the problem."

"I wouldn't be surprised," said Vera slowly. "It sounds like something the lizardmen would do."

"We should see if we can find out what or who is responsible for the poisoned water," suggested Cyril. "If you want to, that is," he added carefully.

"Sure," said Vera. Originally, she would not have dreamed of attempting such a thing, but the cyclops' presence made her feel safe and secure. She was no longer a little girl. She was a level one cleric. If she wanted to become confident in herself, she had to take the initiative. The cleric pointed ahead to a side passageway. "This looks like it might lead somewhere. Let's go down here."

"Lead the way," ordered Cyril.

Chapter 15

Rebecca woke with a start. She tried to sit up, but the sudden pain in the back of her head forced her to fall back with a groan. A nearby hissing noise forced her to open her eyes.

At first everything was blurry, but as her eyes began to focus, Rebecca saw something that made her sit up despite the pain. Staring at her was a number of lizardmen. It took a moment for her to realize that she was separated from them by a set of bars. Looking around, she discovered that she was in a crude holding cell. The lizardmen were in an adjoining cell.

The lizardmen hissed when they saw her sit up. Rebecca folded her arms across her chest and stared back at them. She hadn't expected to find lizardmen like this, but it was a start. It never occurred to her before how ugly these creatures looked. Their lizard-like faces and beady eyes made them look as devious as they were said to be.

One lizardman was staring at the dwarf as he spoke. "You should have waited for Brind, Lynch."

The lizardman called Lynch spun on the leering one and hissed. "And let that elemental escape? Not on your life!"

"You let it escape anyway," countered the leering one.

"That's because the orcs interrupted our spell, you idiot!" snapped Lynch. "We would have had him!"

"Perhaps," admitted the leering one, "but without the proper magical skill level, I doubt we could have held it for long."

"Long enough for Brind to take over," argued Lynch.

"Of course. Then Brind would get all the credit for capturing the fire elemental," added the leering one.

"Shut up, Lyrr!" growled Lynch. He stomped to a corner of the cell and sat down. It was then that Rebecca noticed the shackles the lizardmen wore. Their hands were shackled behind their backs to prevent them from casting spells.

An orc guard came up just then and checked on the prisoners. After a moment's surveillance, he departed. A few of the lizardmen hissed as he left but he appeared not to notice.

Rebecca looked around at her cell. The cell had two solid rock walls. The other sides were made of thick, rusty bars of dwarven origin. One side joined to the cell of the other prisoners. The other side looked out across the walkway. In the corner was a short keg of water. The dwarf doubted it was suitable for drinking. The bed she was sitting on was a crude slab of rock. Beside her, the dwarf was amazed to find her pack. One strap appeared to have come undone when she was put into the cell. Why the orcs hadn't taken it away was a mystery to her.

She picked up the pack and carefully went through its contents. Everything was there, including her maps and dagger. She grinned. Any orc who touched the dagger was in for a big surprise. The dwarf wondered how many had tried to steal it while she was unconscious. The only things missing were her hand axe and crossbow.

Opening up her map, Rebecca traced out where she had last been. Unfortunately, she had no idea where she was now. She had to start a new map with her present location as the reference point. Surveying the surroundings beyond her cell, the dwarf studied each detail and jotted it down on her new map. Adjacent to the cells was a walkway that curved away on both sides. It disappeared from view in either direction. The walkway was several feet wide and beyond that the floor dropped away. On the far side of the drop, somewhat lower in elevation, a large area almost circular in shape was lit by numerous torches around its circumference. Four walkways led onto the platform at ninety degree angles. The orc cavern was quite large, the ceiling almost endless in height. By comparison, the platform was almost tiny. Several orcs were on the platform talking and gesturing with each other. Occasionally a couple of orcs got into an argument, resulting in some pushing and shoving. This disorganized form of communication continued for some time.

Above all this, several caves were visible, with their openings overlooking the scene below. Most of the larger and more used caves had sentries posted at the openings. The smaller ones remained dark and empty. In one such opening, far above the others, Rebecca thought she caught sight of a light. But when she looked in that direction, the light was gone.

The dwarf carefully jotted down the locations of each cave opening, making sure to note elevation in their coordinates.

"It won't do you much good," said a lizardman suddenly.

Rebecca looked up at the speaker but said nothing.

"They'll kill you and eat you," continued the lizardman.

"That's probably better than what you're in for," said Rebecca.

"How so?" asked the lizardman.

Rebecca decided to follow through on a hunch. "The orcs blame you for the poisoned water. They'll kill you if you don't give them clean water. You've created a problem and now you have to fix it."

"Oh, we will!" sneered the lizardman, "once the humans - and dwarves for that matter - have been eliminated!"

"That's enough!" snapped Lynch from across the cell. "We don't consort with the enemy. Just keep your mouth shut until we get out of here. It shouldn't be much longer."

"How do you know you'll get out of here?" demanded Rebecca.

"Easily," said Lynch. "In exchange for our freedom, the orcs will be given clean water. They can't refuse!"

Lyrr leered and some of the lizardmen hissed in laughter.

"Besides," continued Lynch, "we're too important to kill."

Lyrr smirked and Lynch gave him a dirty look.

Rebecca could only shake her head. Orcs were not inclined to negotiate, but in this case, the lizardman had a point. Water was a precious commodity. Even orcs would have to negotiate with the lizardmen if clean water was at a premium, and lizardmen were the only source to obtain it.

Although they hadn't said so outright, the lizardmen didn't deny it either. Rebecca was quite certain they were responsible for the poisoned water. How they had managed to do it on such a large scale she did not know, but she hoped to find out. As the poisoned water ran across the land, everyone would be affected, from humans to dwarves, and even elves. This was something that needed to be stopped at all costs. But she couldn't do anything as long as she was stuck in a cell. She needed to escape!

Suddenly, stomping feet could be heard and a contingent of orcs appeared on the path to the cells. They stopped in front of the lizardmens' cell and one orc unlocked it with a large, steel key. Rebecca recognized it as being of dwarven origin. Strangely, the crest emblem engraved on its side was unknown to her. She thought she knew most of the nobles' emblems, but this one appeared to be far older, perhaps dating back to the dragon wars.

"Come," ordered a large orc, beckoning the lizardmen to exit their cell.

"It's about time," snapped Lynch, standing and leading his group out of the cell.

Just before exiting, Lyrr turned to the dwarf and said, "See you later." He leered.

The prisoners walked in a single file between the orc guards and marched around the bend out of sight.

A short while later, Rebecca could see the lizardmen being led up to the round platform. An orc with a golden emblem on his breastplate stopped them and ordered everyone to turn and face another path that led to the platform. A moment later, a lizardmage wearing a black cloak with red fringes appeared, flanked by two of his own guards. He nodded to the orc captain.

"The kegs of water have been delivered. Release the prisoners."

Near one of the larger caves above, an orc wearing chain mail appeared. The torchlight from the sentries flickered eerily off the chain mail, giving the orc an unusual glittering aura. The orc made a hand motion and re-entered the cave.

Apparently satisfied, the orc captain signaled his guards to release the prisoners. He handed the keys for the shackles to the black-robed lizardmage.

Lynch turned his back to the lizardmage and exposed his shackled wrists.

The lizardmage just hissed in laughter. He turned around and walked off the platform. The former prisoners scampered after the lizardmage; their shackled hands making them look comical in their gait. Lynch followed more slowly, muttering to himself. Lyrr seemed to be enjoying himself, leering at the orc captain as he passed.

The captain left the platform via a different walkway and the other orcs went about their business. Things became quiet.

Rebecca sighed. She wished she could get away as easily as the lizardmen had. She picked up her pack and retied her shoulder strap.

Suddenly, a short grunt, followed by a scuffling noise, made the dwarf look up. Somewhere down the walkway something was afoot. A yell was followed by a holler and sounds of fighting could be heard. Steel clashed against steel. Yells of surprise were replaced by cries of pain. Some orcs appeared on the walkway, running from something. Behind them, Rebecca saw an unbelievable sight. A disembodied sword flailed madly in all directions. It flew through the air and slashed at the orcs in front of it. Unable to flee, the orcs turned to combat the phenomenon, but to no avail. The sword sliced the arm off one orc before plunging deeply into the abdomen of the other. The first orc screamed in agony while the other one gurgled its last breath, falling to the floor in a heap.

The sword did not hesitate as it swung back and decapitated the screaming orc, silencing the horrible sound forever. Lunging forward, the sword flew in swift motions toward the cells. It stopped of its own accord in front of Rebecca's cell.

The dwarf's neck hairs stood on end and she held perfectly still, hoping the sword would not assault her.

Suddenly, a large key appeared out of nowhere. It flew toward the dwarf and landed at her feet, making her jump.

"Hurry up!" hissed a familiar voice. "Unlock the door while I keep the guards at bay!" Already two more orcs were running up the walkway to do combat with the mysterious sword.

"Alric!" cried Rebecca joyfully. She picked up the key, hoisted on her pack, and ran for the door. Using the dwarven key, she fumbled with the ancient lock in her haste to escape.

"Hurry!" cried Alric. "I can't keep this up much longer!" Two more orcs were down, only to be replaced by four more.

The lock finally clicked and Rebecca exited her prison. She drew her dagger and prepared for battle. Unfortunately, she couldn't help the invisible elf for fear of hurting him by accident. More orcs appeared on the walkway.

Alric swore. "We're not going to get through that way. We'll have to go the other way." He parried several blows by sword wielding orcs.

Rebecca looked in the opposite direction, the same direction that ultimately led to the round platform. "Follow me!" she cried.

The dwarf and elf bounded down the walkway with a group of orcs in pursuit. Along the way, they encountered two more orcs. With momentum on her side, Rebecca stabbed each of them with her dagger before they could react. One fell off the walkway, flailing wildly as its body burned with magical energy. It was dead before it hit the bottom of the cliff.

The other one stared dumbly as the hole the dagger had left in its chest ate away at its insides. Alric grabbed its arm as he ran past and flung the orc after its companion. It fell silently, too stunned to react.

The companions reached the round platform and began to run across to the walkway on their left. As they reached it, they saw a wall of heavily armed orcs marching toward them.

Changing direction in mid-flight, the duo tried the next walkway. Again, a large number of orcs approached.

The companions spun to face the last available walkway and their hearts sank. The orc captain and his guards were already there.

Alric and Rebecca returned to the center of the platform and looked around uncertainly. Their escape routes were blocked. Orcs surrounded them on all sides.

Alric swore. "Where did they all come from?"

Rebecca knew what the elf was thinking. "Your actions were honourable, Alric. It's not your fault we didn't succeed."

Alric withdrew Rebecca's hand axe from his pack and handed it to her. "I almost forgot. You might need this."

Rebecca gripped the axe in her free hand.

"I've got your crossbow in my pack too," added Alric.

"I'll get it later," muttered Rebecca. She eyed the approaching orcs warily.

The orc captain scowled menacingly at the pitiful duo. He took a step forward and was about to speak, when a yell behind him made him turn around. A bright burst of light preceded a low rumbling sound. The light increased in intensity and the rumbling sound increased.

The platform shook and several orcs were thrown to the floor. A moment later, a large fireball blasted down the walkway, striking the orc captain's guards like a tidal wave of fire. An instant later it claimed the orc captain himself, burning his flesh and bones where he stood.

With no time to spare, the dwarf and elf threw themselves to the side, rolling to the safety of a side walkway, right into the path of a group of orcs. Fortunately for the duo, the orcs were fleeing back the way they had come, intent on saving themselves from the inferno that had just claimed their leader.

The fireball flew right across the center of the platform where the dwarf and elf had just stood. It flew to the opposite walkway in pursuit of more fleeing orcs. Those who didn't move quickly enough were swept away by the tidal wave of fire. Moments later, the fireball smashed into the far wall with a loud explosion, ending its existence.

The dwarf and elf rose shakily to their feet, along with orcs on the other side of the platform.

"Come this way!" cried a faint voice.

Rebecca looked down the walkway where the fireball had originated. In the distance she could make out a flaming figure. It was the burning man! She grabbed at Alric's invisible form and managed to grasp his cloak. "Come on, Alric!"

The dwarf and elf ran down the walkway after the elemental, who always managed to stay just far enough ahead of them to light the way. Where there were other intersections the elemental would slow down so they could follow the correct path.

They ran and ran.

Rebecca, not accustomed to running, panted heavily.

Alric, who had expended a lot of energy, was tired as well.

"I can't go any further!" gasped Rebecca.

"Me neither," said Alric. The sword stopped moving as Alric stopped to lean against the wall to catch his breath.

The dwarf staggered to a stop next to him.

The light ahead of them dimmed and vanished.

"Who was that?" asked Alric. He removed his cloak to cool off and made himself visible in the process.

"I think that was an elemental," said Rebecca.

"An elemental!" exclaimed Alric incredulously. "Are you sure?"

"Yes," said Rebecca. "I overheard the lizardmen talking about trying to capture it."

"Isn't it controlled by anyone?" asked the elf. "Usually whoever summons it controls it."

"I don't know," said Rebecca. "This one seems to be acting on its own. When I rescued it from the orcs, it ran away and I didn't have a chance to talk to it."

"You rescued it from orcs?" asked Alric in surprise. "What did I miss?"

Rebecca relayed the events leading up to her capture.

Alric responded by explaining how he had come across the orc cavern. After spying on their operation and stealing some water from their stockpile, (the elf handed Rebecca a fresh wineskin full of water), Alric had been about to go back to the rendezvous when a group of lizardmen prisoners were ushered in. He had spied on them for a while, and not long after he had spotted some orcs carrying Rebecca to a cell next to the lizardmen. It was then that Alric had formulated a plan to rescue the dwarf. He had to wait for Rebecca to regain consciousness before making his move. Alric had thought most of the orcs were gone when he had fought his way to the jail cell. He had been wrong.

"At least we escaped," said Rebecca, "thanks to the elemental."

"We could have been killed by that fireball," reminded Alric.

"True," admitted Rebecca. "But he was still trying to save us."

"I guess," said Alric. "I would sure like to talk to him, or it, or whatever."

"Me too," said Rebecca.

A light appeared ahead of them in the tunnel and the companions braced themselves.

"I'm not running anymore," stated Rebecca.

"Agreed," answered Alric. He readied his sword.

The light increased and a flaming figure appeared at the end of the tunnel. It approached cautiously. "I hope you weren't harmed by the fireball," it began. "My - power - is often much stronger than I expect. It can be unpredictable."

"We're fine," said Rebecca. As a show of good faith she put away her dagger. She looked at Alric.

Alric reluctantly lowered his weapon. He chanted a spell and it shrunk into a dagger.

The elemental paused. It appeared agitated. "Do not try to summon me!" it warned in a low tone.

"We're not using summoning magic!" explained Rebecca quickly as Alric sheathed his dagger.

The elemental relaxed.

"Thank you for saving us," said Rebecca.

"You did the same for me," answered the elemental.

Alric gave the dwarf a sharp glance. He had thought the dwarf had been exaggerating about saving the elemental.

After an awkward silence, Rebecca spoke. "My name is Rebecca." She indicated the elf. "This is Alric, my companion."

The elemental nodded. "My name is Tyris. My gender in this existence is male."

"Pleased to meet you," said Rebecca.

"Why are you both so far from home?" asked Tyris.

"I'm on a quest to find lizardmen lairs and report them to my king," explained Rebecca. "The dwarven army will be dispatched to eliminate them."

"A difficult task," observed Tyris. "And you, Alric? You are much further from your homeland."

Alric was caught off guard. "I - uh - well -."

Rebecca elbowed the elf in the ribs and he continued. "I'm after a particular lizardmage who crossed me not too long ago."

"It seems they're trying to poison the water," added Rebecca. "We have to stop them."

Tyris nodded in understanding. "If your quest is to hinder the lizardmen, then allow me to help. They continuously try to summon me for their evil purposes and I will have none of it. If you wish to neutralize the poison, I may not be able to help directly, but I will aid in whatever way I can."

"Really?" exclaimed Rebecca excitedly. To have an elemental aid her in her quest was more than she could have bargained for. "We'd love to have your help, right Alric?"

"I - uh - sure!" he exclaimed with a weak smile.

Rebecca clapped her hands together happily. "Which way do we go?"

"You're the one with the maps," reminded Alric.

"Oh yeah," said Rebecca sheepishly.

Chapter 16

 can't believe only two of them got paralyzed!" panted Cyril. He ran behind the cleric, whose staff light reflected haphazardly off the uneven tunnel walls.

"Maybe they encountered a cyclops before," said Vera as she stumbled over some loose rocks on the tunnel floor.

Cyril helped Vera steady herself and they continued to run. "I hadn't thought of that," admitted Cyril. After a moment, the cyclops added, "If they keep after us much longer, we may have to stand and fight. I'm getting tired. Do you have any offensive magic?"

The question caught Vera off guard. It hadn't even occurred to her that she could use her magic against the ogres. She quickly recalled some of her latest spells, which, when used correctly, could disable her opponents. At the tower, she had never used any of her spells to harm anyone. Her spells were meant to help, not hinder. Yet there were times when some of those spells could be used in an offensive application.

The cleric was just bringing these spells to mind when they rounded a bend and nearly stumbled into a vast cavern. A rough stone table with dwarven symbols engraved in its side was in the center of the cavern. Seated on the ground around this table were a number of ogres. The cleric and cyclops stumbled to a halt.

Cyril groaned. He turned to head back the way they had come but it was too late. The three ogres chasing them had caught up. The first ogre lunged at Cyril and the cyclops leaned toward him, absorbing the ogre's momentum. Although equivalent in stature, Cyril was stronger than his opponent. With a mighty heave, Cyril pushed the ogre back into his companions, causing them to fall to the floor in a tangle of arms and legs.

Vera, meanwhile, could hear Cyril fending off the attackers to the rear. But her problem was the ogres approaching from the front. They looked displeased at the unwelcome intrusion. Chanting rapidly but firmly, Vera cast a sleep spell while rubbing the appropriate spell components together in her hand. As she finished chanting, some white feathers and dried leaves fell from her hand to the floor. Simultaneously, about half a dozen ogres fell to the floor, fast asleep.

The remaining ogres came forward confidently, assuming Vera didn't have time for another spell. She proved them wrong by casting a shield spell to block the area in front of her. She couldn't extend the shield all the way around herself and Cyril because the cyclops was in combat with the ogres behind them again. To implement a full shield could trap an ogre within the shield with them, or leave Cyril stuck outside the shield.

The first of Vera's opponents stepped dangerously close to her when he suddenly ran into the invisible shield. With a dull thud, he bounced back into one of his comrades and landed unceremoniously on the floor. The other ogres stared at their partner as he scrambled to his feet in rage. With a wild yell, he charged the cleric with his club raised over his head. Again, he ran into the shield and bounced back onto the floor.

Seeing this, a female ogre - the first Vera had seen - cried out a battle cry and started to pound on the cleric's shield with her club. The other ogres in the cavern followed suit.

Vera could feel the pounding from within the shield and chanted some more to strengthen the shield.

Cyril successfully brought his club down on one ogre's head, the spiked end biting deep into its thick skull. It went down with a groan. Unfortunately, the club had become embedded in the ogre's skull. Seizing the opening, the other two ogres threw themselves at the cyclops.

The cyclops' club ripped free and Cyril staggered backward into the cleric, knocking her off balance. The cyclops responded by kicking back one of his opponents and grabbing the other one around the throat. Squeezing tightly, he waited until it stopped struggling before letting it drop to the floor.

Meanwhile, Vera had been knocked to her knees. Her momentary lack of concentration had caused her air shield to weaken enough that one ogre's club managed to penetrate it. It smashed down hard against the floor mere inches from the hapless cleric.

Several bright flashes, followed by short explosions, caught everyone by surprise. A few of Vera's attackers fell to the floor, dead. Their smoking, charred corpses were all that remained. The other ogres spun in unison to face this unexpected attack from the rear. Three more fireballs struck three more ogres in rapid succession. The female ogre's body rolled past the cleric, its body fully engulfed in flames. It struck the wall beside the tunnel and came to a stop, still burning. The remaining ogres tried to flee, but there was nowhere to hide. Fireballs struck them wherever they ran. One ogre, the same one that had run into Vera's shield the first time, ran at her again, thinking her shield was still down. He was wrong. He ran headlong into the shield. This time he bounced off, hit the floor, and lay still.

The battle behind Vera ended at the same time. Cyril lifted his club from the chest of his last opponent and turned to see how Vera was doing. Seeing the dead and burning bodies all over the place he asked breathlessly, "You didn't -?!"

Vera shook her head. "It wasn't me."

Across the cavern, Vera and Cyril could make out a dark cloaked figure lit by a staff adorned with a bright green orb of light. As it came closer, Vera could see that it was a black mage.

The cleric did not lower her shield as she spoke. "Who goes there?" she asked in a quavering voice.

The figure continued to come closer but all they could see was a black cloak. The face was hidden beneath the hood. Suddenly, the cloaked figure threw his hood back, revealing a young man with blue eyes and blond hair. "I am Arch Mage Kazin."

Vera gasped.

"And you are?" prodded Kazin. He stopped walking.

Vera lowered her shield and started running toward the mage, who instinctively held his staff in a defensive pose.

"Kazin!" cried Vera. "I'm Vera, Max's sister! Remember me?"

Kazin was surprised. He allowed his old friend's sister to embrace him before holding her back and looking at her up close. "Vera? Is that really you?"

"Yes!" cried Vera joyfully. "You came just in time!"

Kazin's face darkened. "You shouldn't be running around in these mountains. It's too dangerous."

By now Cyril had wandered up to the two. Kazin looked directly at the cyclops' eye and nodded. "You must be Cyril. I've heard about you."

Cyril, realizing Kazin was looking into his eye, looked away hastily. A moment later he returned his gaze, his eye showing surprise and bewilderment. "Hey! You're not paralyzed!"

Kazin continued to look Cyril in the eye and smiled. "My magical training includes mental discipline. I'm not as susceptible to your magic as most people are. But I'm not immune to it either. If I let my guard down, I can be paralyzed too."

Cyril could only shake his head in amazement. He offered his hand. "I am pleased to meet you. Vera has told me about you. You are her friend. Therefore, you are mine as well."

Kazin shook his hand. "I'm honoured."

Cyril's face momentarily darkened. "I hope you were not sent to take me back."

Kazin shook his head. "No. High Cleric Malachi wishes you were back, but he certainly wouldn't force you to go back against your will."

Cyril's face brightened. "Really?" He looked at Vera.

The cleric grinned. "See! I told you Malachi liked you!"

"We'd better get away from here," interrupted Kazin. He indicated the fallen ogres. "Some of them might wake up any time now. When they do, they won't be happy."

"Aren't you going to kill them?" asked Vera.

Kazin looked at the cleric. "Why? They are not a threat to us right now."

"But they're our enemies!" pouted Vera. "They tried to kill us a moment ago!"

"We are the intruders here," responded Kazin. "To kill them in their sleep makes us no better than they are. I used to be like you, but I have learned a lot in my travels. Not every creature is evil. For example, I knew a minotaur who was not evil. He became one of my closest friends. Cyril is another example. Some people think he is evil just because he is part cyclops. You and I both know otherwise."

Vera sighed. "I suppose you're right, Kazin." The cleric was just frightened, and her fear made her want to lash out. The familiar feeling of compassion suddenly kicked in. "Should we try to heal the ones who are still alive? They might see that we don't want to harm them and -."

"I wouldn't go that far," interrupted Kazin. He chuckled and patted the cleric on the shoulder. "Besides, there is a darker force at work here. The ogres aren't smart enough to be behind it." The mage turned to go and the others quickly followed.

"Where are we going?" asked Vera after they had put some distance between themselves and the cavern of ogres.

Kazin stopped and turned to face the cleric. His face looked greenish in the light of his staff. "You should return to the Tower of Hope at once. The clerics are needed more than ever with this new disease present."

"But I can't cure that illness," lamented Vera. "Believe me. I tried! People were even chasing me away and calling me a fraud!"

"Don't agonize over that," put in Kazin gently. He held the cleric by the shoulders. "I know it can't be healed yet. Even the expert healers can't do it. But once a cure is found, your magical skills will be invaluable."

"The best cure is often found at the source of the trouble," said Vera. "Cyril and I are trying to do just that."

"That is my mission as well," said Kazin. He released the cleric. "But I don't think you know how dangerous a mission this is. There are many evil creatures in these mountains, and the most dangerous ones wield magic." He pointed back the way they had come. "You saw first-hand how dangerous it can get. If I hadn't come along, you might have been killed!"

Vera looked crestfallen.

"Then we should join forces," put in Cyril suddenly. He had been quietly observing the conversation until now. "My - gift - (he looked at Vera as he said this) could prove useful. I am quite strong too." He flexed his arm, causing Kazin to grin in spite of himself.

"And I can heal your wounds!" cried Vera. She looked into Kazin's eyes anxiously.

Kazin's grin vanished. "Vera, I couldn't save your brother, and I don't want your death on my conscience as well. If harm came to you, I wouldn't be able to live with myself. What would I tell your parents?"

"Don't worry about me," said Vera. "I won't hold you accountable for my well-being. I'll take care of myself. If I die, it's my fault."

Kazin sighed. "Alright," he said at last. "You can come with me."

"Yes!" cried Vera joyfully. She jumped up and embraced the mage.

Kazin gently removed the frail cleric's arms from around his shoulders and looked at her sternly. "You'll have to pull your own weight. I can't always watch over you and fight the bad guys at the same time."

"Of course!" said Vera seriously. But her grin returned a moment later. "This will be so exciting!"

Kazin looked helplessly at the cyclops before turning to continue down the passageway.

A short while later, the trio arrived at a major intersection in the tunnel system. The path veered off in five directions.

"Now which way?" asked Vera.

A sudden gust of wind struck the companions from the left and echoed loudly down the tunnel to the right. The spell casters' cloaks rippled around their ankles with the cool blast.

"We go this way," answered Kazin confidently, following the direction of the wind. The mage made a point of marking the walls as he went.

"How do you know this is the way?" asked the cleric as she stumbled down the corridor after the mage. Her sandals slapped noisily on the floor as she went.

Kazin, whose own sandals made echoing noises, turned his head to the side as he spoke. "I'm following the wind. The air elemental instructed me to follow his wind and I don't want to disappoint him."

"Air elemental?" asked the cleric. She looked back at the cyclops, who merely shrugged back at her while keeping his gaze averted.

Kazin did not respond to the question, preferring to concentrate on the tunnel ahead of him.

Suddenly, a rumble echoed through the tunnel, followed immediately by a heaving, shaking motion under their feet. Vera would have fallen had the cyclops not held onto her with a massive hand. Kazin was thrown to one side and fell heavily against the wall.

"What was that?" asked Vera fearfully.

"An earthquake," answered Cyril.

The rumbling occurred again and some loose debris fell on the companions from the tunnel ceiling. Then the rumbling stopped.

"Is everyone O.K.?" asked Kazin.

"Yes," said Cyril.

"Let's keep moving," ordered the mage.

"Are you sure we're headed the right way?" asked the cleric shakily.

"I've followed the wind since I entered the mountain," explained Kazin. "The elemental told me to do it, though I didn't think it applied to the mountain as well. At first I ignored the wind, not realizing that it was guiding me. A couple of times I chose to go opposite the wind to find out if it meant anything. The first time I ended up at a dead end wondering how the wind could have originated there. The second time the wind blasted fiercely into my face and I had to turn back. Ever since then, I followed the wind and have never reached a dead end or trap. The only time I ran into any enemies was when I had to rescue you." The mage paused thoughtfully. "Maybe I was supposed to rescue you."

"Because we were supposed to help you!" finished Vera excitedly.

"Perhaps," said Kazin. He marked the wall and led the others down the tunnel again, his staff lighting the way.

"Do you want me to light the way for a while, Kazin?" asked the cleric suddenly. "Your staff probably needs to recharge."

"No, it's O.K." said the mage over his shoulder. "My staff has an endless supply of energy. It hardly costs me any magical energy to keep it lit."

"Really?" asked the cleric enviously. She eyed the green orb atop the mage's staff. "Is it because of the orb?"

"Yes," said Kazin. He did not elaborate.

"Why are you marking the walls?" asked Cyril.

"It's just a precaution," said Kazin. "If we have to backtrack, the marks will guide us. Sometimes I wish we had a dwarf to guide us. They know their way around the mountains better than anyone."

A good half hour of intermittent rumbling and shaking plagued the companions' journey before the silence reigned once again. Heavy breathing and footfalls were the only noises.

"It seems to have stopped," commented Cyril after a while.

"Yes," said Kazin. He pulled into an alcove with a solid rock wall and ceiling. Using his lit staff, he quickly inspected it for weaknesses and found none. "We'll rest here for a while. I've got some food if you're hungry."

"I have food as well," offered Cyril. He removed his pack and pulled out some rodents and a rabbit. They were still alive but paralyzed.

Kazin blinked. "That's better than the rations I brought with me."

"Help yourself," offered the cyclops. "I can easily get more."

Kazin thanked him and quickly prepared a fire using some porous rock fragments on the floor nearby. He made a small pile and pointed his staff at it. Then he chanted a spell and the rock fragments lit up in a ball of flame.

"That's an interesting spell!" complimented Vera. She held her hands over the flames for warmth.

Kazin produced a pot and some utensils. "Can you cook?" He was looking at the cleric.

Vera returned the mage's gaze when she heard the challenge in his voice. "That's a specialty of mine!" In a few moments she had a delicious meal cooking for them.

"This method of cooking uses very little water," explained the cleric as she worked, "which is good since our water is in short supply. The magic draws most of the needed water from the surrounding air. I've combined a spell meant to help someone who is dehydrated with a spell to cool the body and restrict perspiration. The spells are almost identical, but when combined produce this interesting effect. I don't know if anyone else has managed to figure this out, though." The cleric smiled. "I like to think of it as my own little secret."

"Impressive!" complimented Kazin. He accepted the bowl of rabbit stew and carefully tasted the hot meal. "Impressive!" he repeated.

The cleric beamed and handed a bowl to the cyclops.

Cyril took a spoon full. "Mmm!" he mumbled loudly.

After finishing supper and engaging in small talk, the companions continued their journey. On the way Kazin told them of his adventures leading him to the mountains.

"So you really spoke with the air elemental?" asked Vera for the fifth or sixth time.

"Yes," said Kazin. "And I hope to speak to him again. He needs our help, and so do the earth and water elementals."

"I hope we can find the fire elemental," said Vera, "if he - it - hasn't already been captured by the lizardmen."

"It won't be that easy for them," said Kazin. "The only magic that can capture it is summoning magic. Most other magic won't affect it."

"Wait a minute!" said the cyclops suddenly. The others stopped and turned to look at Cyril. He had a strange expression on his face and a distant look in his eye.

"What is it?" asked Vera.

"What does the fire elemental look like?" asked Cyril.

"I don't know," said Kazin. "I haven't seen it yet."

"Would it look like a man who is on fire?" asked the cyclops.

"Perhaps," said Kazin. "Why?"

"I remember seeing a fiery figure shortly after entering the mountains. It looked at me before running away from me down a tunnel. After you mentioned that elementals were immune to most magic, I remembered that it looked directly into my eye before it ran. I thought that was odd at the time. I tried running after it but it was long gone. It sure moved fast!"

"That could have been it!" exclaimed Vera. She looked at Kazin for confirmation.

"It's quite possible," admitted Kazin. "You say it looked like a man?"

Cyril nodded. "A human on fire. Where his eyes should have been were dark holes. I couldn't tell if he wore clothes or not because his fire was too bright. But he didn't appear to be in any pain."

Kazin nodded. "That was very likely a fire elemental. If he moves as fast as you say, he may very well still be on the loose. If we find him, I hope we can convince him to help."

"Can't you summon him?" asked Vera.

Kazin shook his head. "I don't know how to do that. It seems the only ones still capable of such ancient magic are the druids and lizardmen. But if we can talk to him, he might help us; especially when he realizes the impact his capture would have on the entire world. If the lizardmen control all of the elementals, the forces they unleash will not only wipe out humans, it will destroy all life, including the lizardmen themselves. The water elemental and earth elemental are already under the lizardmages' control, as indicated by the poisoned water and earthquakes. Because the air elemental has been captured, the air might soon become contaminated, with uncontrollable winds to spread the contamination around the world. If the fire elemental is captured as well, fires will consume everything the lizardmen wish to burn and then some. Even the lizardmen will not be able to stop the destruction then! So you can see how critical our mission is!"

Vera swallowed nervously at this vision of doom. Even Cyril was frightened by the possible scenario.

Kazin tried to ease their fear with a relaxed smile. "Don't worry. It hasn't gotten that bad yet. We still have a chance to change things. I've been in worse scrapes before."

Vera had difficulty visualizing a worse situation than the one Kazin had described. Her look was not lost on the mage.

Kazin laughed. "Remember the wars a few years back? My companions and I put a crimp in most of the necromancer's plans and we eventually won the war. We beat the odds then and we can do so again. You'll see."

"I hope so," said Vera uncertainly.

"Absolutely!" boomed the cyclops' voice behind her. He laid a hand gently on the cleric's shoulder. "The air elemental thought so."

The cleric looked up at the cyclops, who deliberately looked at her pendant. Cyril's face had a new expression on it. It was a look of determination and resolve. Vera drew strength from her friend's expression. She returned her attention back to the mage with a determined expression of her own. "Lead the way, Kazin!"

Kazin held up a fist in victory and turned to lead them on their important and exciting quest.

What suddenly happened next caught everyone off guard. A deafening rumble was followed by a loud cracking noise. The tunnel behind them rose sharply, dumping its hapless travelers like sand down a chute. They slid helplessly down the tunnel and bounced off a couple of corners on their way down. After a third corner, the trio approached a massive, gaping crevice that separated their half of the tunnel from its continuation on the other side. With too much momentum and no handholds, they were incapable of stopping their descent. The companions tumbled unceremoniously from the tunnel into the black and forbidding nothingness.

Down, down they fell as the heaving mountain changed its form and reconnected the tunnel high above them. Large chunks of rock could be seen breaking off from the sudden impact.

Kazin was trying to complete a complex levitation spell when he heard Cyril cry out. In the dim light of his staff, the mage saw the cyclops frantically pointing below them and looked to see what was wrong. It was too late. This type of landing was not what Kazin had in mind . . .

Chapter 17

lric rose to his feet and brushed the dust from his clothing. He shook his head to rid his hair of more dust and flipped up his hood to cover his head. "Does this sort of thing happen often in the mountains?" he asked the dwarf as he helped her to her feet.

"From time to time," answered the dwarf. She brushed her own clothes clean and checked her pouch for a comb. "I've never experienced such a heavy, continuous earthquake before, though." Finding her comb, she proceeded to brush her hair, taking care to accentuate her silver streak.

"It was indeed an uncharacteristic quake," put in Tyris. "Something doesn't seem right."

"It will take more than an earthquake to stop me from my objective," said Alric resolutely. "I'm going on regardless."

"Absolutely," said Rebecca. Satisfied that her hair was in order, she put her comb back into her pouch and withdrew her maps. Unrolling the current map, she held it so the others could see. Tyris leaned as close as he dared to provide additional light.

"See this path?" asked Rebecca, pointing to a spot on the map.

"Yeah," said Alric. "What about it?"

"It is directly over us by about a hundred feet. We were there about a half hour ago."

Alric scratched his head. "And?"

"That means we're going deeper into the mountain," stated Rebecca. She drew a line from a different part of the map across to the path in question. "This is the path we are on right now." She continued the line through the other one and stopped it abruptly. "And here is where we are now."

"But how can you tell that the line you crossed is above us?" asked Alric. "It looks like the two paths intersect."

"Do you see the difference in darkness in my lines?" asked Rebecca.
"Yes."

"That means the paths are at different altitudes. The light line is the path above us. The dark line runs below it, not through it."

"I see," said Alric uncertainly. "So you have to write darker the deeper you go."

"Only on this map," said Rebecca. "On the next piece of parchment that I use to continue the map, the dark lines become the light lines, and any deeper lines I make will be darker. One can only make the lines so dark, after all."

Alric looked confused.

"Some dwarves use different colours when there are lots of elevations to contend with."

Alric looked lost.

Rebecca smiled. "It's O.K. Alric. It's not easy for most people to understand." Changing the subject, the dwarf pointed to the dark line. "Hopefully, if we continue on this present path, we will enter a different part of the mountain farther west than we've gone thus far."

"So what?" asked Alric impatiently.

"That means we're getting farther away from the dwarven realm, which in turn means we will have a better chance of encountering lizardmen." Rebecca rolled up the map while she let this sink in.

"That sounds reasonable," said Tyris.

Alric shrugged. "Lead on, dwarf."

"My name's Rebecca," said the dwarf sternly.

"Sorry." The elf beckoned ahead. "After you, Rebecca."

The dwarf led the way, followed by the elf and fire elemental. The path had a very slight downward slope, and the going was easy. They passed a tunnel on their right that was dark and cobwebbed. It didn't appear to have been used in some time. As they passed it, however, they heard a noise from within. As one they stopped, giving one another quizzical glances.

Rebecca shrugged. "I don't know. Tyris?" She looked at the elemental.

Tyris moved toward the entrance and stuck his hand into it. The flames on his hand wavered and flickered. "There is a draft," he said slowly. "This tunnel is not a dead end."

"I'll check it out," said Alric. He pulled his invisibility cloak from his pack and put it on, turning himself invisible. Rebecca and Tyris watched as the cobwebs in the tunnel parted and clung to the elf's invisible form.

"Be careful," said Rebecca.

"I will," was the answer.

They waited about five minutes before they detected motion in the tunnel again. An instant later, the elf reappeared as he removed his cloak and brushed off the cobwebs.

"Well?" said Rebecca anxiously.

"It goes for quite a ways," said Alric. "I heard more noises the further I got. A pile of rubble part way down the tunnel must have been a cave-in at one time. My guess is that the last earthquake loosened the rocks and re-created an opening to the other side. I didn't go any further because I think we should investigate what's on the other side together."

"Then let's go," said Rebecca. She led the way with the others in pursuit.

As Alric had explained, they reached a massive cave-in. Near the top, they could see an opening just barely big enough to crawl through.

Alric turned to the dwarf. "Are you up to a climb?"

"Of course," answered Rebecca. She freed her hands and began climbing.

The footing was unstable and many rocks were kicked down the side of the cave-in as they advanced, but progress was made. Soon they were at the opening. Tyris' flames flickered noisily as the air from the other side came through.

"I'll go first," offered Alric. He quickly threw on his cloak and disappeared, noisily crawling through the opening. Rebecca followed, with Tyris behind her.

On the other side, they discovered that the tunnel here was virtually identical to the side they had come from. The trio continued down the new path and noticed a considerable incline as they walked.

"We're going uphill," said Alric, stating the obvious.

"I'll keep that in mind when I mark it on the map," said Rebecca.

The tunnel leveled off and made several minor turns, ending at an opening. A large canyon loomed before them, dropping to an unknown depth. On the far side, they could see a path that was illuminated by several torches. A cave entrance was evident on either end of the path.

"Interesting," said Alric slowly. "Someone's using -." His voice trailed off as some movement at one cave entrance caught his eye. The companions ducked back into the shelter of their tunnel and Tyris stepped back a fair distance to prevent his glowing light from being seen by the individuals below.

An orc appeared, followed by two armored orcs carrying spears. Behind them, pulling a wooden wheeled cart, were two more orcs. They were bent over, laboring to pull the cart, which was laden with a large, wooden barrel. The cart rumbled along the path, bouncing and creaking as it rolled over the uneven surface. Two more guards followed the procession, their spear tips glinting in the torchlight.

The two guards in front communicated in their guttural language, laughing and drooling. At one point, the orc in front turned and gave them a sharp command, eliciting silence. A few minutes later they finished following the path to enter the opposite cave entrance. Silence followed.

"They must be hauling water," surmised Alric. "Too bad we can't get over there and find out where they're going."

"Or, more importantly, where they came from," said Rebecca. "It could possibly lead us to the lizardmen."

"That's true," said Tyris, who had returned to join them. "Following the orcs will only lead us to their territory."

"Good point," said Alric.

Tyris peered down into the canyon. Despite the blackness below, he could make out a narrow ledge not far below them. "I wonder if we can reach that ledge down there."

The others looked to where the elemental was gazing.

"What good would that do?" asked Alric.

"There is a large peninsula down there that almost reaches the other side," explained Tyris, pointing. "If we could reach that location, we should be able to jump across to the other side. There is also another ledge that runs right above the orcs' ledge. If we go across there, we can get very close to the first cave entrance."

Alric and Rebecca looked at one another uncertainly.

"Orcs don't wield magic," said Tyris. "Unless they can throw their spears accurately over such a long distance, they cannot harm us."

"They could be armed with bows or crossbows next time," said Rebecca. "Or they could call for help from orcs that are armed appropriately."

"I will take care of that problem should it arise," stated Tyris. "My fire balls will be difficult for them to evade on that narrow path."

"Well," said Alric, looking pointedly at Rebecca. "What do you think?"

Rebecca considered. "I have rope in my pack which may come in handy." She looked at Tyris. "I don't think that will help you, Tyris."

"Do not concern yourself with me," said Tyris. "I can change my form to match my surroundings. I will not fall."

Rebecca took a deep breath. "Well, I guess we might as well try it. At least there is a good chance that we can find some lizardmen."

"We should be able to get across safely," put in Alric, "provided there are no more earthquakes."

The others glanced sharply at the elf at this sinister reminder. Nevertheless, they proceeded anyway.

Using the rope, the elf and dwarf safely lowered themselves to the ledge below them. Then Tyris allowed himself to 'slide' down to where they were by making himself into a blanket of flames. Once on the ledge, he resumed his human form and led the others to the peninsula jutting out across the canyon. At the tip of the peninsula they stopped to assess the safest place to jump across.

"It's a lot wider than I thought," said Rebecca uncertainly.

"You can do it," said Alric confidently. "If you like, I can attach the rope to your waist so if you slip, I can pull you back to safety."

Rebecca shook her head. "That's not necessary. I can do it." She backed up a few paces and took a run at it. With a grunt, she sprang across the gap and landed on the other side, rolling to her feet upon arrival, as her combat instructor had trained her to do in a combat situation. The dwarf beckoned the elf to come across.

Alric used the same strategy as the dwarf, but nimbly landed on his feet. "Long legs," he said to the dwarf.

Rebecca harrumphed.

Tyris was about to make his crossing when one of the things they all feared would happen did happen. Another contingent of orcs exited the first tunnel and headed directly toward them, albeit somewhat beneath them.

Tyris looked around frantically for a place to hide, but he was out in the open. The orcs hadn't seen him yet, but if he attempted to make the jump right then, he would surely draw their attention. He decided to lie down and make himself as flat as possible. By so doing, he knew he was hidden from their line of sight. Unfortunately, he could not extinguish his flames, eliminating the flickering light that could still betray him.

Alric and Rebecca ducked for cover and waited tensely. The orcs hadn't seen them yet. They were trudging along the path below them unaware they were being watched. Some long minutes later, when the orcs were nearly across the path, one of them made an exclamation. The party stopped and looked to where he pointed. Tyris had been discovered!

The elemental rose to his full height just as a guard threw a spear in his direction. The spear fell well short, so Tyris responded by throwing a fireball in the general direction of the party. The fireball exploded between the cart pullers and the front guards, causing all of them to jump out of the way. One guard lost his footing and tripped into the canyon, screaming until he could no longer be heard. Simultaneously, the cart pullers accidentally knocked the cart off its course and it rolled toward the edge of the ledge. The pullers lunged after their load and tried to stop it from reaching the canyon's edge, but it kept going. Somehow during the mad scramble, one orc's arm got caught in the side of the cart and he was being dragged with the load. The other orc tried in vain to hold back the cart but it was too heavy. The two rear guards ran to help, but it was too late. Almost in slow motion, the cart toppled over the edge with its hapless victim in tow. Unlike the first orc, this one fell to his death in silence. The cart shattered when it hit a rocky obstruction on its way down, exploding its contents in a myriad of directions. The side of the canyon was bathed in a glistening sheen of water.

The lead orc was not impressed with what had just transpired and was shouting orders at the four remaining orcs. The remaining front guard tried to throw his spear at Tyris but threw it too far to the left. The spear sailed harmlessly into the canyon.

The lead orc knew it was pointless to stay where they were and gave one last command before running for the nearest tunnel. The front guard and remaining laborer ran behind him while the rear guards turned and fled back to the first cave entrance.

Tyris was already casting fireballs after the rear guards to prevent them from summoning help.

Alric picked up several sharp stones from nearby and began throwing them at the first orcs.

Rebecca was about to tell him that he would never succeed at stopping them when the elf chanted some elven magic. Each of the stones transformed in mid-air, becoming short but deadly arrows. Their speed increased and they changed direction as needed to hit their marks.

The guard and laborer fell down with arrows in their necks, while the lead orc was struck in the leg. He fell down on one knee and howled in rage. His cry was cut off as a fireball struck him in the head, claiming his life.

Alric and Rebecca saw the rear guards lying on the path, their bodies smoking in ruin. Tyris had eliminated them. They turned to see Tyris just as he jumped across the gap and landed next to them. "Nice going," he said to the elf.

"That's one of my favourite spells," said Alric.

Rebecca harrumphed. She had her mini crossbow in her hand but never had a chance to use it.

"You'll get your chance," said the elf consolingly.

Rebecca cheered up slightly. Not wanting to put a damper on things, she suggested they push the bodies off the ledge to prevent any following parties from sounding the alarm. The others agreed. Finding a way down to the ledge, they quickly went to work.

When that task was completed, they dashed for the first tunnel entrance and explored it as swiftly as they could. Several side passageways appeared to be well used and they chose one to explore. It wound around in a sharp bend and there was a steep incline. Soon they could hear a muffled noise ahead of them.

At this point Alric stopped the others. "I'll go ahead and explore," he whispered. He donned his invisibility cloak and went to see what lay ahead.

After a brief jaunt he came to a short landing where two orcs stood, illuminated by a wall torch on either side. They faced away from him, looking down on something that was happening well below them. Noises could be heard below but Alric couldn't make out the sounds. He needed to get a closer look.

The elf crept forward quietly, secure in the knowledge that he was invisible. However, as he got closer to the orcs, one of them sniffed loudly.

"Do you smell that?" asked the orc.

"Smell what?" asked the other one.

The orc sniffed again. "It smells like - I'm not quite sure. Kinda like a human but not quite."

"Your nose is fulla rotting flesh," said the other orc sarcastically.

The first one growled.

Alric knew he could not get closer without his scent giving him away for sure. Suddenly an idea occurred to him. With a quick jab, he poked the second orc with his dagger.

"Ow!" exclaimed the orc. He rounded on the first one. "What'd ya do that for?"

"Do what?" asked the first orc.

The second orc tilted his spear and jabbed the first one in the leg. "That!"

"Ow! What's the matter with you?!" exclaimed the first orc, readying his own spear.

"You did it to me!" said the second orc.

"Now you're imagining things!" said the first orc.

"It wasn't my imagination!" argued the second orc.

"I didn't stab you - yet!" cried the first orc. He raised his spear in a threatening manner.

The second orc growled threateningly, ready to do battle.

Alric couldn't contain his laughter any longer. His laughter gave him away, but it so startled the orcs that the elf had no difficulty eliminating them. His lightning-quick movements, along with his invisibility, gave him the opportunity to slit each of their throats. The orcs fell to the ground with a soft thud.

Looking past the landing, Alric could see the scene below unimpeded. What he saw made the hair on the back of his neck stand on end. After watching the scene for a time, he hurried back to fetch the others.

When Tyris arrived at the landing, he spotted the torches on the walls and an idea occurred to him. He sprang into the flames of one of the torches and allowed himself to be sucked in. The torch's flame became considerably brighter, but the elemental was well disguised.

Alric and Rebecca stared at one another in amazement.

"That's a clever trick!" exclaimed the dwarf quietly.

"Nifty, huh?" said the torch.

"It talks too!" laughed Alric.

The torch chuckled.

Rebecca diverted her attention to the scene below and gasped.

"Could you hold me closer to the edge?" asked the torch. "I can't see very well from here."

Alric obliged by taking the torch from the wall sconce and holding it closer to the edge.

What Tyris saw made him flare up momentarily. A relatively large cavern was illuminated by torches on all sides. Three tunnels bisected the cavern. There were six orc guards standing to attention, two flanking each tunnel entrance. Near the wall opposite the tunnels was a cart manned by two laborers. Accompanying them were four guards and a leader. The laborers were rolling a heavy wooden barrel up to the cart. With some difficulty, they rolled the barrel up some planks onto the cart bed before standing the barrel on end. Then they lifted the planks and used them to seal the rear of the cart so the barrel could not fall out.

Behind the laborers, the companions saw the most interesting feature of the cavern. The wall, directly across from the middle tunnel, wavered and shimmered with a blue-grey light. Standing next to the shimmering light were two lizardmen. One was a fierce-looking lizardmage, wearing a dark brown robe and carrying a smooth black staff. The other wore a breastplate and wielded a three-pronged trident. The robed lizardmage turned to the wall and stepped into the swirling light, disappearing from sight.

Rebecca gasped. "A portal!"

"Yes," said the torch. "Through there lies the realm of the lizardmen."

By now the contingent with the cart was leaving via the middle tunnel. Almost as soon as they left, another contingent arrived from the left tunnel, pulling an empty cart. They stopped in front of the shimmering portal.

The leader gave a sharp command and the two laborers in the party hastened to the portal, warily eyeing the breast-plated lizardman as they passed. They disappeared into the portal.

A short time later, a barrel burst from the portal, followed by the laborers and the robed lizardmage. The laborers proceeded to load the barrel. When that was done, the robed lizardmage approached the leader of the caravan. "This is the last one. You will be given more when you pledge more troops to our cause. We will meet here again in two hours."

The lead orc grumbled and ordered his party to depart. They left by the middle tunnel like the previous group.

The lizardmage nodded at his counterpart and they both stepped through the portal. A moment later, the portal flickered out of existence, leaving a bare stone wall in its place. The orc sentries by the tunnels relaxed.

For the companions, it was time to formulate their next plan of attack.

Part III

The Cure For What 'Ales' Ya

Chapter 18

General Larsen rode his shiny black stallion through the ranks of civilians crowding the gates at the Tower of Hope. He brushed his graying hair from his eyes and then scratched his bearded chin. He suspected he looked as disheveled and rough as everyone else these days. But unlike these people, who were sick and dying, he was still healthy and strong, albeit dead tired.

The general genuinely felt sorry for these people, but his duty was to protect the Tower of Hope. Several civilians had raised a commotion trying to enter the tower's courtyard, and he had been called upon to intervene. Calming people who were desperately seeking healing was not an easy task, especially when explaining that the clerics in the tower were unable to help their suffering anyway. The only thing the clerics could do was offer fresh water to drink and herbs to reduce pain. Clerics lined the tower's battlements, chanting healing spells in concert. But all they could succeed in doing was to slow down the progression of this plague. People died daily, the dead being hauled to mass graves a few miles away. It was not a pretty sight, and people everywhere were losing hope of recovery for themselves and loved ones.

General Larsen was worried. His men had their hands full dealing with the sick and dying, delivery of water and herbs, and the security of the tower. Should there be an attack by creatures from the mountains, they would be overrun in minutes. The tower didn't stand a chance.

Larsen looked up at the battlements and spotted several skink warrior guards. Proficient with crossbows, these frog-like lizardmen were unaffected by the poison. If they were immune, could their lizardmen relatives in the mountains be immune as well? If so, the lizardmen could easily subdue the Tower of Hope using magic. The black mages had suffered a severe blow of their own, and it was unlikely they would be able to come to the tower's aid should a war break out.

The dragon mage, Kazin, was said to have been away from the Tower of Sorcery when the disease broke out there, but could one lone arch mage, even if he was able to change into a dragon, do enough to save them? General Larsen grunted. Probably not. The general arrived at the gate and his men pushed back the crowd so he could ride through. The gate opened briefly and he rode through. During this time, a commotion arose as civilians tried to burst through the guards and enter the tower's grounds while the gate was open.

The noise dissipated as the gate closed behind Larsen and the general rode his horse to the stables. Once there he dismounted, wincing as he put weight on his left leg. An injury sustained a decade or so ago at the battle near the Tower of Sorcery had left him with a slight limp. While fighting his way back to a safer location, several high-ranking clerics had spotted him and immediately went to work on his injury right in the field of battle. He had never let them finish their healing before barging back into the battle when he saw his men losing ground to the undead legions they faced. Now he paid the price, with an injury that would nag him for the rest of his life.

As Larsen limped back to the tower, he saw more of the skink warriors moving into position along the battlements. He didn't trust these creatures, but High Cleric Malachi was adamant to the contrary. The skink warriors used to be noncommittal when war broke out, opting to fight for the losing side in order to even the odds and prolong the battle. Then, when the upper hand was achieved for the side they fought on, they would switch sides and shoot their former allies! This side-changing would continue indefinitely until the war was over.

According to Malachi, a special deal had been reached between humans and skink warriors. Apparently, Arch Mage Kazin had done them a favour, and the skink warriors had pledged allegiance to the Tower of Hope. Now they always fought for the tower. In exchange, their injuries were attended to by the clerics. Nevertheless, the general did not like or trust these creatures. But he tolerated them for now. He was expected to.

He was at the tower's entrance when there was once again a commotion back at the gate. A messenger was let through. General

Larsen recognized him as an outpost messenger, so he waited for the man to approach.

Actually, the messenger was barely a man; he was probably only fifteen years old. But General Larsen needed new recruits, and he wasn't choosy in this day and age. He also knew that training from a young age could produce a superior soldier. This boy was young and agile, and both traits were valuable.

The messenger spotted the general and ran up to him breathlessly, his blonde hair bouncing on his head as his feet touched the ground. "Sir!" he called, slowing to a halt in front of his general. He gave the customary salute.

"Ensign." General Larsen returned the salute, pleased that the boy had remembered to salute him. Too many new recruits either forgot, or didn't have the proper respect to follow through on that formality. "Status report?"

Still out of breath from his run, the boy began his report on the goings on at one of the outposts near the Old Dwarven Mountains. "We have a problem, Sir."

"What's wrong?"

"Two days ago outpost two failed to send a runner to outpost three at the designated time. A dispatch was sent out from outpost three to investigate. When they got there - to outpost two that is - they found that it had been overrun by orcs. There were signs of battle, but the bodies had been removed." The boy paused.

"Is there any possible motive for the attack?" asked Larsen.

"All of the food and water supplies were taken," said the boy, "along with a few weapons."

General Larsen cursed. "Is there any indication as to the orcs' whereabouts?"

"Yes, Sir," said the messenger. "It appears that the orcs have returned to the mountains again. Despite the heavy rain and perpetual darkness, our trackers have confirmed this by following the tracks."

"Were they only orcs?" asked Larsen. "No lizardmen or ogres?"

The messenger shook his head. "Only orc tracks could be seen."

Larsen nodded.

"Sir!" said a voice suddenly to Larsen's right. Larsen turned to see one of his lieutenants saluting him. Larsen returned the salute, as did the messenger. "Lieutenant Breen."

The lieutenant was a young, able-bodied man with a wiry build and dark hair. Larsen had promoted him to lieutenant after he had proven his mettle in the battle by the Tower of Sorcery. Unscathed after the battle, Breen had tirelessly helped to carry the injured back to the healing tents. As a result, many lives were saved both on and off the field by this man's fortitude.

"Am I interrupting?" asked the lieutenant.

"Actually, your timing is impeccable," said Larsen. "I have a task for you to perform."

"I am always at your service," said Breen, standing to attention.

"I need you to gather a contingent of soldiers to replace the guards in outpost two," said Larsen. "They were overrun by orcs two days ago."

Breen's eyes widened but he said nothing.

"So far it appears to have been a random attack," continued Larsen. "They targeted the food and water supplies. It seems they have bad water to contend with just like us. Whether they take our water to weaken us or to supply themselves, we must be wary of another attack. You must proceed with caution."

"Yes Sir," said Breen

"I also want you to assign a grey mage to each outpost," added Larsen.

"Sir?"

"I want them to set wards around each outpost to warn of any intruders. That way everyone can be aroused and a surprise attack can be averted."

"Yes, Sir," said Breen.

"Send two extra soldiers to escort the grey mages to the outpost towers and they can supplement the forces stationed there upon arrival."

"Of course, Sir."

Larsen turned to the messenger. "You have done well, ensign. Report to the barracks and inform the next messenger on the roster to report to Lieutenant Breen. You are off messenger duty for now."

"Yes, Sir!" shouted the ensign excitedly. He saluted the two men and hurried off for the barracks.

"He needs a rest," said Larsen.

"It's just as well," said Breen. "The duties around here are starting to become repetitive. The messenger and soldiers will welcome the change."

"I'm sure they will," said Larsen. "Just remember it's much more dangerous manning the outposts these days. If things continue the way they are, there could be a delay in supplying the outposts with supplies or reinforcements should the need arise."

"I suggest we change shifts at the outposts more frequently," suggested Breen.

"I agree," said Larsen. "That will get more men away from here more often and keep morale up."

"When do I leave?" asked Breen.

General Larsen considered. "If you can get water and supplies together for all nine outposts before dark, you can get started at first light. A heavier contingent of soldiers is less likely to be ambushed, and supplies will get safely delivered to each outpost."

"Understood, Sir," said Breen, saluting.

General Larsen saluted back and dismissed his lieutenant. Breen had not taken two steps when Larsen suddenly called out. "Breen?"

Breen turned. "Sir?"

"Tell the grey mages to wear black robes, will you?"

"Sir?"

"They're magic users, and if the orcs think they're black mages, it might catch them off balance. That would put the element of surprise back in our favour."

"Very good, Sir," said Breen, saluting again.

Larsen knew Breen liked the idea when he saw the momentary grin at the corners of the lieutenant's mouth before he turned and left to carry out his orders.

x x x x x

William Farnsworth, known by his friends as Billy, sat in his favourite worn out chair watching the flames in the fireplace as his dwarven guest, Henry Woodworker, poured a couple of glasses of homemade dwarven ale. He handed one glass to Bill and sat down in another worn out chair beside him.

"This stuff is made from pure wildhorn leaves," said Henry proudly. "I made it myself, using my great granddad's recipe. It's the cure for what ails ya."

Billy took a sip of the brew and smacked his lips. "Well, I'll be, Henry! This stuff's better than your last batch!"

Henry chuckled jovially. "It's the same batch, Billy-boy! It's just aged a little more."

Billy looked at his brown-bearded friend in surprise. "Really? I can't believe it!"

Henry nodded. "'Tis true, Billy, 'Tis true!"

Billy took a good sized gulp of the ale. "You're in the wrong profession, my friend."

"Aye," muttered the dwarf. "Carpentry ain't as fun as it used to be." He downed his glass and refilled it with more ale.

"It's more profitable than farming," said Billy, allowing Henry to refill his glass even though it wasn't empty yet. The room was getting warmer.

Wildhorn leaves grew on the side of the mountain, and many were aware of its special sight-giving ability in dark conditions. Most humans ate the leaves to be able to see their way through the perpetually dark tunnels in the mountains. This freed their hands of torches, which were cumbersome to carry, particularly in cramped conditions. Carrying a stockpile of wildhorn leaves would get you farther, faster, than having a torch with a limited life span. Elves and dwarves, however, were able to see exceptionally well in the darkness, and did not require the use of wildhorn leaves. For them, if they ingested these leaves, it could lead to blindness. The same fate would result for the humans if too large a quantity was consumed at once. Remarkably, in a fermented state, wildhorn leaves were safe to consume. Thus, some brave dwarves found a use for the leaves more to their liking in the form of one style of dwarven ale. Unfortunately, the sight giving property of the leaves was lost in the brewing.

"How many head of cattle do you have left?" asked Henry, breaking into Billy's thoughts.

"Less than one third of them are still alive," said Billy sadly. "Those that live don't look so good."

Henry shook his head. "That's too bad. I wish there was a way that I could help."

"Don't fret about it," said Billy. "There's nothing you or anyone can do about it. Even the clerics are unable to help."

"Aye, it's a mess," said Henry. He downed his glass again and rose somewhat unsteadily to his feet. "I'd better be headin' home. There's still some work for me to attend to come morning. You finish off the rest of the ale. I reckon you'll be needin' it."

Billy raised his glass to his friend. "Take care, my friend."

"You too," said Henry, staggering toward the door. Donning his coat he added, "Say hi to the missus for me."

"Will do," said Billy.

"I hope she gets well soon."

"So do I, Henry, so do I."

The dwarf left and Billy rose, glass still in hand. He added some more ale to it and climbed upstairs to check on his wife, Elsie.

There were two lit candles on either night stand when Billy entered the bedroom. Elsie lay in bed, almost motionless. Billy approached the bed and leaned over to kiss her glistening forehead. Perspiration from her face had made her pillow damp so he changed it for a dry one. This caused her to wake up momentarily.

"Bill." The word was barely a croak as her parched lips opened to speak.

"Hush," said Billy gently. He laid a gentle finger to her lips. "You rest. I'll take care of you, don't you fret now." He reached over to the night stand for the glass of water but it was empty. The water jug was empty too. Billy cursed under his breath. He had forgotten to refill it. He looked around helplessly for a moment and almost spilled his ale.

"Water," moaned Elsie.

Billy didn't want to keep his wife waiting while he ran downstairs for more water, so he held his glass of ale to her lips. "It's the cure for what ails you," said Billy calmly, quoting Henry's earlier remark.

Elsie drank the liquid slowly, coughing slightly as it went down her parched throat. She drank nearly half the glass before stopping. Her lips betrayed a slight smile as she drifted off to sleep.

"Good night, dear," whispered Billy quietly. He kissed her again and put his glass on the night stand. Then he took the empty water jug and turned to the bedroom door, berating himself for not keeping the jug full of the fresh water that his son had brought from the Tower of Hope. He was startled by the presence of someone standing in the doorway.

"Sorry, father. I didn't mean to startle you."

"That's O.K, son."

"How's mom?"

Billy led his son, Jim, from the room and closed the door behind him. "Still weak, I'm afraid." He spoke softly, so as not to disturb Elsie.

Father and son went downstairs to continue their conversation. Billy went to the water keg to refill the water jug and Jim followed.

"When do you return to duty at the tower?" asked Billy.

"First thing in the morning," said Jim.

"Then you'd better go back to bed. You'll need your strength to deal with all that rabble at the tower."

"I wish I could stay and help you here," said Jim.

"There's nothing you can do here, son. You're more useful at the tower. Besides, you have to bring us some more of the tower's clean water. You can't do that moping around the house, can you?"

"I guess not," admitted Jim. He yawned. "Good night, father."

"Good night, son." Billy gave his son the water jug. "Could you bring this to up your mother's room for me? I'll be up shortly."

"Sure," said Jim, taking the jug from his father.

Billy watched his son go back upstairs and then he sat in his favourite chair again. The dwarf's bottle of ale sat beside him. His glass, unfortunately, was still upstairs. "Who needs a glass?" muttered Billy, grabbing the bottle. He put the bottle to his lips and drank.

Next thing he knew it was morning. The smell of fresh coffee greeted his nostrils and he smiled softly. "Ah, that smells good." He rose and headed for the kitchen. "Son, you make a sweet smelling -" his voice trailed off as soon as he entered the kitchen. He blinked several times before he could believe his eyes.

He had expected to see a tall man dressed in a lieutenant's uniform. What he actually saw was a frail, emaciated woman in a nightgown. Billy's lips moved but he couldn't speak.

Jim entered the kitchen a moment later. "Dad, did you -?" His voice trailed off like his father's.

Elsie turned to face the two men in her life. Her eyes were sunken and her face was pale. "Good morning, boys," she rasped. A thin smile played across her lips. "That's potent ale Henry concocted, isn't it?"

Billy and Jim Farnsworth exchanged surprised looks.

Elsie burped.

Chapter 19

 few more rocks bounced off the hastily erected shield that Vera had magically generated and fell into the black abyss below them. Then all was still.

The orb on Kazin's staff still glowed, lying a few feet to his right. He tried in vain to reach for it but was bound fast. He looked down at the sticky white substance that held him in place. He and the others lay on a vast, white net, stretching into the darkness.

"Where are we?" asked Vera fearfully. She was entangled not far from Kazin's feet.

"It looks like we're in some sort of net," said Kazin. He noticed one section to the left that had several large holes, obviously made by the falling rocks from above.

"Cyril?" said Vera suddenly, looking around anxiously. "Cyril, where are you?"

"I'm here," said the cyclops a short distance away. He was lying on his back, barely visible in the staff's light.

"Are you O.K.?" asked Vera.

"Yes, thanks to your shield," answered the cyclops.

Vera breathed a sigh of relief. "Good. I wasn't sure my spell could protect us all." She canceled her shield spell now that the rocks had stopped falling.

Kazin struggled with the binding strands of the net again with no success. "I can't get free."

"Me neither," said Cyril. "Maybe . . .," his sentence was cut short when Vera let out a blood curdling scream. Not far away from her, barely visible in the gloom, a large black object approached her trapped form.

As it got closer, Vera shrieked, "A spider! It's a - a giant spider!"

Kazin needed no further urging. He struggled frantically to reach his staff, while Vera tried in vain to crawl away from the giant creature.

Cyril, seeing that Vera was in danger, surged against his bindings with a super human strength he never knew he had. Wrenching his arms free, he tore the bindings from his legs and rose awkwardly to his feet. Strands of the white stuff clung to his body as he forced his way to Vera's side, balancing precariously on the bindings. He stepped between the spider and Vera and faced the creature. "Look into my eye!" he intoned in the typical mesmerizing chant of a cyclops.

The spider had either never encountered a cyclops before, or it forgot what a cyclops was capable of. It looked into Cyril's eye and froze in position.

Cyril stared at it for long moments before determining that it was indeed paralyzed and not pretending. Then he turned to free the cleric from her bindings, ripping apart the white strands with his bare hands.

"Thank you, Cyril," said Vera gratefully, hugging the big one-eyed man warmly. "Now we're safe."

No sooner had she said this when there was a screech to Kazin's left. They all looked in that direction but saw nothing.

"There are more of those things?" said Vera tremulously, her voice quaking in fear.

"Where is it?" asked Cyril as he approached Kazin.

Kazin caught a glimpse of something out of the corner of his eye. "It's below us" he cried. A black tentacle with razor sharp claws running along its length reached up toward him from below. The mage braced himself for the assault when some strong arms ripped him from his bindings. The black tentacle slashed the open netting where Kazin's body had just been. The owner of that arm shrieked in rage.

"Thanks, Cyril," whispered Kazin as he lunged for his staff. He instantly turned to confront his assailant with magic, but Cyril already had it under control. The spider was paralyzed. The cyclops ripped the netting that its legs were attached to and it fell silently into the darkness below.

Vera screamed again and Cyril and Kazin spun around. More spiders were approaching them from behind.

"This is a giant web!" exclaimed Kazin in disbelief. Instinctively he made his staff light up brilliantly to illuminate their surroundings.

Dozens of spiders shrieked in the brightness and recoiled in agony. The light was unbearable to them.

Kazin made his staff even brighter and some of the spiders retreated a short distance. The mage briefly wondered why some retreated from the light while others were unaffected. Then he realized that Cyril had paralyzed them by looking them in the eye.

Vera fearfully grabbed Cyril's arm. "Should -should I shield us from them?"

"No," said Kazin finally. "We need to get out of here. The shield will just trap us here." Some of the spiders were overcoming their fear of the light and were inching closer. Kazin chanted and blasted them with fireballs. Their bodies were engulfed in flames and they screamed in agony as they died. One spider was boldly crawling along underneath the web and Kazin barely had enough time to blast it with a lightning bolt.

"Which way do we go?" stammered Vera.

"Follow me," said Cyril confidently. He led them away from the largest concentration of spiders.

The going was slow, as they often became tangled and stuck to the web. The spiders followed eagerly, and Kazin had to shoot fireballs and lightning bolts at them a number of times when they got too close. The companions finally reached the wall and stopped. The cliff face loomed before them, a vertical wall extending both up and down as far as the eye could see in the staff's light. There was no way anyone but a spider could climb those walls.

"Now what?" said Vera, turning to look behind her at the slowly approaching spiders. The spiders had them trapped and they knew it. They made hissing and clicking noises in anticipation.

"There's only one choice," said Kazin. The others looked at him questioningly. "Stay close to the wall," ordered the mage. "When I call for you, come to me at once."

Vera and Cyril nodded.

Kazin approached the spiders, casting spells left and right. The creatures scurried out of his way. When he was far enough away from the wall, the mage chanted a spell to light up his staff with a brilliant green light. It was so bright it forced even the bravest of spiders to back up in fear. Then a transformation began to take place. Kazin's body grew in size, and his human features disappeared. His countenance took on that of a dragon. Scales, claws, and wings grew out of his body.

Cyril and Vera watched the transformation in awe. Though they knew about Kazin's ability, they had never seen it for themselves before.

"Incredible!" exclaimed the cyclops. Vera was speechless.

Suddenly, the web began to sag and Cyril and Vera clung to the sticky web to maintain stability. The dragon soon became too large for the spider web to support it and it began to give way.

"Kazin!" cried Vera.

The dragon opened its wings and a fantastic fireball emerged from its giant, gaping maw. The flame instantly incinerated the front ranks of spiders, and seared the next few rows of spiders with intense heat and flame. The shrieks of pain and agony were deafening, echoing loudly off the canyon walls. The web between the dragon and spiders gave way and the spiders on the far side that survived scrambled to maintain hold.

The dragon looked behind him as his side of the web sank. "Hurry! Get on my back!"

Cyril grabbed the trembling cleric and jumped down to the dragon, who was by now below them on the falling web. They landed on the dragon's back and barely managed to hang on. Fortunately, the strands of webbing that clung to them also helped them to stick to Kazin's back.

Kazin leaped free of the webbing and opened his wings wide, allowing the air beneath him to lift them up and away from the canyon's unknown depths. Some spiders, who had been trapped on the same side of the web as the cleric and cyclops were, tried to save themselves by jumping onto Kazin's back. Most of them missed and fell to their doom. But two succeeded. One landed squarely on Kazin's back and clicked and hissed angrily at the cyclops and cleric.

As Kazin flew, belching flames to light his way, Cyril quickly climbed atop the dragon's back. He swung at the spider with his club. The spider jerked back and raised its front legs to do battle.

Meanwhile, Vera was having a little more difficulty. A spider had landed on Kazin's tail and was approaching her cautiously.

The cleric had a hard time standing up on the back of the flying dragon, and had to fight from a kneeling position. "Kazin, shake your tail!" cried Vera as she jabbed at the spider with her staff. Kazin did as he was told and Vera almost lost her own balance. The spider paused but did not lose its position. Vera could see that Cyril was busy and knew she was on her own. A spell came to her mind and she wasted no time gathering the spell components in her pouch. The spider was moving toward her and she chanted hastily. When the 'weakness' spell was complete, the spider stopped its advance. Vera grabbed firm hold of the dragon's back this time before shouting, "Shake your tail again, Kazin!"

Kazin complied, and this time the spider toppled over the side and disappeared.

Vera turned ahead to see Cyril still trying to land a blow on the spider. But the spider's reflexes were quick and it easily avoided each of the cyclops' attacks. It was also intelligent enough to avoid the cyclops' gaze. It was concentrating so hard on its fight with Cyril that it didn't notice Vera sneaking up behind it.

Vera carefully gathered some spell components from her pouch and chanted the 'stun' spell. The spider froze in place and Cyril successfully landed a blow to the spider's head. The spider staggered under the impact and one of its eyes burst open, emitting fluorescent green ooze. Vera made a face but helped Cyril roll the stunned creature off Kazin's back.

The dragon looked back over his shoulder. "Are you guys O.K.?"

Vera nodded. "Now we are."

"Good," said Kazin. "I've spotted a place where we can land. Hold on." Kazin landed on a ledge at the entrance to a cave and let his companions climb off. Then he transformed back into his human form. "Whew! That was close!"

Vera shuddered. "Those spiders were huge!"

A shriek sounded above them and a giant spider whizzed past them to the depths below.

"Let's get out of here!" said Kazin. They entered the cave, anxious to leave the canyon behind. Three tunnels led from the cave. The decision of which tunnel to take was made for them by a faint gust of wind. "It's not as strong as before," said Kazin with concern. "We'd better hurry."

Vera followed the black-cloaked figure in front of her with newfound respect. Kazin was indeed a powerful mage. The stories she had heard about him were almost too fantastic to be believed, but now she believed them, having seen for herself the majesty of his transformation. She longed to learn more about him. Several questions formed in her mind and she was about to ask him something when he suddenly stopped walking. The cleric bumped into him and looked past him to see why.

The first thing she noticed was that the tunnel they were in had just ended, but another tunnel ran to the left and right at ninety degrees. In both directions, the tunnel was much narrower than the one they were in. The other thing that grabbed her attention was the sudden change in Kazin's staff. The green light the orb emitted was replaced by a bright orange one.

"Hmm," murmured Kazin. "Interesting."

"What's wrong?" asked Vera.

"We are at a lizardman portal," said Kazin. "This is the way into the lizardmen's realm."

"Which way?" asked Cyril.

Kazin turned to face the others. "Directly ahead. But for now, I think we'll go this way." He chose the left tunnel and led the others along the narrow path. His staff returned to its light green glow. Vera gave Cyril a curious glance but the cyclops turned his gaze away in time.

They walked for what seemed like eternity. At last they came upon a mid-sized cavern that contained some elevated alcoves along one wall.

"I think this will be a good place to rest," said Kazin. "We could all use some sleep. I'll take first watch."

Cyril yawned and stretched. "That's the best advice I've heard all day. I was wondering when we were going to stop." He pulled a blanket from his pack and proceeded to one of the alcoves to lay it out.

Wrapping himself up in it, he was soon asleep judging by the sounds of his snoring.

Meanwhile, Vera and Kazin had chosen their alcoves and prepared their resting places as well. Kazin then set wards around the perimeter of the cavern and returned to the center of the cavern to begin his vigil. He found a flat rock and sat down.

Vera was about to turn in when she changed her mind. So as not to disturb the soundly sleeping cyclops, the cleric padded over to the mage in her bare feet and sat down in front of him. She stared up at him like a pupil eying her teacher.

"You should sleep," said Kazin.

"I'm not that tired yet," said Vera. "I have too many questions floating around in my head to be able to sleep properly."

"What would you like to know?" asked Kazin quietly.

Vera's eyes betrayed her adoration for the arch mage. "How do you do that - transformation - into a dragon?" she blurted. "I didn't see you cast any spells or anything."

Kazin shook his head. "It isn't that kind of magic. It is a magic powered by the mind. If I will it to happen, it does."

"How did you acquire that power?" asked Vera.

Kazin smiled. "Long ago, I defeated a dragon that lived in a cave far to the south of here. Your brother, Max, helped me to defeat it. When the dragon was destroyed, I obtained the orb, but not without your brother's sacrifice." Kazin shook his sadly. "I wish it had never happened. I'd sooner have Max back and give the dragon back his orb." The black mage looked hatefully at the orb atop his staff. "But then," continued Kazin, "we might not be here today. Too many important things have happened after that to regret my personal loss."

"The orb gave you the power to transform?" pursued Vera.

Kazin looked at the cleric and realized that she had come to grips with her brother's death. She was intent on learning, not reminiscing. "Not all at once," said Kazin. "It transformed me physically over time. When my first transformation occurred, it nearly consumed me. The orb has a life of its own. It speaks to me with the spirit of the dragon whose spirit it contains."

"A dragon lives in the orb?" asked Vera incredulously.

"Yes," said Kazin. "During the dragon wars, when magic was much more powerful among men, the black mages managed to find a way to contain the dragons' life essence by trapping it inside magical orbs. This way they could control the dragons for use in battle against the enemy. When the dragons were killed, their life force remained trapped in the orb. What the mages didn't realize was that the dragons' magic was also trapped in the orb. After the death of the dragons, any mage holding the orb became linked with the dragon, becoming able to magically become a dragon in mind and body. Most mages didn't have powerful enough minds to resist the dragon's mind control, and became permanent dragons. They wreaked havoc on anyone and everyone who stood in their way. Needless to say, they were hunted down and killed, and their orbs destroyed to prevent that catastrophe from happening again. Thus dragon orbs, like the one in my staff, were highly sought after. Few are known to still exist. After the dragon wars, large bounties were given to any man who killed a dragon and brought back the orb. Many lost their lives in such a quest for glory. Unfortunately, some real dragons were killed in the process too. That's probably why any that survived disappeared from us forever."

"Does anyone know what happened to the real dragons?" asked Vera.

"They disappeared without a trace," said Kazin. "The occasional seaman who returns from a major voyage occasionally claims to have seen a real dragon way to the south or east, but reports are rare and sketchy."

"Why are you in control of the orb?" asked Vera. "It hasn't consumed you."

Kazin smiled. "Not yet, anyway."

Vera's eyes widened. "You mean -?"

Kazin chuckled. "Don't worry. My mind is still strong. When I first transformed, I didn't quite know how to deal with the dragon's spirit, but as time went on, I was able to suppress its urges. That's one of the reasons today's mages are always looking for dragon orbs. Our mental training is superior to that of our ancestors. Our magic is much weaker, but our minds are stronger. The modern mage is more capable of resisting magical assertion than a mage from the dragon war period. Now our mental training is an integral part of our studies in the Tower of Sorcery. It wasn't all that prominent back then. Back then, if you could cast spells, it was all you needed to become a member of the tower. Also, in the past, magical spells were cast for every little thing. Now, it is used in moderation. We are more in control of our spell casting these days."

"This mental training," commented Vera, "is that why you can look into Cyril's eye without becoming paralyzed?"

"Yes," said Kazin.

"Can you teach me?" pleaded the cleric.

Kazin smiled. "It won't happen overnight. It's an acquired skill."

"That's fine," said Vera. "I want to learn."

"Very well," said Kazin. He raised his hands and chanted softly.

✗ ✗ ✗ ✗ ✗

Cyril took the second shift since he had little trouble getting back to sleep. It seemed like moments after Vera had taken her shift, however, that he was roused to wakefulness in the morning, if one could call it that in the mountains. It seemed to the cyclops that Vera glanced directly into his open eye for a split second, but she was not paralyzed, so he figured it was only his imagination. "Is it time to get up already?" he lamented.

"Yes," said Vera softly. "It will be a busy day today. I can feel it."

When they had their gear packed, Kazin led them back to the intersection where his orb had turned orange the day before. The orb turned orange again and Kazin concentrated. Suddenly, the wall before them shimmered and undulated.

Vera gasped. Kazin had not spoken a word of magic. "How did you do that?" she whispered.

Kazin did not answer her question. "Follow me," he ordered. He stepped into the portal and disappeared from sight. The others quickly followed.

They took a few effortless steps and arrived in a small cavern with three branching tunnels. Kazin turned and the portal disappeared, displaying an ordinary stone wall. His staff continued to glow orange. The mage made a slight mark on the wall to reference their passing. A short gust of wind materialized out of nowhere and echoed down the right tunnel. "Follow me," said the mage again. He led the others down the right tunnel. His staff returned to its original green glow. The trio exited the cavern and walked for nearly an hour, the wind guiding them whenever they were faced with a choice of direction. Several light tremors raged through the mountain as they went.

"The wind gusts seem to be a little stronger in the lizardmen's realm," commented Kazin. "We must be getting closer."

The cleric and cyclops remained silent, content to let the mage lead the way. They were glad the mage had bumped into them. They were in over their heads, but the mage's presence was comforting.

At one point, the companions passed another spot where Kazin's orb changed colour.

"Another portal?" asked Vera.

"Yes," answered the mage. "I suspect it leads back out of the lizardmen's realm." A slight breeze urged them to continue the way they were going. Kazin made a mark in the opposite wall. "Perhaps we can come back to it." He turned to continue their original course.

The path began to drop steeply and curve to the left. Not much further, Kazin's staff changed colour again. This time, however, it turned pink.

"A portal?" asked Cyril.

Kazin looked perplexed. "Yes. But there's something different about it." He concentrated. The concentration became strained and beads of sweat appeared on the mage's forehead, but he persisted.

Vera was worried that Kazin was overdoing it, and was about to break his concentration despite the risk of retribution, when the portal finally opened.

Kazin breathed a big sigh of relief. "It was magically locked. Now that I know what I'm dealing with, it should be easier next time." He looked at the others. "Be prepared for trouble," he cautioned.

Vera and Cyril nodded silently.

As one, they stepped through the portal.

The companions ended up in a winding passageway that went left and right like a never-ending snake. After moving along the passageway swiftly but cautiously, they could hear running water.

Carey Scheppner

Shortly after, light could be seen ahead of them. Kazin chanted a quick spell. "We are temporarily invisible," he explained to the others when they didn't see anything obvious happen.

"I can still see you," murmured Cyril, his low voice barely audible above the sound of running water.

"With this particular spell, invisible people can see one another," answered Kazin.

Cyril nodded in understanding.

The trio crept silently forward and reached the area that emitted the light. The sound of splashing water was much louder here. Before they knew it, the companions wound up in a circular chamber lit by torches with several passageways leading away from it. In the center of the chamber was a spectacular fountain of water. The fountain shot a good twenty feet straight up to the ceiling. At its zenith, the edges of the water returned to the floor in perfect symmetrical formation. The water on the floor ran in deep grooves around the fountain and drained into a large hole in a never-ending spiral to disappear from sight.

Vera quickly chanted a spell and grinned. "It's clean water!" she exclaimed. She grabbed her nearly empty wineskin and stepped forward.

Kazin stopped her and did a spell of his own. Satisfied, he turned to the cleric. "It's safe to proceed. There are no magical wards protecting the fountain."

Everyone filled their wineskins, drinking deeply and refilling their wineskins repeatedly.

Suddenly, a lizardman came upon them from one of the passageways. Vera was about to cry out when she remembered they were still invisible.

Cyril snuck up behind the unsuspecting lizardman and grabbed his head. With a quick motion, he snapped the creature's neck. The creature sagged to the floor, never knowing what had just killed him.

Vera looked away from the brutal scene. She was never comfortable with grizzly brutality like that, but she also knew she had to get used to it in the days ahead.

"We'd better dispose of the body," said Kazin.

The cyclops nodded and threw the dead creature over his shoulder.

186

Unfortunately, another lizardman happened upon the scene right then and saw his companion hanging in mid-air.

Kazin muttered and cast a fireball into the surprised lizardman just as more appeared in the chamber rolling a couple of barrels.

"Retreat!" shouted Kazin to the others. He waited for Vera to run past him back the way they had come. Cyril dropped his useless baggage and sprinted after the cleric. Then Kazin followed, hot on his heels.

Fortunately, Kazin's voice was sufficiently muffled by the fountain that the lizardmen scurried down the wrong passageways in pursuit. This gave Kazin the time to cancel the invisibility spell and unlock the portal they had entered by. They passed through it only to hear someone coming toward them here as well. That forced them to backtrack further.

When they reached the portal they had bypassed earlier, Kazin stopped and looked at the others. "What do you think?"

Light suddenly appeared ahead of them, answering Kazin's question for them. They were surrounded. The mage concentrated, opened the portal, and they were through.

The passageway that materialized before them curved sharply to the right. It also went down at a significant angle. The three companions paused when they heard a large number of voices some distance away.

Kazin looked back at the others, who nodded. They knew forward was the only way to go.

They traveled a few more minutes, the voices getting louder. An occasional roar could also be heard. At last, flickering light could be seen ahead of them. Creeping cautiously, the companions arrived at a platform jutting out from a rock face overlooking a vast chamber below. Keeping back so as not to be seen, Kazin, Vera, and Cyril looked below them.

Vera gasped. "Are those all ogres?" she whispered incredulously.

Kazin eyed the spectacle below in awe. "Incredible! There must be thousands of ogres gathered here! I've never seen so many all at once!"

Cyril pointed. "Look over there!"

The others looked where Cyril pointed. On an upper ledge at the far end of the chamber they could see a massive ogre, along with two much smaller robed figures.

"That must be the ogre chieftain," said Kazin.

"Who are the mages?" asked Vera. Her question was answered when one of the cloaked figures threw back its hood. The cleric gasped again. "A lizardmage!"

"Yes," said Kazin somberly. "I wonder what they're up to."

"Look!" exclaimed Cyril. Behind the lizardmages a portal opened. A small contingent of lizardmen appeared, hauling a cart laden with barrels. The portal closed and one of the lizardmages beckoned the ogre chieftain. The chieftain turned to his followers and shouted out an order. A few moments later another ogre came up to the platform. He lifted the lid off one of the barrels and grabbed a mug that hung on the side of the cart. He dipped the mug into the barrel, brought the mug to his lips, and paused uncertainly. The crowd below became silent. The ogre chieftain gave a nod and the other ogre drank. A moment of silence passed, followed by another. At last the ogre who drank put the cup down and nodded to his chieftain. The chieftain said something, but his voice was drowned out by the cheering of the crowd below. The chieftain shook hands with one of the lizardmages and turned to the crowd to speak. The crowd fell silent once again. This time the ogre chieftain's words could be heard across the entire chamber. Kazin assumed the lizardmage had amplified the ogre's voice to carry farther.

"In exchange for good water," bellowed the chieftain, "we will cease our hostilities toward the lizardmen. We will then join them in their war against the humans - the true cause of our suffering!"

Vera gasped again while the crowd murmured loudly.

"Also," continued the chieftain, "I have been informed that the human magic users have been disabled! With the lizardmen and their magic, we will encounter minimal resistance!" The crowd roared while the chieftain spoke on. "The spoils of war are ours to do with as we please!"

At this, the crowd went berserk. "Let us prepare for war!" screamed the ogre chieftain.

The ogres filed out of the chamber's many exits, excitedly yelling and cheering. The lizardmen left via the portal, leaving the cart and barrels for the ogres to take with them. In a matter of minutes, the chamber was empty.

Kazin and Vera looked at each other. They had to stop the ogres from launching their attack! With black mages dying and clerics overloaded with patients, the humans didn't stand a chance!

"Someone has to alert the Tower of Sorcery and the Tower of Hope!" said Vera anxiously.

"Don't look at me," said Cyril. "Who's going to listen to a cyclops?"

"We're too far into the mountain," said Vera. "If I go, how will I open all the portals we went through? Besides, even if I could get back to the first portal entrance, I still couldn't get out the way we came in, remember? I'd be lost."

"Relax," said Kazin. "There are outposts along the base of the mountain that can alert General Larsen of an impending attack. The troops there are also equipped with homing pigeons, so word is bound to get through. An advance warning from us would make little difference. We have a better chance of stopping things at the source. If we can find and free the trapped elementals, we might be able to persuade them to purify the water and undo some of the damage they've caused since being controlled by the lizardmages."

"I agree," said Cyril. "The elementals need our help. If we don't save them, no one will be safe from the consequences."

Vera nodded. "O.K. What are waiting for? Let's get those lizardmen before it's too late!"

Chapter 20

ll clear," said Alric, removing his invisibility cloak. He came back to the scene of a recent, but short-lived battle.

"Great," grunted Rebecca, dragging the last of the orcs to the side to join with the others.

"Clear this way," reported Tyris from another tunnel. He turned his attention to the wall where the lizardmens' portal had been. "Now we have to find a way to activate this portal."

"I'll try some of my magic," offered Alric.

"By all means," said Tyris. He stepped aside so the elf could have access to the wall. "In the meantime, I think I'll dispose of the bodies." He turned to the dwarf. "That's good enough, Rebecca. I'll take it from here. Stand back."

Rebecca backed away from the elemental and the pile of dead orcs. The elemental strode into the pile of bodies and raised his arms. Instantly, the mass of dead orcs lit ablaze in an intense inferno. There was a momentary stench, but it was ventilated from the chamber by a convenient gust of wind originating from one of the tunnels.

Alric, busy casting a spell, glanced only briefly at the inferno before turning his attention to the wall. Rebecca averted her gaze as well, her eyes stinging from the brightness.

A few moments later the bodies were turned to ash, as were the orcs' clothing and weapons. All that was left was a pile of dust.

"There!" said Tyris, satisfied with his handiwork.

Alric was still trying various door opening spells, all without success. "It's no use!" he said at last. "The magic the lizardmen used must be different somehow." He turned to the elemental. "Can't you help somehow?"

Tyris shrugged. "I'm afraid not. I can't cast spells."

"Can't you burn your way through the door?" asked Rebecca.

"I could eventually burn my way through that rock," said Tyris, "but it won't do much good. You see, portals like that are designed to transport the individual or individuals to another place entirely. The other end of the portal may lie halfway across the mountain."

"Oh," said Rebecca dejectedly. "So, now what?"

"Now we wait," said Tyris. "The lizardmage said he would be back in two hours. Time is almost up."

"There are bound to be orcs showing up to meet the lizardmen," said Alric. "We should hide."

"I agree," said Rebecca. "We need the element of surprise."

"Yes," agreed Tyris. "The orcs are bound to show up before the allotted time, so we'll have to deal with them quickly before the lizardmen show up. We'll use the same strategy we used to take out the guards."

"Sounds good to me," said Alric. He donned his cloak. At that same instant, the portal in the wall began to materialize.

"The portal is opening!" whispered Rebecca. There was no time to hide. All three of them braced themselves. "Lizardmen!" she growled menacingly, charging toward the portal to join Alric. The elf cast a spell on his dagger to make it into a sword.

When something other than a lizardman stepped out of the portal, the dwarf was caught off guard. In fact, she became frozen in her tracks.

The elf did not take the time to identify the intruder. He sank his blade into the intruder's shoulder and pulled back to take another swing. A short scream was followed by a chant and as Alric swung his sword again, it clanged off an invisible barrier that protected the intruder. Seeing another smaller figure nearby, the one, he surmised, who had cast the spell, Alric instinctively lunged at her with his sword outstretched. The spell caster, dressed in white, stepped back while chanting another spell. She pointed a staff in Alric's direction.

Suddenly, Alric was no longer able to proceed as a sleep spell struck him with full intensity. The elf crashed headlong to the ground and lay still. Meanwhile, two of Tyris' fireballs whizzed past him toward the intruders.

Another spell caster, dressed in black, held his staff in front of the white-robed intruder, the orb of his staff absorbing the fireballs that flew his way.

Tyris already had another volley of fireballs flying in the opponents' direction.

"Stop!" cried the black-robed mage, his attention on the flaming figure in the background. One fireball got past his staff and struck the white-robed spell caster. With a cry she went down, the amulet around her neck flaring brilliantly.

"Vera!" cried the cyclops, who had suffered at the hands of the invisible sword wielder. Released from the shield spell when Vera had cast the sleep spell on Alric, he bent over the cleric and cradled the unconscious figure in his massive arms.

"Stop!" cried the black-robed man again. "We don't want to harm you!"

"Release my friends!" ordered Tyris, "or suffer the consequences!"

"O.K.!" cried the mage. "Tell them to stop attacking!"

The cyclops looked up at the fire elemental, angrier than he had been since leaving the Tower of Hope. It only frustrated him further that the flaming man was immune to his paralyzing ability. He growled at the flaming man, but looked down when Vera came to with a moan. She opened her eyes and Cyril quickly looked away, but not before the cleric smiled at him while looking directly into his eye for a split second.

The cyclops helped the cleric to her feet while the elemental repeated his order. "Release my friends!"

"Be patient!" snapped Kazin suddenly. "You injured the one who can release your friends."

Tyris was taken aback by the sharpness of Kazin's tone. "You dare to talk to an elemental that way?" intoned Tyris angrily.

"I meant no disrespect," said Kazin, a little more calmly. "You injured my friends. I'm as upset as you are."

Vera was standing on her own now, and Tyris was amazed that she was alive at all. She looked at the elemental. "I will release your friends now. You must promise us that they will not harm us."

Tyris nodded, still amazed that the cleric was unharmed.

Vera freed the dwarf first. Rebecca resumed her charge and skidded to a stop when she heard Tyris shout, "Stop!" Waving her axe threateningly, and without taking her eyes off the cleric, she said, "What? Who?"

"Do not harm them," said Tyris.

The dwarf looked around, disoriented.

Vera then went to deal with the invisible sword-wielder. "Hmm. This one should be interesting." She felt around until she could feel the body. Grabbing hold of what she thought was an arm, she chanted a wake spell on the individual.

"Relax, Alric!" called Tyris. "They mean you no harm."

"Huh? What?" said the elf. He rose groggily to his feet.

"Show yourself!" ordered Kazin.

"Why should I?" snapped Alric, looking in the direction of the speaker. He almost gasped when he recognized Kazin as the human mage who resided in Greenwood. He couldn't allow Kazin to see that he had possession of the cloak!

"I like to see who I'm dealing with," responded Kazin.

A cry from the cleric gave Alric the reprieve he needed. Everyone looked at Vera, who had just now remembered Cyril's stabbed shoulder and looked to see his arm covered in blood. "Cyril! Your wound!"

"It's nothing," said Cyril stoically.

"Nonsense!" said Vera sternly. She began to administer her healing magic to the wound.

Kazin turned back to the elf, who was busily jamming something into his pack. When the elf rose, he locked eyes with the mage.

"There, uh, now you can see me," stammered the elf. "Satisfied?"

Kazin knew the elf was hiding something. He decided to keep a close eye on him. He turned back to the fire elemental. "I've been looking for you."

"Don't even think of trying to summon me," growled Tyris.

Kazin shook his head. "I don't plan to. But I do need your help."

"Why?"

"Because the air elemental told me to come and find you."

"Why would the air elemental want me?" asked Tyris.

"Apparently, you are the only elemental still free of the control of the lizardmages," said Kazin. "We must try to free the others before the lizardmen find a way to control you. If they capture you as well, the entire world could be destroyed."

Rebecca gasped. "That explains the earth quakes and poisoned water."

Kazin nodded. "Yes."

"Then we're on the same side!" exclaimed the dwarf. She indicated the cyclops with her thumb but avoided looking at him this time. "But I don't see why you chose to put up with the likes of him."

"Hey!" snapped Vera, pausing in her healing chant. She shook her staff at the dwarf. "Cyril is a good man!"

Rebecca didn't look convinced.

Kazin laughed. "I think we should introduce ourselves. It should ease the tension."

Introductions were made, and when Rebecca found out who Kazin was, her eyes almost popped out of her head. "You're Kazin? The same Kazin who helped Uncle - I mean - King Harran in the wars a decade ago?"

"Yes," said Kazin. "Harran is a good friend of mine."

The dwarf ran forward and embraced the mage in a bear hug. "It's wonderful to finally meet you!" cried the dwarf. "And to think we almost killed one another!"

Kazin gently released the dwarf. "You say Harran is your uncle?"

"Not exactly," said Rebecca. She briefly told Kazin of her uncle, Horst Hammarhold, and his interaction with King Harran.

"I see now," laughed Kazin. "I'm sure Harran is happy to be your 'unofficial' uncle. He's a fine fellow. I know him well."

Rebecca turned to Tyris. "He's O.K., Tyris. We can trust him."

Tyris relaxed.

"Someone's coming!" interrupted Alric suddenly. At the same instant, a contingent of orcs entered the cavern, catching the group unawares. Orcs could be heard coming down the other tunnels as well.

Kazin and the others sprang to life. "Rebecca, you and Alric take the far entrance! Tyris, can you block the entrance on your right?"

Tyris nodded. He sprang into the opening just as some orcs tried to get through. The elemental burst into an inferno, burning the orcs in front and causing the remaining ones to jump back.

Cyril insisted on fighting, so Vera cast a 'slow' spell on the orcs that had circled around Kazin to attack him from behind. This allowed Cyril to reach them before they could attack the mage. Then Vera cast a strength spell on Cyril. Swinging his club with his good arm, the cyclops literally swatted the orcs like flies, sending them flying into the walls on either side. His super human strength was amplified by his dislike of orcs.

Kazin, meanwhile, was blasting fireballs into the charging orcs. With Cyril taking the orcs in close, the mage was making headway toward the third tunnel. More orcs were trying to get into the cavern, but the mage's fireballs were keeping them back. Kazin looked over his shoulder and saw that Rebecca and Alric were losing ground against the surging orcs. More were slipping into the cavern. "Vera!" shouted the mage, "Can you block this entrance with your shield?"

Vera cast weakness on some of Alric and Rebecca's attackers and came running to the mage. "Ready!" she shouted.

Kazin sent a volley of fireballs into the orcs and Vera cast her shield. The orcs could not get past.

Satisfied that the way was blocked, Kazin checked Tyris' entrance and concluded that the elemental had things under control. Not so for Alric and Rebecca. Cyril was already working his way through the orcs in the chamber to aid the dwarf and elf.

Kazin was forced to fight in hand to hand combat and his experience paid off. His staff thrust, jabbed, and clobbered the orcs senseless. He made sure none got past him to attack the vulnerable cleric, who was busy maintaining her shield.

Finally Cyril made it to the elf and dwarf, who stood back to back fighting for their lives. Alric hadn't even had time to don his cloak, so he was a visible target. His arm had been cut and he was bleeding openly. The dwarf made her attacks count as orc after orc was singed by her dagger. Her hand axe flew just as effectively in her other hand.

Kazin eliminated the last of the orcs in the cavern and began pelting the orcs entering the last tunnel with fireballs. He had to make the fireballs smaller to avoid hurting the dwarf and elf. Cyril paralyzed and smashed his way through the orcs. The dwarf, elf, and cyclops moved in to seal off the last tunnel.

Looking around, Kazin saw that all was secure in the chamber. He noticed that Vera was straining to maintain her shield all by herself. The elemental seemed to be doing fine, but Kazin didn't know how long Tyris could keep it up. Even elementals could tire out. The sounds of battle continued in the last tunnel, but the mage knew that at least two of those who fought were injured. It was time to withdraw while they were still in reasonable shape. He turned to the wall that contained the portal and knew that was the only way out. Concentrating, he opened the portal.

"Vera!" shouted the mage.

"Yes?" said Vera, looking back at the mage with a strained expression. She was breathing heavily.

"Can you control the shield from over here?"

"Yes," answered the cleric, the strain in her voice evident. "But it is harder to maintain."

"I know," said Kazin, "but we have to retreat. I'll help you." He chanted his magic and boosted the cleric's shield. Shield magic was one of only a few spells shared by both the white and black mages.

Vera slowly backed away from her tunnel toward the portal, maintaining her shield with Kazin's help.

"Cyril, Rebecca, Alric, get ready to run through the portal on my mark!" shouted Kazin.

"O.K.!" said Rebecca, her dagger scorching another orc that had gotten too brave.

"You too, Tyris," said the mage.

Somewhere within the wall of flame a voice responded. "I will go last. You must all clear the cavern."

Vera had reached the mage. "Hold your shield until the others get here," said Kazin. Vera nodded.

"Now!" ordered Kazin. As the elf, cyclops and dwarf came running, Kazin showered their pursuers with fireballs to slow them down. The three fighters dove through the portal.

"You next, Vera!" ordered the mage.

The cleric disappeared through the portal, wondering how Kazin could be operating the portal, holding the shield by himself, and casting fireballs at the same time. Her respect for the mage increased even more.

"Come on, Tyris!" cried Kazin. The orcs were surging into the room too fast for him to contain them.

"Go first and I'll follow!" called Tyris, his form beginning to change.

Kazin dove into the portal. He knew he could sustain it from the other side. His only fear was that some of the orcs would get through before the elemental did. Screams of agony reached his ears just before he disappeared to the other side, where the heavy breathing of his companions was the predominant sound.

A few moments later, the elemental arrived in his human form, unscathed. "I wouldn't go back there for a while," he said calmly. "The smell of roasted orc flesh is almost unbearable." He looked around at the unlikely group that was assembled before him. Vera and Alric sat on the floor, the cleric busy healing the elf's arm. The cyclops was leaning against the wall, fatigued as a result of the heavy fighting. Kazin and Rebecca were still breathing heavily from their own exertion. On the ground nearby were two dead lizardmen.

The elemental directed his attention to Kazin. "Are we now in lizardman territory?" He indicated the fallen lizardmen.

Kazin nodded. "These two were guarding this portal when we stumbled upon them. I figured there was something important through the portal, so we investigated it. That's when we ran into you guys."

Tyris nodded. "This portal leads to the orcs' realm. This is where the lizardmen delivered several barrels of water to them in exchange for troops for some battle or other."

Vera, finished with Alric's wound, stood up. "They're recruiting orcs? Oh, no!"

Rebecca raised an eyebrow. "Huh? Did I miss something?"

The cleric looked at the dwarf. "They're preparing to attack the humans! The ogres have already agreed to fight for the lizardmen! Now the orcs are joining them! With the mages out of commission, and the clerics overwhelmed by all of the sick and dying, we don't stand a chance!"

"The mages are out of commission?" asked Rebecca uncertainly. She looked searchingly at Kazin. "How?"

"There was an intruder at the Tower of Sorcery," explained Kazin. "Most of the mages have been poisoned."

Rebecca held a hand over her mouth. Her eyes widened in fear. Then she lowered her hand and whispered, "Who could have done such a terrible deed?"

Kazin shook his head. "I don't know."

Alric was just as stunned as Rebecca. It was he who had done that deed! Now he knew what he had been manipulated to do. He was glad no one was looking at him. His guilty expression would have betrayed him.

"We should alert the dwarves," said Rebecca. "They will help, I'm sure!" She turned to face the red-faced elf. "You should alert the elves!"

"There's no time," said Kazin. "We have to stop the lizardmen before they get their plan off the ground."

"How do we do that?" asked Rebecca.

"We have to save the elementals," said Kazin. "Hopefully that will thwart the lizardmens' plans before they launch their attack."

Alric, who had been somberly silent until now, rose to his feet. His fists were clenched. "Let's get going, then. I'm not letting these lizardmen get away with this! The lizardmage behind all this is going to pay! Dearly!"

Kazin was surprised by the elf's vehemence. Although he was not sure about the elf's motives, he was sure of one thing: their goals coincided.

Chapter 21

o you really think the orcs would know where the fire elemental might be?" asked a lizardman. He looked sidelong at their leader as he walked down the tunnel beside him.

"Even if they have seen it, what makes you think they will tell us?" asked a female lizardwoman behind them. "They have no reason to trust us."

Lynch rounded on the two who challenged his plan. "They will answer our questions truthfully! If they want additional water, they'll do anything!" With that outburst, he turned on his heel and continued down the corridor.

The group of lizardmen marched on in silence, allowing their irate leader to lead on. Bringing up the rear was Lyrr. He said nothing, because for once he thought Lynch had come up with a reasonable plan. Days of aimless searching had shortened Lynch's already short fuse. After giving several suggestions to Lynch, Lyrr finally convinced him to ask other mountain dwellers if they had seen the elemental.

Lyrr was pulled from his reverie when he nearly bumped into the lizardman in front of him. The group had stopped. Pushing past the others, Lyrr made it to the front to see what was up.

Kneeling beside a prone lizardman body, Lynch was examining it for a cause of death. Lynch rose to his feet and faced the others excitedly. "He was killed by a fireball! It could have been our elemental!"

"Almost anyone can cast a fireball," challenged another lizardman. "What makes you think he was killed by an elemental?"

"Why would another lizardman kill some guards protecting a portal to the realm of the orcs?" challenged Lynch in return. He pointed at another lizardman nearby. "That one's dead from the same cause."

"Maybe the orcs can tell us something," suggested the lizardwoman.

"That's what I've been saying all along!" snarled Lynch. The leader looked at Lyrr and pointed to the portal's location. "Lyrr, would you like to do the honours?"

Lyrr leered. He knew Lynch had trouble with portal magic and was afraid to admit it. Nevertheless, he stepped forward and activated the portal. Everyone stepped through and Lyrr went through last. He closed the portal behind him.

The air around them was thick with the smoke of charred flesh, and the gore of orc remains lay sprawled about the cavern. The stench was almost unbearable.

"Uggh!" gasped the lizardwoman. "What happened here?"

Lynch turned to face her, his expression elated. "Don't you see? It was here! The elemental was here! We're getting close!"

Lyrr looked around at the carnage and had to agree. The devastation was more than any lone lizardmage could cause, even Graf himself. This was the work of a more powerful being.

"Attack!"

The battle cry caught the lizardmen off guard. Streaming in from every direction were hordes of orcs.

The lizardmen let loose with a number of fireballs and magic arrows, but the number of orcs was too great.

Lyrr turned to reactivate the portal, but was surprised to see it had already been opened. Lizardmen, armed with staves and spears, appeared in the cavern. Seeing their fellow lizardmen in trouble, they immediately entered the fray, doling out additional offensive magic. The front rows of orcs were killed, but not before killing four of Lynch's party. Some bolts fired from orc crossbows found their marks in the newcomers.

"Fall back!" shouted an armed lizardman, who appeared to be a lieutenant, judging by the insignia on his breastplate.

Lynch's party fell back to the portal while the lizardmages provided cover with fireballs. Soon, all of the surviving lizardmen had returned to their own realm. The portal closed, sealing them off from the enraged orcs.

The lieutenant spun on Lynch's party. "Who is in charge here?"

"I am," said Lynch. He was rubbing his left shoulder which had suffered a blow from an orc's club.

"What was going on in there?" demanded the lieutenant.

"The orcs came out of nowhere and attacked us," said Lynch sourly.

"Why?" asked the lieutenant.

"How the hell should I know?" retorted Lynch. "We just entered the cavern and before we knew it, they attacked."

"Did you kill all those orcs?" asked the lieutenant, unfazed by Lynch's attitude. "The orcs that were burned?"

Lynch shook his head. "No. They were like that when we got there."

The lizardman pointed to the two dead sentries who lay nearby. "What about them?"

Lynch shrugged. "They were dead when we found them."

The lieutenant's eyes narrowed suspiciously. "Why didn't you report this to a command post? You know the rules!"

Lynch shrugged again. "We decided to see if the orcs knew anything. It would have been better to report the incident with some idea of what had happened." He was playing it cool.

The lieutenant was not convinced. "You realize this is a restricted area? What is your business here? Do you have permission to even be here?"

Lynch pulled out a document and thrust it angrily into the lieutenant's face. "Here! My mission is to find and capture a fire elemental whatever it takes! The document is signed by Graf himself!"

The lieutenant read the document. "Lynch," he said at last. "Of course! You're known for getting into trouble. Do you know what trouble you've caused this time? You may have broken the alliance we've worked so hard to achieve with the orcs! I should report you!"

"Go ahead!" retorted Lynch. "I didn't do anything wrong! If anything, it's that blasted fire elemental who did this. Every minute I waste talking to you gives the elemental more time to escape! Do you want to be responsible for any further damage that the elemental causes?" Lynch grabbed his documents back. "If you're finished your interrogation, I've got work to do!" With that, he turned and headed down the tunnel, his remaining party in tow.

The lieutenant stared after him. "You realize I still have to report you!"

Lynch said nothing and raised and lowered his arm in a gesture of dismissal. Lyrr leered at the lieutenant and said, "Thanks for your assistance." Then he turned and followed his party. He knew that Lynch was going to be in trouble for his actions sooner or later, but he also knew Lynch would suffer endless ridicule if he returned empty-handed. The elemental had to be captured, and for once, he felt like they were on the right track.

✕ ✕ ✕ ✕ ✕

"The council recognizes Narla," said the speaker below Graf's alcove.

Narla spread her fish-like lips into a sensual grin. "The air elemental is still under control, but somehow succeeds in making the odd crack through which some of his magic occasionally escapes. Fortunately, we catch the openings before he can escape or release any of his magic against us. His power is great, and should greatly assist us in the upcoming battle."

Murmurs of approval filtered through the hall below.

"I have also determined," continued Narla, "that under the present conditions, the elemental's power will likely be limited. In trying to escape, it is depleting its energy at a phenomenal rate."

"What do you propose?" asked Graf.

Narla looked up at her leader. "If we had more lizardmages available for summoning, the elemental would not be resisting us, and would obey us willingly. That would allow the elemental to gain strength instead of wasting it trying to escape."

Graf stared. "You already have more spell casters than you need! Why do you need more?"

Narla hesitated. "There appears to be some unexplained resistance. It's as if someone else is trying to summon that elemental."

Graf was surprised. Who could be trying to summon the air elemental? The black mages in the human realm were not known to use summoning magic, and they were by now too few to accomplish this anyway. Could it be the clerics in the Tower of Hope? Doubtful. Something else was going on here. "Recruit more lizardmages as necessary," said Graf sullenly, "but don't give me any more excuses."

Narla nodded. "Thank you." Then she sat down.

General Slong rose and the speaker announced him.

"One of my lieutenants has reported an incident," began the general. His bronze breastplate glistened in the torchlight.

Graf nodded. "Carry on."

Slong continued. "Apparently, one of the portals to the orcs' realm has been breached."

Murmurs of surprise shot through the throng below. Graf stiffened in his chair. "Go on."

"They discovered two sentries, murdered, and went through the portal to investigate. In the orc cavern, they came upon a battle in progress between some lizardmen and numerous orcs. Reacting quickly, our troops extracted our people and returned them to our side of the portal. There were several casualties."

The murmurs and hisses in the crowd were starting to get too loud and Graf yelled for silence. The crowd settled down and Graf said, "Who were these lizardmen, and why were they in orc territory?"

Slong cleared his throat. "It was a party legally in the process of tracking down the fire elemental. They were led by lizardman Lynch."

Graf's eyes widened. "What! What was he trying to do?"

Slong shook his head. "I don't know. My lieutenant had no choice but to let him continue on his way. He had written permission to leave no stone unturned in his quest for the fire elemental."

Graf threw his hands up in despair. "But what does this have to do with a security breach?"

"The sentries who were killed were killed by magic," explained Slong. "Fireballs, to be precise."

"And?"

"Numerous orcs on the other side of the portal were also killed by fire magic."

"I assume Lynch took them out?" asked Graf.

"I don't think so," said Slong. "My lieutenant claims that Lynch and his team came upon a massacre that had already occurred. The orcs that they saw massacred in the cavern numbered in the dozens. It was as if they had been overwhelmed by an enormous inferno."

"The fire elemental?" hissed Graf in surprise. The crowd began to make noise again, but Graf rapped his staff on the floor to restore silence.

"Perhaps," said Slong. "Further investigation is hampered by the throngs of blood-thirsty orcs that are waiting in the cavern. I think they blame us for the assault."

Graf swore. "And you think the fire elemental has entered our realm?"

"It's possible," said Slong. "That explains the dead sentries on our side of the portal."

Graf swore again. The crowd was becoming restless again.

Graf rose to his feet. "Anyone who discovers the whereabouts of the fire elemental must report to a senior official as soon as possible. Slong, you increase the number of patrols and guards and bring a lizardmage along who knows how to summon a fire elemental. We can't let one lone elemental thwart our plans."

"Yes, Sir," said Slong.

"Are the other factions of orcs aware of this incident?" asked Graf.

Slong shook his head. "No. Not yet, anyway."

"Good. Make sure it stays that way. Offer the angry orcs more water and explain to them that we're on the same side. Tell them the elemental was a last-ditch effort by the human mages to shatter our alliance."

"Yes, Sir," said Slong. He hesitated. "There was one other security breach. It occurred in one of the fountain chambers."

"What?!" exclaimed Graf. "The fire elemental again?"

The crowd below hissed in consternation.

Slong shook his head. "I don't think so. There were some fireballs cast at our people, but no one could see who fired them. Several lizardmen were killed by fireballs, and one died of a broken neck. The intruders were nowhere to be found."

The crowd became even noisier at this news.

"You let them escape?!" shrieked Graf.

"They knew how to activate our locked portals," explained Slong hurriedly. "By the time security forces arrived, the intruders were long gone."

"Then double your security at once!" snapped Graf. The crowd was much too noisy by now so Graf bellowed, "Silence!"

With relative quiet in the hall, Graf continued, "How are things with the ogres?"

"Everything is going according to plan," said Slong. "The ogres are preparing for the assault, as are the goblins and a contingent of cyclops."

"Good! I'm hoping get started soon!" Graf turned to address the crowd. "You all know what to do! Any intruders are to be neutralized at all costs! In a few days we march!"

The crowd hissed and murmured and filed from the hall. As if in anticipation, the mountain rumbled ominously. Even Graf stumbled as he exited the council hall.

Graf stopped at a grub depot and filled a large sack with food. The lizardwoman maintaining the stash eyed him suspiciously. She had seen him do this on several occasions, but knew better than to question him on his peculiar actions. Graf nodded at her when he was finished, and departed.

Along the way, Graf spotted a messenger. The messengers in the lizardmen's realm were young, energetic lizardmen and women who were anxious to serve their kind. Graf told her to summon Brind to his quarters at once. The messenger nodded and ran to do as she was ordered. A quick response would put her in a favourable light with the leader of the lizardmen.

Arriving in his quarters, Graf crossed the room and entered his study. A hulking figure in the corner observed his approach through three sets of eyes. Graf threw the sack down in front of the hydra and sat down at his desk.

The hydra opened the sack with two of its heads and dumped the contents on the floor. "Is that all?" exclaimed the middle head.

"Quit complaining!" snapped Graf. "If you all shared, you wouldn't be so hungry the next time! Besides, you'll get plenty to eat in a few days."

The three heads paid no heed to the lizardmage and ate ravenously, gorging themselves as fast as their jaws could snap. Graf took the opportunity to cast a spell to clean up the mess the big creature had made. He wrinkled his nose. Soon the hydra would be sent out to aid in his plan.

A knock sounded at Graf's front door so he got up, left the study, and locked the study door. He set a spell to hide the sounds of the eating creature within. Then he answered his front door. It was Brind, the lizardmage who specialized in fire magic.

"You sent word that you wanted to see me?" said Brind.

"Come in," said Graf.

Brind entered and Graf offered him a chair. Then he sat down in a chair facing the fire mage. "Brind, I'm going to get right to the point. It appears that this Lynch character is unable to find the fire elemental. I want you to take charge and organize a more extensive search."

Brind nodded, a sly grin appearing on his lips. "Of course!"

"I also expect you to find out who else is trespassing in our realm."

Brind's smile vanished but he said nothing.

"I don't believe the conclusion Slong came to that the elemental breached our security alone. Elementals don't have that kind of magic."

"You think someone let him in?" asked Brind.

"Yes," said Graf. "It was definitely a spell caster. At first I thought that idiot Lynch may have let him in by accident. He could have killed the sentries to hide his mistake."

"Lynch wouldn't stoop that low, would he?" asked Brind.

Graf shrugged. "It's possible, but not likely. Lynch doesn't appear to be that smart. Besides, there's the breach in the fountain chamber to explain too."

"Could it have been a human?" asked Brind.

"Perhaps," said Graf. "So far, I don't know of any humans or elves that know how to activate our portals. Only one human mage I know of could be capable of that magic, and I was hoping he was afflicted along with his cohorts. I don't know for sure if he was affected, so we'll have to be extra cautious, just in case. He is a dragon mage, with very powerful magic."

Bring gasped. "If he's loose in our realm, he could upset all of our plans!"

"Precisely!" said Graf. "I suggest you find a way to deal with any intruders - even if it's not the mage that I speak of - with long range weaponry."

"Yes," said Brind thoughtfully. "A dart tipped with our new poison should do nicely."

Graf grinned. "A devious suggestion. I like it!"

Brind rose. "I'll get started right away!"

Graf rose too. "Don't be surprised if you discover an elf in our midst."

"What?" Brind looked confused.

"I know of a determined young elf who is capable of sneaking into secure locations. He is also able to make himself invisible."

"Someone like that could easily sneak through an open portal!" exclaimed Brind.

Graf nodded. "I suggest you use a 'detect magic' spell from time to time. It will indicate the presence of an invisible magical object or activated spell. It won't give you the exact location of an invisible person, but it will alert you to unauthorized magic in your vicinity."

Brind nodded. "Good idea. I'll keep my eyes and ears open."

After Brind left, Graf sat down. He opened a book of magic that lay on the table but couldn't concentrate on the magical spells listed within. The puzzle of who had breached their realm nagged at him.

Chapter 22

Malachi eyed the jug on the table doubtfully. "You say this stuff rejuvenated your mother?"

"Yes!" said Jim Farnsworth excitedly. "It made her strong enough to get out of bed! I wouldn't have believed it if I hadn't seen it!"

"Is she cured?" asked Malachi.

"Well, not exactly," admitted Jim. "The effect only lasts for several hours."

"Then what?" asked Malachi.

"Then she reverts to her original condition. When she starts to become weak, I offer her more of the ale and in an hour or so she's up and at it again."

Malachi looked over at General Larsen, who sat at the table with them. "What do you think about this?"

"At first I was skeptical too," said Larsen. "Lieutenant Farnsworth convinced me to let him give some to one of my ill soldiers. That particular soldier was bed-ridden for nearly a week, but this ale gave him the energy to get out of bed and perform some menial tasks. He was as drunk as a sailor, but the very fact that he was out of bed tells me to give that concoction some consideration."

"What is it made of, Lieutenant?" asked Malachi.

"According to my father, it contains fermented wildhorn leaves. A dwarven friend of his made it from an ancient recipe."

"Wildhorn leaves, eh?" said Malachi thoughtfully. "We have some of those leaves in our inventory and have tried them for healing this illness, without success. We never tried them when they were fermented, though."

"Fermented in dwarven spirits," reminded Jim.

"Yes," said Malachi, nodding thoughtfully.

"A partial cure is better than no cure at all," said Larsen.

208

"I agree," said Malachi, "but I have a problem with a bunch of intoxicated people running around."

"I would sooner be drunk than dead," said Larsen.

"We don't know if it prevents anyone from dying," argued Malachi.

"It doesn't help to reduce abdominal pain either," said Jim. "My mother said the pain was still present even though she could walk around. She did say that the more ale she drank, the less she noticed the pain, however."

"Undoubtedly," said Malachi sternly. After a moment, he said, "Is this all you have of this ale?"

"Yes," said Jim. "The dwarf who made it is making more for my father."

"See if you can get him to produce this ale on a larger scale," said Malachi. "It may be the beginning of a cure, but I'll need a lot more for study."

"He'll want compensation," warned Jim. "He is a dwarf, after all."

"Give him what he wants," said Malachi. "We have money, if that's what it takes. The money by itself is not much use for healing, but it may buy us the ingredients we need to cure thousands of afflicted people."

"Yes, Sir," said Jim.

He looked at General Larsen, who nodded. "Make haste, Lieutenant. Lives hang in the balance."

"Yes, Sir!" said Jim again, saluting.

After the lieutenant departed, General Larsen asked, "What are your plans, Malachi?"

Malachi sat back and sighed. "I'm hoping to find a cure from that dwarven ale. I never thought I'd see the day that dwarven ale would be used for healing, but I'm all out of ideas. All of our healing spells are cast using well-known herbs, and it's time we tried casting spells using something different. This ale may just be the thing that we need to cure the disease."

"I hope for all of our sakes you're right," said Larsen. He rose to his feet and pushed the jug of ale toward the High Cleric. "If I were you, I'd be tempted to sample some of that stuff. Just don't use it all up."

Malachi laughed heartily. "Don't think that idea hasn't crossed my mind, General."

Larsen chuckled and left the room.

Malachi picked up the jug and sniffed the contents. He coughed and held the jug away from his nose. "That stuff's powerful enough to raise the dead!" Chuckling to himself, the High Cleric left the room by a different entrance and arrived in a hallway. This hallway had doors to rooms that bordered the outer wall of the tower. On the other side of the hallway was a triangular chamber meant for only the high clerics. Malachi walked down the hallway and stopped at a door to one of the outer rooms. He withdrew a set of keys and produced the one for the door. The key worked smoothly and the High Cleric entered the room.

In the room was a triangular table with a chair at each of the three sides. On the table was a round holder containing a clear orb about twelve inches in diameter. This was the orb room where communication between the towers could be initialized.

Malachi sat down on one of the chairs and ran his fingers through his brown hair. He chanted a spell and a white mist began to swirl within the orb. Soon, a face appeared in the swirling mists. It was a dark-haired, middle-aged man. The face broke into a smile when it recognized the High Cleric.

"Malachi! It's good to see you!"

"Hello, Valdez," greeted Malachi.

"How's the situation down there? I hope you have good news."

Malachi sighed. "No change, I'm afraid. People are still getting sick and dying, and the number of afflicted is still rising. We're not getting much sleep these days."

Valdez shook his head. "That's terrible. Our own efforts here in Priscilla are fruitless. The clerics and druids here are not as skilled as the clerics in the Tower of Hope, but their determination is unmatched - especially now that we have patients of our own to contend with. Barbarians in the outlying areas have been coming into town suffering from the same symptoms as the people in your area. It's definitely a result of the water coming from the mountains. A general advisory not to drink the water is in effect."

"Do you have clean water to offer them?" asked Malachi in concern.

"For now our wells in the city are uncontaminated," said Valdez. "We have covers on them to prevent the poisoned rain from getting in. It's not easy to do, considering the heavy rains we've been getting. It has rained nonstop for three days now."

"We've had the odd storm pass through here," said Malachi. "It's most forbidding near the Old Dwarven Mountains. The dark clouds are generating such heavy rains and thunder that the guard outposts can hardly function. Something is causing this chaotic weather, but I don't know what. I sure wish Kazin was here to check it out."

"No doubt he's in the thick of things, as usual," said Valdez. "According to his unicorn, Kazin is in the mountains as we speak. Apparently he's on his way to find and rescue some elementals."

"Elementals!" exclaimed Malachi. "That certainly explains why we're having this unsettling weather!"

"It also explains the tremors we've been experiencing of late," added Valdez.

"Yes, we've experienced them too," said Malachi. "If elementals are involved, then the tremors are the result of the earth elemental's imprisonment."

"And the rain and poisoned water means the water elemental is being controlled," added Valdez. "Not to mention the heavy winds."

Malachi nodded. "The air elemental, of course. That can't be good. The only ones I can think of that might be able to summon elementals in the mountains are the lizardmen. If that's true, I'd hate to see what they're planning. They must know we're at our weakest right now."

"Undoubtedly," said Valdez. "I hope Queen Milena's upcoming trip to the Tower of the Moon produces some results. Apparently the druids need her assistance."

"I hope they find a cure," said Malachi. "The closest I've come to a cure is from a very unlikely source."

"Which is?" prodded Valdez.

Malachi held up the jug for Arch Mage Valdez to see. "Dwarven ale."

"What?!" Valdez was aghast. "You can't be serious!"

Malachi grinned. "Apparently, a couple of sick people have tried this ale, made from fermented wildhorn leaves, and have regained enough energy to walk around after being bed-ridden."

"Amazing!" exclaimed Valdez.

"Unfortunately, the effect of the ale wears off," said Malachi. "The patients then return to their sickened state unless they consume more of the ale. It's not a cure, but at least it's something to work with, even if it means being drunk all the time."

Valdez laughed. "That's incredible! How do you deal with all the drunken patients running around?"

"I haven't got enough ale to know the answer to that," said Malachi. "I hope I don't have to find out, either," he added wryly.

Valdez laughed again. "What made you think of trying dwarven ale?"

This time Malachi laughed. "It was something someone did by accident. They just brought it to my attention."

"I'd like to have a sample to study," said Valdez.

"I'm getting a larger quantity delivered to me very soon," said the High Cleric. "Unfortunately, I have no way of getting it to you. The mountains that separate us are still a nagging issue that needs to be dealt with."

"I could ask the unicorn to go there to retrieve some samples for me," suggested Valdez. "The other day he brought some samples of your herbs for our experimentation, along with a patient. He didn't know we already had patients of our own. The unicorn could be there in a couple of days' time, I'm sure."

Malachi nodded. "That would work. I'll have a sample ready for you."

"Good," said Valdez. He sighed. "I'd better go. The queen was waiting for me in the council chamber. As her advisor, I'm going to have plenty of work while she's gone."

"Wish her well for me," said Malachi. "I miss her ever since she left us to become a druid."

"Will do," said the Arch Mage. "She always tells me to put in a 'hello' for her anyway."

Malachi smiled. "Keep in touch, Valdez. I always look forward to our little chats. It gets my mind off of the stresses of the job."

"Likewise," said Valdez. "Goodbye."

Malachi sat back as the orb cleared. It was time to begin preliminary tests with the ale. But first - he looked around even though he knew no one was there. Then he took a sip of the ale - and almost choked.

✗ ✗ ✗ ✗ ✗

Martha sighed. She lifted the covers to conceal the body of yet another casualty. "It's terrible, absolutely terrible."

Adriana came up to her from behind. "Another one?"

Martha nodded sadly.

"I'll get the treemen to dispose of the body."

Martha turned to face her counterpart. Her usual jovial expression was replaced by a haggard, tired look. "How many more do we have to bury before this is over?"

Adriana reached out and touched Martha's arm consolingly. Ever since she almost lost Martha to the summoning magic, she was always nearby, making sure Martha wasn't overdoing it as she was apt to do when things got tough. "You should rest. I can take care of the sick for now."

"Are you sure?" asked Martha.

"Of course!" said Adriana. "I just took a break. Now it's your turn."

Martha reluctantly nodded. "Very well. I'll send for the treemen. Call me if something comes up."

"I will," lied Adriana.

"Remember. We need to try summoning the air elemental again in one hour."

"You shouldn't bother wasting your energy with that," cautioned Adriana. "We won't succeed in summoning the elemental anyway - not while it is under someone else's control."

"Our summoning attempts will make it more difficult for the lizardmen to fully control the elemental," explained Martha. "I know this because I can feel their magic falter when we do our summoning magic."

Adriana knew Martha was right, but wished she wouldn't push herself so hard. "Milena will be here soon. We'll let her take on that job when she gets here."

Martha's face brightened at the mention of Milena's name. "I can't wait to see her again!" Then her face darkened as she scanned the room full of beds laden with mermaids who were close to death. "It's unfortunate she has to come home under these circumstances. I wish she didn't have to see this."

"I have already seen it," said a voice behind them softly.

The druids spun around to see the speaker. Standing there was a fair-haired woman with a regal appearance dressed in the brilliant blue cloak common to those who wielded druid magic.

"Milena, my child!" cried Martha happily. She pounced at the newcomer and gave the fair-haired druid a bear hug. "I've missed you so!"

"Uggh!" gasped Milena. She detached the robust druid gently. "I'm happy to see you too." She looked at Adriana. "Both of you."

Adriana smiled, an expression that rarely crossed her face, especially of late. "Milena. I'm glad you could make it."

"The griffin flew swiftly," said Milena. "You chose a larger, more experienced one to fly me. I barely had time to explain my instructions to Arch Mage Valdez, my advisor."

"That's because time is in short supply," said Adriana. She gestured to the numerous beds behind her. "This plague is deadly."

"I know," said Milena. "Some of my people are suffering too. The spread of the poisoned water must be stopped."

"The lizardmen are behind it," said Martha. "The elementals have been captured, one by one. Recently the air elemental was yanked from us even though we had already summoned it."

"I know," said Milena again. "The unicorn told me. Did you try summoning him back?"

Martha nodded. "Yes, but the magic holding the elemental is too strong to overcome. The most we've been able to accomplish is to weaken the lizardmens' magic enough to momentarily give the elemental an opportunity to break free."

Milena nodded. "I'll help you next time. The magic from all three of us might be more productive. What about a cure?"

"We were hoping you might have some ideas that could help us," said Adriana. "With the water elemental beyond our reach, our healing magic is rather limited."

"You mean you can't summon the water elemental?" asked Milena. "You obviously made contact with the air elemental even though it is controlled by others."

Adriana shook her head. "Both the water and earth elementals were under the lizardmens' control for too long. Our magic isn't capable of finding them. The air elemental hasn't been controlled for long enough to be subdued by the lizardmen."

"Yet," put in Martha bluntly. "That's why we need to continue our efforts to summon it. As long as we keep interfering with the lizardmens' magic, the summoning will not be complete."

"What about the fire elemental?" asked Milena. "Can you summon it?"

Adriana shook her head again. "The fire elemental walks the world freely. We can only summon from the spirit dimension. The air elemental is the only one left with ties to the spirit dimension."

Milena's eyes widened. "This is more serious than I thought!"

Adriana nodded. "That's why we called for you. Maybe together we can stop this madness before it's too late."

"I'll do what I can," promised Milena. She undid her packsack, embossed with her royal emblem, and swung it around to a nearby table. Some treemen shuffled past to retrieve the dead mermaid. "Here is what I've got so far," said Milena. She filled them in on information concerning fermented wildhorn leaves, and dwarven ale.

"Fascinating!" exclaimed Martha when Milena was done. "Ale that can potentially cure disease! I'll have to find some information on these ingredients in our library."

"I'll check the spell books," offered Adriana.

"What do you want me to do?" asked Milena.

Adriana looked back at the patients while a treeman carried in a new mermaid patient.

"Never mind," said Milena. "I'm on it." She went over to examine the patient while the other druids hurried off to check their stores for information.

Chapter 23

I really don't like the looks of it," muttered Vera.

"It's perfectly safe," explained Rebecca. "It was made by dwarves a long time ago. That's why it's still here today."

"But it's so - ancient!" argued Vera. "Are you sure it will hold us after all these years?"

"Of course!" said Rebecca confidently. She walked a little way out onto it and turned to face the others. "See?"

Vera looked doubtful. The ancient swing bridge was made of planks interwoven with rope. There was a dangerous gap between the planks where someone could easily fall through if not careful. Either side of the bridge was lined with rope railings the full length of the bridge. These railings were frayed at intervals as a result of age and dryness common in these warmer depths of the mountains. As Rebecca walked back to the others, the bridge swayed and creaked. The cleric turned to the mage. "You can't fly us across?"

"No," said Kazin. He pointed out across the vast canyon to the cave on the other side. "There's no place to land. It would be easier to use the bridge."

"I cannot cross or the bridge will be consumed with fire," informed Tyris. He turned to the cleric. "However, if the good cleric will permit it, I could ride on the tip of your staff."

"You can do that?" asked Vera in surprise.

Tyris withdrew his form into a ball of flame and soared through the air to land on the cleric's staff. "Nothing to it!" said the staff cheerfully.

"Impressive!" exclaimed Vera.

"I will go first," offered Cyril. "If the bridge holds me, it will certainly hold any of you."

"It'll hold," insisted Rebecca.

Kazin nodded. "Very well. We've checked most of the tunnels on this side. The cave at the other end seems to be the next logical place to go."

Cyril wandered out onto the bridge. It groaned and creaked ominously but held firm.

"I told you it would hold," said the dwarf. She waited for Cyril to be several paces ahead of her and stepped onto the bridge after him.

Vera looked at Kazin, who nodded. "Go ahead. I'll be right behind you." The cleric gulped and followed the dwarf.

"I'm here too," comforted the staff.

Kazin waited until the cleric was a few paces ahead of him and then stepped out onto the bridge.

Alric took the rear, carefully grasping the now shaky railings.

The companions marched steadily, careful not to look down at the bottomless gorge below. Tyris shed enough light for all of them to see where they were going.

Vera was approximately in the middle of the incredibly long bridge when it happened.

A rumbling occurred deep below them and ran up the walls of the canyon like a shivering spine. The companions paused momentarily. The rumbling built in volume and intensity and the swing bridge began to vibrate and shake.

"Hurry!" cried Kazin.

Everyone started moving with haste.

A faint yelp, barely audible above the rumbling of the canyon, made Cyril turn around. Rebecca had lost her footing and had rolled under the railing to the edge of the bridge. She had barely managed to grab hold of the rope between two planks with one hand to save her fall. "Help!" she cried. The cyclops, seeing that Vera was too far back to help, made his way as fast as he could to assist the struggling dwarf.

Meanwhile, Vera had seen the dwarf fall. This distracted her from her concentration on the planks and she stepped into the gap between two of them. With a cry she went down, dropping her fiery staff in the process. To make matters worse, one rope tying the two planks together snapped apart. The gap opened wider and she fell through up to her armpits.

"Vera!" cried Kazin. He sprang forward to reach her but stepped awkwardly between two planks himself. The elf arrived quickly to help him get untangled.

Tyris, meanwhile, knew Vera was in trouble and nobody could reach her. He was still sitting atop the staff as it lay across the bridge's planks behind the cleric.

Vera was losing her hold on the planks and slowly slipped downward. She was struggling so hard to hold herself up that she couldn't even cry out for help. Tyris knew he could pull her to safety, but not without burning her. The bridge also stood a good chance of catching fire if he returned to his human form. Seeing the cleric slip even further down, the elemental made up his mind. He changed form and reached down just as the cleric lost her grip.

Rebecca strained to pull herself up. Her right hand burned from the strain of holding all of her weight. The harsh, frayed rope didn't help matters any. Suddenly, a giant, greenish yellow hand reached down and firmly grabbed the dwarf's arm. With relative ease, the cyclops lifted the dwarf back up to the bridge so she was standing safely between the rope railings.

Rebecca looked gratefully at the cyclops, who avoided her gaze. "I take back what I said earlier. You are good to have around."

The cyclops wasn't paying attention. His eye widened and he cried, "Vera!"

By now, Alric had helped free Kazin and they looked ahead of them on the bridge.

The elemental had just managed to pull the cleric to safety. Her amulet glowed fiercely, protecting her from fire damage. But Tyris had set the bridge on fire. Moreover, the elemental seemed to have gone berserk. He increased in size and intensity until he was at least three times the size of the cleric. His form coalesced and he began to float up above the bridge.

"Aieee!" he screamed. "I'm being summoned!"

"Look up there!" shouted Alric. He pointed high above them to a cave overlooking them from the side of the canyon they were leaving. They couldn't have known it was there from their original vantage point at the start of the bridge. In this cave opening, they could see a number of lizardmen chanting a spell. The fire elemental's form rose slowly toward them.

The mage began casting fireballs in the direction of the lizardmen but they were too far distant. The fireballs fell hopelessly short. A sudden jolt on the bridge brought their attention back to their own predicament. The fire on the bridge was now out of control. One railing had snapped, and the spot where Tyris had been was burning like kindling. The bridge was about to split apart entirely.

"Get off the bridge!" yelled Kazin. "The bridge is going to collapse!"

The cyclops, dwarf, and cleric were already running for the far side of the bridge for safety.

Kazin turned to the elf. "We'll have to go back."

Alric nodded and sprinted for the near side of the canyon.

"Aieee!" screamed Tyris again.

Kazin stopped and looked up. He had to try to free the elemental. It was of paramount importance that the lizardmen did not control the fourth and final elemental. If they did, it could mean the end of everything. But he had to wait until everyone else had made it to safety before doing anything.

Just as the last of the companions cleared the bridge, a loud groaning and snapping noise occurred. Kazin transformed just as the burning bridge split apart and crashed into the lower canyon walls. The mage sprouted his leathery wings and flapped hard to gain altitude. The lizardmen above were no longer visible in the cave entrance but he flew up there anyway. As he reached the opening, he blasted it with a fierce flood of his fiery breath. He was secure in the knowledge that the elemental would not get hurt in the blast, being naturally immune to fire damage, but he hoped he could destroy any unwary lizardmen nearby. Unfortunately, he was too late. The lizardmen had already gone with their prize.

The ledge was wide enough to land on, so Kazin landed and returned to his human form. He turned around and looked down to where the others were gathered on the other side of the canyon. The mountain was still rumbling, so trying to call down to them was pointless. He made hand motions indicating that he was going after Tyris and hoped they understood.

He couldn't signal his intentions to Alric, who was on the same side of the canyon as himself, so he turned and hurried after the lizardmen. He didn't have time to find a way to reunite the companions right now. They were on their own. Tyris was the one who needed help.

The cyclops, cleric and dwarf saw Kazin's hand signals and realized what he was going to do.

"He can't leave us behind!" wailed Vera. "How are we going to find our way in this place?"

"Relax," said Rebecca calmly. "I know how to find my way in the mountains. We won't get lost."

"But what if we need to get through a portal?" asked Vera, "assuming we can even find one?"

"We'll just have to do without portals," said Rebecca coolly. "It looks like we're in lizardman territory now, anyway."

"What about Alric?" asked Cyril.

The trio looked across the canyon at the tunnel they had earlier vacated. One half of the bridge hung uselessly down the side of the canyon, the bottom section still on fire. The tunnel entrance was empty.

"He'll be okay," said Rebecca. "He can turn invisible, so he'll be better off than we are."

"That's true," said Cyril, rubbing his healed shoulder gingerly. He remembered the disembodied sword that had pierced him previously.

Vera saw Rebecca's sore hand. "Your hand is injured! Let me heal it."

"It's all right," said Rebecca modestly, but she held it out for the cleric anyway.

Vera pulled some spell components from her pouch and chanted a spell. The wound healed over almost instantly.

"Wow!" exclaimed Rebecca. "That was fast!"

"I'm a level one cleric," said Vera proudly. "Healing wounds like these is a prerequisite to becoming a full-fledged cleric."

"Thanks," said Rebecca. "I'm glad you're stuck on my side of the canyon." She glanced at the cyclops, who looked at the floor. "Both of you."

After a moment of awkward silence, Rebecca added, "Come on. Kazin wouldn't want us to stand here moping around. He'd want us to do everything we can to stop the lizardmen from succeeding. Once he gets Tyris back, he'll come looking for us. I'll leave the odd mark for him to follow so he'll know it was us."

"You're pretty confident he'll get the elemental back," commented Vera.

"I'll tell you some of the stories my uncle - I mean king - told me about Kazin," said Rebecca. "There's a lot more to him than meets the eye."

"I'll vouch for that," said the cyclops. "He met my eye without getting paralyzed."

The women laughed.

✗ ✗ ✗ ✗ ✗

Alric returned to a passageway they had ignored because it appeared to be unused and difficult to navigate. The upward slope, however, meant that it could lead up to the cave where the lizardmen had performed their summoning spell. His keen elven eyesight helped him to traverse the passageway successfully, and it opened up wider the further he went. He stopped to pick up some loose pebbles that were undoubtedly the result of the mountain's quakes. He needed them for his magic arrow spells. Had he had some in his possession previously, he could have sent his magical arrows up to where the lizardmen had been. He was sure his arrows could have outdistanced Kazin's fireballs. At least now, if he encountered more than one lizardman at a time, he would have long range capability.

Up, up he went, his agile form sprinting along rapidly. The tunnel almost spiraled up to where he knew the lizardmen had been. The elf's heart pounded in excitement. He was happy to finally be getting close to the heart of the lizardmens' realm. Though he preferred to work alone, he hoped to find Kazin. The mage was the only one who could open the lizardmens' portals, and get him closer to the lizardmage he sought.

Before he knew it, Alric reached the cave where the lizardmen had been. The walls and floor were black and steaming, the result of fire damage. It could have been either Tyris or Kazin. There was no sign of the lizardmen or Kazin. The elf swore. Not including the cavern directly ahead, there were only two ways into the cave. He had arrived by one. That meant Kazin had probably gone the other way in pursuit of the lizardmen. Or, Kazin had found a portal the lizardmen had used to escape and gone after them the same way.

Alric swore again. If the latter were true, he had no way of finding either the lizardmen or the mage. He had to assume his former reasoning was correct. The elf sprinted into the opposite tunnel and would have disappeared if he wasn't already invisible.

✗ ✗ ✗ ✗ ✗

Kazin looked around at the empty cave. Should he go left or right? He tried a magical spell check and the right tunnel glowed. "That was easy," he muttered. He followed the trail of magic as fast as he could. The lizardmen were not far ahead. The mage reached a wide intersection branching into three other directions. He was about to cast another spell check spell when a gust of wind blasted down the left path. Kazin grinned. The air elemental was resisting the lizardmens' magic again. Hurrying down the left tunnel, the mage could hear sounds ahead. Soon light could be seen reflecting off the walls. He was close!

Rounding a final bend, Kazin reached a well-lit cavern. Several hissing lizardmen holding torches surrounded a giant translucent box with a clear liquid sloshing around in its walls. The light emitting from it was a brilliant orange in hue. The lizardmen were in the process of stepping through a portal in a nearby wall. Before Kazin could think of how to proceed, the last lizardman disappeared through the portal and the portal vanished. The cavern reverted to darkness once again.

Kazin lit his staff and moved forward cautiously. There were two more tunnels with access to this portal junction. He wondered vaguely what lay at the end of their depths, but knew he had no time for exploring. He had to free Tyris at all costs. He began to concentrate on the portal. It began to shimmer.

The mage suddenly heard a noise behind him but had no time to react. A 'whoosh' noise was followed by a sharp pain in his neck. Sudden dizziness overwhelmed him before everything went black.

A hooded figure in a red robe approached the prone mage and hissed menacingly. "So! A human mage! We can't allow humans in our realm! Those who meddle in our affairs must suffer the consequences!" He withdrew a dagger from his cloak and took another step toward the mage.

A noise behind him made him turn abruptly. Someone was coming! He turned back to the unconscious mage and lifted his weapon to deliver a killing blow. Before he could make his move, a one word chant instigated a magical arrow. The arrow streaked across the cavern and struck the lizardman's dagger on its downswing. The dagger was thrown from the lizardmage's hand, and the lizardman jumped over Kazin while hissing a spell of his own. He cast a fireball spell in the direction the arrow had come from, but another arrow was already flying at him from a different direction.

The lizardman was struck in the left arm and he responded by hissing in pain and raising a magical shield to protect himself from any further arrows. Then he opened the portal and dived through, with more arrows in pursuit. Some of the arrows bounced harmlessly off his shield. The rest bounced off the bare wall as the portal closed.

Alric quickly checked the area for any further intruders. When the area was secure, he hurried over to the mage and dragged him from the cavern to a spot a short distance away down a tunnel. He was thankful he had spotted a lizardman skulking around at the four-way intersection. By following the lizardman, the elf had deduced correctly the path that Kazin had taken. Kazin would have been killed had he not come along to save him.

Alric laughed inwardly at this. He stole from this man, and had saved his life too. If he didn't need the mage so much, he could have let him die. Alric shook his head quickly. No, that was not his way. He was a thief, not a murderer. He looked down at the unconscious figure. The peaceful expression on Kazin's face did not indicate an evil person. Kazin appeared to be a good man. All the stories he had heard about this mage backed this up. Just over a decade ago, Kazin had saved not only the human race, but all of the races, including the elves. Many elves would mourn his death should something happen to him. Alric owed this man his allegiance. Indeed, they were allied in their present quest. Their goals were the same. Alric suddenly felt honoured to be working with Kazin. If they lived through this quest and succeeded in saving the world, Alric's own name would be adored by his elven brothers and sisters. The elf considered his personal goal in this quest. Fame was one thing, but revenge was another. His part in unknowingly helping the lizardmen was a part he wished to correct. His reputation had been tarnished. The lizardmage who had taken advantage of him had used him to help cause the disaster that awaited them right now. It was up to him - and the others in his group - to stop this threat before it was too late. True, up to now the humans had suffered the worst of the damage. But the lizardmen wouldn't stop there. Once the humans were defeated, the elves and dwarves were sure to follow.

A low moan brought Alric back to the present. It was time to move on.

Chapter 24

raf closed the portal behind him and walked quietly down the corridor, stopping in front of a wall that barred his way. Silently, he pulled his hood over his head and concealed his gloved hands within his robe. Then he spoke a word of magic and stepped through the wall as though it wasn't even there. He entered a large room with a grey stone table in its center. A number of hooded figures were present and they turned to suspiciously watch the newcomer.

Graf spoke his secret password and the figures in the room relaxed. The lizardman approached the others and they waited for him to identify himself.

"Inferno," said Graf in a low voice.

"Welcome," responded a cloaked figure nearest him. "Ice Blade," he continued, indicating himself. The others followed suit with names like Sawtooth, Cleaver, Ropeburn, Sparky, and Multibolt.

When the introductions were concluded, Graf spoke. "How are things progressing?"

Ice Blade held up a hand. "Let's wait until Longspike gets here."

"I'm here," said a voice behind them.

Everyone turned to face the newcomer. Other than the fact that he was very tall, he looked like an ordinary cloaked figure like the rest of them.

They started to identify themselves but Longspike held up his hand. "I know who you are. Is everyone here?"

"Affirmative," said Ice Blade.

"Then we should proceed," said Longspike. He thrust his pack on the table and opened it, withdrawing a stack of marked papers. "Have we got enough information concerning the humans' magic?"

"I think so," said Ice Blade. "Many of the spell components are common in our realm but rarer in the humans' world. We can reduce or block movement of those goods to restrict the use of many of their spells."

"Good!" said Longspike.

"I've studied the spell inflections and hand motions of their magic," put in Sparky. "Most of the spells can be identified soon enough to give us time to erect counter measures. Arch mages are still a threat since they can cast even complicated spells with lightning-quick speed, as well as cast numerous spells at once."

Longspike sighed. "I wish we were able to do that. That's why I dislike human spell casters so much. We'll have to deal with their arch mages one at a time. Working together, we have the power to defeat them."

Graf (Inferno) chuckled. "No problem!" he muttered under his breath. When everyone turned to look in his direction, Inferno realized he needed to change the subject quickly. He pulled a scroll from his cloak and placed it on the table. His hand swiftly returned to his pocket. "Here is a scroll that should interest you."

Longspike took hold of it and unscrolled it. After a moment, he gasped. "A 'pass through rock' spell!" He turned to Inferno. "Where did you get this?"

Inferno shrugged innocently. "It was lying around in a pile of spells in my study. I figured it might come in useful."

"Let me see!" exclaimed Sparky. She held out her hand.

Longspike passed it to Sparky for inspection.

Sparky studied it for a moment before exclaiming, "It's an ancient elven spell! I've only ever heard of this spell being used in the time of the dragons! The spell was thought to have been forgotten shortly afterward when the dragon wars ended! A spell like this could prove useful indeed! This is a rare find!"

"How long have you had this, Inferno?" asked Longspike.

Inferno shrugged again. "It's only one of hundreds of scrolls I inherited a while back. Most of them are self-explanatory, but this one in particular looked intriguing. I figured it was interesting magic, so I put it aside to study later. It must have fallen behind some books on my shelf, because I forgot about it until just now when I was reorganizing my library."

"I'll have to study it and see if we can cast this spell ourselves," said Sparky.

"Help yourself," offered Inferno.

"That's settled then," said Longspike. "Is there anything else to report?"

"Support for our magic continues to increase," said Ropeburn in a feminine voice. "Especially once word spreads of the poisoned water caused by the human black mages and their foolish experiments. We tell people that black magic is the only way to defend ourselves against them. Recruitment is steady, with the majority being younger and eager to learn."

"Many of those apprentices are defying the laws and openly casting their magic," added Multibolt. "Several have even been arrested."

"As long as they aren't traced back to the guild," said Longspike sternly.

"They're only being detained overnight with stern warnings, or fines if damages were incurred," stated Sawtooth. "So far there is no indication that the authorities are interrogating them."

"That will change soon," said Cleaver. "I have it on good authority that a priority will be placed on infiltrating the guild." Sawtooth gave Cleaver a sharp glance but said nothing.

"Then we have to increase the screening and limit new members with a questionable background," said Longspike.

"Consider it done," said Ropeburn. "We will keep apprentices away from confirmed mages until they have proven themselves."

"Very good," said Longspike. "Is there anything else to report?"

"More wells have become contaminated," said Ice Blade. "Several communities in the northern part of the realm have been affected."

"Is there any progress being made in counteracting the poison?" asked Longspike.

Ice Blade shook his head. "No. Some of our mages are experimenting with black magic to see if anything may have been missed by our ordinary magic, but so far we have come up empty."

"I still think the key lies with the humans' magic," put in Inferno. "The fact that the disease started within the Tower of Sorcery proves beyond a shadow of a doubt that the human black mages unleashed this plague upon the world. They are the ones who should be held accountable for this gruesome act."

There were murmurs of agreement among the others.

"Furthermore," continued Inferno, "if we plan to do something about it, now is the time to act. The black mages are presently in a seriously weakened state."

"I've taken that into consideration," said Longspike. He spread his papers out on the table. "Here is the plan. . ."

× × × × ×

"I can't believe I didn't see it coming," lamented Rebecca. "I should have been more alert."

"Don't blame yourself," said Vera consolingly. "We were all caught off guard." She looked over at the cyclops, whose head was covered with a sack. His hands were bound behind his back via shackles attached to the wall. His head hung down, an indication that he was unconscious.

"I don't even know where we are," complained Rebecca.

"At least we're together," said Vera. She knew she didn't sound very reassuring so she stopped talking. Instead, she recounted in her mind their swift capture.

Crossing under an overhang, they hadn't been aware of their captors until they had been jumped from above by a number of lizardmen guards. A sack had been thrown over Cyril's head just before he was knocked unconscious. Rebecca had gotten swarmed before she could draw a weapon. She had also been hampered by a slow spell. Meanwhile, Vera had been too surprised to cast a spell to help her friends. Her staff had been yanked from her hands and several spears had been aimed at her throat. From there, the ladies had their packs taken away and were led away from the area with bags over their heads, while some of their captors had the delightful task of carrying the unconscious cyclops on a stretcher.

They had walked for what seemed like hours, and Vera's head swam with all the twists and turns they had made en route. But even had she kept track of where they were going, the magical portals they had passed through would be difficult, if not impossible to find without Kazin's help.

They had finally been shoved into a cell, and Cyril had been tied up in an adjacent cell. The heavy iron doors had been slammed shut, and Vera and Rebecca were then free to remove the sacks. It had made little difference.

The cells were almost as dark as the sacks were. The only light came from a distant torch in the hallway outside the cells. It shone eerily through the grate in the cell door. Heavy iron bars separated the dwarf and cleric from Cyril's cell. They were unable to aid him from where they were.

Vera discovered enough spell components in her pocket to be able to cast a spell for Cyril. Her staff would have made the spell stronger and more accurate, but it was not at her disposal this time, so she chanted the spell and waved her hand in Cyril's general direction.

"Hopefully that takes care of his headache when he wakes up," explained the cleric when the dwarf gave her a questioning glance.

Rebecca nodded.

"Do you need any healing?" asked Vera.

The dwarf shook her head. "I didn't even have a chance to fight."

"I'm sorry I couldn't undo the spell they cast on you in time," said Vera sadly. "I wasn't prepared."

"None of us were," said Rebecca flatly. "We walked right into that one. I should have been wearing my talisman. It tells me when magic is nearby."

"Wouldn't my staff interfere with it?" asked Vera.

Rebecca nodded. "Probably, but it would vibrate even more with more magic present. At least I could tell if we were getting close to another magic source."

"I see," said Vera. She felt for her pendant and discovered it was still around her neck. Somehow the lizardmen had failed to discover it. She sighed. Unfortunately, it wasn't particularly useful right now.

A moan from the other cell alerted them that the cyclops was regaining consciousness.

"Cyril? Are you O.K.?" asked Vera anxiously.

"Vera?"

"I'm here," said Vera. "I'm in an adjoining cell."

Cyril yanked at his chains and winced. "I can't move!"

"Don't struggle," said Vera. "Rebecca and I are O.K. We're working on a way out of here." She looked at the dwarf.

"Maybe we can jump them when they come to check on us," said the dwarf. "They didn't tie us up."

"Maybe there's a way out of these cells," commented Vera. She got up and pushed on the cell door, making it rattle noisily.

"That's dwarven workmanship," said Rebecca. "It won't be easy to break out."

"How would lizardmen have access to dwarven iron?" asked Vera. "Could they have stolen it?"

"It looks pretty old," said Rebecca. "I'd guess these cells predate the lizardmen. These cells probably belonged to the dwarves when they still resided in these mountains before the dragon wars."

"So the lizardmen moved in when the dwarves moved out?" asked the cleric.

"Not right away," said Rebecca. "A few decades probably passed before the lizardmen called this home. I'm sure it was occupied by goblins and orcs in the meantime."

Vera shuddered. "I don't know how you dwarves manage to live in the mountains with all these evil creatures running around."

"In the outside world you have bears and boars and the like," countered Rebecca. "And thieves and bandits are commonplace. What's the difference?"

"I suppose," said Vera.

"In many ways, the mountain is peaceful," added Cyril in a muffled voice.

"I prefer the sun on my face and the breeze flitting through the green grass," said Vera defiantly. "This darkness is too forbidding. Even this gold engraving the dwarves put in this cell door doesn't shine as brilliantly as it would in the outside world."

Rebecca was about to respond when her eyes, now accustomed to the faint light, spotted something familiar within the engraving that Vera had pointed out. She got up and went nearer to examine it more closely. It was an ancient dwarven emblem. She had seen this emblem before. Where? Then it occurred to her. It was the same as the one on the key that she had used to open her cell in the orc's realm! The dwarf frantically felt in her pockets and a shiver went down her spine. It was still there! She had kept it!

"What is it?" asked Vera, watching the dwarf's movements curiously.

Rebecca withdrew the key and held it aloft. "This key matches the emblem on the door!" whispered the dwarf excitedly. She carefully slid her arm through the cell doors' grate and reached for where the keyhole should be. Then she groaned in dismay and pulled her arm back. "I can't reach that far."

"Let me try," offered Vera. "My arms are longer."

Rebecca handed her the key. "Don't drop it," she cautioned.

Vera nodded and slid her arm slowly through the grate. Consternation marked her features as she tried to plug the key into the key hole. "I - I think it's in the hole," said the cleric finally.

"Turn it and see!" whispered Rebecca excitedly.

"Just a minute," said Vera. "I need to get the circulation back into my arm." She pulled her arm back and shook it to restore blood flow. "O.K. now," she said, returning her arm through the grate. She felt for the key. "Oh, no!" moaned the cleric.

"What is it?" whispered Rebecca, her eyes wide.

"I can't find - Oh! Here it is!" There was a loud click and the cell door opened.

"You did it!" cried Rebecca, embracing the cleric even while she was still trying to disentangle her arm from the grate.

Then the dwarf slapped the cleric's arm. "Next time don't scare me like that!"

"Sorry," said Vera sheepishly.

The escapees quickly opened Cyril's cell. They removed the sack from his head, but discovered that Rebecca's key would not unlock the chains binding the cyclops' arms.

"What do we do now?" asked Vera.

"We'll have to go and find the shackle keys," stated the dwarf.

"Don't worry about me," said Cyril. "Save yourselves."

"We're not leaving you," said Vera flatly.

"We'll come back for you as soon as we can," added Rebecca. "We have to find the keys first." She looked at Vera, who nodded.

"Sit tight, Cyril," ordered the cleric.

"Do I have a choice?" said Cyril.

Vera giggled.

The dwarf led the cleric from the cell area and together they slunk along the torch-lit hallways. Before long they found the guardroom where three guards sat at a table. Peeking around the corner, beyond the guards on the floor, lay the companions' packs and weapons.

"Did you hear the air elemental has been contained?" asked one guard.

"Yes," said the second guard. "I heard they used the earth elemental to create a wall of solid rock to imprison it."

"Ingenious!" declared the third guard, a female with bluish lips and an ugly wide grin. "That way the magic needed to control it is minimal."

"My cousin is part of that group," said the first guard. "She told me there is a mysterious force pulling at the air elemental. They can't seem to get it to do what they want because it keeps phasing in and out of our realm. She thinks someone else may be trying to summon it."

"Who could possibly be capable of such magic?" asked the second guard.

"I think the black mages may be trying to summon it," said the female guard. "The humans claim they aren't capable of such magic, but I wouldn't put it past them. Remember the human necromancer a few years back? Humans weren't supposed to have an understanding of necromancy either."

"You're probably right," admitted the first guard.

"I wonder how Brind is doing with the fire elemental?" asked the second guard, changing the subject.

"If anyone can catch it, it's Brind," said the female guard dreamily.

"You're just in love with him, aren't you?" nagged the first guard.

The female guard spun on him. "He's the best fire mage there is! I wish I was his apprentice!" Then she calmed down a bit. "Besides, that klutz Lynch couldn't cast a spell if his life depended on it."

The guards laughed.

The dwarf and cleric withdrew from the scene to converse.

"What now?" whispered Vera. "How do we get our packs without the guards noticing?"

"We need to create a diversion," whispered Rebecca. "You have to get them to chase you while I sneak in and grab my weapons."

"Why me?" asked the cleric. "Why don't you get them to chase you? Once I have my staff and components, I can stop them with magic."

Rebecca considered. "Maybe you're right. Maybe you will have a better chance of stopping them than I will. It's difficult to get close enough to lizardmen to fight them in close combat."

Vera nodded.

The plan started out as expected. Upon seeing the dwarf, the lizardmen sprang to their feet and ran after the escaped prisoner. On cue, Vera virtually flew into the guard room and grabbed her spell components and staff. Then she was off to aid her companion. She followed the noise of the pursuit and quickly caught up, thanks to the slow, awkward gait of the lizardmen. When all three guards were in sight ahead of her, she cast her spell. It had the desired effect. All three guards stopped in their tracks.

Vera was jubilant at her success, but it was short-lived. One of the lizardmen suddenly turned around and cast a spell in her direction!

There was no time to react as a fireball struck Vera full in the chest. Miraculously, it fizzled out as though it wasn't even there, thanks to the pendant that had saved her life a number of times now.

Vera prepared a chant to retaliate, when there was a savage cry followed by a grunt. The dwarf had jumped the lizardman from behind.

The cleric approached the struggling combatants and pointed her staff at the lizardman's head. When Rebecca saw what Vera was up to, she tried to hold the lizardman still.

The cleric chanted and the lizardman stopped struggling.

Rebecca rose to her feet and they looked down at the victim. It was then that they noticed it was the lizardwoman. Her face was contorted in a scowl, and her lips were an even darker shade of blue.

"She looks frozen," panted Rebecca as she endeavored to catch her breath.

Vera nodded. "I cast a freeze spell on her. It didn't succeed the first time, so I tried again just to see if casting a spell twice would work. I figured that if it didn't work I had time to try something else."

Rebecca examined the remaining two guards who were frozen in place. Then, satisfied the danger was over, she checked their pockets for keys. The only ones she found were the same as her own.

Vera stood up after examining the lizardwoman for keys. "Any luck?"

"No. You?"

"No."

Rebecca cursed under her breath. "Well, I'd better get my pack and weapons. I feel naked without them."

Vera accompanied the dwarf to the guard room and they picked up their belongings, including Cyril's large pack.

"I might be able to free Cyril," said Rebecca suddenly.

"How?" asked Vera.

The dwarf pulled out her dagger. "With this magical dagger."

"Let's try it!" said Vera.

"There's only one problem," said Rebecca. "This dagger could kill him if it gets too close."

Vera turned pale. "What do you mean, too close?"

"It's a long story," said Rebecca. Then the dwarf looked at the cleric. "Can you shield him from magic?"

"Yes," said Vera. "But I learned at the Tower of Hope that some magical artifacts are more powerful than defensive magic."

"That's what I'm afraid of," said Rebecca. "Maybe I can cut the chains from the wall. The wall isn't part of him."

"I'm willing to try that," said Vera.

"Let's go."

On the way, Rebecca dispatched the guards in the hallway using her dagger.

When Vera saw the magic of the dagger, she had second thoughts about using the dagger to free Cyril.

As the companions neared the cell, they stopped in horror.

"Did you leave Cyril's door open?" whispered Rebecca.

"No!" hissed Vera.

They looked at each other in alarm. Tiptoeing slowly, the dwarf and cleric approached Cyril's cell. Looking through the doorway, they could see a lizardman standing with his back to them. There was no sound or movement. Rebecca and Vera gave each other a curious glance. It was too quiet.

After an agonizingly long pause, Vera suddenly giggled. "It's safe." She walked into the cell and stepped around the prone figure. "Good work, Cyril."

Cyril looked at Vera for a split second and then looked down. He noticed that she had met his gaze again without getting paralyzed. He wondered if the effect of his ability was wearing off.

Rebecca looked at the paralyzed guard uncertainly. He held a water jug in his hands. Hanging at his waist was a set of keys.

"Hey!" cried the dwarf. She grabbed the keys and examined them. "Those look like they just might work!" She went over to the cyclops and with the third key the shackles came undone.

Cyril stretched his arms and stood up to his full height. "That feels better!"

At that moment, the mountain rumbled and shook vehemently.

"Let's get out of here!" cried Vera.

They locked the paralyzed lizardman in the cell. Vera spell-checked the water in the jug and discovered it was good, so they poured it into their flasks and hastily made their departure, happy to be free once again.

Chapter 25

ou have no right to do this!" hollered Lynch. His face was livid and his words were spat out with such gusto that Brind had to wipe the irate lizardman's saliva from his face.

"Graf told me to take over this task and I'll do it," said Brind calmly. He wiped his scaly wet hand on his dark red cloak.

"But I was the one who caught it!" protested Lynch. "I'll not have you receive credit for capturing the fire elemental!"

"I'll be sure to mention it to the council," sneered Brind.

"I don't believe you," snarled Lynch.

"Believe what you like," growled Brind. He turned to the contingent of lizardmen who were chanting around a large box that undulated with a bright orange glow. The fire elemental was trapped inside. "Follow me," ordered the red-robed mage.

Lyrr leered at Lynch as he passed the angry lizardman and followed Brind and the others down the passageway. Lynch ran behind, still protesting.

Moments later, the passageway became dark.

No sooner did the darkness prevail when a greenish light began to materialize at the passageway's other end. Soon Kazin and Alric came into view.

"They're not far ahead!" whispered Alric.

Kazin held up a hand. "Let me rest for a minute," he panted. He leaned against the wall and tried to catch his breath.

"You must be poisoned," said Alric anxiously. "We need to get you back to the others. Maybe Vera -."

Kazin shook his head. "She may not be able to help. I think it's the same poison we're trying to stop. The only way to help me is to stop the lizardmen. Our best chance lies with the fire elemental. We have to free Tyris not only to help us, but to prevent all four of the elementals from causing the destruction of the world."

As if in response to Kazin's words, the mountain rumbled ominously. A gust of wind surged past the human and elf down the passageway.

Kazin's eyes widened. "Let's hurry! The druids are still fighting for control of the air elemental! That means that all of the elementals are not entirely under the control of the lizardmen yet! If the druids stop or take a break before we free Tyris, it could all be over!" With a surge of renewed strength, Kazin sprang down the tunnel after the lizardmen. Alric followed, not entirely sure what Kazin meant about druids and the like, but understanding the urgency of the situation.

As luck would have it, Lynch had stopped Brind and the others to argue with the stubborn lizardmage.

"I won't let you get away with this!" bellowed Lynch. He began to chant.

His chant was only partially completed when Brind leveled him with a thrust spell, sending the hapless lizardman tumbling unceremoniously down the passageway. "Get away from me!" he snarled.

Lynch amazingly recovered enough to complete his spell. He aimed his staff at Brind and a lightning bolt surged toward the lizardmage.

Brind was not prepared for this comeback, and dove to the side just in time to avoid being singed. Unfortunately, the lizardmen who held the box with the elemental were directly behind him. The lightning bolt struck the two lizardmen in front and they let go of their end of the box as they fell, shrieking in agony. The box fell to the ground, but miraculously remained intact. The other lizardmen chanted frantically as they surrounded the box, trying to contain the elemental inside.

Lyrr stepped around the commotion to help Brind to his feet.

Brind glowered at Lynch. "You fool! You nearly allowed the fire elemental to escape!"

Suddenly, a sharp cry sounded from the circle of chanting lizardmen and women. Rapidly, one lizardman after another fell to the ground as a hail of magic arrows and fireballs struck the occupied party. The magic holding the elemental wavered and the box began to shake and rumble.

"The elemental is escaping!" shrieked a lizard woman. She sprang away toward where Lyrr and Brind stood.

Seeing the imminent explosion, Lyrr chanted a haste spell on those closest to him. "Let's get away from here!" he cried. Without waiting for the others, he fled down the tunnel as fast as he could. The expected explosion threw him off his feet. A strong gust of fire and heat surged over his head. A shower of rocks and boulders fell all around him. Moments later, all was still. Coughing in the dusty air, Lyrr rose shakily to his feet. He looked around. A moan nearby told him that someone else had survived the blast. Tracking the sound, he discovered the individual's arm and pulled him to his feet. It was Lynch.

"Lynch?" said Lyrr in astonishment. He was surprised his spell had reached Lynch, who had been way down the passageway when his spell had been cast.

Lynch coughed. "I'm all right," he mumbled.

Lyrr knew better than to expect a 'thank you' from Lynch. He looked around as the dust settled, and his eyes became accustomed to the darkness. He spotted the female lizardwoman under some debris and went to see if she was still alive. She was. Some investigation proved that her leg was broken. "Come give me a hand," said Lyrr. "She needs healing. We'll have to carry her between us."

Lynch grumbled under his breath but assisted anyway. "At least we're rid of Brind," he muttered.

"You wish!" snarled a voice behind him.

Lynch spun around to face the speaker. "Brind!"

Brind appeared from out of the gloom, a luminescent shield surrounding his body. His red robe was amplified by the shield, lighting the caved-in passageway with a flickering red light. It appeared as if the walls were flowing in blood.

"You really messed up this time," spat Brind as he approached the others, stumbling over rocks and boulders.

"I thought it was your job!" put in Lynch slyly. "I caught the elemental, but it was in your custody when it escaped!"

"You're the one who helped it escape, you idiot!" retorted Brind.

"Enough!" growled Lyrr. "Let's take care of our injuries and regroup. If we work together, we can catch the elemental again. Then Graf doesn't need to know of anybody's failures."

Brind and Lynch glared at each other.

× × × × ×

Alric called a halt to the party and lifted Kazin's arm from around his neck. He gently lowered the mage to the ground with his back leaning up against the wall. "We should be safe for the moment."

The fire elemental watched anxiously. "Is there nothing you can do?"

Alric shook his head. "No. This poison is undoubtedly the same as the one affecting the mages in the Tower of Sorcery. There is no cure unless the lizardmen have an antidote that we don't know about."

"So what are we going to do?" asked Tyris.

Alric suddenly realized that he was being looked to for leadership. Kazin was too weak and barely conscious. The elf clenched his jaw. That was why he preferred to work alone. No one got in his way that way. He looked at the helpless mage. If Kazin wasn't so important in his quest to find the lizardmage responsible for this entire mess, he would consider leaving the mage behind. The mage's ability to locate and open the hidden portals used by the lizardmen was without a doubt his greatest asset. Even if there were someone else to take care of the mage, Alric could only explore the tunnels and caves he could see. He could end up walking right past the enemy's lair without even knowing it. The elf looked at the elemental. Tyris was unable to take care of the mage. A simple touch would set the mage's cloak ablaze. That left Alric. He was now the leader and caretaker all rolled into one. He sighed. "We have no choice but to go on, Tyris. That may be the only way to help Kazin and stop the lizardmen."

"Which way do we go?" asked Tyris. He pointed to the junction ahead.

Alric hesitated. He had absolutely no idea. A sudden gust of wind whipped past the trio and down the right passageway. Tyris' flames momentarily flared up.

Remembering what Kazin had told them about the wind, Alric said, "we go right." He turned to help the mage to his feet but was surprised to see Kazin already standing.

The mage winked at the elf. "That rest was nice. I should be able to move under my own steam for a while. Lead the way, Alric. I'll let you know if we encounter a portal."

Even Tyris was surprised. "Just when I think you can't go on, you get another burst of energy, Kazin."

Kazin smiled wryly. "The dragon inside of me is trying to take control. Every time it starts to gain strength, so do I. Somehow I'm deriving strength from it. I just have to be careful that it doesn't take over completely."

"What if it does?" asked Alric.

"Run. Hide if you have to," said Kazin. "The dragon will be unpredictable and very dangerous."

Alric stared.

Kazin smiled again. "Don't worry. I'm still in control. You're safe for now."

Alric didn't look convinced. "Just make sure you warn me in advance."

"I will," said Kazin seriously.

× × × × ×

"I don't know which is worse," grumbled Larsen, "sick people or drunken ones."

"We are doing what is necessary," said Malachi consolingly. His words sounded empty to his own ears.

The two men stood atop the battlements surveying the thousands gathered there in the hopes of being cured. Tents and shelters were sprawled far off into the distance. Camp fires flickered eerily off the faces of those who were huddled near for warmth. Those not by the fires staggered around under the influence of the dwarven spirits that were handed out earlier in the day.

"At least when they were sick they stayed in one spot," continued Larsen. "The drunken ones keep getting in the way of my soldiers."

"It's far better being in the way than being dead," said Malachi. "The spirits give us hope and extra time to find a cure. Already the numbers of dying have decreased."

"I suppose you're right," admitted Larsen.

Malachi looked up at the moon, briefly visible through an opening in the perpetual clouds of the past several days. "Our magic is more powerful each day we get closer to full moon, and it helps when the moon's rays are able to get through these clouds. I should get back inside to assist in the healing magic. It's been a productive day. Perhaps the night will prove fruitful as well."

As the high cleric turned to go, Larsen stopped him. "I don't want to end the day on a negative note, Malachi, but there is one more issue that has come to the forefront that requires your attention."

"What is it, Larsen?"

"Our food supplies are dwindling," said Larsen. "As you know, many domestic animals have succumbed to the same disease that is affecting the people. As a result, good food is in short supply. As of today, we have begun to ration supplies to the people. Many who lined up today opted for dwarven spirits instead of food so that those who are weakest would not go hungry."

"You mean some of the people drank dwarven spirits on empty stomachs?" asked Malachi incredulously. "Do you know how spirits affect the body when there is no food to absorb some of it? How could you let that happen?"

"I cannot force people to eat," said Larsen calmly. "The people are free to do as they choose."

Malachi groaned. "Well, tomorrow we're supposed to be getting food supplies shipped up from the far south, including the elven realm. Also, any day now the dwarves are due to deliver fresh supplies of the spirits we requested. The dwarf whose recipe we're using is doing an admirable job overseeing the production of his brew."

"Good," said Larsen. "That settles that problem for now."

"Is there something else?" asked Malachi.

"Well," began Larsen slowly, "it's something that just came to my attention today."

"What is it?"

"Some of my soldiers have tried an experiment where they sampled the dwarven spirits in an effort to see if they will remain immune to the disease. They plan to drink only a certain percentage of the spirits daily. I was going to put a stop to it, but have decided to allow it. I'm thinking they might be on to something. The spirits won't cure the disease, but maybe they will prevent it from being acquired."

Malachi considered. "Good thinking. Let me know how it turns out. Things can't really get any worse than they are right now anyway, can they?"

At that moment the ground shook. The sudden upheaval was so violent that the two men had to grab hold of something to keep from being thrown off their feet. Below them, several tents collapsed, and screams of surprise could be heard over the rumbling.

As suddenly as it had begun, the rumbling stopped. A strong gust of wind suddenly blasted out of the north, and the smell of ozone could be sensed in the air. Thunder and lightning was evident on the northern horizon.

Malachi and Larsen looked at each other in alarm.

"You were saying?" said the general.

Chapter 26

A horn sounded far off in the distance. The dwarf immediately held up a hand for silence as she and her companions came to a stop. "It seems our escape has been detected," she whispered.

Vera's staff light reflected ominously off the tunnel's walls. "We'd better keep moving," said the cleric silently.

"And quickly," added the cyclops.

Rebecca hesitated. "I just wish we were going the right way. We could be heading into even more danger." Noticing the worried expressions on her companions' faces, she attempted to cheer them up. "I think the way we're going is our best option. We're going away from the more heavily traveled routes, so we're not as likely to get caught. Besides, I'm wearing my magic-detecting talisman. Any change in magic level warns me that there are lizardmen nearby. We won't get caught off guard this time."

This did not seem to reassure the others, so Rebecca said with exaggerated confidence, "Follow me." She trudged off in the direction they were originally heading and the others followed without saying anything.

They had taken no more than a few steps when another earthquake struck the mountain. Everyone lost their footing and debris showered from the ceiling. The mountain rumbled and shook so violently that the tunnel behind them caved in, foiling any would-be pursuers. The trio tried to rise to their feet, but the shaking was so vehement that they couldn't regain their footing. Then the tunnel in front of them caved in. At the same instant, the wall to their right began to crack, threatening to crumble like the rest of the passageway. They were about to be crushed! But instead of caving in on them, the wall simply fell outwards, tumbling in many various sized pieces into an unknown gorge below them. The place where the companions lay was like an alcove, protected on all sides from the shower of stones coming from somewhere above them.

Finally the mountain stopped rumbling. The companions coughed in the dusty aftermath of the earthquake, trying to fill their lungs with clean air. It was a full five minutes before they regained their composure.

Cyril helped the others to their feet. "Is everyone O.K.?" he gasped.

Rebecca and Vera confirmed they were alright. Vera found her staff and held it aloft to examine their surroundings. The dust reduced visibility, but they were able to determine the alcove they inhabited was solid and intact. Where the wall used to be on their right, was now a steep drop down to what sounded like an underground river. The staff light was not bright enough to illuminate the depths below.

"Now what?" asked Vera uncertainly.

Rebecca, after confirming the tunnel was hopelessly blocked, stated the obvious. "We'll have to go down."

Vera stared at the dwarf in horror. "We don't even know if we can go down!"

Rebecca withdrew her rope from her pack. "I'm open to suggestions."

Vera looked hopelessly at Cyril, who looked away.

"Don't worry," said Rebecca. "I'm a skilled climber. I grew up high in the mountains. I'll set you both up so we can go down in unison. We'll be tied to one another so if one of us has trouble, the others can come to their aid. The rope will be permanently fastened to the alcove we're in, so it will be supporting our weight. The lanyards tied to your chest will keep you within range of the rope, but allow you to move down unrestricted." Rebecca glanced at Cyril. "It is the finest rope available in the dwarven realm. It will even hold up a cyclops."

"Like the rope on the swing bridge?" asked Vera uncertainly.

Rebecca gave the cleric a glowering look. "It's much newer than that! This rope is even somewhat fire resistant, if that's what's bothering you."

Vera sighed. "I guess we don't have a choice, do we?"

Cyril laid a gentle hand on the cleric's shoulder. "We'll be fine. You'll see."

Vera gave the cyclops a wan smile. She held her staff over the edge again and this time the air was clear enough to see the river below. It was not as far down as she had first thought. The cliff was not as anticipated either. The rocks from the earthquake had made the slope much more manageable.

It took nearly an hour for the companions to descend to the river because the rocks were loose and unstable, but they managed without incident.

At the bottom, Vera approached the river and tested the water with magic. It was more contaminated than any water sources she had tested so far, and the stench was almost unbearable. "This is awful!" she gagged.

Rebecca was holding her nose too. "We'd better get away from here!" she said in a nasal voice.

Suddenly an idea occurred to Vera. "Wait a minute!" She did another spell test and the water close to her glowed with a faint greenish light. "Just as I thought!" she exclaimed.

"What is it?" asked Cyril.

Vera looked at the cyclops and he looked away. "Whatever magic is causing this is not far upstream! The magical signature in this water is noticeable for the first time since I've been checking it. When we were farther away, the magical signature in this poisoned water was already gone, but here it is still evident. That means we are near the source of the contamination!"

Rebecca's eyes widened. "That means we can finally find out what's causing the poisoned water and put a stop to it!"

"Finally we have a trail to follow!" put in Cyril excitedly. "Let's go!" He turned and headed upstream without waiting for the cleric and dwarf to respond.

Rebecca and Vera glanced at one another before running to keep up with the cyclops' long strides.

Suddenly the cyclops yelped and began hopping around on one foot. The others hurried to catch up and see what the matter was.

"What's wrong?" asked Vera in concern, as Cyril held his foot and continued hopping on his other leg.

"I stepped on something sharp!"

Vera turned to where the cyclops had been but the dwarf was already there. She had a strange expression on her face. She held onto the talisman around her neck. "There's something magical here!" she exclaimed.

Vera held her staff closer to the area in question and immediately picked out a shiny object protruding from the river's edge. Rebecca saw it too and reached down to touch it.

"It's some sort of steel spike," said the dwarf slowly. "It seems to be embedded in the ground." She tried to pry it loose but it wouldn't budge. "Let me try something." The dwarf withdrew her magical dagger and began to chip away around the object. The moment it made contact with the silvery tine, there was an instantaneous flash. She touched it again but this time there was nothing. "Odd," she muttered. The dwarf continued digging and succeeded in prying away the shale slabs encasing the object. Another spike was revealed. Soon others came into view. The spikes were all sticking out from a central piece shaped like a ball. Rebecca began digging more furiously. "I think I know what it is!" she exclaimed.

Before long, the entire head of the item had been revealed. The spiked ball gave way to a portion of a handle, and Rebecca grabbed it with her tiny hand and pulled. Still, it did not budge.

"Let me try," offered Cyril. He had overcome his momentary pain and was as curious as the others over what he had stumbled onto. His huge hand grasped the handle near the spiked ball and pulled. The remaining shale shattered and fell away. The cyclops lifted the item up into the light.

"Just as I thought!" cried Rebecca joyfully. She enjoyed finding treasure, as did all dwarves, and this was the second time on this adventure it had happened to her. "It's a mace!"

Cyril hefted the exceptionally large mace with ease. "It's very light!" he exclaimed.

"Let's see!" said Vera. She took it from Cyril's hand and nearly dropped it. "Uggh!" she exclaimed. "What are you talking about? It's extremely heavy!"

Cyril gave the cleric a strange look, while trying not to look into her eyes.

"Let me try," offered Rebecca. Vera gladly handed off the weapon to the dwarf. Rebecca grunted with the exertion of holding the weapon. "You must be awfully strong if you consider this mace to be light, Cyril." She passed the mace back to the bewildered Cyclops.

Cyril, meanwhile, hefted the mace and swung it in the air with exaggerated ease. "But it's light!" he insisted.

"That must be part of the magic," said Rebecca. "I wonder why it is only light for you."

Cyril looked at his trustworthy club on the ground a few feet away. "I guess I won't be needing you anymore." He glanced quickly in the dwarf's general direction. "If that's O.K. with you," he added.

Rebecca shrugged. "You were the one who found it. You're the only one who can make use of it. It's too heavy for me anyway. It's yours as far as I'm concerned."

The companions celebrated their find for a few more minutes before continuing on their adventure. With a new trail to follow, and a new weapon at their disposal, they had renewed hope of acquiring their objective. Things were beginning to look up. If only the rest of their party fared as well.

× × × × ×

"The forces are gathering in the great caverns," said Slong. "The ogres, goblins and cyclops are anxious to get started."

"Good," said Graf, "but until the orcs get here and the rest of the army is assembled, we can't march. I want to make a coordinated attack."

"Understood," said Slong. "I will tell them." He turned to go.

"Wait," said Graf suddenly, an idea forming in his mind. "Maybe we can let them get a taste of battle to build morale."

"Sir?"

"Why don't you let them eliminate the human outposts near the mountains? The outposts are lightly guarded. If those outposts are destroyed, the humans won't know when we will proceed with an all-out attack on their precious Tower of Hope. They will no longer have an early warning system in place."

"And we will have the element of surprise!" filled in Slong, "along with creating an element of fear."

"Precisely!" said Graf. "This attack will mimic the previous one, but seem like we're testing the strength of the humans. They won't know we are already capable of destroying them."

"Excellent," said Slong.

"Bring the earth elemental with you," added Graf. "I want to know how obedient it is when we are using it in battle. It is a suitable test."

"Understood," said Slong.

"And take out some of the most remote northern human settlements," added Graf. "There will be more spoils for the army to divide among themselves."

"Yes, Sir," said Slong.

When the general had departed, Graf made his way via several magical portals to a place near his home. There he spotted a lizardmage holding a trident and wearing a blood red robe. It was Brind.

"Brind!" exclaimed Graf. "What are you doing here?"

Brind had a dour expression on his face. "I would like to report on the fire elemental."

"Proceed," said Graf. He was not inclined to let Brind into his quarters because he sensed bad news.

"We briefly had the fire elemental in our possession," stammered Brind nervously.

"And?" pressed Graf impatiently.

"We were attacked and lost control of it," stated Brind. "I think it was the human mage you were talking about."

"You think?" growled Graf.

"I am fairly certain of it," said Brind. "I saw him as he was attempting to open one of our portals."

"Why didn't you stop him?!" shrieked Graf.

"I did," answered Brind. "I shot him in the neck with a poison-tipped dart."

Graf started. "You what?"

"I shot him with a poison-tipped dart," repeated Brind. "He went down right away."

Graf clapped his hands together and hissed. "Excellent! What happened next?"

"I was moving in for the kill when an accomplice of his ambushed me," continued Brind. "I couldn't see who it was but they were casting magical arrows at me. The portal was my only escape."

"Were they invisible?" asked Graf.

"Quite possibly," said Brind. "Do you think it was the elf we talked about?"

"I'm not sure," said Graf. "It would be a most unlikely alliance, but it's possible." He shook his head as if clearing his mind. "It doesn't matter. The mage has been poisoned! It is only a matter of time before he dies. You have done well, Brind!"

Brind gave a weak smile. "Shall I continue to search for the fire elemental? Once I see it, I'm sure I have the power to summon it by myself using my trident to channel the energy. It is easier to summon on this plane than the one beyond."

"Yes," said Graf. "But hold onto it this time. We may be able to use it in our war."

"Of course," said Brind, relieved. He turned and left. Brind had told his story in the wrong order, but it had worked out for the better. At least Graf was pleased about the poisoned mage.

Meanwhile, Graf entered his quarters. He cast a spell to silence everything in the room from possible listeners outside. Then he began to laugh. His hissing laugh let decades of stress go. He lifted his face to the ceiling and cried, "The dragon mage is poisoned! He is as good as dead! Next come the human clerics and mages! Then the dwarves and elves! The world will be ours at last!"

From the study doorway, three sets of eyes watched the outburst with incomprehension. Little did the hydra know what plans Graf had in store for it.

Chapter 27

lric wiped the dust from his clothes and rose shakily to his feet. The partial cave in that had resulted from the earthquake had filled the tunnel with dust and debris. He coughed to clear his lungs. The elf looked around in the falling dust, visibility only slightly enhanced by the light emanating from the elemental.

Tyris had survived the cave in handily, being able to 'flow' through the debris by conforming his body to the shapes of the falling rocks. His area was affected more than the others, judging by the size of the boulders around his feet.

Kazin had suffered the most. His weakened state had left him unable to shield himself from the falling rubble. His head was cut and bleeding. Fortunately, the amount of debris that had fallen on him from above was limited. He struggled to get to his feet and Alric helped him up. Kazin slapped the dust from his cloak. "Thank you, Alric," he said between coughs.

The arch mage sat down wearily and attempted to catch his breath. He lifted his wineskin to his lips but it was empty. It had gotten torn by a falling rock.

Alric offered him his wineskin. "Here."

Kazin looked at the elf. "Are you sure -?"

"Drink!" ordered Alric. "I've got another wineskin in my pack," he lied.

Kazin was doubtful but drank anyway. After a few gulps he handed the wineskin back to the elf. Then he staggered to his feet. "Let's keep moving."

"Are you sure -?" began Alric.

"Yes," interrupted Kazin. "The longer we delay, the weaker I'll become."

Alric was amazed at the mage's determination, but said nothing.

251

He followed the others quietly, Tyris leading the way through the dusty darkness over the cave-in rubble to the tunnel beyond.

A good hour of uneventful travel passed by before Kazin's staff began to glow orange. The trio stopped in front of the tunnel wall and Kazin concentrated. A few moments later, a portal opened before them. Alric and Kazin exchanged determined glances and stepped through, followed by the elemental.

They stopped immediately after stepping through because they had arrived in a tunnel similar to the one they had vacated.

Tyris looked to either side of them. "Which way?"

Kazin waited for the familiar gust of wind but there was none. He grew concerned. "The wind that has been guiding us is no longer present. I hope the air elemental is O.K."

"Maybe we shouldn't have gone through the portal," suggested Alric. "We could be going the wrong way."

Kazin considered. Perhaps Alric was right. "Alright. Let's go back through the portal and check." He turned around but stopped with a puzzled expression. He looked at the orb atop his staff.

"What is it?" asked Alric.

"Did you notice when the staff light changed to pink?"

Alric looked at the staff and was surprised to see it was a pinkish hue instead of the usual orange one. "Is that a problem?"

Kazin shook his head. "No. It's just curious that it's magically locked."

"Locked?" asked Alric. He looked at Tyris. "How can that be? We just went through it a moment ago!"

Kazin shrugged. "I don't know all of the magical workings of lizardman magic. This is new to me."

"Could someone have locked it after we went through?" asked Alric nervously.

"That is unlikely," said Tyris. "I would have sensed magic users in our vicinity at the time."

"Can you open it?" asked the elf.

Kazin nodded. He closed his eyes and concentrated. Beads of sweat began to form on his forehead and he had to pat his face with his cloak hood to reduce the stinging of sweat in his wound.

At last the portal opened and Alric was about to step through but Kazin held up a hand. He opened his eyes and Alric noticed a strange glow in the mage's eyes. Kazin's expression was one of surprise. His staff still glowed pink. Kazin closed his eyes and concentrated some more. Suddenly, the wall behind the companions glowed and undulated. There was a portal behind them!

"Well, what do you know!" exclaimed Tyris. "Who would have guessed that another portal would be located right opposite the first one?"

"A clever strategy," commented Alric. "Anyone pursuing a lizardman into this tunnel would never guess that there was another portal so close by. I'd wager that there are traps at either end of this tunnel."

"You could be right about that," admitted Kazin.

Alric looked at Kazin. "Which way now?"

Kazin grinned despite being weakened by the magic. "I didn't open the portal for nothing." He turned and stepped through new portal with the others close on his heels.

They entered a vast cavern with many converging tunnels. Torches flickered in wall sconces all around the cavern, shedding considerable light on the scene before them. In the middle of the room, a jumble of rocks was piled in a circular fashion.

"I wonder what happened here," muttered Alric, moving past the rubble to look for signs of lizardmen and danger. Kazin went around the other side to magically confirm that the room was secure.

Tyris approached the rock pile and placed his hand on some nearby rocks. He cried out and instinctively sprang away from the rocks. The mage and elf snapped to attention and gave Tyris a fearful stare.

"What is it?" asked Kazin, alarmed. Though weak, he moved to the elemental's side quickly.

"These rocks!" gasped Tyris. "They were magically created by the earth elemental!"

Alric studied the rock pile curiously. "What for?"

"I - I sense other magic here," said Tyris. "This is bad! Very bad!"

Kazin inspected the pile of rocks using magic, but other than the usual glow of magical light, he could learn nothing.

Tyris cautiously approached the rocks again and seemed to concentrate. Then his eyes widened. "No! It can't be!"

"What is it?" asked Kazin in concern.

Tyris turned his gaze to Kazin. "This pile of rocks was used as a barrier!"

"A barrier for what?" asked Alric. He was becoming impatient.

Tyris turned his burning gaze on the elf. "A barrier to prevent the air elemental from escaping!"

Kazin was stunned. "You mean the air elemental was imprisoned here?"

Tyris nodded. "Yes."

"The barrier is broken," stated Alric. "Isn't that a good thing?"

Tyris shook his sadly. "Not likely. The barrier does not appear to have been broken from the inside out. I sense no signs of a struggle. If the air elemental had escaped, there would certainly be more damage to this cavern. You underestimate the power of an elemental."

"So you think the elemental is still under the control of the lizardmen?" asked Kazin.

"Probably," said Tyris.

"If that's the case," said Kazin, "the lizardmen no longer needed to keep the air elemental trapped to control it. We're too late to help it." He sat down and was overcome by a fit of coughing. His breathing became more laboured and he was getting sicker and sicker. The quest was getting nowhere.

"Take a look at this," said a voice from one of the tunnels. Kazin sighed and got to his feet. The tunnel Alric had drawn their attention to opened up into another cavern. "It looks like they were mining something here," said the elf.

The cavern looked like it had been mined, but it was perfectly symmetrical in every dimension. "The earth elemental's magic was at work here," stated Tyris.

"What were they mining?" asked Alric.

Tyris shrugged. "I don't know. Perhaps this is where the earth elemental obtained the rocks for the barrier."

The cavern led nowhere, so the trio returned to the main cavern. It was then that Kazin's staff glowed pink again.

The mage approached the nearest wall and the staff glowed brighter. Out of curiosity, Kazin started walking around the circumference of the cavern. As he expected, each time he centered himself between tunnel exits, the staff became bright pink. The portal they had arrived in, however, made the staff glow orange. The mage pondered for a few moments, and suddenly an expression of understanding dawned on him.

"Of course!" he exclaimed.

"Of course, what?" asked Alric.

"That's why lizardmen were thought to be nearly extinct! Their magic allows them to live in a parallel plane of existence!"

Alric looked at the mage blankly.

"Each time we go through a portal - usually the ones with magical warding - we enter their realm by going into a separate plane of existence!"

"We're in a different plane of existence?" asked Alric.

"Yes," said Kazin. "At the moment we are."

"I don't sense anything different," said Tyris.

"You probably won't," said Kazin. He gestured around the cavern with his arm. "This cavern is still in the mountains, but it is removed from where we were before we came in here. It is a magical place of this world but not of this world." The mage slapped the wall beside him. "Each of these portals leads back to our plane of existence, and at least one of each of the tunnels we see is associated with each portal on the other side. This is a central location for various parts of the mountain all glued together. The lizardmen created it using their magic. They use it as a means of refuge from the other races, and as a means to travel a great distance in a short time - something like the portals connecting Marral and Warral to Sorcerer's Island." (The Tower of Sorcery had portals that mages used to get to the mainland east and west of Sorcerer's Island.)

Alric shook his head. This was a bit much for him to comprehend. "So we're in the lizardmens' realm. What does that gain us?"

Kazin coughed and pointed to the unchecked portal nearest him. "This is the perfect opportunity to 'jump' to a number of other lizardman locations and try to find the source of the poison. If one portal doesn't lead us anywhere, we'll come back here to try another route. We found the spot where the air elemental had been held captive. They must have felt secure here. It stands to reason that the other elementals are being held in caverns similar to this one."

"I'm all for that," said Alric. "But if this is a central hub as you claim, wouldn't it be more heavily travelled? Where are all the lizardmen? They should be going through here in droves. It's too quiet."

"I thought about that," said Kazin. "I have no answer. Something is seriously wrong here. Where are the lizardmen? Where did they take the air elemental? Where -?" The mage broke off in another fit of coughing. His head swam and his insides ached. The world spun, and, with his strength completely sapped, Kazin passed out.

✗ ✗ ✗ ✗ ✗

The downpour had reduced to a light deluge as the gates to the Tower of Hope creaked open. Muffled sounds became an audible roar as the masses gathered outside pressed in against the army in an attempt to gain access to the tower's courtyard. The ranks of soldiers held their ground as the convoy of supplies were ushered in. About forty wagons came rumbling into the courtyard, laden with food, water, and emergency supplies. Many grey mages accompanied the convoy in order to protect it on the long journey from the Tower of the Sky.

Amidst the first two wagons rode a tall, slender grey mage. She threw down her hood and exposed her long brown hair and eyes. She had a stern expression and an old scar on left cheek. Although no longer young, she had the bearing of someone who derived strength from hardship. The plight of the people outside the tower made her suddenly thankful that her life wasn't so bad after all.

The grey mage surveyed the courtyard and the bustle of activity surrounding the supply wagons as they were eagerly unloaded by soldiers and clerics alike. The skink warriors sat atop the battlements watching the work below. Their presence was eerie from the grey mage's standpoint, and by the look of her travelling party, she surmised the others felt the same way.

A cleric came bustling up to the grey mage. "Excuse me," stammered the cleric. "Are you the leader of this expedition?"

The grey mage nodded. "Yes."

"Please come with me," said the cleric. His voice was muffled within the hood of his cloak, which was pulled tight over his head to keep out the rain.

The grey mage dismounted and landed in a sizeable puddle. She looked down at her muddy boots but showed no reaction. It had rained for most of her journey, so she was wet to the bone already anyhow. She followed the cleric into the shelter of the tower where she was told to wait.

While waiting, she noticed the statue of a balding, grizzly looking man nearby. Everyone who walked past seemed to be ignoring him.

"Mara!" exclaimed a heavy set, white robed cleric. His brown hair had specs of grey and his paunch jiggled as he strode toward her in haste. "I didn't expect you to deliver the supplies personally!"

Mara smiled as she gently embraced the cleric. "I wanted to ensure that everything arrived intact and on time." She pulled back from the cleric and her smile vanished. "I had no idea things were as bad as you led me to believe, Malachi. I thought you were exaggerating when you told me what was going on. Now I see that you weren't stretching the truth at all."

Malachi sighed and spread his hands. "I'm glad you responded so quickly. There are many people in need of your supplies. You have no idea how good it is to see you."

Mara smiled again. "It's good to see you too, Malachi. It's been a long time since we met face to face."

"That's true," said Malachi. "It's too bad we have to meet under these circumstances." The High Cleric beckoned the leader of the grey mages to follow. "Come. Your cloak is drenched. I'll get you to your quarters and have a spare set of dry clothing brought to you."

"Thank you," said Mara. As they walked, Mara asked Malachi whether there was any more progress with the disease.

"We recently discovered that healing magic with the faelora herbs helps offset the internal pain most of the people are enduring," said

Malachi happily. "Combined with the dwarven spirits, many people are moving about when ordinarily they would have been bed ridden."

Mara stopped walking. "I'm sorry. Did you say - 'dwarven spirits'?"

Malachi turned around. Seeing the incredulous expression on the grey mage's face, he couldn't help but laugh, his paunch jiggling merrily. After his fit of laughter, Malachi responded. "Yes. That was my first reaction when I heard the idea." He put his arm around the mage and led her to her room. "I'll explain it when you've settled in. First, you need to get out of your wet clothes before you catch cold."

They had just reached Mara's room when a young cleric came bounding up to the High Cleric.

"Excuse me, Sir!" panted the cleric. "A sentry from one of the outposts has arrived and needs to see you at once!"

Malachi grunted. "Very well." He turned to Mara. "I won't be long. You can -."

"I'm coming with you," said Mara sternly.

Malachi looked into the mage's eyes and saw the resolve. "Very well," he said at last. "Come on."

Outside, the sky seemed to have gotten darker. A sentry stood surrounded by a number of other soldiers who talked excitedly. Malachi approached them just as General Larsen arrived from another direction.

Seeing the High Cleric already present, Larsen spoke. "Out with it, Milani!"

The sentry turned to face his commander with a pale face. "We have been attacked, Sir!" stammered Milani.

"Attacked? By whom?" demanded the general.

The soldier shook his head for lack of words. Finally he answered. "All sorts of creatures! Ogres, lizardmen, cyclops, creatures made of stone, everyone! A handful of us barely managed to escape with our lives!"

"What about the other outposts?" asked Larsen.

The soldier fearfully shook his head. "There were so many!" He shook his head again. "God help them all!" he said in a terrified whisper.

Larsen and Malachi exchanged fearful faces. Mara looked between the two men and her face became ashen as well. If these men were worried, she was even more so. She had brought numerous mages to assist with the distribution of supplies. Now it appeared as though they would be needed for battle instead. Hopefully there was still enough time to ship more mages up from the Tower of the Sky via North Lake. The black magic the grey mages wielded was no match for the powerful magic of lizardmen, but every little bit they had was better than nothing. For not the first time, Mara wished that grey magic was more powerful than it was.

✕ ✕ ✕ ✕ ✕

Martha exhaled with a great huff. "It's no use. I can't sense it anymore. We've lost it for good this time."

"It was too little too late," said Milena. She sat down on the roof of the Tower of the Moon and disappointment spread across her features. "If I had just come sooner."

"It's not your fault, child," said Martha consolingly. She sat down beside the druid and put her arm around her. There was a cold wind and in the distance storm clouds were brewing.

"All together we could have summoned the air elemental right into our plane," lamented Milena. "Then the lizardmen wouldn't have been able to summon it away from us."

"What would we have done then, child?" countered the rotund druid. "Using all of our magical energy to hold onto an elemental while those who need us are dying all around us? No. It makes little difference in the end. The lizardmen would have prevailed eventually. If we were dealing with the earth or water elemental, on the other hand, we wouldn't need to use nearly so much energy. Those elementals are what provide much of our druid magic. But we use air magic less, so our magic is not as powerful when it comes to summoning an air elemental."

"As long as it gave Kazin time to find the fire elemental," interrupted Adriana. She stood across the altar from the others. She was as disappointed as they were.

Milena brightened at the mention of the dragon mage. "Kazin will do it. He'll succeed."

Adriana wondered what everyone saw in the mage, but knew better than to question his abilities now. He was perhaps their only hope. Amelia, the oracle who had resided among them up until a few years ago, had determined this with her ability. As usual, she had been right. Before she died, she had also instructed them to send Rubin's ship south to a small port near Rist. He was to assemble troops and give passage to some important people. Who those people were was unspecified. There were no reasons given, just a command. Reluctantly, Adriana had complied - and not a moment too soon. Some of the sailors were regaining consciousness and they had to be sent off before falling under the lure of the mermaids in the lagoon.

Milena stood up. "Well, since we're not getting anywhere with summoning, let's concentrate our energy on healing the sick." She turned to Adriana. "What have you discovered so far regarding the herbs?"

Adriana shrugged. "The only thing that seems to work is the faelora herbs. They tend to lessen the pain when I use the right spell incantations. It doesn't eradicate the disease, but it makes the patients more comfortable."

Milena turned to Martha. "And you?"

Martha sighed. "I've studied the books on wildhorn leaves until my eyes practically fell out. Not one book mentions wildhorn leaves that are fermented. Leave it to a dwarf to come up with such a preposterous idea."

"That preposterous idea could lead to the cure we need," stated Adriana. "We need to create a similar substance to experiment with."

"Do you know how long it will take to ferment wildhorn leaves?" retorted Martha. "Not to mention, we've got a very small supply of it in our stores. And even then, we still need the ingredients to make the ale."

Adriana nodded. "I see what you mean." She rubbed her chin. "I guess we'll have to settle for what we've got. The quantity of faelora in our stores will last for a while. I suggest we use it to keep our patients comfortable until we come up with the right spells and components to cure them."

"Agreed," said Milena. "The next things I think we should try are fermented forms of the herbs we have. Maybe something other than the wildhorn leaves will have the right healing properties."

Martha rose. "I'll start looking for spells that are known to cure poison. There are a few books on detoxification that I haven't looked at yet."

"Good idea," said Milena. "Let's get at it."

Just as they re-entered the tower, the clouds rumbled ominously and the rain came down in torrents.

Chapter 28

The chanting grew louder as the trio crept along the bank of the river. The path was narrow and rocky, and the going was tough. In the distance, light could be seen reflecting off the poison river's surface. The ceiling here was lower, and the stench was compressed in the confined space, making breathing difficult. At last the dwarf called a halt. She stroked her hand through her hair and the silver streak shone in Vera's staff light.

"If we wish to continue," said the dwarf quietly, "we'll have to get our feet wet."

Cyril shook off his right foot. "I'm already wet anyway." He had slipped into the water several times already.

Rebecca addressed the cleric. "Do you want to go on?"

Vera looked down at her muddied white robe. "We might as well. It looks like we're headed in the right direction. If we want to find the source of the poison, we have to keep moving."

Cyril looked back the way they had come. "I don't think I want to go back that way if I can help it. It was a long walk." They had travelled for several hours without finding any routes that led away from the river. It was pointless to go back. Cyril turned forward. "I'm with Vera. I say we go on. We knew we would have to face lizardmen eventually. I for one will do what I can to stop them from their mad experiment." He clenched his mace so his arteries protruded from his arm.

"Alright then," said Rebecca. She turned to lead the others into the water. She was not happy about getting wet - dwarves rarely were - but ahead was where they would find their answers. If it meant getting wet, so be it.

The going was even slower as they waded through the water. They constantly helped one another to their feet when one of them stumbled. As luck would have it, they rounded a bend in the river and found a dry surface at the edge of the river to walk on again. The trio paused to shake the water off of them and continued.

A chanting noise could be heard ahead and the companions knew they were getting close. Judging by the sound, the chanting was that of the lizardmens' magic. Light now flickered off the walls as well as the water. There was even enough light that Vera could put out her staff light.

The river curled around to their left and the trio crept along slowly, straining to see around the bend. At last they caught a glimpse of a well-lit cavern ahead. They stopped and surveyed the scene in awe. A vast cavern housed the source of the river, which widened out closer to the center. Around the circumference were numerous torches, and a set of stone-carved stairs rose up and away around the edge at least as far as they could see from where they stood. Several small tunnels could also be seen, leading away from the area at just above the water level.

Around the water's edge were several dozen lizardmen and lizardwomen. They were the source of the chanting that could be heard. About a dozen of them chanted in unison, directing their attention to the object in the water. The object in question was breathtaking in its beauty. It was completely blue in colour, as bright a blue as one could imagine. Although easily five times the size of a human, its features resembled that of a human woman; but not just any woman. This creature was the image of perfection. From the smooth cheeks, finely curved chin, and slender nose, to the literally flowing long hair, to the perfect shapely figure beneath the head, no man could stare at her without falling in love. Some who had witnessed this creature claim that it was by her that mermaids were created.

Vera gasped. "That must be the water elemental!"

Cyril could only stare with his jaw agape. "She's beautiful!"

They watched for a few minutes and saw the elemental pushing the water, which came out of the ground in front of her, downstream in the direction of the companions. As she did so, the water turned brown and dirty. Although beautiful, her expression showed genuine fatigue. She was half-heartedly contaminating the water. It didn't take the companions long to realize that the lizardmen were controlling her actions.

Rebecca was the first to come to her senses. She nudged the others back out of visual range of the cavern. "Do you see what's happening?" she whispered.

The others nodded. "Lizardmen are making her contaminate the water!" whispered Vera hoarsely. "That's the source of the poison! We have to stop them!"

"There are quite a few of them," commented Cyril. "I doubt we can kill them all, and I doubt I can fool enough of them to paralyze them first."

"Maybe we can interfere enough to allow the elemental to escape," suggested Vera. "I know for certain lizardmen can't cast more than one spell at a time according to some magic books I've read."

"Good idea," said Rebecca, "but we'll have to act quickly. Once they turn their magic against us, we'll have to get out of there fast! The safest way is back downstream. We know there's no one down here for miles."

An idea occurred to Vera. "How well would we do if we were against non-magic users?"

Rebecca gave the cleric a sharp glance. "What have you got in mind?"

A small grin crept across Vera's lips. "It's just a thought. It might not work, and I won't be able to protect us with my shield."

"That's O.K." said Rebecca. She winked at Cyril, who turned away just in time. "I'm sure Cyril and I can handle a bunch of lizardmen on equal terms."

Vera rummaged through her pockets and successfully found the components she needed. The only thing lacking was her confidence.

The pressure was on. The entire world counted on her spell to succeed. It was a difficult spell to master, even for an experienced cleric, and Vera had never attempted it before, and certainly not on such a large scale. Surprisingly, she remembered it from her text book back at the Tower of Hope. Having it come to her at such a critical time was a stroke of fortune she would not soon forget. The cleric readied herself and looked at the dwarf.

"Ready?" asked Rebecca.

Vera nodded nervously.

Cyril got up and stepped ahead of the dwarf. Rebecca sprang after him, but knew too late that the cyclops had taken the honour of being the one to lead the charge. Once again, she was glad he was on her side.

The lizardmen were unprepared for the unexpected interruption in their magical spell. As they chanted, the water elemental slowly stopped what she was doing. She turned to regard her captors with curiosity.

A tall lizardmage standing off to one side straightened. "I didn't tell you to stop!" he snarled. "Get back to work!" A number of lizardmages in the second row began to chant, joining their voices with those of their partners in the first row.

The elemental turned to look at the speaker, whose blue-green robe wavered in the light of the cavern. "I shall not!" she retorted, her voice shaky and exhausted.

"Continue to poison the water!" ordered Relg the lizardmage. He shook his gnarled staff as he spoke. The third row of lizardmages added their magic to the others. There was no effect.

"I am tired," stated the elemental wearily. "I am going to rest. I am leaving you."

"No!" cried Relg. "You cannot disobey! You are under our control!" More lizardmen pitched in with their magic.

"I am not under your control," intoned the water elemental. This time her voice had an edge to it. She was getting angry.

"No! It cannot be!" shrieked Relg. He began chanting himself.

"Fools!" muttered the elemental. She began to sink into the river.

Unusual sounds and cries of pain at the edge of the gathered lizardmages drew their momentary attention. The elemental paused to see what was going on.

"Concentrate on the summoning magic!" cried Relg. He could not afford distractions. The elemental should be easy to summon within sight of them all.

By now, most of the lizardmages were trying with all their might to regain control of the elemental. The rest - the ones who were closer to the commotion, directed their attention that way.

Bashing through the ranks of lizardmages was an angry cyclops and a ferocious dwarf. Instinctively, some of the lizardmages tried to cast spells against the intruders. Their spells failed to materialize. They tried several different spells, all without success. The mace and dagger silenced their babbling faces.

Vera was overjoyed that her 'silence' spell had worked. Not only did it free the elemental, it prevented the lizardmages from counterattacking with their magic. The cleric ducked out of sight to let the fighters do the battling. The initial rush was successful, but the lizardmages had regrouped and started to gain the upper hand by surrounding the cyclops and dwarf, who had moved too far from the river's exit.

The angry lizardmages were restricted to jabbing with their staves. Their weapons were cumbersome, but their strength in numbers was superior by far. They soon landed blows with their staves and pressed in from all sides. Vera wished she could help her friends, but knew her spells would also fail.

By now Relg knew what was happening. He saw the fighting and knew that was a diversion. He was too intelligent to miss the fact that someone had cast a silence spell on him and his helpers. He looked around for tell-tale signs of a spell caster and spotted Vera peeking around a large boulder. Her mostly white cloak had given her away. Relg's pointed snout spread into a sinister grin. He pushed past the other lizardmages, some of whom were still trying to regain control of the elemental, and worked his way toward the undefended cleric.

Things were looking dire for the companions, when several fireballs blasted into the crowd from above. High up, at the top of the stairs that wound around the cavern, was Tyris!

"Tyris!" exclaimed Vera in a whisper. The fire elemental had come to their rescue! Her joy was cut short when she brought her gaze back down to the chaos below. Right in front of her stood Relg. His shimmering robe seemed to be blacker and more forbidding up close. He seemed even more fearsome since he wasn't the least bit intimidated by the fire elemental's fireballs.

"You are a fool!" snarled Relg. "You think you can just come here and stop us so easily? When you are dead, my minions will once again be able to cast spells. Your feeble attempt to hinder our plans will amount to nothing. I will enjoy killing you!" He raised his staff and swatted Vera with uncanny ease. She flew back and landed in the river. The strike, combined with the ice cold water, knocked the wind from her lungs. The cleric tried feebly to pull herself back to the river's edge.

Relg took a step forward to finish the cleric, but froze when he heard a menacing voice behind him. "Pick on someone your own size, you slimy lizard!"

Relg spun on the speaker and swung his staff at the same instant. His staff flew through open air. The only thing he saw when he came to a stop was a sword pointed at his chest.

"Nice try," said the voice venomously, "but not good enough." The sword plunged into the lizardmage's chest and twisted around. All Relg could do was gurgle as he dropped to the ground. He dropped his staff and his greenish blood flowed into the river, poisoning it further.

Invisible hands grabbed the cleric firmly by the arms and pulled her ashore. "Wait here."

Vera knew the voice but was too winded to respond. She merely nodded. Alric had shown up just in time. She would thank him later.

Meanwhile, the tight quarters that Rebecca and Cyril had experienced had lessened off a bit. Many lizardmages were escaping down some nearby tunnels, while others were more interested in doing away with the intruders. By now most of the lizardmages had given up the summoning spell to help their friends or save their own skins. Fireballs continued to rain down on them from above, and some of them rolled into the water, making the water elemental hiss in agony. The clash between the elemental forces coming into contact with one another caused instant steam. Within minutes, the majority of the cavern became a dense fog. This made fighting difficult for both sides.

Alric moved stealthily among the lizardmages, killing as he went. Rebecca and Cyril continued to fend off attackers with their backs to each other.

Tyris stopped casting fireballs into the fray, sensing he was hurting the water elemental unintentionally. He did not notice the figure who had snuck up behind him from the portal. The summoning magic was so swift and methodical that Tyris barely had time to cry out. Before he knew it, he was trapped between the tines of a trident.

Brind chuckled. "This time you won't escape, my fiery friend."

Watching him from the shadows was a black-cloaked figure. Had Brind seen how weak and frail that figure was, he would have stayed and fought. A lightning bolt struck the trident from his hand with the same ease that he had used to capture the fire elemental. Brind was torn between fighting with the shadowy figure, retrieving his trident, or escaping.

Some more lightning bolts flew at him, but his hastily erected shield fended them off. Because Brind had to cast the shield spell, his summoning spell was negated and the elemental surged out of the trident and turned on his aggressor. Left with no other choice, Brind canceled his shield spell and opened the portal. He dove through the portal and vanished. One thought went through the lizardmage's head. Shouldn't the human mage be dead by now?

On the other side of the portal, Kazin was already unconscious.

Tyris hovered over him, painfully aware that he was unable to do anything to help. He was as helpless as the mage.

Back at the river, Vera caught her breath and got to her feet. The fog gave her an advantage with her white cloak. It wasn't perfect, being wet and dirty, but it wasn't bad either. Screams echoed eerily through the fog as the cleric crept toward the water elemental, making sure to avoid being seen by the lizardmages, most of who were on the other side of the river contending with her friends. At the river's source, the cleric could just make out the decaying form of the water elemental. Unafraid, Vera jumped into the water with the elemental and waded out to her.

Suddenly, the elemental raised her head, ready to destroy the intruder in her space. She would have drowned Vera with a simple flick of her wrist, but stayed her hand, surprised to see a human cleric before her.

"Are - are you alright?" stammered Vera. The fierce blue eyes washed away her courage like a tidal wave. The elemental was fearsome to behold when angry.

The elemental sighed. "I have done a terrible thing," she moaned.

"The lizardmages controlled you," objected Vera. "You had no control over that."

"I should have resisted," countered the elemental.

"You can't resist summoning magic," said Vera. "That's beyond your control."

The elemental shook her head.

"You're free now," said Vera consolingly. "Can you fix what you were forced to do wrong?"

The elemental looked up at Vera with a sad expression. The expression was so intense that Vera's eyes watered. "I cannot interfere with the goings on in the world unless I am summoned," said the elemental. "That won't be for some time, as I need to recover." She spotted Vera's staff. "But I can help you make a start if you wish it. I owe it to you for rescuing me."

"I would like to help you any way I can," said Vera. Tears rolled down her cheeks uncontrollably now. This gentle giant was so awe-inspiring that Vera's emotions were in turmoil. She wanted to hold the elemental and weep endlessly.

The elemental took hold of Vera's staff and her hand seemed to caress it and meld into it. The white colour washed out of the staff and swirled down the river, leaving it devoid of any colour whatsoever. "Simply touch the staff to any contaminated water and it will be cleansed," said the elemental.

Vera raised her transparent staff out of the water and examined it with curiosity.

"I must go now," said the elemental.

"Thank you," whispered Vera as the giant water elemental sank into the water and became one with the river. A great sense of loss swept over the cleric and she wept.

Most of the commotion had finally subsided, and Alric located Rebecca and Cyril as they contended with the last few lizardmen. The elf stabbed the lizardmen in the back and called out to the others. "Are you O.K.?"

Rebecca's heart leaped to her throat. "Alric, is that you?"

"Yes," said the elf. He waved his sword around so they could see where he was.

"You found us!" exclaimed Rebecca joyfully. Then she winced. Her left arm was cut and bruised, and there was blood running down the side of her face.

Cyril lowered his mace. His right leg was ripped open and the blood ran down to his feet. His left elbow was gashed and bleeding as well. "You came just in the nick of time," he panted. He looked around suddenly. "Where's Vera?"

A splashing noise came from the water and the three companions bolted for the sound. Instead of lizardmen, they encountered Vera. Judging from her red eyes, she looked as though she had been crying.

"What's wrong?" asked Cyril in concern. He stumbled forward to help her away from the water.

Vera looked up at the cyclops (who looked away) and was about to respond when she saw him wince in pain. "You're hurt!" she exclaimed. She discovered his wounded leg and immediately began to use her healing magic. When it didn't work, she sighed. "I can't heal you here. My silence spell is still preventing magic from being cast here." She looked up at the dwarf and the disembodied sword. "We have to get away from here."

"Silence spell," murmured Alric. "It's no wonder the lizardmages weren't casting spells." Then he realized they were looking to him for an escape route. "Follow me."

The others followed the sword as the elf led them to the stairs at the edge of the cavern. Lizardmage bodies were strewn about all over the place. Tyris' fireballs had claimed most of the lives, the bodies burned almost beyond recognition. Many more were stabbed and lay in grotesque poses on the floor. Alric brought his sword down on one of the bodies that still moved. At least 30 lizardmages had been killed, and an equal number had fled into the many caverns.

As they wended their way through the carnage, Rebecca asked, "Where's Kazin? I saw Tyris up in the alcove, but I didn't see Kazin."

"He's up there with Tyris," explained Alric. "Tyris had to stay up there so he wouldn't get too close to the water elemental. Apparently, if elementals get too close, they could hurt one another. Kazin was too weak, so Tyris elected to guard him so I could come down and help you."

"What's wrong with Kazin?" asked Vera.

Alric realized the others didn't know what had happened to the arch mage. "Kazin was poisoned by a lizardmage dart."

"What?!" gasped Vera and Rebecca together.

"I got there just in time to scare off the lizardmage," said Alric, "but the damage had already been done. The dart hit Kazin in the neck, so I think the poison had a stronger effect than if he had ingested the poisoned water. He's in pretty bad shape."

Vera gave Rebecca a fearful stare but said nothing.

They had reached the stairs and the sword bounced up them, matching the elf's long strides. Cyril winced with each step and Vera held him on one side while Rebecca held him from the other. The going was slow, but as they neared the top on the far side of the cavern, they could see a light orange glow. It was Tyris.

"Who goes there?" demanded Tyris.

"It's just us," called Alric. "We're all alive but some are wounded."

At the alcove, Vera saw Kazin on the ground where he had fallen. She ran up to the mage and lifted his head off the floor. She looked up at the elemental. "What happened?" she demanded.

"I was captured by a summoner," said Tyris, indicating the trident lying on the ground a short distance away. "Kazin used the last of his energy to rescue me before collapsing. I am in his debt."

Alric was surprised. "You were summoned?!" He looked at Vera. "I thought you cast a silence spell that prevents spell casting?"

Vera looked confused. "Yes. Maybe my spell didn't cover the entire cavern. It was the first time I had ever cast it."

"That would explain why my magic to change my dagger into a sword was successful," commented Alric. "I did that spell up here before I headed down to help you."

An idea suddenly occurred to the cleric. She got up and tried to heal Cyril's leg. The spell worked. "It works!" she exclaimed. Cyril's wound began to close and heal. The cleric then went to work on the other injuries. With that completed, she used her magic to revive Kazin. Tyris leaned forward so the cleric could see what she was doing.

The arch mage stirred. He opened his eyes and winced, shutting them again. "Tyris, you're awfully bright," rasped Kazin.

Tyris stood back. "Sorry."

"Kazin!" murmured Vera, hugging the mage.

Kazin tried to sit up and gently pushed the cleric away. "I think I'm dying," he said with a hoarse voice.

"No, you're not!" insisted Vera. Tears started forming in her eyes again. "It won't be long before a cure is found. I can purify the poisoned water. I'll cure the poison in your body if it's the last thing I do."

Everyone's ears perked up at Vera's statement. "What was that?" asked Rebecca. "What did you just say?"

Vera looked up at the dwarf. "I'll cure the poison in your body if -."

"No. Before that," said Rebecca.

"Oh," said Vera, understanding the question. She relayed the encounter with the water elemental to the others, showing her clear staff as proof.

"Well done," complimented Kazin. He coughed and pulled the cleric closer. "Now go find your way out of the mountains and save the world. Cyril can sense the outside world. He can guide you. Rebecca will see to it that you don't become lost."

"What about you?" demanded Vera. "You're going with us! I'll carry you myself if I have to!"

Kazin coughed and shook his head.

Suddenly a commotion sounded below and everyone looked down into the cavern. Lizardmen were returning with reinforcements. Their torch light was showing through the thinning fog.

"Alric," murmured Kazin.

"Yes?" said Alric, leaning close to the mage to hear.

"Do you remember what I was telling you about the dragon within me?"

Alric nodded but realized no one could see him. "Yes," he said belatedly.

"It is time."

Alric stepped back in alarm. "Are you sure?" The others looked at Alric's sword with curiosity.

"Yes," said Kazin. "Take care of the others." The arch mage pointed his staff at the stone wall that was the portal. Moments later it shimmered. "Now go! All of you!" shouted Kazin.

"I'm not leaving you," insisted Vera. Tears were now streaming down her face.

"You must!" rasped Kazin. He began coughing uncontrollably. He pulled away from her as she grabbed onto him.

Cyril knew the signs and pried Vera away from the arch mage as gently as he could. "Come," he said softly. He nodded at Kazin and added, "I will always remember you, my friend."

The companions stepped through the portal, Tyris the only one without tears in his eyes. Alric was glad he was invisible so no one could see his own moist eyes. Cyril and Vera were the last to step through. The cleric looked longingly at the mage before the magic whisked her away. The portal closed. Soon the only sounds came from below.

Kazin looked down into the cavern, which was rapidly filling with lizardmen armed to the hilt. The laughing of the dragon spirit raged within Kazin's head. It sensed Kazin's weakness and tried to overcome his will. It wanted to gain control. Slowly, perhaps more slowly than ever before, he began to transform. His body became more and more reptilian and less human. After agonizing minutes, he stood on the ledge, with barely enough room to stand. The crowd below had now spotted him, his enormous body impossible to hide. With an ear-splitting shriek, the dragon unfolded its leathery wings and plummeted into the masses below. . . .

Chapter 29

yrr peered around the corner. "He seems to be busy eating."

"Is there enough room to sneak around him?" asked Lynch. He cowered in the shadows, content to let Lyrr risk his life spying.

"I think so," said Lyrr. "There are enough bodies piled up that we should be able to move undetected."

Lynch shuddered. It was hard to fathom so many dead lizardmen in one place. "We have to get past it in order to track the fire elemental. It was up the stairs by the portal. The longer we wait, the colder the trail will become."

Lyrr sighed. He didn't think it was a very good idea to try to summon the fire elemental with the rest of their team out of commission. With just the two of them, it was doubtful their magic would be strong enough to capture an elemental. Still, chasing the elemental was preferable to fighting in the war against the humans. "We should disguise ourselves," said Lyrr.

"What do you suggest?" asked Lynch.

"There are plenty of rats around here," said Lyrr. "If we look like rats, maybe the dragon will ignore us. We wouldn't be worth pursuing. Not with the feast he's got in front of him right now."

"Good point," said Lynch. "Let's do it."

Lyrr chanted softly while Lynch held his arm to allow the spell's effects to encompass him as well. In moments, the two lizardmen were replaced by two rats.

"How do I look?" asked Lynch.

"Ugly, as usual," said Lyrr. "I've seen more attractive rats." His leering expression was not lost in his new form.

"Shut up," snapped Lynch irritably. "Let's get moving."

The two rats scurried around the outskirts of the cavern. They ducked in behind the charred remains of the lizardmen. Steam still rose from the bodies, an indication that they were freshly killed. The sound of chomping became louder as the rats neared the dragon. Whenever the great beast paused, so did the rats.

The dragon spit out the bones and sniffed. It smelled rats nearby. Undoubtedly they were there to feed on the carcasses. 'Oh, well,' it thought. There was plenty of food to go around. The dragon resumed eating, tearing lizardmen flesh from bone. It never noticed the stealthy rats scamper by on their way to the stairs.

They had almost reached the stairs when another rat jumped out in front of them. It squeaked and ran up to Lynch, sniffing him from every angle. Lynch tried to jump out of the way but the female rat pursued him.

"Get lost!" hissed Lynch irritably. He jumped up the stairs to try to escape. The rat followed.

Lyrr leered. "I guess you're more attractive than I thought." He followed the others up the stairs.

Halfway up the stairs Lynch was breathing heavily. "I didn't think it was so far to the top." The female rat caught up to him and that spurred him on.

"We're just smaller," said Lyrr. "That's why the distance seems longer." He paused to catch his own breath and looked down at the dragon in the cavern below. The dragon was gazing up at them curiously but gave no indication it was going to attack them. Lyrr continued his ascent.

Lynch finally reached the top and turned to let Lyrr know they were there but didn't get a chance to say anything. The female rat sprang up the final step and landed squarely on the hapless rat. They locked together and tumbled end over end, stopping at a large stick. Lynch struggled to free himself from the female rat and stumbled to his feet.

Lyrr stood by, leering. "You don't waste any time, do you?"

"Shut up, Lyrr!" snapped Lynch. "Are we clear to change back again? I'd like to get rid of this nuisance." As he spoke, the female rat was sauntering up to him in a suggestive manner.

"Are you sure you don't want to -?" began Lyrr.

"Change us back!" ordered Lynch furiously.

"Very well," said Lyrr. He looked over the edge to see the dragon engrossed in his feast. With a word of magic, the two lizardmen reappeared. The female rat was not ready for this surprise and shrieked, jumping way up and back.

"The rat liked you better the way you were," said Lyrr nonchalantly. Lynch growled and Lyrr leered.

The dragon looked up toward the alcove, irritated by the noise. After a moment, it resumed eating. 'Silly rats,' it thought.

The lizardmen breathed a sigh of relief. They were not spotted because they stood back from the edge. It was then that Lynch saw the stick he had bumped into earlier. It wasn't a stick.

"What have we here?" he whispered, bending over and picking it up.

"A trident," said Lyrr.

"I know it's a trident, you fool!" snapped Lynch.

"Then why did you ask?" said Lyrr, leering.

Lynch knew Lyrr was toying with him so he didn't respond to the remark. "I wonder why it's here."

"Maybe someone else was here trying to capture the fire elemental," suggested Lyrr.

"Don't be silly," snapped Lynch. "There was no way anyone could survive the attack long enough to summon the elemental. Besides, the lizardmages who had survived the attack said magic wouldn't work here at the time due to a suspected magic nullification spell."

"Maybe so," admitted Lyrr, "but the trident is perfect for containing a magical being. With a trident, we can contain the fire elemental with minimal magic."

Lynch gave Lyrr a sharp glance. "Then we'd better bring it with us." He pointed to the portal. "What are we waiting for?"

Lyrr chanted and opened the portal. The lizardmen stepped through and disappeared.

The dragon paused and looked up toward the alcove. Did he hear talking a moment ago? He listened, but there was only the sound of the river beside him. Then he saw a rat bounding down the stairs. "Stupid rats," he murmured. He returned to his feast. It was getting cold. One good blast of fire warmed things up again and he ravenously devoured his meal.

× × × × ×

Frosty landed atop the Tower of the Moon and furled his wings. Soon they blended into his body and were gone. He looked around, his proud bearing and shiny white horn an image of pure beauty. No one else was on the roof at this time.

A strong gust of wind reminded him to make haste with his delivery. It seemed to him that he was strictly a messenger these days. He would have preferred to be with Kazin, but the circumstances surrounding recent events made that impossible. Once the elementals were freed, he could contribute more directly. For the moment, he did what little he could to help.

Approaching the roof door, which led down into the tower, the unicorn concentrated and the latch unlocked. The door opened outward and admitted the four-legged beast. Few creatures could overcome locked doors like Frosty, and even druid magic could not keep him out. He entered the opening and disappeared inside, the door closing and locking behind him.

The unicorn found Milena and Adriana in the main hall, scurrying from bed to bed tending to the sick mermaids. They did not notice him until he whinnied. Then they looked up in surprise.

"Frosty!" exclaimed Milena, running forward to embrace the mythical creature.

"How did you -?" began Adriana. Then she threw her hands up in despair. "Oh, never mind. I don't even want to know."

"I have some supplies for you," said Frosty when Milena finally let go of his neck. He turned to locate a pouch that was slung over his back. Then he picked up the pouch in his teeth and turned to Milena. "Here," he said through clenched teeth. "Just what the druids ordered."

Milena took the pouch and grunted under the weight. "What's in here?" she asked.

"Wildhorn leaves and dwarven ale," answered Frosty. "I've always wanted to be an ale runner," he added sarcastically.

Milena laughed. Even Adriana cracked a quick smile.

"You always find a way to lighten the mood, Frosty," said Milena. Frosty whinnied again.

Adriana tucked in a mermaid and came forward to help Milena with the pack of ale. "I'll do some experiments straight away."

Suddenly a voice behind them cried, "I've got it!"

Everyone turned to see Martha run into the room out of breath. "Hi, Frosty," she said briefly. She did not seem the least bit surprised he was there. She held a book in her hand.

"What is it?" asked Milena.

Martha paused to catch her breath. "I think I know how we can create a cure for the disease!" she blurted at last.

"Out with it, Martha," said Milena excitedly.

"It won't be easy," said Martha. She turned to a page in the book. "Apparently, we can create the antidote by using the faelora and the dwarven spirits."

"How?" prodded Milena.

"That's when it gets more complicated," continued Martha. "First, according to the book, we have to get an experienced representative of black, white, and grey magic, together with at least one druid."

"O.K.," said Adriana. "That's not too hard. And then?"

"Then we have to summon the water elemental," said Martha.

Adriana groaned and threw her hands up in the air again. "So much for that idea."

Milena's hopes faded. "We just can't seem to win."

"You should try to gather the mages together anyway," interrupted Frosty.

"What's the point?" asked Adriana. "The water elemental is out of reach."

"Not necessarily," said Frosty.

"How do you know?" asked Milena.

"My magic is strongly related to the four elementals," said Frosty. "My magical strength is weaker if an elemental is being controlled on our plane. My power was at its weakest when the air elemental was taken from you. I've recently noticed an increase in my strength. It could be that one of the elementals recently returned to its own plane of existence. Perhaps it was the water elemental. That elemental was in our plane of existence longer than any of the others. If it was pushed too hard, it could have burned itself out and perished in its summoned form. If that is so, the elemental is very weak. You won't be able to summon it until it becomes stronger."

"How long will that be?" asked Adriana.

"I don't know," said Frosty. "You'll just have to try summoning it from time to time."

"In the meantime," interjected Martha, "we need to get the mages together."

"Do you think you can find Kazin?" asked Milena.

"I'm about to find out," said Frosty gruffly. "As his familiar, I've sensed him in danger a few times, but the feeling keeps getting weaker. My magic isn't as potent in the mountains, so I have no choice but to search for him. I'm getting a bit concerned."

"If he's O.K. but too busy looking for the source of the poison," said Milena, "you can fetch Arch Mage Valdez. He's our only alternative for an experienced black mage. It will leave my country with no leader for the short term, but this is a higher priority."

"Understood," said Frosty.

"I'll dispatch a couple of griffins to gather a white and grey mage," offered Adriana.

"I'll study the necessary spells for the cure," said Martha.

"You'd better get going," said Milena to the unicorn. "We've got lots of work to do, and you have to find Kazin. I sure hope he's O.K."

"Me too," said Frosty.

"He's O.K." said Adriana with an unusual air of confidence. She had just opened a bottle of the ale and sniffed. Her face immediately contorted into a gruesome expression. "Phew! They say this can be used for a cure?"

Frosty smirked. "The dwarves say it's the cure for what 'ales' ya."

Everyone but Adriana laughed.

x x x x x

"You never told us you could do that!" exclaimed Rebecca.

Cyril shrugged. "I guess it wasn't important at the time." He continued walking ahead of the others, leading the way.

"You could have led us deeper into the mountain without the aid of the magical portals," said Rebecca.

"Perhaps," said Cyril, "but that probably wouldn't have gotten us closer to the lizardmen and the trapped water elemental. Now that our quest is completed, our task is to find our way out of the mountain. That is easy for me since I can sense the outside world. We'll be out of here in no time. I just hope it's somewhere we can descend the mountainside in safety."

"Me too," said Rebecca. "Without my rope, it will have to be a manageable climb."

The ground shook and the companions paused to brace themselves. It was a common occurrence now, happening several times an hour, but the tremors were not as strong as the ones they had experienced earlier.

When the tremors faded, Rebecca looked back past the glowing elemental. "Is everyone O.K.?" The section of tunnel they were in was long and straight.

"Yes," answered Alric in the back of the group. He saw that Vera was fine in front of him. "We're fine."

The cleric had rarely spoken since departing the cave where they had abandoned Kazin. She wept silently now, not wanting to dampen the spirits of the others. For the earlier part of their journey, either Cyril or Rebecca had walked with her, their arms around her shoulders. Murmurs of encouragement had done little to lift her spirits. After a time, they had all decided to give her some space. Only time would heal her sorrow.

A slight gust of wind from ahead of them wafted past them, causing Tyris to flare up briefly.

"We're closer than I thought," commented Cyril.

"Wait!" said Tyris suddenly in a hushed tone. "I sense magic wielders!"

Alric spun around to scan the tunnel behind them, his sword drawn and ready. "Are you sure?"

"Yes," whispered Tyris nervously. He did not want to be summoned again.

Alric turned to the others. "Go on ahead as though nothing is wrong. I'll investigate." He hurriedly pulled his cloak from his pack and donned it, becoming invisible. He wasn't worried about the others seeing him now that Kazin was no longer with them. Then he shrank his sword into a dagger and hid it behind his cloak, making it disappear as well. "I'll catch up with you later."

Rebecca stepped past Tyris and Vera and took up rear guard while Cyril led the way. The fire elemental's light shone brightly and warmly behind him.

Alric waited silently at the last corner for less than a minute before a couple of cloaked figures came into view. One carried a dimly lit staff while the other carried a trident. Alric's friends were not very far down the tunnel yet and Tyris' light was still visible.

The two figures moved just past the invisible elf when they spotted the elemental ahead of them.

"There it is!" whispered one of the hooded figures excitedly. "Start the incantations!"

The other figure held up the trident and began to chant.

Alric could tell by the voices they were lizardmen. He immediately withdrew his knife, but made the mistake of changing his weapon into a sword while being too close to his adversaries. They heard his almost inaudible chant, and the first cloaked figure spun around to face this uninvited guest. A shield spell was in place before Alric could bring his sword down on them. It clanged harmlessly off the shield.

The other figure continued concentrating on his summoning spell. The fire elemental wailed as his essence was being drawn into the trident.

Alric growled and slashed at the shield in a futile effort to stop the lizardmen.

By now, Alric's companions had concluded that things weren't going as planned. They were running toward the lizardmen to aid the elf.

The cloaked figure casting the summoning spell was aware of the attacker behind them, but was more concerned by the ones coming toward him. One was a white magic wielder judging by the colour of her cloak. The reports of the 'magic nullifying' spell back at the water elemental cavern indicated that a white mage (cleric) was likely present to have cast that spell. It seemed extremely doubtful that a human white mage would be so deep within lizardman territory, but here was evidence to the contrary.

The fire elemental was now half absorbed into the trident, but the effort to summon it in its entirety was too intense. The white mage would be in range to nullify his spell before he could complete it.

Opting to save his life and that of his companion, he discontinued his summoning spell and hastily pulled a piece of parchment from his pocket. He read the words written on it and grabbed his companion who maintained the shield. As he did so, his hood fell back. He turned and leered at the disembodied sword. The lizardmen sprang through the solid rock at the side of the tunnel, disappearing from sight. The piece of parchment fluttered to the floor.

Alric slashed frantically at the wall but his sword would not penetrate it. By now Vera, Cyril and Rebecca were at Alric's side. They stared at the blank wall, breathless from their run.

Alric bent down and picked up the parchment. The words were not in lizardmage dialect as he had expected. They were in elven! He read the words silently and looked up at the others in surprise. "It's an elven spell scroll! It's some sort of 'pass through rock' spell!" he cried excitedly.

His excitement waned when he looked back down at the parchment. The words were starting to fade. The spell scroll was intended to be used only once and then fade away. Alric tried to memorize it as best he could before it disappeared altogether. Luckily, he had some background in elven black magic. A normal elf wouldn't have even had a chance to identify the spell, let alone understand it.

Meanwhile, Tyris had pulled himself together into human form again and awaited the outcome back down the tunnel. He had no intention to be so close to a couple of summoners.

"We'd better get out of here," cautioned Cyril.

"Good idea," said Rebecca.

The group hurried to rejoin Tyris, and Cyril led them away at a brisk pace.

Less than an hour had passed when Cyril finally led the companions out of the mountains. As luck would have it, they were already at the tree line, and the descent to the bottom of the mountains was a short trek.

It was drizzling and lightning could be seen arcing across the sky. The thunder rumbled ominously, drowning out all other sounds. Verbal communication was hampered, so hand signals were used to navigate down the mountainside.

At the bottom, a small path showed signs of recent heavy usage. They followed this for a time and came upon one of the Tower of Hope's outposts. It was destroyed almost beyond recognition. The companions looked at one another in alarm. Signs of destruction were everywhere, but there were no signs of bodies or weapons. The battlefield was picked clean of anything valuable.

Vera bent over to examine something white on the ground and discovered it was a human finger bone. A sudden realization of horror crept over her, making the hair stand up on the back of her neck. The victims had been eaten! She hid behind a pile of nearby rocks and retched.

Alric instinctively knew this was the work of the lizardmage he was after. If the lizardmen were already at war with the humans, the lizardmage would undoubtedly be among them. The only way to find out was to follow the trail of destruction.

No one wanted to stay near the grizzly scene, so Cyril led them southeast toward the Tower of Hope. He wasn't expecting to return to the tower again, and after what he had just witnessed, he might not see it again anyway. At least, not the way he remembered it . . .

✗ ✗ ✗ ✗ ✗

The black smoke billowed up from the old farmhouse. There wasn't much left of it other than one wall and a few scattered pieces of furniture. The rest of it had been consumed in the fire several hours before. Lynch and Lyrr approached cautiously. Being out of the mountains was a little disconcerting for them. It felt like they were exposed. From a distance, they had seen movement within the structure and were curious as to who might be hanging around in the ruins.

As they reached the remaining wall, the door suddenly squeaked open. They tensed but discovered there was no one there. It was merely the wind blowing the door on its rusty hinges.

"I guess there isn't anyone here," said Lynch.

"Let's go in," said Lyrr. He held the door open and peeked inside. The main floor of the house was a pile of wreckage, but to the left was a stairway going down into the basement. He led the way down with Lynch maintaining a safe distance.

"There's nothing here, I tell you," insisted Lynch.

"We'll see," said Lyrr. He got to the bottom, and in the smoldering darkness he saw a figure moving in the shadows. When it saw the intruders, is dodged behind a partial cupboard.

Lynch coughed. "I can't breathe. There's nothing here."

"I saw something," hissed Lyrr. He made his way to the cupboard and looked behind it. Cowering in a tight ball was a goblin.

"Get up!" ordered Lyrr.

The goblin got up, shaking fearfully. "Don't hurt me! I'll share!" It looked past the lizardman to a pile of torn clothing and bones.

Lyrr looked at the bones and saw the remains of a human. He wrinkled his nose. "You can keep it. We just want to ask you a few questions."

"W-what?" asked the goblin.

"We're looking for a fire elemental," said Lynch. "Have you seen it?"

"I - I don't think so," stammered the goblin.

"Did you see anything or anyone unusual pass by here?" asked Lyrr. He looked at Lynch like he was a moron. The goblin probably didn't know what a fire elemental even looked like.

"There was a group of people who went by but they were far away," said the goblin. "There must have been lots of them because they had lots of torches."

Lynch and Lyrr exchanged glances. That could mean the presence of a fire elemental.

"How long ago was this?" asked Lyrr.

"About an hour ago," said the goblin, shrugging.

"We are closer than I thought," said Lynch.

"We aren't close enough," said Lyrr. "They're too close to the Tower of Hope now. We aren't safe anymore."

Lynch growled. "If I don't bring back that elemental, I'll never be able to show my face again. I'll be ruined!"

"We can't do anything more," said Lyrr. "The elemental got away and there's nothing we can do about it. We have to go back."

Lynch kicked the cupboard with vengeance. "That dirty invisible guy! If it wasn't for him, we would have the elemental in our custody."

"It was something you couldn't have foreseen," said Lyrr. "Come on. Let's go back and rethink what we're going to do next. It's not safe here. Human patrols could appear at any moment."

Lynch looked crestfallen as he followed Lyrr out of the farmhouse.

✗ ✗ ✗ ✗ ✗

Sawtooth left the meeting of the dark magic society of the elves in haste. She had a worried expression. The plan to infiltrate the Tower of Sorcery had been pushed ahead. Most of the other senior members of the society were happy with the plan, but she had reservations. Inferno had been acting strangely for some time now, and his insistence to get revenge on the human mages seemed out of place for his character. He was rarely vocal about issues that were beyond the realm of the elves, and he never used to be so eager to wage war before. Sure, the human mages were the first to be affected by the poison, but more study was needed to confirm that the humans were indeed responsible for it. Launching an all-out assault was a risky venture for all of them, especially since it could reveal many of their identities. But the plan seemed to be almost too good to fail, and Inferno's input into the planned assault was devious and cunning.

Cleaver was another one to watch out for, but not for the same reason. He was putting his efforts into finding spies within their midst, and Sawtooth was commissioned to assist him. She used her special magical perfume to obtain confessions from spies during interrogations. Sawtooth had contacts within the existing government, and he was relying on her to locate the leaks in their organization.

What Cleaver didn't know yet was that Sawtooth was a spy herself, sent to keep the king of the elves informed of the goings on within the dark magic society. Sawtooth had to find the occasional scapegoat to keep Cleaver from suspecting her as a spy. The king knew her job was critical, being included in the upper ranks of the society, so he supplied a few scapegoats for her to turn in from time to time. So far it had worked.

But now there was an event planned that the king would have to know about. It wasn't time for her appointed information briefing with the king, but she had to tell him what was going to happen right away. He needed to make a decision on whether or not to act.

If he acted in time, it would thwart a plan that was likely to create a rift between the humans and elves. It would involve a large number of the king's secret forces, and expose some of the principal figures in the dark magic society. It would almost surely expose Sawtooth herself. She would be expelled from the society by the survivors of the failed conspiracy. They might even kill her. Worse still, the king's secret forces would see her as just another black mage without her dark green ring. It was her insignia of her allegiance to the king, and without it she was indistinguishable from the other black mages. Someone had stolen it, she was sure, but she had no idea who the thief was. The ring also had the power to instantly summon a dozen of the king's secret forces with the proper incantation.

On the other hand, if the king didn't act, innocent people could get killed, and the elves would be blamed for the atrocities committed against the humans for no apparent reason. The peace the elves shared with the humans would disintegrate into enmity and war. The dwarves would remain neutral, but make huge profits supplying both sides with arms. With the present allies feuding, the creatures in the mountains would become bolder and begin to re-assimilate the outside lands bit by bit. True, the humans would suffer the worst of this, but sooner or later the elves would have to deal with the monsters, and no one would come to their aid. Humans could be negotiated with. Monsters could not.

Sawtooth passed through the last magical door and climbed some stairs. At the top, she pushed up the floor board of a local barber shop and stepped into the back room. It was dark, but her keen eyesight helped her navigate her way to the front door. Then she undid the lock with a quick spell and stepped into the dark streets. The door closed behind her without a sound, and she relocked it using the same magic. Sawtooth turned to face the uncanny damp early morning air. It was so damp that she was drenched even though it wasn't raining. But instead of heading in the direction of home, she turned and headed for the king's castle. The king had to know. He wouldn't like being disturbed at this odd hour, but there was no helping it. The only question left in her mind was - should she tell him about the stolen ring?

Part IV

The Gathering of Evil

Chapter 30

The dragon was in a bind. The cavern where he had eaten his fill of lizardmen had many tunnels leading away from it, but none of the paths were large enough to accommodate his great bulk. The only way out of there was to follow the underground river. It wasn't the most comfortable path to travel, but he could handle getting wet. The stench of the poisoned water was dissipating, now that the fresh water was running down the underground river to replace the poisoned water that had run before it. Several smaller streams had diverted from the river, but the tunnels they followed were too small for a dragon to traverse. Hours later he had reached the end of the line. The river did not end below ground, as he had expected, but was actually a little above sea level. He knew this because he could smell the fresh air coming in as the flow of the river exited the mountain. He could also hear the river's water splash into the waters of North Lake not far below.

But that was as far as he could go. The river tunnel opening was too shallow for him to go past. The water here actually reached the top of the ceiling before exiting the mountain with a fairly loud roar. If he attempted to go out with the rushing water, he would be crushed like an ant against the unrelenting cavern roof. He couldn't even get close enough to the opening to see if it was night or day outside. The river's flow was simply too strong.

In rage, he blasted at the opening with his fiery breath. This did nothing to the surrounding rock other than blackening it somewhat. A moment of steam from the water was instantly dissipated by the inflow of air. He was trapped and there was no escape.

The dragon sat on a flat rock at the side of the river for a number of hours trying to think of a way to escape the grip of the unrelenting mountain. At last he fell asleep.

He did not know how long he had been asleep when he sensed

something nudging him. He awoke with a start. Beside him on the rock sat a unicorn.

"Good morning," said the unicorn politely.

"Who are you?" asked the dragon sleepily. He was not pleased at being woken up.

"You know very well who I am," said the unicorn.

"Oh, yes," said the dragon in recognition. "You're Frosty."

"Very good," said Frosty. He looked intently at the dragon but said nothing.

At last the dragon spoke up. "What do you want?" he snapped. He did not like being stared at.

"I need you to come with me," said Frosty calmly.

"Where?" demanded the dragon.

"You'll see," said Frosty. "First, you have to change back into a human."

The dragon laughed. "I can't. The mage is dead. I'm a dragon for good." He looked at the unicorn and sniffed him. "You know, you smell like a delicious meal. Maybe I'll have you for breakfast."

"I think you'd better let Kazin take control," said Frosty frostily. "You can't stay like this forever."

The dragon laughed again. "He's gone! Dead! That's why I'm in control."

"Kazin is still alive," said Frosty. "I can sense him."

"He's dead," insisted the dragon.

"He's alive," insisted Frosty. "You just don't want to admit it."

"He's dead!" growled the dragon menacingly. "And so are you in a moment!"

"Look within and you will see Kazin is still alive," said Frosty calmly.

"No," said the dragon.

"Yes," countered Frosty.

"I'm not going to waste time arguing with you!" snapped the dragon. He opened his jaws and blasted Frosty with a flurry of flames. When the smoke cleared, the unicorn stood there unharmed and unmarked.

"You can't harm me that easily," said Frosty with infuriating calm. "Now let Kazin take control."

"No!" snapped the dragon. "You can't make me do it!"

"Do you want to get out of here?" asked the unicorn.

"Yes!" cried the dragon. "Help me get out of here and I'll let you live!"

"Let Kazin take control or I'll let you sit here until you die."

"You wouldn't!" shrieked the dragon. "You wouldn't abandon Kazin!"

"So you admit Kazin is still alive," said Frosty matter-of-factly.

"I didn't say that!" cried the dragon.

"You knew my name," said Frosty.

"So?" said the dragon

"How do you know?" asked the unicorn.

The dragon paused to reflect. "I'm not sure."

"Kazin told you," said Frosty. "He's within you. Don't you hear the voice inside your head?"

"What voice?" asked the dragon.

"Can't you hear it? I can."

The dragon listened. Then he heard it. It was faint but noticeable. The mage was still alive. "Nooo!" shrieked the dragon. "It can't be!" He spun on the unicorn and blasted him with another series of flames. He continued until his breath was spent. Panting in exhaustion, the dragon saw the air clear and the annoying unicorn standing before him unharmed.

"Do you give up yet?" asked Frosty.

The dragon lost his patience and lunged angrily at the unicorn, but Frosty was ready. He sprouted wings and flew aside. The dragon could not stop his forward momentum, and splashed headlong into the river. The current grabbed the immense beast and propelled him helplessly toward the cavern opening.

The dragon couldn't fight the current and knew he was doomed to die if he kept his form. There was no chance to think. Without any other choice, he transformed into the human mage due to his overwhelming desire for survival. Only the mage's small body would have a chance to survive the exit from the mountains.

Frosty plunged into the water with the mage and grabbed hold of the inert body of Kazin. As they cleared the opening, Frosty sprouted his wings and lifted the mage clear of the waterfall to avoid plummeting into the depths below. A moment later, the unicorn was airborne and flying toward the Tower of the Moon as fast as he could go.

✗ ✗ ✗ ✗ ✗

Malachi surveyed the activity below and wondered if the effort would be worthwhile. The rain had stopped momentarily, but the dark clouds remained. The wind had also increased, whipping the cleric's robe about his ankles. In the distance, he could see another contingent of soldiers herding villagers from the communities up north to the safety of the Tower of Hope. Their torch was particularly bright in the darkness.

"I'm amazed at the progress they're making," said Mara.

Malachi jumped and turned to look at the grey mage. "Oh - Mara! You startled me."

"Sorry," said Mara. "I can't blame you for being jumpy."

Malachi sighed and looked northward toward the dark clouds. "This is a troubling time," he said. "I don't know if we'll make it through this time."

"I have some news to cheer you up," said Mara.

Malachi returned his attention to the grey mage. "I'm listening."

"All of the available grey mages at the Tower of the Sky are on their way. The ships departed from the western ports and should be here in a day or so."

Malachi sighed dejectedly. "I just hope they arrive in time. If they're late, they'll find the Tower of Hope in ruins. There's no knowing when the enemy will get here, or even if they're coming. I'm amazed they haven't already shown up. It shouldn't have taken them so long to travel this way. My scouts haven't reported any sightings, but I don't expect we'll have much advance warning either way. The uncertainty is driving me up the wall."

"You've weathered battles like this before," reminded Mara.

"Sure," said Malachi. "But this time our magical ability may not be enough to defend against the magic of our attackers. No offence intended," he added.

"Our magic may not be as potent as the black mages' magic," said Mara, "but my people can combine offensive and defensive magic quite effectively. We just need to change our tactics and concentrate on our strengths."

Malachi nodded. "That's why we're building a moat. It prevents us from going on the offensive, but also hinders the enemy from charging the tower. It's primarily intended to hold back the earth elemental, against whom we have no defense. The earth elemental won't cross water."

"I think it's ruthless," said Mara, "to use an elemental to fight their war for them. It's inhuman."

"Lizardmen aren't human," reminded Malachi.

"Obviously," said Mara.

"The moat is almost complete," said Malachi, changing the subject. "It's almost time to fill it with water from North Lake."

"How did you manage to get so many people to pitch in?" asked Mara. "There seems to be a lot of people working on it."

"We offered additional rations of clean water," explained Malachi, "as well as more dwarven ale. Most people were only too eager to help. There are also plenty of other volunteers that are arriving in droves from other parts of the land. By now word has spread everywhere and people are bolstering General Larsen's army. We need every able-bodied soldier we can get."

"And still you don't think it will be enough?" asked Mara.

Malachi sighed. "I don't know. We need a miracle. A dragon would be nice."

"You mean like Arch Mage Kazin?" asked the grey mage.

"Yes," said Malachi. "Ever since he went into the mountains, we haven't heard from him. Even his familiar has no idea where he is. I hope nothing has happened to him."

"The familiar was the unicorn I saw yesterday?"

"Yes," answered Malachi. "I sent the unicorn off to the Tower of the Moon late yesterday with some samples of the dwarven spirits, as well as a stash of wildhorn leaves and faelora. Hopefully it's enough to get them to find a cure for the disease." The high cleric clenched his jaw. "If I could just stop the dying."

"There's no point fretting about things that are beyond our control," admonished Mara. "Let's concentrate on things we can do to win this war."

Malachi seemed to gain some strength from Mara's optimism. "Quite right, Mara. Quite right."

The high cleric was about to lead the way back down the steps into the courtyard to continue handing out extra rations, when he noticed the latest contingent of soldiers escorting some people past the usual assignment posts for newcomers. As they approached the tower's gates, he could make out a white-cloaked figure and a large figure with light greenish skin among them. He couldn't believe his eyes. Taking the steps two at a time, the high cleric worked his way down to the gates. They were just opening as he arrived and he huffed and puffed from the exertion of his run.

Mara caught up to him shortly after and watched the small group of people enter the courtyard with interest. A cleric with a dirty white robe entered, followed by a cyclops, a dwarf, an elf, and a brightly flaming figure who shifted nervously in the presence of so many magic wielders. The last figure was the most unusual and drew the most stares from those who had assembled to gawk at the newcomers.

"Vera!" exclaimed Malachi when he recognized the cleric. He stepped forward and embraced her warmly. "Thank heaven you're alright!"

"I'm fine," said Vera with a weak voice.

Malachi looked over at the cyclops without fear of being paralyzed, but the cyclops looked away out of habit. "Cyril! I've missed you! How are you doing?"

"I'm fine," said Cyril, not sure how to react now that he was back.

Vera introduced Rebecca and Alric and Malachi shook their hands warmly. Alric had a disappointed expression on his face, as though he did not find what he had been looking for.

When Vera introduced Tyris, it was Malachi who was unsure how to react.

"Do not use summoning magic," said Tyris in a low voice.

"You are safe here," said Malachi. "We do not even know how to summon a being like yourself. It has been generations since we had the ability, if ever."

Tyris nodded.

Malachi then introduced Mara to the others.

"A pleasure," said Mara with a friendly nod.

"Did you run into Arch Mage Kazin by any chance?" asked Malachi. "He went looking for you after you left so suddenly."

Vera looked crestfallen. "He found us alright, and helped us immensely while we were looking for the source of the poison. But he got poisoned. He – he didn't make it."

Malachi gasped and his eyes widened. "That is grievous news indeed! He will be sorely missed by everyone. I was counting on him as much as everyone else."

"He instructed us to carry on, and that's what I intend to do," said Vera fervently.

"His good advice will be heeded," said Malachi seriously. "Come! You must be tired and hungry. You shall all be washed and fed and we'll discuss your adventures inside!" He led the way into the tower and filled everyone in on the latest events at the tower.

Chapter 31

azin opened his eyes and tried to adjust to the bright daylight coming in from the window to his right. It wasn't exactly bright to the other occupants in the room, considering the dark, dreary cloud cover outside, but for someone who had been unconscious for a long time, it was more than enough. He closed his eyes again. Beside him, he heard some voices chanting softly.

"He's awake!" whispered a feminine voice nearby.

The other voices stopped chanting and Kazin felt someone lean close over him. "Are you sure?"

"I just saw him open his eyes for a second," said the first voice.

Kazin took a deep breath and opened his eyes again. He squinted at the familiar face of Vera.

"Kazin? Kazin!" cried Vera excitedly. She turned to the others behind her. "It's true! He's awake! We did it!" She suddenly started weeping uncontrollably, hours of strenuous healing magic taking its toll on her frail body.

"Now, now, child," said an older woman calmly. She put her arm around the cleric and gently led her from the room.

"Martha?" murmured Kazin, recognizing the voice of the druid.

"Yes," said another voice above him. It was the first voice he had heard.

Kazin let his eyes adjust for a few more seconds. "Milena?"

"I guess I'll let you two talk," said a new voice. It was Adriana. She stood up and left the room, closing the door behind her.

"Hello, Kazin," said Milena softly when the other druid had gone. "Welcome back to the land of the living."

"Where am I?" asked Kazin. He tried to sit up but his strength hadn't returned yet.

Milena puffed up his pillow and gently pushed him back down on the bed. "Rest for a while, Kazin. You'll gain your strength faster that way. In answer to your question, you're in the Tower of the Moon. Frosty brought you out of the mountains. You were in rough shape."

Kazin tried to recall the events since the dragon took control of him. The images that came to mind were fuzzy and intermittent. He shook his head in an attempt to clear his mind. "It's good to see you again," said Kazin, concentrating on Milena's face instead. He remembered their previous adventure where Milena had achieved her status as a druid.

"I'm happy to see you too," said Milena. "It's been a long time. Too bad it's during another emergency. You have a habit of getting into the thick of things."

Kazin tried a weak smile. "That's me." His smile vanished and he looked more closely at the druid. Her face was haggard looking and she appeared exhausted. "You look awful."

Milena smiled a warm smile, despite her condition. "I've been in healing mode since I got here." Then she frowned. "Mermaids are dying in droves."

Kazin shook his head sadly. "How did Vera get here?" he asked, changing the subject.

"She caught a ride on a griffin," said Milena. "So did Mara, the head grey mage."

"Why?" asked Kazin.

"We have a plan to create an antidote for the poison," said Milena. "We need an experienced representative of each branch of magic to succeed. We sent the griffins to pick up Mara and Vera. I'll represent the druids. That leaves the black mage. With you awake, we're just about ready to make our attempt."

"You said 'experienced representatives'," interrupted Kazin. "You and I are experienced, and so is Mara as a grey mage, but are you sure Vera is up to the task? Not to speak against her, but she's only a level one cleric."

Milena nodded. "I thought the same thing when she first got here. But it was the griffin who chose her. Apparently, the griffin was unwilling to let any of High Cleric Malachi's senior clerics mount it. It only stood still when Vera neared it. She was the only one it would allow on its back. In retrospect, it may have had to do with the fact that she had met the water elemental previously. The griffin knew the water elemental was going to be summoned, and a cleric who had previous contact with that elemental was preferable to one that did not. Those griffins have the strange ability to sense these things. They're smart creatures, but they can be very stubborn at times."

Kazin nodded. "So you were just waiting for me to wake up." The mage's strength was rapidly returning and he pushed himself up to a seated position. This time Milena didn't stop him.

"There is one more attendee we need at this event," said Milena. "You're not the only one we needed to work on."

"Who's that?" asked Kazin.

"The water elemental," answered Milena. "It's critical to have that elemental present for the cure to be created. We've attempted to summon it a few times while you were on your way here, but without success. It must still be weak from its time in the mountains. But Frosty senses the elemental is getting stronger all the time. He figures we will succeed very soon."

"Then we should give it a try," said Kazin. He started to get out of bed, but this time Milena pushed him back down. "Not so fast. It's our turn to get some rest now. We put in a considerable effort in reviving you. None of us are ready to perform a summoning spell at this point in time. While we rest, you should too. Apparently, you'll need to channel a lot of your magical energy to help create the cure."

Kazin looked around and spotted his staff in its sheath nearby. The green orb atop the staff was still intact. A moment of trepidation swept over him but disappeared as quickly as it came. He was in control now. The dragon's voice inside his head was a mere whisper. It would not take over again anytime soon if he could help it.

Milena started for the door. "I'm glad Frosty was right about the poison."

"What do you mean?" asked Kazin.

The druid stopped and turned to regard the mage. Her face held a look of surprise. "You mean you don't know?"

Kazin shook his head and stared at her blankly.

Milena's face became thoughtful. "Now it's starting to make sense," she mumbled.

Kazin looked at her quizzically.

"The poison was never a threat to your life, Kazin."

Kazin wrinkled his eyebrows. "Huh?"

Milena took a few steps closer to the bed. "The poison doesn't affect lizardmen, right?"

"Yeah, so?"

"Why do you think you're able to open the lizardmen's portals?" continued the druid.

"I use magic," said Kazin.

"Where does that magic come from?" asked Milena.

"It comes from within," said Kazin. "I guess the dragon within me -." He broke off, his eyes opening wide as the realization crept over him.

"Dragons are physically related to lizardmen," said Milena.

"And by taking on the form of a dragon, my immune system cleared the poison from my body!" finished Kazin. "If I had just thought of that sooner!"

Milena nodded. "I thought you had figured that out when Vera told me you sent her away because you were planning to change into a dragon. She thought you were going to die, and so, apparently, did you."

Kazin put his hands over his face and groaned. "I'm such a fool!"

Milena patted his shoulder. "Nobody's perfect. I'm just glad you're still alive. If the dragon hadn't asserted itself, you could have died, never knowing the cure was within your grasp."

Kazin pulled his hands away from his face. He looked grim. "That doesn't make me feel a whole lot better."

Milena laughed. "I suppose you're right. Even my bedside manner is failing. It's time I got some rest. I'd better go." She turned and left the room.

Kazin lay back on the bed but he was not the least bit tired. The 'revive' magic the druids had used on him made him too energetic to lie around. He decided to get up and walk around instead.

He threw the blankets aside and stood up. His robe was on the dresser so he threw it around his shoulders. His shoes were nowhere to be found so he padded over to the door in his bare feet. The stone floor was cold but not unduly so. Opening the door, he peeked into the hallway. Nobody was around. The mage entered the hallway and finally had his chance to explore the Tower of the Moon at a leisurely pace. He passed several closed doors and peeked into the open ones. Most rooms had beds with unknown figures hidden beneath the blankets.

A treeman suddenly appeared in the hallway ahead of him, and Kazin wondered if it had enough room to get past him. Instinctively, he pressed himself against the wall as the treeman approached him. With practiced ease, the treeman deftly stepped around the mage. Not a single branch or twig made contact with Kazin as the treeman glided past. Only a slight breeze indicated the treeman had passed by. Kazin marveled at the magical creature. The druids had such command over the forces of nature that it still boggled his mind.

A while later, Kazin paused at the room with the heavy, expensive lavender carpet and the walls full of paintings. He studied the scenes of dragons and soldiers and intense battles that were a depiction of the dragon wars many generations ago. His eyes were drawn to the painting prominently displayed over the fireplace. It was the one he had noticed the last time he was here. It still gave him the creeps. The wizened old mage had such a fierce, intense expression that Kazin was instantly afraid of him. But at the same time, he looked familiar. Kazin knew this mage. He had seen him before, but where? No arch mages looked like that. There were no master mages with the kind of magical aura that this mage had.

A noise behind him made Kazin turn. A treeman went past, carrying an inert form bundled in a blanket. A visible piece of tail fin protruded from the blanket, giving away the identity of its occupant. Another mermaid had perished.

Kazin sighed and followed the emotionless treeman until he came to a tight hallway that led to the stairs of the roof altar. He let the treeman continue down the main hallway, while he took the secondary path. He climbed the stairs and attempted to open the trap door to the roof. Fortunately, it wasn't magically locked or otherwise. As soon as the door was pushed up, a strong gust of wind wrenched it from the mage's hands and blew it open the rest of the way.

It hit the roof with a loud bang that was louder than the howling wind itself. Kazin climbed onto the roof, fighting to keep the wind from ripping his cloak away.

On the roof, he saw Mara, the grey mage, struggling to prepare some items in preparation for the summoning spell. He went over to assist her. When the grey mage saw Kazin, she immediately stood up as a sign of respect for the arch mage.

Kazin smiled. "Hi, Mara. It's been a really long time, hasn't it?" He had to yell to be heard above the wind.

Mara smiled back. "Yes. Last time we met, you were just an ordinary, impulsive mage. Now look at you."

"A lot has changed," yelled Kazin. A sustained gust of wind tried to roll over a heavy sack at Mara's feet and Kazin and Mara struggled to push it back into position. A nearby stone slab was the only convenient item, so Mara held the bag while Kazin pulled the stone up against it to support it.

"Let's go inside!" yelled Mara when that task was done.

Kazin nodded and followed the grey mage inside. Another battle with the wind ensued as Kazin attempted to close the trap door. He finally won that battle and the door slammed shut, eliminating the outdoor noise with it. At the bottom of the stairs, Kazin rejoined Mara and they walked down the hallway. As they went, Mara told Kazin of the latest events as she had perceived them on her journey north to the Tower of Hope.

Kazin was shocked at how widespread the poison was. He was also surprised at the effects of the dwarven spirits. "That's fascinating, Mara! Those dwarven spirits may be part of the answer to a cure!"

"That's why the druids had me prepare the spirits as well as the faelora herbs for the summoning. If the water elemental is truly that weak, we may need to have those ingredients ready at the spur of the moment in order to create the cure."

"Good thinking," said Kazin. "I guess the druids had time to think things through."

"I just hope we can pull it off," said Mara.

"So do I," said Kazin. "I hate seeing so many lives being lost."

"Me too," said Mara. "I just hope it will be worth the effort."

"What do you mean?" asked Kazin.

Mara stopped and turned to the arch mage. "We may be saving people from the poison in time to be massacred by the creatures emanating from the mountains." She went into detail about the loss of the outposts north of the Tower of Hope.

Kazin was aghast. "I'll bet that was what they were planning all along! They needed to weaken the human mages in order to have the upper hand when they attacked! Their strategy was so successful they spread the poison across the whole land! Now all they have to do is walk in and seize control!"

"Not if the grey mages can help it," intoned Mara. "We are more numerous than black and white mages combined, and fewer of us were affected by the poison. We were far enough south that we had enough advance warning, so we took the proper precautions. Most of the grey mages are poison free."

Kazin nodded. "That's encouraging news, Mara. Your mages are the last line of defense for humankind."

"High Cleric Malachi has sent a plea to the dwarves and elves for military aid, but there was still no reply when I left," added Mara. "I doubt they will be able to help in time anyway. The High Cleric expects the attack at any time. Scouts were sent out to investigate the edge of the mountains for activity. Not very many returned, but those who did encountered a darkness so fearful and a wind so powerful they fled in terror. Something is going to happen and we won't see it coming until the last possible moment."

"I would be more useful there," said Kazin. "By flying as a dragon, I would be extremely useful in scouting as well as fighting."

Mara gave the arch mage a curious stare. "Are you sure you want to change into a dragon again so soon?"

Kazin shook his head. "I don't want to, but wanting to and having to are two very different things. I have the ability, so it should be used if it's needed."

"That's true," admitted Mara, "if you look at it that way. But I'm guessing you're needed here first. I'm sure the druids will let you go as soon as the cure is completed."

"As long as the water elemental can be summoned," said Kazin. "If it takes too long, I may have to leave anyway."

"It won't come to that," said a voice behind them.

The mages spun around to face the speaker.

"Frosty!" exclaimed Kazin. "I understand I have you to thank for rescuing me!"

Frosty held his head high at the instant recognition and praise. "Of course! Saving you from yourself is no easy task!"

The irony was not lost on Kazin. "I owe you big time for this, Frosty."

"Naturally," said Frosty sullenly. "It's not easy being your familiar."

"I'm sure it isn't," said Kazin humbly.

Frosty affectionately nudged Kazin with his nose and Kazin avoided the clear, white horn. Making contact with the magical tine would result in a painful, hot sensation. There was more magic stored in that horn than Kazin wanted to know.

Kazin petted the soft white mane of his familiar. "How did you know I was still alive when you came to rescue me, Frosty?" he asked.

"If you were dead, I would cease to exist," said Frosty. "I'm your familiar, remember?"

"Oh, yeah," said the mage.

"While I was looking for you, I was tracking your essence," continued the unicorn. "That led me to the dragon. The dragon claimed you were dead, so I tricked it into sensing your spirit within. As soon as the dragon sensed you, so did I. Let's just say the dragon didn't take it very well when he found that out."

Kazin could only shake his head in amazement. "And you determined that the dragon was my cure for the poison."

"It was the only conclusion I could come up with," said Frosty. "I'm surprised you didn't make the connection yourself."

"Nobody's perfect," said Kazin bashfully, using Milena's line.

✗ ✗ ✗ ✗ ✗

In the gloom below, Graf surveyed the gathering forces with

305

satisfaction. Thousands of orcs, ogres, goblins and lizardmen had congregated at the foot of the Old Dwarven Mountains. Many more were still arriving. The scene was even more imposing with the violent thunder and lightning, and driving torrents of rain. Torches sputtered and flickered in the perpetual gloom. Suddenly Narg, the lizardmage in charge of the earth elemental, appeared. Narg's nostrils flared under the strain of summoning magic, but he had help. He led a throng of lizardmen who chanted their magic around a large, brown, rock-like creature some thirty feet high. Its face was similar to a human female.

The creature - the earth elemental - was no longer encased in ice, and was now totally under the control of the lizardmen. As it exited the protection of the mountains, it looked up at the thunderous skies above and moaned. The moan was so loud and sorrowful that it sank deep into the earth. The resulting earthquake was so severe that most of the gathered forces below fell to the ground. Graf himself would have fallen had it not been for Slong, his general, who caught him before he fell.

Graf re-established his footing and yanked his arm from Slong. He glowered at his general with a look of hatred. "When I need help, I'll ask for it!" he hissed.

"As you wish," answered Slong indifferently. He knew Graf well enough to know that he wasn't going to show any gratitude.

Though the earth elemental had a woman's face, the rest of the body was less defined. The body was made of rocks and earth, and tended to grind and undulate as it moved forward. The arms and legs were huge, and mighty fists at the ends of the arms were like giant battering rams. The ground shook as it walked to a designated spot behind the army.

The air elemental made its debut next. If the appearance of the earth elemental was terrifying, the appearance of the air elemental was unnerving. The air elemental emerged from the mountains with a similar crew of summoners surrounding it. Emanating from a cylindrical bowl in the middle of the summoners, the air elemental seemed to be gliding along of its own accord. It wasn't hard to see this elemental from a distance, because it stood about five times higher than everything around it except for the earth elemental. It undulated so one couldn't make out its features clearly, and the whirlwind it emitted was so intense, the lizardmages who surrounded it had difficulty walking with their robes whipping about their feet. Upon exiting the mountains, the air elemental seemed to grow as it absorbed the surrounding air as though feeding on it. It virtually doubled in size. It was a formidable sight to those who had already been assembled. .

Following the procession was Narla, the lizardmage in charge of the air elemental. Her navy cloak with purple trim whipped mercilessly around her ankles, but she strode tall and proud. She looked up to where Graf stood with his general and grinned with her fish-like lips. She was showing off her skills as a summoner and appeared to be enjoying herself.

Graf barely grinned back and turned to his general. "How long before the forces are ready to march?"

"We should be ready by noon tomorrow," answered Slong. He squinted into the foreboding sky. It was only a few hours after noon, but the dark skies hid any sunlight, making it seem like night rather than day. It wasn't going to get any lighter.

"You should raze any farms and villages," stated Graf. "Let the army seize whatever spoils they wish. Try to recruit dissatisfied humans by offering them clean water. Attack the Tower of Hope and then head east for the Tower of Sorcery."

Slong nodded. He did not need Graf to repeat his orders.

"Meet me there as soon as you can," continued Graf.

Slong straightened at this comment. "Aren't you coming?"

Graf gave a sinister grin. "I'm going to soften up those puny human mages for you."

"By yourself?" asked the general incredulously.

Graf continued grinning. "Not alone, but with some unlikely allies."

"May I ask who?" asked Slong.

"You'll see soon enough," said Graf cryptically.

Slong sighed. Graf wasn't letting him in on his plan. It didn't really matter; as long as he succeeded.

"I have to prepare," said Graf after enjoying his assembled army for a few more minutes. He turned and entered the tunnel behind him as another earthquake rocked the mountain. The deluge he left behind him came down even harder.

At the outer edge of the gathered forces, two sets of eyes watched with interest as Graf departed.

"He's not going?" asked Lynch.

Lyrr shook his head. "I don't think so. It looks like Graf has other plans."

"I wonder what he's up to," said Lynch.

Lyrr looked over at Lynch. His own curiosity was aroused as well. "Why don't we try to find out?"

Lynch shrugged. "What would it gain us?"

"We might learn something that can give us an edge over the other senior lizardmages. It might also give us an opportunity to help Graf and make him forget about your failure to catch the fire elemental."

Lynch looked at Lyrr. His goal of moving up in the hierarchy of the lizardmen's realm was always in the back of his mind. "Who said anything about helping Graf?" To him, Graf was just in the way of the ultimate goal – being the ultimate ruler of their kind.

This hint wasn't lost on Lyrr. He leered.

"Let's see what we can find out," said Lynch. He led the way back into the tunnels nearby.

Lyrr's leer became even wider. This was going to be fun.

Chapter 32

s the contingent of grey mages disembarked just west of the Tower of Hope, Jerrin, a grey mage, studied the preparations that had been made for the inevitable war. Thousands of people scurried about in various duties in and around the tower. The moat, now full of water, lay north of the tower. It spanned some fifty feet across and stretched well past the tower to the west. At various intervals, archer towers were hastily erected to enhance the protection of ground troops. Large bunkers were constructed on both sides of the moat. That meant the bulk of the fighting force would start ahead of the moat and only fall back behind the moat if a retreat was ordered. The makeshift bridges across the moat were designed to be collapsed once all allies were safely back across the water barrier. It wasn't exactly professional looking, but it did look effective. Considering what little time was available, it was a major feat nonetheless.

Jerrin set foot on the muddy shore of North Lake and sloshed through the muck toward the tower, along with hundreds of other grey mages. It wasn't raining at the moment, but the wind was bitterly cold as it cut through his drenched grey cloak.

At the tower, Jerrin presented a letter to the sentry at one of the check in booths. He was then separated from his companions, who were led off to the thousands of tents sprawled around the Tower of Hope. Most of the tents were set up south of the tower, away from where the fighting was to occur. A number of grey mages had provided a large supply of new tents for everyone as Mara had requested.

Jerrin was led to the tower gates where another guard, a senior ranking official, inspected the note. With a grunt, Jerrin was admitted past the portcullis into the tower's courtyard. From here, a cleric took charge of the guest and led him to the tower itself.

The tower was awesome to behold, especially by someone who had never seen its glass-like pinnacles before. The interior of the building was spectacular in its own right, the shiny white walls lit by the shafts of light that filtered down from above. The unique design of the tower allowed it to be brighter inside than out, and even a murky day like this one provided adequate light to see by.

Jerrin's heart filled with sorrow at the thought of this great structure being lost to the war. He resolved to do his part in trying to preserve this great piece of history.

The grey mage was told to wait in the main lobby, so he looked around at the paintings on the walls. A strange statue of an older man stood off to one side and Jerrin wondered what significance it had. His examination of the realistic features of the man was cut short as a heavy set cleric hastened toward him.

"Good afternoon!" panted the cleric. He proffered his hand. "My name is High Cleric Malachi. I understand Mara sent for you specifically?"

Jerrin shook the high cleric's hand. "Yes. My name is Jerrin."

Malachi nodded. "I understand you have a sound understanding of warfare and sieges?"

Jerrin nodded. "Yes. I've studied many writings dating back to ancient times and have some actual experience fighting at the Tower of Strength and the battle at Marral."

"Good!" said Malachi. "Your experience as a grey mage warrior is sorely needed. It will be up to the grey mages to save the Tower of Hope. Are you aware of the fate of many of the black mages?"

Jerrin nodded. "I've already been briefed."

"Good," repeated Malachi.

Jerrin looked around. "Where's Mara?"

"She's on an important mission," said Malachi. "Her services are required with the druids in the Tower of the Moon. They need her magic to help create a cure for the plague."

"The 'Tower of the Moon'?" asked Jerrin. "It actually exists?"

Malachi smiled patiently. "Yes. Its location is still somewhat of a mystery, but -."

His comment was cut off when a deep-rooted tremor suddenly shook the tower and its battlements. The high cleric instinctively grabbed hold of Jerrin's shoulder to keep from being thrown down. Minor debris tumbled from the ceiling above them.

Malachi had a look of horror on his face. "That's the first time in a while we've had had such a tremor! I fear the time is near at hand." He looked into Jerrin's eyes. "What do you know about elementals, Jerrin?"

Jerrin narrowed his eyes. "Not much. Why?"

Malachi put his arm around Jerrin's shoulders and began leading him away. "Because, my son, that is what we're up against."

"Tell me what you know," said Jerrin anxiously. Whatever preconceived ideas he had before arriving here were about to change drastically.

Meanwhile, outside, soldiers had the gruesome task of cleaning up the bodies of several skink warriors who had fallen off the battlements during the latest earthquake . . .

✗ ✗ ✗ ✗ ✗

The wind had diminished considerably as the spell casters gathered atop the Tower of the Moon in preparation for the summoning spell. The sky was still mostly overcast, but the twilight created by the setting sun still gave off enough light to see by. Torches were lit a short distance away from the altar to provide light when the sun finally set. The supplies of dwarven ale, wildhorn leaves, and faelora were ready beside the altar. The three druids were dressed in their usual dark blue robes. They stood around the altar, separated by each of the other mages. Vera had on her white robe, almost glowing clean since her exit from the mountains. Her robe was as white as Frosty, who stood back, well out of the way of the summoners. Mara wore her grey cloak while Kazin wore his black one. Behind the mages on the ground lay their staves, which were needed later.

"Is everyone ready?" asked Martha, who stood to Kazin's right.

"I think so," said Vera. She stood between Adriana and Milena, who was on Kazin's left.

"Then let's hold hands," said Martha. She took hold of Kazin's right hand and Mara's left hand. Everyone else followed suit, taking hold of the hands of those next to them.

Adriana, who was directly across from Kazin, began a soft chant. Milena and Martha joined in. Their spell was uniform in pitch and loudness, rising and falling like a large wave in North Lake. The mood created by this was mesmerising, and made more eerie by the disappearing daylight. Kazin felt as though his very spirit was floating with the spell. Vera and Mara experienced similar sensations.

Unlike the air elemental, who was difficult for the druids to summon, the water elemental was a more familiar entity that they had experience calling to their plane of existence. Kazin half expected to see the druids sweating with the exertion of the spell as he had seen when the air elemental was called into being. But that was not the case with the water elemental.

Before long, a layer of water began to appear on the altar. It rose and fell with the chant of the summoners. With each rise it grew larger. Its form soon began to materialize. The entity's head rose above its humanoid torso. Even its features became evident. Kazin always thought mermaids were alluring, but this elemental was breathtaking in comparison.

"Why have I been summoned?" demanded the elemental when it was fully formed. Its body melded into the pool of water that rested atop the altar. The water should have run off the altar's surface, but seemed to be attached to the elemental by some unknown force.

Adriana stopped chanting and looked up at the magnificent being. "Greetings. We are the druids of the Tower of the Moon. We require your assistance to aid us in creating a cure for a lethal disease."

The elemental turned to look at the speaker. "I am aware of the disease of which you speak. It was I who was used against my will to create it."

"We know," said Adriana. "You cannot be held responsible for causing it. We are interested in curing it. You have been summoned that we might create a spell capable of healing those who are sick and dying."

The elemental paused before speaking. "You speak the truth," she said at last. "I know the order of the druids and I know you. You care about nature above all else. I sense your feeling of loss and grieve for you. I will help you in your endeavor. It is a noble cause and will balance the damage my magic has caused during my last summoning. But take heed! My strength is not fully returned! Your magic must be strong enough to enhance mine in order to create a spell of such significance!"

"We understand," said Adriana.

"You must gather the spell components," said the elemental. "They must be things you know to make even a slight difference to those who suffer this disease."

"We have the components ready," said Vera. Adriana seemed agitated when Vera spoke out of turn, but said nothing.

The elemental turned to regard the cleric. She recognized her immediately and her eyes widened. "You! Are you the cleric who saved me from the lizardmen?"

Vera looked embarrassed. "It wasn't just me. I had help."

"From the druids?"

Vera shook her head. "No. From my companions. They all contributed."

"Are they here?" asked the elemental.

"Only one of them," said Vera. She nodded her head in Kazin's direction. "Kazin."

The elemental turned her attention to Kazin and regarded him closely. "Curious. I did not expect a black mage to be one of my rescuers."

"I really didn't do much," said Kazin. "In fact, I was almost unconscious when you were released from the lizardmen."

"We wouldn't have been there if it wasn't for you, Kazin," interrupted Vera.

The elemental looked between the white and black mage with interest. "Such modesty! It is rare indeed to discover that no one wishes to claim that they rescued an elemental! Bring me your staves."

Vera let go of Adriana's and Milena's hands to pick up her staff while Kazin did the same. This left Milena chanting on her own. Thankfully, it didn't break the connection with the summoning spell. Seeing this, the others stopped holding hands as well.

As Vera presented her staff, the elemental asked what her name was. "Vera," said Vera.

"I am Ella," said the elemental.

Ella reached out and touched the clear staff for a split second. Then she put her arm down. When she spoke, it was with a deep, serious voice. "Vera the cleric, you now have increased ability with water-based spells. Those spells will be more potent, and less taxing to cast. You can learn all spells related to water, regardless of your rank as a cleric."

Vera stared at her staff in wonder. "Thank you!" she whispered in reverence.

The elemental turned to take hold of Kazin's outstretched staff but recoiled when she saw the orb atop the staff. "A dragon mage!" she exclaimed. "Do dragon mages still exist in this day and age?"

"I'm the only one that I know of," said Kazin quietly.

The elemental's eyes narrowed and she seemed to look right through the black mage. "There is some resemblance. Yes. It is unmistakable. You are the dragon mage." She straightened. "It is destiny that we meet here and now. You will need this!" With a movement so quick it was instantaneous, she swatted Kazin's staff with her right hand. On contact, a thick layer of mist sprayed everyone near the altar. When the mist settled, Kazin still stood there with the staff in his hands. The elemental undulated, its form unsettled, but soon reformed when Martha and Milena increased their summoning effort.

The elemental nodded. "There. Now your staff is enchanted. You must receive enchantment from the other elementals to ready yourself for your most difficult task."

"I don't understand," said Kazin.

"You will," said Ella, "in time."

"Ah, speaking of time, we need to work on the cure," interrupted Adriana.

The elemental turned to the druid. "Quite right. What ingredients have you got?"

Mara opened the nearby bags she had set up and drew out a sample of each thing. She described each item as she went. "We have faelora, which helps reduce the pain of suffering. And wildhorn leaves, which, when fermented as in this dwarven ale, cause the sick person to gain enough strength to get up and walk around. Of course, a side effect is intoxication."

Ella examined the contents in Mara's hands thoughtfully. She did not seem the least bit surprised at the discovery of the dwarven ale as a healing agent. "We can use the faelora and dwarven ale. The wildhorn leaves by themselves are useless."

"But we need three items to make the spell work properly," said Martha suddenly. The robust druid had stopped chanting. Immediately Adriana picked up where Martha had left off, adding her magic to Milena's.

"Yes," said the elemental. She turned to the black mage. "We have it right in front of our eyes."

"I don't understand," said Martha.

The elemental turned to Martha. "Lizardmen are immune to the poison. Their blood is part of the cure. Dragons are related. If we use a vial of Kazin's blood, we can accomplish our objective just as well, but with one added benefit. By using dragon blood, which is high in magical energy, we will only need to use it once. Once the spell is created, we can cast it with only the two other ingredients and achieve the same effect."

"Of course!" exclaimed Martha. "In the past, spells were constantly created using dragon blood, so that the spells could be cast with fewer ingredients thereafter!"

"Exactly," said Ella. The elemental turned to Vera.

"May I borrow your staff?"

Vera nodded and handed her the staff.

The elemental turned to Kazin. "I'll have to ask you to transform into a dragon for me in order to obtain the dragon blood. Only when you are in dragon form is your blood correct for this spell to work."

Kazin gulped. He wasn't entirely ready to do his transformation so soon. He was still leery of the dragon's previous control of him. Nevertheless, he knew this was too important to be postponed. He walked over to the edge of the tower to give himself more room. Then he transformed. He stretched out his neck so his head was directly in front of the elemental. The two beings were nearly the same size.

Calmly, the elemental used Vera's staff to touch Kazin's cheek. A word of magic was uttered and the bottom of Vera's staff turned red as it filled with Kazin's blood.

"Now pour a cup of dwarven ale and place a few faelora herbs in it," said Ella. She turned to regard the dragon's face. "You can change back again, Kazin."

Relieved, Kazin transformed back into his human form and approached the group while Mara quickly prepared the cup of ale and herbs and placed it in front of the elemental.

Then the elemental touched Vera's staff to the cup and spoke another word of magic. The blood in the staff poured into the cup to mix with the other ingredients.

"Do you have some magical words to use for the spell?" asked Ella.

"Yes," said Martha, "but I'm not sure of the order of the words or the proper inflections."

"Give me the words and I will sort them for you," said Ella. "Then you must listen to how I pronounce each syllable and repeat it after me." She looked at the two summoners. "You can stop your summoning. I will help of my own free will. You needn't worry that I will depart from you if you stop. We must work together on this."

Adriana and Milena stopped chanting.

"Ah, that's better!" said Ella in relief. "I should have just enough strength to do this." She looked at each of the gathered spell casters as she spoke. "You will need to channel your magic into the cup, one for each of the schools of magic - white, black, grey and druid. The remaining ones - I count two - will have to chant the spell correctly, over and over a total of ten times. After that, we won't know if the spell works unless we try it on someone who is sick."

"Already taken care of," said a voice behind them.

Everyone turned to see Frosty, his white coat reflected in the torchlight. No one had noticed how dark it had gotten since the elemental had been summoned. The clouds above parted for a moment, allowing the moon to shine down on the Tower of the Moon. The additional brightness revealed a mermaid lying at Frosty's feet.

"Perfect," said Ella. She turned to Martha. "The words?"

Martha said the words as they came to her.

"Very good," said the elemental. "This is how you cast it." She pronounced the words the way Adriana and Martha were supposed to say them with the proper inflections. They repeated them until the elemental was satisfied.

"One question," stammered Vera suddenly.

Everyone turned their attention to the cleric.

Vera looked ashamed as she spoke. "How do we channel our energy at the cup?"

Everyone looked at each other uncertainly and the elemental laughed. "Good point! What each of you must do is cast a powerful spell of your choosing at the cup, provided the spell is continuous and strictly from your school of magic. For the grey mage, your spell must consist of an equal combination of black and white magic. The more potent your magic is, the better the created spell will be. Do not worry about damaging the cup - I have already enchanted it. Your spell will not seem to affect the cup once the druids have begun. O.K.?"

Everyone murmured in understanding.

"Good," said Ella. "Let us begin." She nodded to Martha to begin. Adriana and Martha chanted the spell once, directing their magic at the cup. Then the elemental nodded to Kazin. "You may proceed."

Kazin raised his staff and pointed it at the cup. He had decided to use his favourite lightning bolt spell. It felt strange to cast it at a cup of ale with faelora floating on top, and despite the elemental's words, he expected it to blow up into a thousand pieces. That was not the case when the lightning bolt struck the cup. Instead, the energy seemed to be consumed within the liquid inside.

Martha and Adriana finished chanting the spell a second time and Kazin could feel the energy of another spell merge with his. Mara was casting a spell which mixed with his, traveling along his bolt spell and into the cup. He couldn't make out the spell she was casting.

The druids chanted a third time and then Vera cast her spell. It was a water-based spell that flowed along Kazin's bolt toward the cup. What happened next caught Kazin off guard and made him nearly stop his spell. His bolt of lightning had nearly vanished!

"Do not stop!" warned the elemental. "Your spells are from

different sources of magic and will seem to cancel each other out, but are still very much present."

Kazin obeyed. He knew his spell was working. He could feel as the energy left his staff.

The druids finished the spell for the fourth time and Milena cast her druid spell at the cup. Any lingering magic that was being cast at the cup was now completely invisible.

The four spell casters held onto their spells with all their might as the older druids repeated the main spell six more times. Upon completion of the tenth casting, all spell casting ceased at once. Everyone was startled by this instantaneous stoppage, expecting their spells to go on. It was then that they realized that a silence spell had been cast by the elemental.

Ella gracefully picked up the cup of ale. "It is finished. You may now use the ingredients to enhance the spell's effects." She held it out for Vera to take.

The cleric took the cup and approached the mermaid in front of Frosty. She dipped her hand into the cup and withdrew some moistened faelora. Then she squeezed out the ale while she shakily spoke the same words of healing magic that the druids had been chanting.

At first nothing happened and Vera was about to cry out in despair. Then the mermaid moved. The mermaid took a deep breath and opened her eyes. "Where am I?" she asked in a clear voice.

"You are at the top of the Tower of the Moon," said Frosty. "We tried to heal you. How do you feel?"

The mermaid smiled seductively. "I feel fine. May I go back into the water now?"

Vera turned to the others with tears of joy. "It worked!"

Mages and druids hugged one another with joy and relief. Countless lives had been lost since the outbreak, but now countless lives could once again be saved. They could now move forward to combat the disease across the entire land and sea. There was a new sense of hope in the air.

When the happiness of the moment had subsided, the mages and druids profusely thanked the water elemental for her help. Then the elemental left them and returned to her own realm to rest.

Adriana and Martha began to make preparations for healing the sick in the tower. Milena gathered what supplies the other druids could spare and prepared to fly a griffin back to her land where her people waited for her.

Kazin knew he was needed at the Tower of Hope, where war could already be underway. Mara and Vera chose to go along with him, anxious to spread word of the cure so that many others could be saved before it was too late. They rode on Kazin's back.

The dragon mage flew as fast as he could, his faithful familiar Frosty by his side.

Chapter 33

The scout galloped through the construction zone and across the moat bridge at full speed, the nostrils of his steed flaring with exertion. People scrambled to get out of the way as the horse and rider came thundering through. The sentries had seen his approach and the portcullis into the tower's courtyard was already open. The rider galloped through the opening and reigned in his horse. He jumped to the ground and approached the general, who was standing near one of the stairways that led up to the battlements.

General Larsen turned to the scout and braced himself for what he expected was bad news.

Jim Farnsworth stopped in front of his general and saluted. With a grim face, he said, "They're coming."

General Larsen needed no further information. He looked up to a soldier atop the battlements and bellowed, "Sound the Horn!"

The lone trumpeter raised his shiny brass trumpet to his lips and blew the dreaded notes that signaled everyone it was time to prepare for war.

Soldiers ran to the armoury to obtain their weapons, while clerics rushed to bring the most critically ill people into the shelter of the courtyard. Civilians were directed away from the construction sites to several tents housing various types of implements designed for construction and farming. These tools were now distributed with a different purpose in mind - battle.

Things appeared a bit chaotic at first, but everything became more organized as lieutenants saw to it that everyone knew what they had to do.

Skink warriors, grey mages, and clerics paced along the battlements, the last line of defense for the Tower of Hope. Many of the mages wished they had been assigned to the ground force to fight alongside their comrades. It was luck of the draw that they wound up here. But their job was just as vital as anywhere else.

General Larsen's archers were occupying hastily erected towers along the moat to assist the ground forces where needed. The towers were vulnerable near the front lines, so a cleric was positioned with each contingent of archers to provide a shield from opposing magical forces.

The ground forces were set up so that at least one soldier was accompanied by three or four civilians. There was also at least one mage, grey or white, among every six groups of soldiers and civilians. Some people argued that by splitting forces like this they were weakening themselves too much, but both General Larsen and High Cleric Malachi knew that the large scale magic the lizardmen were capable of could easily damage a strong, tightly grouped fighting force. Splitting them up would force the lizardmen into using individual magic to eliminate opposition one at a time, making it harder and more time consuming for them to advance. There would be more one-on-one battles fought, giving the white and grey mages a fighting chance.

Malachi observed the commotion from the optimum vantage point along the battlements. The ranks of soldiers and fighters formed rapidly, and their formations looked impressive from above. Malachi grew even more impressed as the forces continued to gather. In a matter of minutes, the thousands assembled below swelled to tens of thousands. The high cleric had to use his looking glass just to see the forces making up the front lines. It was the biggest force he had ever witnessed since becoming a cleric many years ago. Even the war a decade ago was on a smaller scale. It was enough to make him feel confident about the upcoming battle.

Of the civilians gathered below, many were given extra rations of freshly brewed dwarven ale. The dwarf who made the stuff had graciously offered the tower his recipe so the ale could be made in mass quantities. With the assistance of magic, the grey mages were able to speed up the fermenting process greatly. No one asked what handsome amount the dwarf was offered for the recipe, but speculation abounded amongst those who consumed the liquid. For now the ale was in abundance, and its effects allowed people to take part in the battle when they would otherwise be too weak to stand.

High Cleric Malachi felt somewhat out of place among the skink warriors. He was not going to be fighting alongside them. He would not even be watching the battle commence. His job was to manage the tower inside, where the halls would surely fill to overflowing as the injured and dying were ushered in for healing. Many women, children, and older folks were milling about in front of the main gates, anxious about their task of transporting injured people to the tower using makeshift cots. They knew that lives hung in the balance, and that everyone had a part to play in the defense of the tower.

Meanwhile, in the front lines, Rebecca fingered her hand axe nervously. She was grouped with a handful of farmers who looked too feeble to be of any use in battle. Two of them staggered under the influence of the dwarven ale. One was equipped with a pitchfork while another wielded a pick axe. Rounding out her team was a farmer with a wood axe and another one with a picaroon. The only consolation for the dwarf was that Cyril was in an adjacent group.

The cyclops' team was as debatable as Rebecca's. Two old men, one young man in his twenties who could barely stand he was so drunk, and one old woman whose wrinkled face was almost fearsome to behold. She held a vicious looking spear.

Some other groups near the dwarf and cyclops fared better, with able-bodied civilians accompanying soldiers and a couple of grey mages. But one thing that was common among all that were assembled were their grim expressions of determination. They were united in their cause, regardless of age or ability.

For Rebecca, this was not her battle. But honour, a value highly regarded by dwarves, demanded that she help these people in their time of need. Perhaps her contribution would go unnoticed and her life would be lost with no one the wiser in the dwarven realm. But to abandon them would mean certain disgrace if she were found out. Even if no one ever found out, it would nag at her for the rest of her life. She would never be able to live with the shame.

Cyril's motives were slightly different, yet similar. This was the perfect opportunity for him to prove that he was a good person. By fighting the forces of evil and by fighting his own kind, he could show that he was more human than cyclops. He didn't fear death; he almost welcomed it. By dying on the battlefield, he would be remembered as a hero. Besides, the Tower of Hope was his home. It was worth dying for. The only drawback about dying was that Vera would be deeply grieved. Cyril didn't want her to suffer that way. It was the only reason not to die, but it was enough to make him desire to live. Thankfully, the cleric was not taking part in the fighting. Cyril could concentrate on fighting without having to protect her at the same time. Of course, she was the one better equipped to protect him. Nevertheless, Cyril could now devote all of his attention to offensive tactics. The cyclops took a deep breath and flexed his muscles. He would give it his best shot. He would not let his guard down if he could help it.

One thing both the dwarf and cyclops wondered was where Alric had disappeared off to. They had no doubt he would be using his invisibility skill in this fight. They hoped he fared well wherever he was.

The welfare of his companions was the farthest from the elf's mind. Alric was sorely disappointed upon his arrival at the Tower of Hope. The fact that the lizardman army hadn't arrived yet meant that Alric's encounter with the lizardmage was delayed once again. He had no doubt the evil lizardmage was a big player among his own kind. If there was going to be a war, the lizardmage would surely be involved. Alric was rapidly losing hope of getting back at the lizardmage when word arrived of an approaching army. With his hopes rising, the elf made plans and preparations for his renewed opportunity. He needed to find a way to penetrate the ranks of enemies in order to gain access to the lizardmage he sought. His invisibility cloak was essential in achieving this objective. The next thing he did was bathe in the cool waters of North Lake, as well as wash his clothing. The sensitive noses of orcs would have a harder time sensing his presence that way. Alric's agility was inherent, and there were some spells that he could cast that would aid him in his quest. Excitement stirred in his blood as he waited just out of visual range of the tower. The enemy would undoubtedly pause near here before attacking. That would give him time to scout for his intended victim. All that remained now was to wait.

Malachi was part way to the stairs down to the courtyard when everyone first felt it. It was a minor shuddering at first. After a short pause, it continued. Then another pause. Each time it occurred, it was louder and more noticeable. It was a deliberate pattern, shaking the ground like a heartbeat. Everyone looked northward in anticipation, wondering what was causing that noise.

A good five minutes of tremors cycled through the assembled forces before the first of the enemy finally appeared on the northern horizon. The first few were soon flanked by many. Those many quickly expanded across the horizon like a shadow. The shadow swelled, devouring the land like a black cloud.

One figure appeared to grow as it neared. The shadow grew with it, matching the steps of the monumental creature. It towered above the other minions, making them seem like ants in comparison.

Within the next few minutes, the oncoming force grew to match the size of the defending forces. And still they continued to advance. Little by little, the defenders grew more discouraged as they saw the number of enemies increase. Now the sound of the attackers could be heard, their march matching that of the gigantic creature. It was terrifying to behold. The hearts of the defenders pounded, but the marching of the attackers drowned it out. Mortar even fell in white puffs as the tower's battlements shook.

When the attacking force finally called a halt, they outnumbered the defenders by five to one. A lizardman dressed in chain mail stepped forward from the sea of darkness and used magic to amplify his voice. "As you can see, you have no hope of winning this war. Surrender, and we will give you fresh water and let you live. Join us and you will be richly rewarded. Resist, and you will die!"

Lieutenant Farnsworth stepped forward and spoke with the assistance of a grey mage's 'amplify' spell. "We would never join you! You have poisoned the water and land! If we surrender, you will continue to destroy everything in your path! That we will not allow!" He turned and stepped back into his spot in the front center of the defenders.

"You are fools! You deserve to die!" bellowed Slong. He returned to his spot at the front of his forces. Then he signaled the giant creature. The creature - the earth elemental - raised a leg and stomped the ground with such vehemence the shock wave knocked friend and foe alike to the ground. Two of the archer towers collapsed, drawing first blood in what looked to be a one-sided war. With a blood-thirsty cry, the attackers surged forward. The defenders braced themselves, grim determination and fear on their faces.

The attacker's momentum was momentarily hampered when the front lines fell into hidden pit traps in random places across the battlefield. Bodies piled into these holes in droves as those in front were pressed from behind. But numbers didn't seem diminished as the attackers navigated around these obstacles.

The next thing caused the attackers to falter again as a war cry could be heard originating from North Lake. Unseen previously because of a 'mirror image' spell cast by a group of grey mages, were legions of sailors lining the shores of North Lake. The spell hid them because it mirrored the shoreline of the lake and made it appear to be empty. Newly invented cannons, mounted on the sides of the ships, and supplied by the grey mages, made their debut. The cannons were cylindrical wooden carriers made from trees harvested from the southern borders of the Black Forest. Those trees were harder and more durable than any other and were suitable for the high pressure of this application. Boulders were tucked into one end and magical fire sticks were inserted into the other end of these specially designed tubes. The boulders were then ejected at high speed with a few words of magic. As the rocks flew from the cannons toward the enemy, they exploded into hundreds of tiny, lethal fragments in the enemy's right flank. Orcs, goblins and ogres were torn to pieces. Lizardmen among them weren't ready for this diversion, and subsequently were unable to cast any defensive magic. These cannons were an invention of the grey mages, spearheaded by the grey mage Jerrin himself.

The attackers were further hindered when hidden archers raked their front row with arrows when they were close enough. The archers each got up to three shots away before they backed up to avoid the inevitable clash between the front lines.

Yells, cries, and sword clashes sounded all across the battlefield. The defenders were pushed back somewhat but still held firm, unfazed by the numbers they were pitted against. The attackers were caught off guard by this determination. They expected the ill-trained civilians within the ranks to break and run. For the defenders, it became apparent the dwarven ale had another positive effect - courage. Many people who were already dying fought with wild abandon, knowing they would likely be dead soon anyway. At least this way they died a meaningful death.

Rebecca swung her hand axe valiantly. The orcs who charged into her were quickly slain. Surprisingly, her team fared well with the initial onslaught, taking care of their opponents in quick succession. But they didn't have time to enjoy their momentary victory as an ogre suddenly barged into them with a vengeance. It killed one of the farmers, but couldn't avoid an attack from two sides as the other drunken farmers stabbed it and hacked its arms from its body. The ogre sagged to its knees while the remaining farmer sliced its head from its body with a wood axe.

Cyril's team didn't fare as well, losing the two older farmers with the first clash. The drunken young man fought like a maniac and effectively held off a couple of orcs singlehandedly. The old lady wielded her spear effectively, stabbing an orc and an ogre in vital spots, killing them instantly. Cyril swung his mace with equal effectiveness, taking down an ogre and two goblins. Then he swung it at the orcs who had killed the old farmers. It was then that he noticed a new feature to his enchanted mace. As he swung it at the orcs, he missed them, yet the mace seemed to send a surge of magical power radiating outward from it. The surge struck the orcs like a jolt of lightning, killing them on the spot. On the back swing, another orc pushed into range and was struck by another magical jolt. The old woman noticed the strange effect of the weapon and stepped behind the cyclops to give him more room to swing.

Some lizardmen approaching the fighting cast some fireballs into the front ranks of the humans. Most of the fireballs bounced harmlessly aside as they struck the shields of the sporadic grey mages and clerics. The few fireballs that managed to penetrate the unshielded areas did minimal damage. It appeared that the strategy of spreading out the magic users was working.

Another strategy that played itself out well was when General Larsen appeared on the defenders' right flank with his full complement of cavalry. His task was to prevent the attackers from circling around the moat on the east side where moat construction had ceased. He charged the enemy's left flank at full speed, taking out a large swath of enemies. The cavalry did a sharp U-turn and continued their attack at full speed. As quickly as the cavalry appeared, it vanished around the back of the battlements. A hidden doorway constructed within the walls opened up, allowing the cavalry inside. The door closed again, any evidence of an opening vanishing entirely. General Larsen planned sporadic attacks like this as the war raged on. He had to use the cavalry wisely to make them last as long as possible.

Unfortunately, the numbers of attackers were still too great. The humans were still being pushed back toward the moat.

The youth fighting alongside Cyril was openly bleeding in several spots, but didn't seem to notice as he slashed at a sea of green ugly creatures. Cyril continued swinging his light magical mace with ease, killing monsters without even touching them. Any creatures that got too close had to contend with the old woman's spear. She repelled attackers so Cyril could swing his mace to full effect.

Rebecca lost two more farmers, leaving the drunken one with the pick axe. He was a big man who had little difficulty swinging the pick axe, but he was still sweating with exertion. Both his size and the fact that he was sweating meant the ale's effect was quickly wearing off. His blows were becoming more accurate, and any creatures who approached were wary of his fierce expression. With hardly anyone on either side of her, Rebecca discovered more and more creatures pressing in on her from all sides. She withdrew her dagger and was forced to fight with the hand axe in one hand and the dagger in the other. Her training at home had covered one-handed attacks, and she was grateful for every technique she had learned. Her axe and dagger were a blur of motion as the dwarf danced and spun with amazing agility. Every time the dagger penetrated the flesh of her enemies, the blinding flash and blood curdling screams of orcs, goblins and ogres rang across the battlefield.

Meanwhile, Cyril was having fun killing several opponents at a time with his magical mace. He didn't notice the fireball intended for him until he staggered off balance, stumbling over a dead body. The fireball whizzed past him and struck the drunken youth in the chest. The youth fell down and lay still. Angered, Cyril turned to face the spell caster who stood only a few feet away. The lizardman scowled and prepared to cast another spell. Cyril growled and moved toward the lizardman, staring at its ugly expression. It wasn't until his third step that Cyril noticed something interesting. The lizardman wasn't moving. He was paralyzed! The cyclops stopped and turned to the old woman. Without looking at her directly, he said, "He's all yours."

The woman pursed her lips and thrust her spear into the lizardman's chest. The spell caster fell to the ground silently. The old woman gave Cyril a satisfied expression but the cyclops had turned to face some new adversaries. These opponents were what Cyril had been waiting for - fellow cyclops.

There were two of them and they were both bigger and stronger than Cyril. Cyril didn't care. He almost laughed when they intoned, "Look into my eye!" Did they actually think he was susceptible to that magic? With a lightning quick lunge, he launched himself at the closest one. It caught the cyclops off guard. In the collision, Cyril and the cyclops fell to the ground. Cyril thrust his elbow into the cyclops' throat and sprang to his feet. With his trusty mace still in hand, Cyril jabbed its handle into the standing cyclops' midriff. Then, while the cyclops was gasping for air, Cyril brought his mace down hard on the first cyclops' head. The skull caved in like a melon. Then Cyril swung his mace around to do combat with the second cyclops. That cyclops brought its own club up to parry Cyril's mace and the weapons came to a dead stop. Then the cyclops with the club gurgled and blood trickled from the corners of its mouth. It had a surprised expression as it looked down at its chest. Protruding from between its ribs was a spear. Cyril didn't hesitate long, and clobbered the cyclops over the head with his mace, putting it out of commission for good. The old woman stepped forward and retrieved her undamaged spear. Cyril marveled at this old woman's skill and bravery but said nothing.

The next challenge for Rebecca and Cyril was something they had never encountered before. A group of brown creatures made of earth lumbered toward them. They were a magical creation of the earth elemental known as golems.

A well-placed spear thrust by the old woman penetrated the golem's chest. It did nothing to hurt or injure the golem. Cyril stepped forward and bashed the creature with his mace. Chunks of the creature sprayed in all directions, yet it kept coming. Cyril wasn't quick or agile, but compared to the golem, he was fast. He took a couple more swipes at the golem before it punched him in the chest with a rock hard fist. The cyclops staggered back, winded, but sprang back to swing his mace hard against the golem's head. The head shattered into bits of rock and clay and the body stopped moving. Then the body crumbled into a pile of dust at Cyril's feet.

Rebecca had a similar experience. She sliced off the golem's arm with her axe and then dodged the golem's other arm as it tried to punch her. Swinging around, the dwarf sliced off the golem's outstretched arm leaving it unarmed. The creature stood there uncertainly, long enough for the dwarf to slice her axe deep into its neck. In what seemed like slow motion, the golem's head toppled from its shoulders. Then the body collapsed just like Cyril's opponent, into a pile of dust.

Across the battlefield, screams and yells could be heard as the inexperienced farmers stabbed and hacked at the golems in a futile effort to kill them. Rebecca and Cyril had discovered how to defeat the golems, but there was no way for them to communicate that to anyone in the midst of battle.

A sudden, burning light appeared behind the defenders, causing most fighters to glance in the light's direction. A gigantic flaming figure stood high above the crowd. It was Tyris. He spread his fingers and from his fingertips sprang numerous bolts of flame. These bolts became tiny figures of flame, like miniature fire elementals. They ran through the fighters with incredible speed, seeking out orcs, goblins, ogres, lizardmen and cyclops. When they found them, they set the creatures ablaze. Even the lizardmen couldn't defend themselves, since magic was useless against elemental magic. When the mini fire elementals encountered the golems, they attempted to set them ablaze, but the golems were fireproof. The fire elementals were simply absorbed by the golems. But that wasn't the end of the fire elementals. They continued to burn inside of the golems. Eventually, the golems became red hot - then white hot. Finally, the heat was so intense the

Carey Scheppner

golems became like molten magma. The golems could do nothing as their bodies built up with so much heat they exploded in a shower of stones and debris. All fighters from both sides ran to avoid being showered with molten debris. When the scene settled, both the mini fire elementals and golems were gone. The earth elemental continued making golems while Tyris made more mini fire elementals to help the sides they fought for.

The introduction of Tyris' flame creatures gave the defenders hope and momentum, and for the first time, they pushed the attackers back ever so slightly.

Another ongoing battle was the magical one. The close combat was taking its toll on the grey mages, and their numbers were dwindling rapidly. Lizardmen were doing more damage with isolated fireballs and ice bolts and they were casting more 'slow' and paralyze' spells that were hindering the defenders. The tide was turning in favour of the attackers again.

The new surge of enemies pushed Cyril and the old woman back even further. They now had their backs to the moat. The farmer who had been fighting with Rebecca had gotten lost in the confusion, so Rebecca stood with Cyril as the last survivors of the front lines were forced to put up their most valiant resistance. The battle was intense, but the numbers were too few to fend off the tide of darkness. Lieutenant Farnsworth was bloody and battered when he signaled the retreat. The defenders withdrew across the makeshift bridges of the moat while archers in the remaining towers gave the army a chance to escape. The hordes of darkness followed the humans, showers of arrows raking their number as they pursued.

Once the humans were across, a signal was given at each bridge and the footings were blown using magical fire sticks. One by one the bridges collapsed into the moat and those fortunate enough to avoid the arrows were thrown into the cold waters of the moat. Those who could swim tried to reach the shore without getting hit by arrows. And if that wasn't challenging enough, a number of mermaids in the western end of the moat surfaced to pull unsuspecting enemies down under the water. Very few of those creatures were able to come back for air.

The battle along the shoreline of North Lake surged back and forth as the sailors battled valiantly with the support of the ships' cannons. The cannons were the only thing that prevented the sailors from being overrun, the lethal cannon balls doing damage to large contingents of enemies at a time. Captain Rubin was at the forefront, his sailors fighting as valiantly as their captain. Providing support from behind with her bow was Della the elf. She was too busy to wonder where Kazin was.

Alric tread carefully as he selected his victims. He could only use his dagger to stab a few enemies here and there without being detected. His dagger thrusts were quick and lethal. By the time the body fell, he was long gone in the crowd of enemies. The elf kept this up as he searched for the lizardmage who had used him. Lizardmen were difficult to tell apart, but Alric had a good eye when it came to identifying his targets. His experience with tracking targets he was planning to steal from gave him an edge in that skill. So far, he never saw anyone close, but he still had plenty of territory to cover. Undoubtedly, the lizardmage he sought would be higher ranking and positioned near the back of the army out of harm's way. He was presently working his way to the back. Thankfully, this led him away from the heavily guarded earth elemental, who was now approaching the moat. Even back here the ground shuddered with each step the elemental took. Monsters and humans alike kept falling to the ground like drunken idiots. The elf used this to his advantage by stabbing some orcs and ogres who were trying to get back to their feet. To anyone watching, it looked like the monsters simply fell down with the shuddering ground. No one paid attention when they failed to stand up again.

Not far from Alric another elemental appeared. It rose, swirling like a storm cloud, high above the battlefield. Taking a deep breath, it blew a strong wind in the direction of the sailors and their ships. Several ships broke from their moorings and were pushed out to sea. Some of them even capsized. The heavier cannon ships were blown into disarray, their cannons pointing the wrong way. The stirred up dust and sand gave cover to orcs and ogres, who charged against the sailors. The sailors had nowhere to run with their backs to North Lake and most of their ships adrift.

Meanwhile, the earth elemental had reached the moat. A contingent of lizardmages followed it, chanting their summoning magic. A short lizardmage with a black robe and red trim raised his curved staff and issued commands to the earth elemental. The elemental bellowed and pulled some arrows from its chest. Then it stamped its foot with such vehemence that the remaining archer towers collapsed. With the shower of arrows halted, the elemental moaned and raised its hands. With an ear-splitting grinding noise, the earth below the moat began to rise. It pushed up so that the water that was in the moat was thrown back against the defenders like a tidal wave. The wave washed the defenders right to the wall of the Tower of Hope. Many people died in that onslaught, being drowned or crushed like ants. With a cry of victory, the attackers surged ahead once more.

A shriek that sounded in the sky above was barely audible to the attackers, whose cries of victory sounded across the battlefield. Only when a wide swath of flame and destruction scoured a path through them did they notice the dragon. The first casualties were the creatures who were making headway against the sailors. The sailors eliminated any stragglers and took a breather as they waited for the next ranks of attackers to approach. Many cheered the dragon on when Della informed them it was Kazin.

The next swath of destruction occurred in front of the tower where the heaviest fighting took place. Kazin made sure his flame was directed at the earth elemental and everyone around it. Unfortunately, there were too many lizardmages guarding the elemental, and their shield fended off the blast of fire. Those not close enough to the elemental were incinerated.

Cyril and Rebecca exchanged glances. Who was this dragon? It couldn't be Kazin. He was dead. Whoever it was didn't like lizardmen any more than they did. Thankful they had a dragon for an ally, the duo rallied their forces and began a counterattack.

Now Kazin was at the right flank where General Larsen and his cavalry were caught in a pitched battle. The fighting here was close, so Kazin had to keep his flame directed at the second rank of enemies. It was enough. General Larsen and his cavalry were able to disengage and return to the back of the tower's battlements. This time, they didn't go into the courtyard, but changed direction to charge the enemy once again. This time Frosty joined them as well, his horn striking any creatures that got close.

Kazin had turned around by now, so he gave the enemies another blast of flame. This disoriented the front lines and made it easier for General Larsen's cavalry to strafe the enemy. The general signaled his thanks to the dragon.

Seeing things under control on that front, Kazin made a brief landing in the courtyard to allow Mara and Vera to disembark with their supplies. Then he flew up and over the battlements where skink warriors were firing their crossbows at enemies who were already within range. As Kazin looked across the battlefield, his heart sank. There were enemies as far as the horizon. Ten dragons wouldn't be enough to stop the tide of monsters. Nevertheless, he knew he could make a difference. He lunged toward the earth elemental and blasted the area with fire. The result was the same. Magic protected the elemental, but destroyed those who were not close enough to the shield protecting it. At least this allowed the ground forces to get nearer to the elemental to have a chance to attack the lizardmen who were summoning it.

Kazin blasted enemies left and right with his flames. How long he could keep this up he did not know. He had never run out of flame breath before, so he didn't know his limit. He was sure he would find out before long.

The dragon approached the air elemental and blasted it with flame. As usual, it was protected by a magical shield. He turned over the open water of North Lake and made another attempt. This time, the air elemental blew directly at Kazin, forcing the flames back onto the dragon. Thankfully, Kazin was flying too fast to feel any substantial effect from the flame. He circled and made another attempt at a lower altitude. The elemental blew back at his flame again, but Kazin changed direction and flew straight up. The flames missed him, but surged across the battlefield, wiping out a nearby contingent of orcs. The damage was more than Kazin could have caused on his own, and he realized the extra air gave his flames additional potency. Kazin expanded on his idea. He flew down low and blasted a swath as far as the earth elemental. Then he turned left and flew until he was close to the air elemental. Once within range, Kazin let out his fiercest breath of flame. As predicted, the air elemental blew at the dragon again. Kazin soared straight up, but this time he was a bit too slow. He felt the searing flame on the underside of his belly as he gained altitude. Despite this one drawback, his plan worked perfectly. His flames were amplified and sent roaring across the battlefield toward the earth elemental. All creatures in the path of the flames were burned alive. As the flame struck the shield surrounding the earth elemental, most of it was absorbed. But some of the fire got through because it was enhanced by elemental magic. Some of the lizardmages within were set on fire, and their concentration of the 'summoning' and 'shield' spell were broken.

Fortunately for Narg, there were still enough lizardmages able to control the earth elemental and maintain the shield, but barely. With nostrils flaring, he commanded the earth elemental to put some distance between it and the air elemental. The elemental complied, moving closer to the left flank. As it walked, the shuddering ground shook the battlement walls, causing cracks to appear in its surface. Narg told the earth elemental to stomp the earth again and the cracks widened. A section of the battlements went down, taking several skink warriors with it.

Narg didn't have time to improve on that success. A number of soldiers and grey mages, flanked by mini fire elementals, advanced on him. It was then that he noticed that he was exposed on all sides. The dragon had burned everything beyond his shielded area. Then he remembered his shield. The humans wouldn't get through. The only threat was the mini fire elementals. He gave the earth elemental a command and a number of golems within the shield wandered out to do battle with the mini fire elementals. The human soldiers kept coming. At the edge of the shield, the human attackers and a cyclops began beating at the shield with their weapons. Narg laughed at the futile efforts of the humans. If it wasn't for the shield, he would have used magic to burn them to a crisp by now.

A small contingent of lizardmen approached from the left and began casting offensive magic at the stupid humans. The grey mages turned and cast their 'deflection' spells to counter the offensive magic. As the fireballs and ice bolts reached them, they were deflected back to the casters. The lizardmen were quickly defeated. Jerrin, the grey mage, turned to Narg and looked him straight in the eye. He smiled wickedly and pointed at the lizardmage. "You're next," he mouthed.

A tap on Narg's shoulder made him spin around. He stared into the eyes of a female dwarf. "What? What do you want?"

"Excuse me," said Rebecca politely. "Are you in charge here?"

Narg took a step back. "Yes. Yes, of course," he stammered. "How did you -?" He didn't finish his sentence because the dwarf had already plunged her dagger into his chest. The searing pain was so intense he scarcely let out a scream. His eyes were wide and his nostrils flared as his body was dissolved by the dagger's magic. Then he fell to the ground in a gory heap.

The earth elemental watched this happen with detached amusement. Some of the other lizardmages who were present reacted by canceling their shield spells so they could combat this new threat.

This allowed Cyril and the other soldiers to penetrate the group of lizardmages. They only had a few moments to attack before Cyril cried out, "Dragon!" He led the humans and dwarf away at a sprint, and the slower lizardmages tried frantically to call up their shield again. It was too late. As Kazin flew over them, he blasted them with his fiery breath. After he passed, many of the lizardmen were ablaze, screaming in agony. Cyril turned around and led the charge back to finish off the lizardmen. The earth elemental felt the release of the summoning magic and was grateful for her freedom. She watched with interest as the last of the lizardmen controlling her was felled. Then Cyril and the other fighters were drawn off to fight some approaching orcs.

The dragon landed nearby and transformed into a human black mage. He put his hands up as a sign that he was not going to harm the elemental. Kazin slowly approached the elemental and reached it the same time as Rebecca.

"Kazin?!" exclaimed Rebecca when he was close enough to recognize. Kazin smiled. "Hi, Rebecca. It's nice to see you again."

"You were dying -." Her voice broke off as she absorbed the fact that Kazin was alive and well.

Kazin directed his attention to the elemental. "Are you alright?" he asked the gigantic creature.

The elemental blinked at the mage. "Of course."

"I was afraid I might hurt you with my flames," stammered Kazin. "I wasn't sure I could help you get free without hurting you."

"Was that your intention?" asked the elemental. "To free me?"

"Yes," said Rebecca suddenly.

The elemental turned to the dwarf. "How did you manage to penetrate the shield, dwarf?"

"My name is Rebecca Mapmaker," said the dwarf. She hated being called 'dwarf'. "I discovered my magical dagger allows me to walk through magical shields like they aren't even there." She held up her dagger so the elemental could see it. "Don't ask me how it works."

The elemental nodded. "Well done. You should be rewarded for freeing me."

Enemies were now approaching the mage, dwarf and elemental. The elemental held up a hand and the earth around them opened up, revealing an infinitely deep crevice. The first few enemies tumbled headlong into the hole and fell screaming to their deaths.

"There," said the elemental. "That should keep them away so we can talk in peace."

"Can you help us fight the lizardmen?" asked Rebecca.

The elemental shook her head. "It is too dangerous. I could fight for you for a while, but the lizardmen here are plentiful. They could easily summon me if they regroup and combine forces with their magic. Then I would be fighting for them once again. Do you want to take that chance?"

Rebecca sighed. "I guess not."

"I have spent too much time in this plane," said the elemental. "My powers grow weak. I have enough energy for one more major thing before I go, but for you I will offer a small gift." She reached down and gently touched Rebecca's head. "From now on, you will have an increased ability to sense mineral deposits and gems as you travel the tunnels in the mountains. You shall change your name to Rebecca Gemfinder."

Rebecca's jaw dropped. "Thank you," she whispered.

Suddenly, a voice inside Kazin's head called his name. Kazin recognized his familiar's voice and looked across the battlefield to see the unicorn staring at him, a stark white figure amidst a throng of enemies. The unicorn fought alongside General Larsen. Everything seemed to be in suspended animation. Nothing moved.

"What is it?" asked Kazin mentally.

"See if the elemental can open a pass through the mountains in the north. Sherman waits with an army to aid us."

"Are you sure?" asked Kazin. Sherman was queen Milena's brother and guardian, and the last thing Kazin had heard was that Sherman was supposed to have gone on a quest.

"Yes," said Frosty. "It is also a perfect opportunity for our realms to join for trade."

Kazin turned to the elemental. "Can you open a pass through the mountains north of here? We have reinforcements waiting there to assist us." Rebecca gave Kazin a curious glance but said nothing.

The elemental paused before answering Kazin. "It is a tall order," she said at last, "but I will do it."

"Thank you, earth elemental," said Kazin, bowing slightly. As he did so, the orb atop his staff caught the elemental's attention.

The elemental's eyes widened. "Your staff has an enchantment upon it!"

Kazin nodded. "Yes. The water elemental put it there."

The elemental's eyes stared at Kazin as though seeing into him. "The enchantment is a powerful one, and it won't be complete until each elemental has cast his or her own enchantment upon it. The water elemental has deemed you worthy of such magic. After your bravery in trying to free me, I believe that trust is not misplaced." The elemental placed her hand on Kazin's staff and hummed in a deep, mesmerizing voice. Then she removed her hand. "There. Now seek out the other elementals. They are both still on this battlefield. When you are away from me, I will open the pass as you requested. Now hurry. Even as we speak, the lizardmen are trying to summon me."

Kazin didn't need any urging. He changed into a dragon and let Rebecca climb onto his back. She was hesitant at first, never having ridden on a dragon's back before, but she wanted to get away from there to let the elemental do her thing. The dragon soared into the air. Kazin blasted the enemy with fire on his way back to the tower to drop off his passenger.

The earth elemental raised her arms into the air and a deep rumbling noise filled the earth and the air above it. Cracks spread out to the north from the place where the elemental stood. Creatures and humans alike fell to the ground as the earth shook. The cracks widened and vast numbers of enemies fell into them to disappear forever. As if by a miracle, the Tower of Hope and its battlements were immune to the earthquake. A loud crack sounded out of the north, and a large crashing noise followed. The earth elemental sank into the ground, and as she disappeared, the rumbling ceased. All was still except the rush of air surrounding the air elemental. The forces on both sides took up arms, and soon the din of battle resumed once again.

By now it was getting dark, but the light generated by Tyris and his mini elementals provided plenty of light for the defenders. The fire elemental had worked his way to the aid of the sailors. With the dragon's absence, the air elemental was once again disabling the ships that had repositioned themselves to fire their cannons at the attackers. But the sailors were seriously outnumbered. The remaining ground forces were scrambling to get on board the last of the docked ships to safety. A group of sailors was cut off from the ships by a gang of ogres, so Tyris ran into their midst and created an inferno. The ogres became flaming torches and ran into the lake to quench their burning hair. Mermaids made short work of them. This gave the sailors the opportunity they needed to retreat to the ships. When the last of the sailors was safely aboard, the ships cast off and utilized the air elemental's wind to establish a suitable distance between themselves and land.

With this accomplished, Tyris ran with incredible speed back to the tower. He had expended a great deal of magical energy and needed rest. He had to move quickly, wary of magic users who could summon him on sight. He reached the battlements and slipped over the section that had collapsed. Then he was behind the wall out of sight.

General Slong saw the gap left by the earth elemental and directed his troops to the middle of the battlefield. The battle on the left against the inadequate cavalry was holding its own and the shoreline was now being secured. Now the siege against the tower could begin. He had lost a lot of fighters when the earth elemental had created the crevices, but they were still more numerous by far. Slong nodded to the lizardmen in reserve. It was time to use their 'shield eating' spell to weaken the tower's defenses. The lizardmen weren't very effective until now because they couldn't concentrate their magic. Now they could inflict maximum damage with a majority of defenders holed up in one spot. The dragon was still a threat, but with enough lizardmen combining forces, he was sure they could combat the annoying creature. There were more of them than one dragon could handle.

Even as Slong schemed, the dragon was blasting another swath through the attackers.

Within the confines of the tower's battlements, Vera was scrambling to heal poisoned people. Some of the other clerics watched the level one cleric closely and learned the spell as she went. Then they began to use the spell themselves to expand her work. Most of the other clerics had their hands full with injured soldiers and civilians.

The wall in the rear section of the battlements suddenly opened and the cavalry forces came galloping in. Their numbers were depleted significantly since the start of the war. Each time they galloped back out to do battle, it seemed like they were starting from scratch. The enemy had such overwhelming numbers.

General Larsen dismounted and led his horse to a trough to drink. The others did the same.

Frosty wandered over to Vera. He didn't even seem out of breath after the intense fighting. "How's it going?"

Vera finished healing a poisoned soldier, who got up and shook her hand in gratitude. "I'm feeling better than I can remember. Thank you."

Vera smiled wanly and turned to Frosty. "Things are coming along alright. But I don't see how it will be enough to prevent the lizardmen from defeating us."

"Don't worry about that part," said Frosty. "Just concentrate on healing people. Let the fighters deal with the war."

Vera nodded and turned to her next patient. It was an old woman with a wrinkled expression. She leaned on her spear while the cleric healed her bloody arm and then cured her of the poison. Then she thanked the cleric and headed back to the portcullis.

Lieutenant Jim Farnsworth turned and saw her. "Mother! Did you get healed?"

"Yes. Yes, I'm fine," said the woman.

Jim embraced her in a joyful hug. "That's wonderful!"

When they separated, Elsie Farnsworth said, "But I'm still fighting. Every fighter is needed in this war."

"But, Mom -."

"No 'buts', son. I'm doing this and that's final. If your father can fight, so can I."

Jim sighed. "I've never been able to win an argument with you. Let's go." He put his arm around her and led her to the portcullis.

Vera derived satisfaction from her successful spell casting. It was something she never expected she would live to experience, considering her ineffective spell casting when she had left the tower. Her determination to find a cure for the disease had paid off, and here she was at the forefront of the healers in the Tower of Hope. By healing the disease, she was giving people hope in the face of evil. The people were seriously outnumbered, yet they still clung to the hope of victory. She was doing her job. The cleric turned to face the eager faces that relied on her to cure them of the disease. There were dozens lined up here, and hundreds more to come. It would be a long night.

After dropping Rebecca off on the battlements, Kazin landed in the courtyard and transformed himself back into a human mage. He strode over to a supply booth to obtain some food and water. His flames were temporarily used up, so he decided to take a short break before resuming his onslaught of the enemy. Even if his flames ran out, he could cast offensive magic as a dragon. But even that was taxing. If he wanted to cause maximum damage, he needed to pace himself.

Blasting a swath of enemies with fire in this war was like harvesting a wheat field with scissors. Only a miracle would stem the tide of monsters. Kazin got ready to transform back into a dragon while Frosty gave him words of encouragement. Then he was off.

As the dragon flew off, the enemy ground troops were inching closer to the battlements. Crossbow bolts rained down on them, but they pressed on. Rebecca used her crossbow as she made her way to the lower level to assist in sealing the breach in the wall. The elite fighters among the defenders remained outside to hold back the attackers as best they could. It wasn't easy to fight in the headwind created by the air elemental, and even though the ground was wet, there were clouds of dust making visibility and breathing difficult.

Back on the battlefield, Alric was furious. He had worked his way through most of the enemies but had failed to see his nemesis. Several times he thought he had seen the elusive lizardmage, but each time he was disappointed. Many lizardmen fell to the elf's dagger. A few times he was nearly discovered, but he kept quiet and moved away from suspicious enemies who jabbed at the air thinking someone invisible may be near. The only place he hadn't checked yet was the group of lizardmen surrounding the air elemental. Most of the spell-casters in the vicinity were lizardwomen, judging by their slightly different appearance and attire, but it was still worth investigating.

The elf was just maneuvering around some ogres to get within range of the elemental when the dragon came into view. He had wondered about the dragon when it had first appeared. He never realized there were other dragon mages still in existence. Perhaps he needed to get out of the elven lands more often.

There was no time to react as the dragon cast ice bolts, lightning bolts, fireballs, 'mass paralysis' and 'fear'. Five spells at once was something only an experienced human black mage could accomplish, and with the magical power of a dragon, it was devastating. Orcs, ogres, and goblins either stopped dead in their tracks or ran in every direction with gut wrenching fear in their eyes. Explosions and fires consumed groups of creatures all around the hapless elf, but thankfully, he was unharmed. A number of lizardmen nearby were also unharmed, and they were casting ice bolts at the dragon. Angered, Alric immediately dispatched them before they could adjust the direction of their magic to match the dragon's course.

The group of lizardmages surrounding the air elemental were unharmed due to a powerful shield created by a number of those within its protection. Alric knew he wouldn't be able to penetrate that shield either, so he decided to wait for an opening.

He watched as the dragon circled around to the north and came in at a low angle. As he let loose with a fiery blast, the lizardmen in charge of the elemental gave an order. As the flame reached the shield, the lizardmages creating the shield stopped chanting. At the same time, the air elemental grew in size and blew at the wall of approaching fire. With a thunderous hissing noise, the fire was repelled and blown back across the battlefield. The flames burned and singed all the forces that had the misfortune to be in its path, but Kazin was already high in the air.

Narla cursed. This strategy was not working. There was only one way to deal with the pesky dragon. The air elemental had to do battle in the air. The lizardwoman hissed to her counterparts. The shield remained down while the lizardmages chanted to control the elemental. Then Narla gave the orders to the elemental. With a powerful blast of wind, the elemental surged high into the sky. Narla pulled her navy cloak tightly about her shoulders to fend off the cold gust.

In the sky above, almost everyone watched in fascination as the elemental created a tremendous turbulence. The dragon was spun around like a scarecrow, unable to control his flight. The elemental raised his hands and then thrust them ahead of him, sending the dragon hurtling across the sky.

Narla's fish-like lips spread across her face into a sinister grin. This was more like it. With the dragon out of the way, the war would be over sooner. The humans had lost!

Narla's grin looked ridiculous as she sagged to the ground. No one even noticed, since their eyes were staring upward. Three more lizardmages were slain in a similar fashion before one of the lizardwomen noticed what was happening. She cried out just as a knife slit her throat. The other lizardmages were torn between defending themselves and keeping the air elemental under control. This indecision played into Alric's hands as he magically expanded his dagger into a sword and slashed the lizardmages with wild abandon. Those still controlling the elemental were straining under the pressure of maintaining the spell as their numbers were being reduced by the invisible imposter.

Up above, the elemental was about to inflict the finishing blow on the dragon. Kazin was being thrown toward the ground at incredible speed. The defenders on the tower's battlements watched in horror as the dragon was about to be smashed into the ground.

Then, with a slight flick of his hand, the elemental stopped the falling dragon in mid-air. He turned his gigantic head to look at the lizardmages who had controlled him for so long. His body, which already twisted in a swirling blue, began to spin even faster. One by one, the lizardmages began to be drawn up into the spinning vortex. The wind was experienced by everyone on the battlefield. As the last of the summoning lizardmages was sucked into the vortex, the air elemental threw the flailing bodies in every direction. Some bodies ended up way out in North Lake, others landed on their allies, and some even landed in the tower's courtyard.

Then the elemental stopped spinning and floated calmly in the sky like a cloud. He had held the dragon far enough away from the vortex he had created to eliminate the lizardmages, so the dragon was unharmed. He turned Kazin upright and drew him near enough to talk to him. No one below was able to hear what was said.

"I knew you would come to my aid," said the air elemental.

Kazin looked at the elemental through reptilian eyes. "You know who I am?"

"Yes," said the elemental. "I saw your staff when we met at the Tower of the Moon. You are the dragon mage. Turn yourself back into your true form so I can see you."

Kazin looked down nervously.

"Don't worry," said the elemental. "I will not let you fall."

Kazin transformed himself back into his human form and sat in mid-air, dressed in his black robe and holding his staff.

The elemental examined the mage for a few moments without

saying anything. Then he spoke. "I sense the enchantment on your staff. You must have proven yourself to the other elementals. I saw you free the earth elemental. I suspect you had a hand in helping the water elemental. I need no more proof that you are the dragon mage of significance."

"I don't understand," said Kazin.

"I can say no more," said the elemental. "Now hold out your staff."

Kazin held up his staff. The elemental waved his hand over it twice. Then he lowered his hand and said, "There. You have received a gift I have rarely given in my existence. I have another gift for the one who killed the chief lizard woman. I could not see who it was because they were invisible, so you will have to seek out that individual and give him the reward."

Kazin nodded. "I think I know who you mean."

"Good," said the elemental. He waved his hand over Kazin's staff again. "Simply touch that individual with the orb on your staff and he will be rewarded with powerful air magic."

"Understood," said Kazin.

"Now change back into a dragon. I am going back to my realm."

"But aren't you going to help us?" asked Kazin, looking at the legions of enemies surrounding the tower. From up there it looked like incredible odds.

"This isn't my fight," said the elemental. "I rarely intervene directly in worldly events. But look to the north."

Kazin looked north and blinked his eyes. The sky was dark and he thought he saw lights twinkling in the distance. Then it occurred to him. Sherman's army was coming!

"You'd better get down there and help your friends," urged the elemental.

Kazin looked back at the tower and saw the black horde attacking the defenders. Apparently they could not hold out long without help. Kazin looked back at the lights in the north. They were still a few hours away at best. He had to help the defenders hold on long enough for Sherman to get there. In an instant, Kazin transformed into a dragon and flew to their aid.

The elemental watched the dragon fly away in satisfaction and then dispersed into thin air. As he dispersed, he gave the clerics in the tower a gift. He blew away the clouds to reveal the full moon. The cleric's magic would be at full strength.

By now, the last of the defenders had retreated behind the wall. The portcullis was slammed shut and an additional barrier was thrown behind it. Skink warriors frantically fired crossbow bolts at the attackers. There were so many monsters crammed together it was impossible for them to miss.

Orcs were climbing over the damaged part of the wall while defenders within beat them back. Ogres were banging at the portcullis with a battering ram. Goblins shot arrows at the defenders. Lizardmen were casting spells at the skink warriors while clerics tried to shield the magic of each attack. The clerics weren't ready to create a mass shield because they wanted their long range fighters to do some damage. A mass shield would protect everyone but also prevent anyone from shooting back at the enemy.

A contingent of cyclops came forward with crudely fashioned ladders and held them in place against the walls while goblins scurried up them to infiltrate the archers and skink warriors. Soldiers and civilians appeared to push the ladders out from the wall with long poles.

As if that wasn't enough, a handful of catapults materialized and fired rocks over the battlements into the courtyard.

Alric paused between killings to observe the spectacle. He was glad he wasn't trapped in the courtyard. It was much safer out here. It had been a close call when the air elemental had sucked up the lizardmages. He had nearly been nearly drawn up in the whirlwind himself. His agility and speed had allowed him to escape the area in time. He had been close enough to the action to see that it was indeed Kazin who was flying around in his dragon form. How he had come back from dying of poison was a mystery, but he was glad the dragon was here now.

Rebecca appeared momentarily by the damaged part of the wall. She was incinerating ogres left and right, her magical dagger flashing with a white light each time it touched them. Cyril appeared beside her, his mace throwing orcs and ogres back without even coming in contact with them.

Alric set his jaw. He didn't care much for the humans, but part of this was his fault. Furthermore, his friends were in there. He hated to admit it, but he had grown fond of the dwarf. Even the cleric and the unusual half cyclops were closer to him than he would have admitted. It was time to act. He scanned the battlefield. His first objectives were the catapults.

Kazin cast lightning bolts in every direction. Explosions and cries of pain were absorbed into the din of battle. A returning lightning bolt narrowly missed the dragon as he circled to repeat his offensive. A white form appeared at his side and he glanced over at it.

"I think you're the primary target out here now," said Frosty. "You're going to need me to shield you from magic."

Kazin nodded his head. "I think you're right, Frosty. It's getting harder to avoid those lizardmen."

"We only have to hold them off a little while longer," reminded Frosty.

"I know," said Kazin. He looked down to see goblins running along the tops of the battlements on the south side where there were fewer defenders. Some grey mages intercepted them and paralyzed them. Then they threw the paralyzed figures over the wall to their deaths.

"It's a good thing the grey mages are here," said Kazin. "Without them we wouldn't have a chance."

"I agree," said Frosty.

Kazin blew a swath of flames at the enemy and one of the catapults caught fire. The inferno was lost from sight as Kazin flew past. He was thankful the darkness made it harder for the enemy to see him coming.

He looked northward but still saw no sign of Sherman's army. He was about to turn around when something caught his eye in the shadows below. It wasn't obvious until he caught a glimpse of movement. It seemed as though the forest was moving. The dragon glanced over at the unicorn with a puzzled expression. "Did you see that?"

Frosty whinnied. His eyes twinkled. "They're closer than I thought."

"Who - oh!" exclaimed Kazin. "But how -?"

"You'll see soon enough," said Frosty.

Kazin gave a joyful laugh. "It's about time!" He swooped around and continued to assault the enemy with renewed hope.

Cyril pushed back one ogre and kicked another one down. A third one raised an axe and swung it at the cyclops' unprotected side. A pick appeared and blocked the attack. The handles of the weapons cracked together loudly. The pick drew back, yanking the axe from the ogre's hand. Muscles rippled in the arms of the man as he brought the pick down on the ogre's head, splitting it in two. Then he turned to the cyclops and looked at his chest as he spoke. "I guess I owe you an apology, cyclops."

Cyril's jaw dropped. He didn't know what to say. His expression was just as surprised when the man raised his pick over his head and swung it right at Cyril. The pick sliced into flesh and bone and a gurgling noise accompanied it. Another ogre collapsed right beside the stunned cyclops.

"Don't tell me you're paralyzed," joked the man.

"Jake?" mumbled Cyril.

The man turned to confront an orc wielding a mace. "That's my name. Don't wear it out."

Cyril came out of his trance and did battle with two more orcs. He was amazed that Jake would fight alongside him after what he had done to him. But he was thankful he had come along when he did. They were on the same side in the battle, and any personal misgivings were set aside. Together, the two gardeners fought like seasoned warriors.

Lieutenant Farnsworth and Jerrin were now fighting alongside the skink warriors atop the battlements. Jim's father fought with them. Beside him fought his friend the dwarf. Henry was now a very wealthy dwarf, and he vowed to help Bill Farnsworth rebuild his farm should they get out of this alive. But they had a war to win, and he wasn't about to let a bunch of monsters part him from his wealth. He fought with the true spirit of a dwarf, hacking the creatures with his battle axe.

Jim and Jerrin issued orders to the defenders to repel the wall scalers. Activity was frantic, but the defenders were prevailing for the time being. Explosions, fireballs, ice bolts, and sounds of battle reverberated around the tower's walls. Injured people were continuously being carried into the tower itself. Healed and partially healed people exited just as quickly. Healing became quicker with the full moon present. Clerics worked tirelessly to get their soldiers back into the fight.

It didn't seem to be enough as the black tide started to overwhelm the defenders. They had gained a foothold on the battlements and pressed the defenders back ever so gradually. Tyris was still afraid of being summoned by lizardmages, so he avoided the battlements where he could be seen and potentially summoned. He elected to stay below, which was just as well. The portcullis had been shattered and enemies came through the opening in droves. The numbers of enemies here were small enough that Tyris was unlikely to be summoned, so he used his powers to maximum effect. With the aid of his mini elementals, he single-handedly prevented the enemies from establishing themselves in the courtyard. Bodies piled up rapidly in the entryway. Tyris' inferno magic kept burning the pile down so more monsters could come in and meet their doom. With the entryway well-guarded, soldiers were freed up to help on the battlements.

Meanwhile, Kazin was in a quandary. He couldn't prevent this advance without putting the defenders in jeopardy. He could only slow down the forces trying to climb the walls.

The fighting was so intense that no one noticed the attack until cries could be heard at the rear of the attackers. Lizardmen and army commanders were being assaulted from behind. Gradually, most of the attackers on the ground turned to see what was wrong. Skirmishing with the commanders were shadowy creatures that weren't there a moment ago. Those who were close enough couldn't believe their eyes. The shadowy figures were treemen, massive wooden figures with dozens of branches that were used like whips and clubs. Fireballs helped shed some light on the scene as lizardmen set the attackers ablaze.

There were an astounding number of treemen, and they were huge, bigger than the ones on the island of the Tower of the Moon. As they advanced, more and more monsters had to turn to contend with these creatures. Gradually, some soldiers appeared alongside the treemen, wielding axes and swords with great skill. Many of these soldiers were big men, known among the humans as barbarians. None were known to reside in this part of the world, yet here they were in full force.

When they saw what was happening, the defenders cried out in joy. No one had expected reinforcements. What had looked like a lost cause had turned into hope for victory. Years after this war, survivors would call this war the Battle of Hope.

A catapult suddenly cast a pile of boulders well short of the tower. It landed in a dense group of lizardmen and killed a majority of them. Commotion ensued around the catapult but no enemies could be found - only dead lizardmen and ogres.

Another catapult failed to launch when a winch rope failed to tighten. Upon closer examination, the rope appeared to have been cut. There was no time to repair it as a group of treemen waded into the scene.

West of the tower, the sailors had regained the shoreline now that the air elemental was gone. With their ships in position once again, they were able to provide cannon support for their ground troops. Slowly, they made headway against the hordes of darkness.

Slong's army was being pushed eastward, but a group of cavalry suddenly appeared, led by General Larsen. It was a small force, but these riders were the elite cavalry that had survived until now. They effectively cut off escape on that side, running down stragglers with ease.

Slong turned to the threat closest to him in the north. Where had these treemen come from? There were no mages here capable of creating so many treemen. Only druids were capable of such magic. He caught a glimpse of some robed figures and was stunned. There were spell casters present! And so many! The lizardman general decided to find the leader of this latest threat. If he could find the leader and kill him, there was a good chance the enemy would falter. His forces were still numerous enough to beat back the treemen and soldiers.

Then he saw the opposing general. He was a large man wearing the full regalia of royal chain mail. Long, shoulder length brown hair protruded from a horned helmet that glistened in the light of the burning trees. The sword he wielded was massive, and he swung it like a scythe, cutting down foes like blades of grass. The muscles on his arms strained and flexed tirelessly as he fought, and his legs were like tree trunks. He stood a full seven feet tall, towering over the ordinary humans who fought at his side.

Slong was no slouch. He was a military commander for a reason. It was time for him to prove himself as he had done many times in the past. He expertly cut through several soldiers and set a couple of treemen ablaze to get closer to his quarry. With a casual wave of his hand, he cast a spell. The din and roar of battle were replaced by dead calm. The battlefield was replaced by an endless wall of blackness. The only things present were Slong and the enemy commander.

The commander paused in mid swing and straightened, his eyes finding the lizardman general. "Wha -? Who -? What is this?" he burst out. His voice seemed faint and distant as the darkness swallowed the sound of his words.

Slong sneered. This was how he dealt with enemy commanders. He preferred to isolate them from the security of their army. Alone, they were rarely confident. Most generals were cowards who boasted of their bravery with large armies at their disposal. When faced alone, they often showed fear and even cowardice.

"You will die here," said Slong.

Sherman raised his sword. "Not if I can help it."

Slong sneered again. "Surrender. You cannot kill me." He indicated the expanse of nothingness around them. "If you do, you will never leave this void. You need my magic to return you to your kind."

"I don't believe you," snarled Sherman.

Slong shrugged. "It's up to you. If I kill you, you will die quickly. If you kill me, you will wander this void until you lose your sanity." The lizardman chuckled. "You can't even die of thirst or hunger. If your forces win the war, they will find your body and see that you are still alive. They will keep you alive by giving you water and food, and maybe even keep you alive with magic. As long as your body still lives, they will not give up hope that one day you will wake up from your coma. You would be trapped in this void for years. And even if a way was eventually found to bring you back, your mind won't be able to accept it. You will be declared mad to the end of your days."

Sherman mulled this over for a moment. Then he asked, "What will happen to you if I kill you here?"

Slong laughed. "That's the best part! I will be removed from this place and reappear on the battlefield. In your mind, I will be dead, but in reality, I will still live on. And even if I wanted to, I could never come back to this place and time in the void. You would be lost forever!"

The big warrior shook his head. "I don't believe you." He raised his weapon.

"That's your mistake to make," said Slong, readying his own sword. "I will live no matter what you do."

Sherman lunged. His swing was vicious, but the lizardman nimbly dodged the attack. Then he quickly counterattacked with his own sword. The warrior barely had time to parry. Sherman lunged again, and again the lizardman danced away. On a backhanded swing, the lizardman sliced into Sherman's left leg. The great warrior stumbled but did not cry out. Sherman faced his opponent squarely this time. It was the first time he had ever encountered such an agile lizardman. He was caught off guard by the skill with which the lizardman handled his sword. This creature was not going to be easy to kill, especially with magic at its disposal. Then something occurred to Sherman. It was something Kazin had once told him.

"You are a liar," said Sherman through clenched teeth. He tested the lizardman with a few quick slashes.

Slong easily parried the blows. "How do you figure?"

Sherman continued his assault and pretended to be weakening. "It's something someone told me once."

Slong parried the blows again. "And what might that be?"

"That lizardmen can't cast more than one spell at a time," said Sherman. He did a couple of sword thrusts to keep the lizardman on his toes.

The lizardman stumbled but kept his composure. "Is that how you want to die? I have a number of lethal spells that can put you out of your misery quickly."

"You can't cast them right now," said Sherman. "After all, you have to use your magic for this little arena of yours." He started to swing at the lizardman with more energy.

Slong grunted with the impact. He was reduced to parrying. He couldn't get in any more offensive swings with his sword. He sneered. "This spell already exists. I can cast a new spell any time I want."

Sherman raised an eyebrow. "Oh, really?" He kept the lizardman on the defensive. "I'm no genius when it comes to magic, but I know a spell of this magnitude requires continuous magic to maintain. Besides, if you could cast magic, you would have done so by now."

Slong was breathing heavily now. The strength of the warrior was becoming too much for him. Nevertheless, he held his cool. "Alright. I'll prove you're wrong." He held out his arm and pointed at Sherman while chanting.

Sherman was fairly certain he was right, but he wasn't about to prove it by letting his adversary kill him. He sliced off Slong's arm and decapitated him on the back swing. An instant later, he was on the battlefield again. The noise of battle was deafening. The leader of the lizardmen lay before him on the battlefield, his head and arm lying off to the side. The encounter with Slong had taken place in the blink of an eye in real time. When Slong's subordinates saw their dead leader, some of them broke and ran. Others put up a fight but were quickly subdued.

The tide of war was turning. Without leadership, the hordes of darkness began losing ground on all fronts. But it was no easy task for the humans to win either. The sheer numbers of the enemy kept fighting on until dawn. Halfway through the night, the tower's battlements were re-secured.

As the sun finally crested the horizon, the last of the monsters was battling their way through the living forest. Most were torn limb from limb. The few that managed to escape fled to the safety of the mountains. They had suffered a defeat they would not soon forget.

Chapter 34

he sky began to clear, revealing the nearly full moon. It was strangely quiet as the raft coasted into the inlet. No sentries were noticeable along the shoreline, but Brind took no chances. He cast a 'detect' spell to make sure he was alone. Satisfied that no one else was in the vicinity, he put the raft ashore. Then he waited quietly. If everything went as planned, Graf was supposed to meet him shortly after midnight. Brind wasn't concerned about whether Graf could find him. It was easy for the lizardmage to locate him using magic.

Brind took the opportunity to explore his immediate surroundings and stepped ashore. In the shrubbery nearby, he discovered the body of a human sentry. He smiled. Graf had definitely been here alright. The lizardmage wondered if Graf's plan was working.

It wasn't long before a rustling sound could be heard as someone approached the inlet. Brind remained concealed and waited. A cloaked figure came into view, barely visible in the moonlight. The figure turned in Brind's direction. "You can come out, Brind."

Brind recognized Graf's voice so he came out of cover. "Graf. How are things going?"

"So far so good," said Graf. "You have the cargo?"

"Yes," said Brind. He led Graf to the raft and climbed aboard. Toward the back of the raft was a large object covered with a tarp. The lizardmage removed the tarp, revealing the sleeping form of the hydra. The creature stirred.

"Perfect," said Graf. "Did it give you any trouble?"

Brind grunted. "It talked too much so I gave it lots of food to shut it up. Then, after all the heads fell asleep, it never made so much as a peep."

"Excellent," said Graf. "Now it's time to put this creature to work."

"I'm not a creature!" protested Frag, raising her head.

"Of course not!" said Graf condescendingly.

"What's going on?" said the head known as Garf.

"Apparently we have work to do," said Frag.

"I'm hungry," yawned Gif.

"You just ate all your supplies a few hours ago!" retorted Brind.

"Oh," said Gif dejectedly.

"You'll have plenty of meat to eat once you've done what I tell you to do," said Graf sullenly.

"What do you want us to do?" asked Frag.

"Just follow me and keep quiet," said Graf. "I'll tell you what to do when the time comes."

"What do you want me to do?" asked Brind.

"Stay here until I get back," said Graf. "I'll be a while, so stay out of sight."

Brind nodded. "Good luck."

Graf grimaced. "It has nothing to do with luck. It's all in the planning. After tonight, the humans will be all but vanquished. With the Tower of Hope and the Tower of Sorcery defeated, the humans will have no choice but to surrender to our superior magic!"

Brind grinned. "I can't wait."

"It won't be much longer," said Graf. "Just be patient." He turned and left with the hydra in tow.

As the lizardmage departed, two creatures with a low profile sprang out of the raft and scurried to safety in the dense brush along the shoreline. Brind had his back to the raft so he didn't see them. Even if he did, he wouldn't have paid much attention to them. No one paid attention to a couple of rats at the best of times.

Brind returned to his hidden spot in the nearby underbrush to wait. Soon all was quiet once again.

In the square near the selling booths lingered a number of cloaked figures. Their dark green capes looked black in the darkness. This worked to their advantage since black robed figures were common on Skull Island. There were only a few people visible at this hour. Most of these were shop vendors who were in the process of closing up and locking their shops. A majority of them headed for their quarters in specially designated apartments. The rest resided in local inns where travelers stayed. These inns sat strangely empty as travelers were few and far between. Most roads these days were not safe, since road patrols were recruited into the war taking place at the Tower of Hope. Civilians were preoccupied with survival and the search for clean water.

"He'd better get here soon," muttered Longspike.

Cleaver looked around. "He'll be here."

"This was too easy," said Sawtooth uneasily. "I don't like it."

"Just wait until we get inside the tower," said Ice Blade.

"I wonder what it's like," wondered Ropeburn.

"This isn't a sight- seeing tour," reminded Sparky. "There will be mages who can disable us if we are not vigilant."

"I agree," said Multibolt. "We're going to have to be alert and watch each other's backs."

"What's our mission again?" asked Ropeburn.

"We have to eliminate all of the arch mages," said Longspike. "Most of them are weak or dead, but we can't take any chances."

"And how do we identify them?" asked Ropeburn.

"They wear rings with a special insignia," said Longspike. "Also, their cloaks have a silver lining. If you're not sure, kill them anyway."

"How many arch mages are there?" asked Ice Blade.

"There are twelve of them," answered Longspike, "but not all of them may be present. Some may already be dead and buried. At least one has escaped the poison, so be alert."

"I'd like to get started soon," said Cleaver impatiently.

"Then we should begin," said a voice behind them. Everyone turned and saw a cloaked figure approaching. It was Inferno. "Is everything secure?"

"Yes," said Longspike. "The patrols were minimal. It didn't take long to take them out."

"Good," said Inferno. "We are ready for the next phase of my - er - our plan."

"Are you sure this will work?" asked Ropeburn nervously.

"Of course," said Longspike. "We know that as unauthorized magic users we will be magically transported to the prisons as soon as we try to enter the tower. Then we use our 'pass through rock' spell to escape the prisons before they can check on us. We then group together in twos and threes and infiltrate each floor and room to find and kill all of the arch mages. Anyone who gets in our way will have to die as well."

"But there are so many mages in the tower," objected Ropeburn.

Longspike nodded. "That's why I invited others to help us." He raised his fingers to his lips and whistled.

In the darkness noises could be heard. A number of cloaked figures appeared and gathered with the seniors of the Dark Magic Society.

Inferno appeared to be agitated. "We didn't need help. I had things under control. The mages are not likely to put up much resistance."

Longspike waved his hand in dismissal. "It doesn't hurt to have help. We don't know what awaits us in the tower. As far as we know, no outsiders have ever come out of there alive."

"As far as you know," muttered Inferno.

Sawtooth wished she had her green ring. She had held off telling the king about it thinking she had time to get one later, but the assault on the Tower of Sorcery had been pushed ahead of schedule once again for some unknown reason. Cleaver told her it was because he suspected someone fairly high up in the Dark Magic Society of being a spy. By moving up the date of the operation, the spy wouldn't have time to interfere. He was right. Now Sawtooth wished she had told the king about the stolen ring in her last meeting. But it was too late to do anything about it now. Her only option was to attempt to foil the plan herself.

Longspike handed out some spell scrolls with the 'pass through rock' spell inscribed on them. "This is to get past the prisons in the tower's basement," he explained. He led the contingent of dark elves past the inns and down the walkway to the mermaid fountain. Magical lights provided mild illumination to the fountain so that the mermaid would never be left in the dark. As the party passed, the mermaid's eyes followed them. It was only a statue, but it seemed to know that something was afoot.

Longspike halted the party before the long, narrow tunnel that was the only entrance to the Tower of Sorcery. In the daytime, the tower was a beautiful obsidian structure with one massive pinnacle in its center. Three domes surrounded the pinnacle, and nine smaller domes bordered the three taller ones. But up close in the moonlight, it was forbidding, its blackness blacker than the night. The entry tunnel seemed even blacker, threatening to swallow anything that considered entering its deep, dark depths.

The leader of the dark elves took a deep breath and strode forward. His chosen army followed. The other heads of the Dark Magic Society looked at one another nervously before following suit.

Inferno took one last look behind him and hoped his instructions were carried out. Then he, too, stepped through and disappeared from sight.

There was silence for several minutes. Then a couple of rats materialized out of the darkness. Their outlines on the ground seemed to be out of proportion to their real size due to the bright moonlight.

"Do you think we can get in?" asked the first rat.

"Only magic users can get in," said the second one. "We should be fine."

"I hope you're right, Lyrr."

"There's only one way to find out," said the second rat. He sprang through the dark opening and vanished.

Not wanting to be left behind, Lynch followed.

Before long, a large figure lumbered into view. It was the hydra.

"I don't know about this," murmured Frag.

"It'll be fun!" said Garf jovially. "Uncle Graf is finally letting us do something important. He said we were magic resistant! The mages won't be able to hurt us! We're going to be heroes!"

"He said there would be plenty of food," added Gif. "Let's hurry!"

"Alright, alright!" snapped Frag. "I'm going as fast as I can!"

The hydra lumbered as fast as it could through the entryway. Then it, too, disappeared from view.

x x x x x

The battlefield was a sea of blood and body parts. One could barely walk without stepping on bodily remains. Clerics wandered through the gory scene searching for signs of life. There were a few people they might still be able to save. When they came across a survivor, soldiers who followed with stretchers were ordered to bring them back to the tower for healing. The grisly task of cleaning up had begun.

In the courtyard, Kazin, Della, Rubin, Vera, Rebecca, Alric, Tyris, Sherman, and General Larsen were together talking. Kazin had just finished explaining his rescue by Frosty and the druids.

Alric immediately recognized Della and tried to keep a low profile. He avoided eye contact with her as she curiously regarded him with interest. When she asked about his reason for being there, he simply answered that he was an explorer who enjoyed an occasional quest.

General Larsen was shaking Sherman's hand. "Thanks once again for your timely assistance! Without you we would have fallen."

"Think nothing of it," said Sherman. "I'm just glad we came in time to help."

General looked at everyone assembled. "Thank you all. I'm grateful for everything each of you has done." Then he turned and wearily went back to work. As he walked away, his limp was even more noticeable than in the past.

"He's a real fighter," said Sherman when the general was out of earshot.

"Yes," said Kazin. "Do you remember when he tried recruiting you way back when?"

"Yeah," said Sherman. "I've learned a lot since those days."

"Incidentally," said Kazin, "how did you get here so fast? I thought for sure it would take a few days for you to arrive all the way from the mountains, let alone from your home city."

"We rode on the treemen," explained Sherman. "We selected the tallest trees with the longest roots from the fringes of the Black Forest, and they were able to move faster than any horse. Don't get me wrong; they moved slowly, but each step they took covered considerable ground in a short time. Also, their massive branches allowed them to carry up to, and in some cases more than, fifty soldiers and a spell caster. It was a bouncy ride, and we had to hold on tightly so as not to fall off. That's why we didn't have any cavalry. The treemen were a better substitute. We had more than enough young spell casters available from Queen Milena's mage schools to activate them. Once we got here, we climbed down and attacked, fully refreshed and ready to fight."

"But how did you know to assemble your army? Did Queen Milena order it?"

Sherman shook his head. "No. You did."

"What?!"

Sherman smiled. "It's a long story. I'll tell you all about it - er - maybe I can't." He scratched his head. "This time travel stuff is confusing," he mumbled.

Kazin gave him a weird look.

A couple of soldiers came by carrying a man on a stretcher. They paused as a gruff voice mumbled at them. They stopped and the man they were carrying tried to sit up. "Cyril," he called in a hoarse voice.

Cyril started when he heard his name. "Huh?"

The man beckoned weakly. "Come here."

Cyril walked up to the man and gasped when he saw who it was. "Jake?!" He quickly averted his gaze to avoid paralyzing the man.

The man's face was disfigured almost beyond recognition. "Yes. It's me."

"What happened?" asked Cyril, concerned.

The man waved his hand irritably. "Never mind that." He coughed before continuing. "I'm dying and I want you to do something for me."

"Just name it," said Cyril.

"I want you to take charge of the tower's gardens," said Jake. "You're better with plants and herbs than anyone I know. As least if you take over, they will have a chance to come back."

Cyril looked over at Vera but turned back before he could make eye contact. "Uh, sure," he said uncertainly.

"Promise?"

Cyril took a deep breath. "O - O.K."

"It will be a big job. There is plenty of damage to undo."

"I - I won't let you down," stammered Cyril.

"Good," said Jake. He motioned for the soldiers to continue. As the soldiers walked away, Jake lifted his head and hollered hoarsely, "And don't forget to water the faelora!"

Cyril gaped after the retreating figure, who smiled and winked. When he turned back to the others, he had tears in his eye.

At that moment, Lieutenant Farnsworth strode by with his mother at his side, along with his father, and Henry the dwarf. When Elsie saw the cyclops, she pointed at him and said, "You should have seen him! He's strong as an ox! He was fearsome to behold! No creature stood a chance against him! Not even the biggest ones!" Her praise carried on even after they were out of earshot.

The cyclops could stand no more. He began to cry. Vera immediately put her arm around the big cyclops' shoulder and held him close. "I told you if you gave people a chance they would like you."

"It looks like you have a talent with gardens," said Rebecca, playfully punching the cyclops in the arm.

"You're all heroes!" said a familiar voice.

Everyone turned to see High Cleric Malachi approaching. With him were Mara, the grey mage, and her general, Jerrin.

"I see you're still alive, Kazin!" exclaimed Malachi. "Everyone thought you were dead!"

"It was a surprise to me too," said Kazin. "I guess it takes more than a little poison to kill me."

"That's great!" said Malachi with a grin. "It's a good thing too. Your help was badly needed this time."

"I see you're finally taking a break," said Sherman.

Malachi nodded. "For the moment. But there is still much to do. I could use some help getting things back into shape around here." He put his hand on Mara's shoulder. "The grey mages have graciously agreed to stay a while."

"I can get my sailors to help," offered Rubin. "Ye'll need supplies and materials. But many will want some sort of compensation."

"I have money," said Malachi. He winked. "I also happen to have a stockpile of ale."

Rubin laughed. "Then ye'll have more help than ye know."

"My army can also help," said Sherman. "All we need is food and shelter. Our own supplies are low since we didn't have much time to prepare." He looked at Kazin as though it were his fault.

Malachi clapped his hands together. "That's wonderful! You are a true hero indeed!"

"I'll do what I can too," said Kazin. "I have nothing better to do."

At this Malachi held up a hand. "Not so fast, Kazin. One reason I took a break was to receive a message from the Tower of Sorcery. It seems there was another break in. The tower has some intruders."

Alric, who had been lurking in the background, snapped to attention.

Kazin gasped. "Who?"

Malachi shook his head. "I don't know. The mage who contacted me had to break the connection rather suddenly. I think you'd better go there and find out what's happening. The quarantine has been lifted now that there's a cure available."

Kazin nodded grimly. "I'll leave right away!"

"I'm coming too," said Alric before Kazin's sentence was even finished.

The mage turned to the elf. "You've done enough, Alric. You -."

"I'm going," stated Alric resolutely.

Kazin could see there was no arguing with the elf.

Rebecca watched the exchange with curiosity. Not wanting to be outdone by an elf, she said, "Me too." There was no way an elf was going to have more honour than a dwarf.

Kazin looked helplessly at the dwarf. He was about to respond when he made eye contact with his wife. If looks could kill, he would be dead a hundred times over.

"Don't even think about leaving me behind this time!" she said venomously.

"I should go too," put in Vera. She looked pleadingly at the high cleric. "No one has gone to heal the mages. They are still dying, and -."

"Yes, yes," said Malachi gently. "You made your point. Go with him. You can train the clerics there to perform the cure spell."

Vera hugged the high cleric. "Thank you, Malachi!"

"Then I'm going too," said Cyril.

Vera turned to the cyclops. "But the gardens -!"

"The gardens can wait," said Cyril. "Besides, you are my friend.

You may be headed into danger. You didn't abandon me when I went into a dangerous place, and I won't abandon you, either."

Vera hugged the cyclops. "Oh, Cyril!"

Kazin looked at Sherman. The big warrior let out a huge breath. "Me and my big mouth."

Kazin grinned. "Don't worry, Sherm. Malachi needs you right now. Your spell casters and soldiers can rebuild things faster than the mightiest of men."

"I guess," muttered the big man. He did not seem happy about being left out.

"You can help us load supplies," said Kazin. "We'll need plenty of faelora and dwarven ale."

Sherman brightened. "Right!" Then he lowered his eyebrows. "Dwarven ale?"

Kazin laughed. "You can let Malachi explain that one to you." He turned to Tyris. "What about you, Tyris?"

"It's time we had a talk," said Tyris. He looked around at the others. "Alone, if you don't mind."

Kazin and Tyris left the others and the elemental informed the mage that it was time for him to return to his other plane of existence. "Before I go," said the elemental, "I would like to offer you something no human black mage has ever had."

"You mean the enchantment on my staff?" asked Kazin.

"That too," said Tyris, "but I'm talking about something else right now."

Kazin stopped and looked at the elemental's coal black eyes.

"Kazin, I want to give you the ability to summon me."

"Are you sure you want to do that?" asked Kazin. "Look what happened when all the elementals were gathered together in a war!"

"That's one of the reasons I want you to have that ability," said Tyris. "If you can summon me, it will prevent others from summoning all the elementals for themselves. It will even out the playing field in your realm a little more."

"But why me?" asked Kazin.

"You're just in your actions, Kazin," said Tyris. "I trust you to do what is right. I can't trust anyone else that I know of. You're my only candidate."

Kazin sighed. "If that's what you want."

"It is," said Tyris. "Now listen closely -." The fire elemental whispered into Kazin's ear.

"That's it?" asked Kazin when the elemental had finished.

"Yes," said Tyris. "Memorize it well and tell no one about it. You won't use it often, but you mustn't forget."

"I won't," said Kazin.

"Good," said Tyris. "Now for the next thing. Once I enchant your staff, the spell will be complete. You will have the power of all four elementals at your disposal. The spell you will wield is called 'lifeforce'. The words to the spell will come to your mind when you need it. It is potent enough to defeat any foe, yet powerful enough to raise the dead. It can only be used sparingly. If you use it for killing, you must wait a full month before using it again. If you use it for bringing someone back to life, you must wait for a full year before using it again. If you do not wait the allotted time, the spell will fail and the enchantment will be gone forever. Note one thing - if the being you are bringing back to life has been dead for more than three days, you cannot bring them back to life. Their spirit has departed and the body is no longer able to be revived."

"That's a lethal magic," said Kazin uncertainly. "I don't know if I'm ready for it."

"You won't need it for many years," said Tyris, "but use it you will."

"How do you know?" asked Kazin.

Tyris merely smiled. "I can't tell you. Just take my word for it."

Kazin took a deep breath. "O.K. Let's get on with it."

Tyris turned to the others who were watching. "I have had a wonderful time with you all. My time here is finished, so I must go now. Take care in your journey wherever it takes you." He waved.

The others waved back.

Tyris turned back to Kazin. "Incidentally, Kazin, I may not appear the same when next you see me."

Kazin gave Tyris a quizzical glance.

The fire elemental touched his hand to Kazin's staff to perform the enchantment. Then his whole body was sucked into the staff and the elemental was gone.

Kazin looked at his staff and waited for something special to happen. When nothing transpired, he walked back to the others. "Let's get ready to go."

"It's about time," muttered Alric. He led the way to the supplies building.

Sherman gave Kazin a questioning glance. "What's got into him?"

"I have a feeling I'll find out fairly soon," said Kazin slowly.

Chapter 35

t was early in the afternoon when the dragon circled the square to search for a suitable landing spot. The journey had gone much more quickly because Mara had offered the services of the grey mages to cast a 'haste' spell on the dragon and his passengers. Kazin had gratefully accepted the offer, and had flown away from the Tower of Hope with incredible speed.

Now Kazin landed amidst a handful of concerned-looking people. The dragon allowed his passengers get off with all the gear before turning back into human form. While the others shouldered the packs of gear, the island residents quickly informed the arch mage of the dead island sentries and how no one had left the tower since the previous day. Two of the shop keepers reported seeing an unusually large number of mages entering the tower sometime after midnight.

Kazin thanked them and led the others to the tunnel entrance. Here he sheathed his staff in his specially designed holster and turned to face them. "Only spell casters can enter the tower. Non magic wielders will simply not be able to penetrate the opening. Spell casters not authorized to enter the tower will get past the opening, but will be magically transported to the detainment cells where they will be interrogated." He looked at each of them. "With special magic, I can take three of you with me. Alric, you and Vera can cast spells, so you will have to go through on your own. As soon as I enter the tower with the others, we'll go down to the cells to free you. Alright?"

Everyone nodded.

Kazin cast the spell and took Rebecca and Della by the hand. Cyril held Rebecca's hand. Then they stepped through the magical barrier and disappeared from sight. Alric and Vera looked at each other and then followed.

Once within the tower's entry hall, Kazin let go of the others and led them to the right into a tunnel that wound down under the entry hall. Another turn to the left guided them to a hallway with steps that went down to the detainment cells. When they entered the cell room hallway where cells lined both sides, they stopped abruptly. A ringing noise was sounding from the end of the hallway signaling the intruder alarm. Kazin was surprised no one had turned it off. The reason for this became apparent when they saw two mages on the floor ahead of them. Kazin hurried up to the first one and rolled him over. The mage was dead.

"She's dead," said Rebecca, examining the other body. "Some time ago, I'd guess."

"Vera!" called Cyril anxiously.

"I'm here!" said Vera from further down the hallway.

Kazin grabbed the keys from the dead mage and he and the others hurried to the cell where Vera was trapped. They released her and found Alric directly across the hall from her. When he was released, Kazin went to the room at the end of the hall and canceled the alarm. Something was amiss. If the guards were overcome, someone would surely have come along by now and turned off the alarm. The rest of the tower would have been alerted and the bodies would have been removed.

"I don't like it," said Kazin grimly. "Something is seriously wrong."

"Then let's investigate," said Alric. "Ughh!" He paused to wipe some rat droppings off his shoe.

"Follow me," said Kazin. He led the others back up to the main hall and chose the left path. At the end of that path, they arrived at another intersection. They went right and passed several classrooms. These rooms were eerily empty.

"Where is everybody?" asked Della. Her voice echoed in the emptiness.

"I'm guessing most of the sick mages are in the residences," said Kazin. But he was proven wrong when they reached the next classroom. Cots lined the floor from wall to wall. Dozens of patients lay in those cots, and a handful of clerics moved between the beds, making their patients as comfortable as possible. They looked up with surprised expressions when Kazin and the others entered.

One cleric came up to Kazin. "Have they been stopped?"

"Has who been stopped?" asked Kazin.

"The intruders," said the cleric as though Kazin should know what she was talking about.

"I don't know," said Kazin. "We just got here."

The cleric gasped when she saw the cyclops. "Don't hurt us!"

Cyril looked away so the cleric wouldn't accidentally become paralyzed.

"We're not here to hurt you," said Vera, stepping forward. "We have the cure for the disease."

"The cure?" said the cleric suspiciously. She took a step back.

"It's true," said Vera. She unshouldered her pack. "We must work quickly to save all the people we can. Which of your patients are the sickest?"

The cleric seemed to be coming around. She pointed. "In the corner."

As Vera headed for the spot, Kazin asked, "Which way did the intruders go?"

"They were looking for the arch mages," said the cleric. "There were at least thirty of them."

"Do you know who they were?" asked Della.

The cleric shook her head. "They were dressed in dark green robes. Their faces were hidden."

At this Alric looked uneasy.

"Which way did they go?" asked Kazin.

"I sent them to the inner chambers," said the cleric. "I don't know if they succeeded in accessing that part of the tower, but ever since they came by, no one else has come along until you arrived."

A chill ran up Kazin's spine. If the intruders made it to the inner chambers, they could potentially access the magic artifact stores. That could be devastating. There was no time to lose.

"Vera," called Kazin.

Vera was in the corner preparing to heal one of the patients. "Yes?"

"Can you teach these clerics the spell quickly? We have to move on and I need you with me."

"O.K." said the cleric. She readied the dwarven ale and faelora and called the other clerics to observe. Then she chanted her magic and healed the first mage. To the amazement of the clerics, the mage awakened from his coma and sat up groggily.

Then Vera let another cleric try the spell. She coached the cleric through the spell and the next mage was healed. After that, Vera was able to let the clerics continue healing on their own. Vera left most of the spell components with them and instructed one of the clerics to take some of the components and pass the spell on to the other clerics within the tower. The more clerics who learned to cure the disease, the better. Then she left with Kazin and the others.

Kazin took a short cut through the tower by cutting across the cafeteria. Alric instantly recognized the room. He shuddered at the thought that he was again within a stone's throw of the spark that had set all these events in motion. The spark that he himself had ignited. He set his jaw. He was determined to make that right again, now more than ever. He wasn't sure he would find the elusive lizardmage, but he was puzzled by the description the cleric gave of the intruders. They wore dark green robes. Were the intruders dark elves? If so, that would explain why they were looking for information pertaining to the human's black magic. Alric ground his teeth. He had supplied some of that information too. Was he being used by the Dark Magic Society? He hated being used. He preferred to be in control. The evil lizardmage wore a dark green robe. Was there a conspiracy within the dark magic society? Was the Dark Magic Society being manipulated by the lizardmen? Were they in cahoots with lizardmen? It hardly seemed possible. Alric vowed to get to the bottom of it.

As the group passed the entrance to the kitchen, a fat cook sprang out at them with a frying pan in one hand and a cleaver in the other. He yelled like a crazed lunatic, swinging his arms in a threatening manner. At the last moment, he recognized Kazin's robe and stopped himself before any damage was done. "Uh - oh - sorry," he said bashfully. "I thought you might be the creature coming back to cause trouble in my kitchen."

"That's O.K. - creature?" exclaimed Kazin.

The cook opened the swinging door to the kitchen area, revealing a scene of utter devastation. Dishes, food, baking ingredients, overturned pots, and all sorts of other paraphernalia were strewn about the entire kitchen.

"What happened here?" asked Rebecca.

"That hideous creature did this!" exclaimed the cook. "All three of its heads ate everything they could clamp their jaws on! Mages cast all sorts of spells trying to make it stop, but to no avail. I had to swat the creature on the behind with my cast iron frying pan to get it to leave! It's going to take days to clean up this mess!"

"Three heads?" asked Della.

"Yeah!" said the cook. "It was the most hideous creature I've ever seen!" He marched back into the kitchen, complaining and muttering to himself.

"What kind of creature do you think it was?" asked Rebecca.

Kazin looked grim. "By what he described, I'd say it was a hydra."

"A hydra?" exclaimed Vera. "But - but, that's terrifying!"

"What's so special about a hydra?" asked Della, "other than it has three heads."

"Hydras are magic resistant," said Kazin. "They're extremely difficult to kill."

"Have you ever encountered one?" asked Cyril.

Kazin shook his head. "Not yet."

Alric started forward. "What are we waiting for? Let's go."

On the way, the companions encountered a pair of clerics carrying a stretcher with a body. As they neared, Vera asked, "Plague victim?"

The cleric in front shook his head. "No. He's injured from the fight with the elves."

"Elves?!" exclaimed Della. "What do you mean?"

The clerics stopped. "The elves are attacking the mages. Didn't you know?"

Everyone exchanged glances. "No," said Kazin slowly. "We just got here."

"Follow us," said the cleric. "We've got proof if you don't believe us."

Kazin and the others followed the clerics to a lecture hall where injured mages were being treated for injuries. A few black mages standing guard snapped to attention upon seeing the arch mage.

"What's going on here?" asked Kazin.

The youngest of the mages stepped forward. "We're guarding the clerics and patients so they can do their jobs. Master Mage Linnal put us in charge."

Kazin knew Master Mage Linnal. He was a younger mage who had taken the mage test a few years ago and was eligible to become an arch mage. If he was in charge, that meant there were no arch mages around to issue orders.

"Are there any elves present?" asked Della.

The young mage nodded. "Yes. We have a few prisoners."

"Show us," ordered Kazin.

The mage led them to a back room where a couple more mages stood on guard. When they saw Kazin, they immediately released the magic on the door so Kazin and his people could enter. Curious stares followed the cyclops as he walked past.

The room had a number of beds where clerics fussed over a handful of injured patients. Kazin walked up to one bed occupied by an elf. The elf glared at Kazin as he approached.

"What's your name?" asked Kazin.

The elf scowled.

"Why are you here?" asked the arch mage. He had a firm edge to his voice.

"To rid the world of those who poisoned the water and land!" snapped the elf.

"You think it was us?" asked Kazin in surprise.

"You humans always experiment with things of this nature!" spat the elf, "especially the arch mages!"

"That isn't true," said Kazin flatly. "It was the lizardmen. Thankfully, we put a stop to it. With the help of the water elemental - who the lizardmen had originally used to create the poison - we were able to come up with a cure. The lizardmages' plan to take over our land has failed."

"I don't believe you," spat the elf.

"You have been misled," said Kazin. "This fight must stop. Who is your leader?"

The elf didn't answer. His eyes stared and he did not blink. At first, Kazin thought the patient had perished.

"Oops!" said Cyril quietly. "He looked into my eye. Sorry."

"Don't be," said a nearby cleric. "This way he won't be in pain for a while."

A patient in another bed moaned and motioned for them to come closer. The companions neared the bed and saw a beautiful female elf with her right arm wrapped in bandages. Alric was instantly smitten by her clear hazel eyes and chestnut brown hair. The smell permeating from her bed was strangely familiar.

"Hi," she said. She looked at Kazin. "Are you an arch mage?"

"Yes," said Kazin.

The elf motioned him closer. When she spoke, she almost whispered as though afraid of being overheard. "I'm sorry this whole thing is happening. What started out as a misunderstanding has escalated out of control."

"Continue," said Kazin quietly. He could sense a strong perfume on the patient and only his expert training kept his mind on the subject.

The elf took a deep breath. "The elves attacking you are dark elves. Dark elves operate independently of the rest of the elves. They believe in the use of offensive magic for the benefit of all elves. Most of the other elves love peace and non-violent magic. The king enforces strict rules of conduct limiting the use of offensive magic. The Dark Magic Society believes otherwise, and operates in secret places unknown to the king. Anyhow, the dark elves have never liked human black mages and were planning some sort of attack to discourage humans from pursuing black magic. When news came of poisoned water and most of the first casualties of the plague had originated in the Tower of Sorcery, the dark elves determined that a more serious thing had to be done to punish the human black mages - particularly the arch mages. A direct assault on the Tower of Sorcery had been planned. All arch mages were to be killed. That leads us to the present."

"Why are you telling me this?" asked Kazin.

"I - can't go into details," stammered the elf.

"What about the hydra?" demanded Della. Her dislike of dark elves was obvious in the tone of her voice.

The patient shook her head. "I'm not sure where it came from. I didn't even know it was part of the plan until I heard about it from one of the clerics." She gave Kazin a sad look. "I was injured not long after leaving the cells. Some mages took me to this place and I've been here ever since. I would have put a stop to this if it hadn't been for the damage to my hand and arm." The elf studied the faces of Kazin's group, wisely avoiding the cyclops' eye. "You see, I lost my -." Her voice broke off and she sat up in alarm. "Where did you get that?" she demanded in a loud voice.

Kazin stepped back, prepared to use magic to defend himself. He didn't complete the spell when he noticed the elf looking at Alric.

Alric came out of his trance. "Huh? What?"

"That ring!" pressed the patient. "Where did you get that ring?"

Alric looked at his hand which wore the green ring. Then he remembered where he had encountered the female elf before - in the dark magic meeting hall. "What, this ring?" he asked innocently. "I found it somewhere," he lied.

The female elf knew Alric was lying. She desperately looked around at those assembled with pleading eyes. "I need that ring! Please! It can stop all of this!"

"I don't think so," said Kazin sternly.

The patient froze for a split second and then fell back against her pillow. "No!" she moaned. "No, no, no!" She shook her head and wept. "This can't be happening!"

Kazin and the others exchanged curious glances.

"Let me talk to her for a moment in private," said Alric quietly.

"Help yourself," said Kazin. "But don't let yourself get seduced by her perfume."

"I won't," said Alric.

"And don't let her get hold of that ring," admonished Kazin.

"Don't worry," said Alric.

Everyone withdrew a short distance while Alric had a talk with the elf. He found her more than attractive enough without the perfume. With the perfume, she was virtually irresistible.

"Why do you want the ring so badly?" asked Alric gently.

"It will help put an end to this nonsense," said the elf.

"You're one of the intruders," said Alric. "Why would you want to prevent this attack?"

"I can't tell you!" wailed the elf. "Please! You've got to trust me! Give me the ring and I'll prove it to you!" Tears welled in her eyes and Alric hated himself for causing pain to such a beautiful elf.

"You know I can't do that."

The female elf looked directly into Alric's eyes. "You stole it from me. It's not yours. You are a thief, and you will be banned from the Dark Magic Society, Windoor."

Alric flinched at the mention of his secret name. "If you take me down, you're coming with me, Sawtooth." He waited while his mention of her name sunk in. "Once the society finds out you were trying to work against their plan, they'll disown you and exonerate me. What do you say to that?"

He regretted his harsh words as soon as he had spoken them. He hated himself even more as Sawtooth began to weep again.

"I'm ruined anyway," cried Sawtooth. She looked up at Alric with a tear streaked face. "Tell me you are not in favour of this attack."

"I can quite truthfully answer that question," said Alric. "Absolutely not."

"Then hear this," said Sawtooth. "That ring is designed to summon a dozen of the king's elite forces to your side as soon as you rub the ring's surface and speak the magic. The soldiers are trained in combat and magic, and even the most skilled dark elf won't be able to stand against these elite fighters."

"Are you telling me you're a spy?" asked Alric incredulously.

Sawtooth covered her face with her hands. "I don't know why I'm telling you all this. You're only a thief. I can't trust you."

Hearing those words from such a beautiful elf made Alric suddenly feel guilty. He wanted the elf to like him, but there was no trust between them. They were on opposite sides, yet she claimed they were on the same side. He shook his head. This was too confusing. He backed away. "I've got to go."

The female elf uncovered her face. "Just remember what I told you about the ring. The words to the spell are etched on the inside."

"I'll keep it in mind," said Alric. He turned to go.

"And be careful," said Sawtooth.

Alric looked back at her. She seemed to be genuinely concerned. He nodded.

"Be wary of the one called Inferno. He's full of hatred. I don't trust him."

Alric nodded again and left to join the others.

When he got back to the group, Kazin was just learning about the existence of a chamber where the dead bodies were put until they could be given proper burials. The room was two doors down from their present location and was kept cold with a special artifact so the bodies would be prevented from decomposing. Kazin asked whether any arch mages had ended up there since the outset of the plague. According to the mage's memory, there were four, the most recent being Arch Mage Krendal. At the mention of Krendal, both Kazin and Della were saddened.

Kazin told the mage to show him to the chamber. At the chamber's entrance, Kazin steeled himself and entered the room with Della at his side. The room contained a number of mages lying on cots. Kazin half expected to see Arch Mage Fildamir present, but there was no sign of him. Good. That meant he was still alive. Then he shuddered as a thought struck him. The arch mage could already be long dead and buried.

But right now Kazin and Della wanted to pay their final respects to the man who had led the Tower of Sorcery since Kazin was a child. Arch Mage Krendal was a stern taskmaster, but he was always there for Kazin as he grew in magical power. He supported Kazin's ascension into an arch mage, a rare opportunity for any up and coming mage.

Kazin and Della went up to the cot where Krendal's body lay in a peaceful pose. His hands were folded together over his abdomen and his old wooden staff lay at his side. The arch mage's weathered face and flowing white beard were the same in death as it was in life. How old this man was Kazin could only guess.

Della squeezed Kazin's hand and remembered the gruff but kind arch mage as he accepted her and Kazin's other companions with open arms. She sighed. "It's a shame we came too late to cure him of the disease. He'd have been proud, Kazin."

Kazin nodded silently.

"It's too bad we can't cure death," went on Della. "I'd sure like to see Krendal the way I remembered him."

It took a moment for Kazin's mind to grasp what Della was saying. He let go of her hand and sprang for the door. He stuck his head out into the hallway and addressed the mage who had guided him to the chamber.

"How long has he been dead?"

"Uh, who?" asked the mage.

"Arch Mage Krendal," said Kazin. "How long has he been dead?"

The mage scratched his head. "Uh - at least two days."

"Not three?"

The mage shook his head. "No. It was two days ago. I'm sure of it."

Kazin tucked his head back into the room and shut the door.

"What is it?" asked Della.

"Let's just call it the moment of truth," said Kazin. He raised his staff and pointed it at the arch mage.

"What are you doing?" demanded Della.

"Quiet!" ordered Kazin. He closed his eyes and concentrated, the words to the spell coming automatically to his mind as Tyris had promised. He began to chant. The orb atop his staff began to glow a brighter and brighter green. Soon the whole chamber was ablaze with green light. Della shielded her eyes, while Kazin's own eyes began to radiate the same green light as his staff. A faint hum could be heard coming from the staff while Kazin chanted the spell.

Suddenly, a piercing blast of white light was emitted from the staff, snaking along its length and jolting into the old arch mage's chest. The arch mage gave a great gasp of air and sat bolt upright on the cot. The 'lifeforce' spell was complete.

Kazin collapsed on the floor and Della opened her eyes. When she saw Arch Mage Krendal's penetrating blue eyes staring back at her, she joined Kazin on the floor, unconscious.

Chapter 36

"ell, well," said the old arch mage. "What have we done to deserve this?"

The people in the hallway reacted strangely when the arch mage opened the door. The young mage guarding the door could only gape with his mouth hanging open in surprise.

Arch Mage Krendal surveyed Kazin's new companions curiously. It didn't surprise him that there was such an odd assortment of characters present. He deliberately looked Cyril in the eye as he spoke. "I think we should find more comfortable quarters for Kazin and Della. They have had quite a shock."

As Kazin and Della were carried to a room where there were spare beds, Rebecca introduced everyone and filled Krendal in on the strange happenings at the Tower of Sorcery. Arch Mage Krendal was surprised to hear about the hydra.

Krendal soon shook off the effects of lying on a bed for a prolonged time and began formulating a plan, when a young mage came running to inform him of the approaching hydra.

"The hydra was talking about getting into the higher levels of the tower to find its uncle," said the messenger excitedly. "Apparently it wasn't able to follow its uncle to the next level since it requires magic, so it was looking for an alternative route."

"Are you saying there is a second hydra here also?" asked Krendal.

The messenger shook her head. "I don't know. I haven't seen one."

The arch mage nodded. "We will have to be wary of that possibility." He then took control of the situation and told everyone what he remembered of the mythical beast.

"Magic won't work," he informed them, "but magical artifacts are another matter entirely. While the magical characteristics may not be as effective, they will still do more damage than ordinary weapons. What it boils down to is brute strength. The key is to make your attacks count. Blinding the creature by stabbing its eyes is often a good practice, but we have three heads to deal with. It's unlikely we'll be able to pierce more than two eyes before the creature gets wise to the tactic. A hydra's biggest weakness lies in the fact that all of the heads need to agree before it acts. If we can get the heads to argue amongst themselves, it may provide one or more opportunities for us to attack."

"So what do you suggest?" asked Rebecca.

"The hydra is between us and the artifact room," said Krendal. "We'll have to make a stand here. Do any of you have magical artifacts in your possession?"

"I have a magical dagger," said Rebecca, displaying her weapon for Krendal to see.

"I have a magical mace," said Cyril.

"Good," said Krendal. He looked at Alric. "And you?"

"I - have an invisibility cloak," said the elf reluctantly.

"Perfect," said Krendal. "Now here's the plan." The companions huddled around the old arch mage. "I'm going to distract the hydra while one of you sneaks up to it." He looked at Alric. "Your cloak will be necessary for this."

"My weapon isn't magical," objected Alric.

"Can you borrow someone else's?" asked Krendal.

Alric shook his head. "No. Rebecca's dagger would kill me, and I've tried to lift Cyril's mace. It's much too heavy for me to wield effectively."

Krendal scratched his beard. "Can anyone other than Alric use the cloak?"

"It's too big for me," said Rebecca. "I would just trip over it."

"It doesn't even cover half of my body," said Cyril.

Krendal sighed. Then he brightened. "Of course! What we have to do is quite simple. There is only one way to unify the cloak and dagger. . .

The hydra marched down the hallway angrily. Mages surrounded the creature in front and behind. They were casting spells at it but to no avail. The hydra was impervious to magic. A mage got too close and Gif's head darted out and snapped up the mage in his giant maw. The mage screamed for a split second before being bitten in two.

"Ptui!" Gif spat out the remains. "These mages are horrible! Where is all the food Graf promised us?"

"We already cleaned out the kitchen," reminded Frag.

Garf snapped at a nearby mage but missed. "I think they taste pretty good once you get past the robes."

"I wonder why Graf sent us here?" commented Gif. "There are plenty of human villages that would have more food than this place."

"He didn't send us here to eat," said Frag. "He sent us here to cause a distraction while he kills off the arch mages."

"But he told us there would be plenty of food!" argued Gif.

"There is!" exclaimed Garf. He thrust his head out and this time his jaws managed to catch a mage by the arm. He swung the screaming mage up into the air and let her fall into his waiting jaws. He chomped the mage a couple of times and then swallowed. "You know, I think the women taste better than the men."

Frag shook her head. Directly ahead of her, she spotted an old bearded mage who stood in the middle of the hallway. He had a serious expression and piercing blue eyes. Something about him made her come to a stop. The mages following the hydra abruptly stopped their magic as well.

Arch Mage Krendal nodded curtly before speaking. "I am Arch Mage Krendal. What is the reason for your visit to my tower?"

"We're here to eat you!" hissed Garf.

Krendal turned to Garf. "Shut up!" Garf's head recoiled at this outburst. "I'm speaking to the center head," continued Krendal. "The center head of a hydra is the most intelligent."

"Listen to him, Garf," said Frag. "He's an arch mage. He knows what he's talking about."

"That's not true!" insisted Gif. "You said arch mages are liars!"

"I agree," said Garf. "We determine intelligence by how strong our magic is, and mine is obviously stronger than yours, Frag."

"If your magic is that strong," said Frag, "how come you can't use it to change us back?"

"I could if I had my staff and arms," argued Garf.

"I doubt it!" snapped Frag.

"It's true!"

"Is not!"

"Is so!"

"Is not!"

Garf snapped at Frag and she retaliated.

Arch Mage Krendal was surprised at how easy it was to distract the hydra. He made a signal and his plan was set in motion. The hydra didn't see it until it was almost too late.

A female dwarf armed with a dagger materialized out of nowhere right in front of the hydra. She took the dagger by the blade and threw it a Frag's head. The weapon flew true and landed directly in Frag's left eye.

Alric pulled his cloak back over himself after letting the dwarf out. He pulled out his dagger and magically changed it into a sword. The disembodied sword bounded up to Garf and slashed at his exposed right side. The blade missed the eye but sliced deeply into the eyelid. Blood squirted from the wound and Garf hissed in dismay. He snapped his head in a sideways motion and sent the sword and its owner crashing into the wall.

From behind the old mage another figure sprang into view. He moved with incredible speed, the result of a haste spell Vera had cast on him. Cyril charged up to Gif's head and began batting the head mercilessly with his mace. The head squealed in pain and tried to snap at Cyril, but the cyclops dodged out of the way. The initial attack left Gif's head smashed on one side. Blood poured from his mouth where some teeth had been knocked loose.

Frag reared her head back in pain and then lashed out at the tiny dwarf below her. Rebecca barely had time to roll out of the way to the left as the head came smashing down on her. Her weapon was magically back in her hand, and thus the dwarf discovered a new attribute of her magical dagger. It could be thrown and would immediately return to her hand after it had stopped flying. Keeping this in mind, she quickly thrust out at Frag's right eye. The blade succeeded in completely blinding Frag. The middle head thrashed and screamed in agony, bumping into her brothers' heads in the process. Fortunately for Alric, the bump prevented Garf from successfully snapping up the invisible sword wielder.

Alric took the opportunity to spring to his feet and hide his weapon. Then he snuck up to Garf and readied his sword. He made a few quick slashes and then concealed his weapon again. Garf's neck was cut open and he hissed in rage. His right eye was difficult to see out of with all the blood in the way, so he blindly snapped at the ground all around him. Alric stayed well back of the enraged head.

The turbulence of the other heads made it difficult for Cyril to land a decent blow, but he managed to seriously damage Gif's neck and nose. The spikes in his mace rent the flesh nearly to the bone. Gif was losing lots of blood and he was beginning to lose consciousness. His half-hearted attacks against his adversary weren't even close.

Rebecca wasn't sure what to do next. Frag was blindly thrashing about like a maniac. The only thing Rebecca could do was stab the middle head's neck. She threw her dagger again and it sank into a major artery in the neck. Frag gurgled a scream and blood trickled from her mouth. She continued lashing blindly at everything nearby.

Alric continued appearing and disappearing, landing sword slashes each time his sword made an appearance. He stayed on Garf's partly blinded side to prevent his good eye from zeroing in on him.

Cyril landed a series of hard blows and succeeded in killing one of the heads. Gif's head hung down limply by its neck, swinging with the heaving of the hydra's body.

Frag was the next to go as Rebecca threw her dagger repeatedly at the bleeding neck. Several major arteries were severed and blood was gushing from the open wounds. Frag had no strength to thrash about any longer and her head crashed to the ground one last time. Rebecca was thrown to the floor as pieces of the floor exploded in every direction. Miraculously, she was unharmed.

Garf sensed the death of his two siblings and took full control of the hydra's body. He turned the bulky body around to retreat, dragging the dead heads like balls on a chain. But the blood loss to the body was too much. Garf staggered and then the hydra crashed to the floor. The last thing Garf saw with his good eye was the disembodied sword coming down to pierce his eye and brain. With a last long hiss, the hydra was dead.

A magical transformation took place and the hydra vanished, to be replaced by two foolish lizardmen and one lizardwoman. On the ground near them, rolling to the side, was a cracked dragon orb.

"Well done!" exclaimed Arch Mage Krendal. To the fighters, he said, "The Tower of Sorcery owes each of you a debt of gratitude." He strode up to the bodies to look at the lizardmen. "Why, they're only young lizardmen children!" he exclaimed. "I should have known lizardmen were involved! That explains why the hydra was looking for its uncle. Lizardmen are responsible for the attack on the tower, and are still on the loose."

While attention was on the bodies, a couple of rats spotted the orb.

"Quick!" whispered Lynch, his nose twitching excitedly. "Let's take it before someone sees!"

Lyrr took a piece of torn robe from nearby and they ran over to the orb. Lynch rolled the orb onto the piece of robe using his pointed nose and Lyrr picked up the four corners in his mouth. He scurried off with the orb tucked safely inside. Lynch followed close behind.

Chapter 37

never expected young lizards to be part of a plan to attack the Tower of Sorcery!" exclaimed Vera.

Krendal shook his head sadly. "They undoubtedly found the dragon orb and handled it, not realizing that its magic was unstable. Damaged orbs in particular are unpredictable." He looked around. "We'll have to store it in a safe place so it won't get into the wrong hands. Maybe it can even be repaired." The arch mage spun all the way around, scanning the floor. "That's funny. I thought I just saw it a moment ago."

The other mages in the vicinity assisted in the search but came up empty. During the search, Alric removed his cloak and stashed it back into his pack.

"What's everyone looking for?" asked a familiar voice down the hallway.

Rebecca turned to see Kazin and Della. "Oh, hi! You recovered fast!"

Kazin nodded. "The clerics here can do wonders."

"Good," said Krendal. "You're just in time. We have work to do." He turned to the gathered mages. "Some of you come with us. The rest of you clean up these bodies. If any of you find the damaged orb, do not touch it. Use a piece of cloth to handle it. Carry it to one of the classrooms and leave it there for me to examine." Krendal turned back to Kazin. "Come with me."

Arch Mage Krendal led Kazin and his companions and a few mages to a doorway that led to a higher level of the tower. Krendal cast a spell on the group and they entered the room.

The room was like a lobby, with many doors leading to other rooms. There was no furniture. Torches powered by mystical magic flickered on the walls. On the floor near one door lay two inert forms.

Vera rushed over to them and examined them. She looked up at the others. "They're dead!"

Krendal stepped forward and recognized one of the ones Vera had examined. "Master Mage Linnal. He had good potential." He turned to the others. "We are losing too many good mages. We must hurry!"

"Which way did the intruders go?" asked Rebecca.

Krendal checked the doors in the room with magic. The door nearest the dead mages glowed slightly. He pointed. "That door was opened using a different kind of magic. Someone overrode our magical lockout. They went through there."

The group quickly opened the door and entered a hallway beyond. More bodies were scattered over the floor here. Three were mages. Two were dark elves. There were signs of fighting. The walls and ceiling were scorched and blackened.

"The fighting was more intense here," remarked Krendal. "We must be getting close."

"The damage here can't all be from our guys," commented Kazin. "Not unless some arch mages are still alive."

"That's unlikely, judging by the reduced number of defenders," said Krendal. "These intruders wield more powerful magic than I thought."

At the end of the hallway were three doors. One led straight ahead, one was on the left, and one on the right. Another spell check indicated the middle door had been used.

Krendal breathed a sigh of relief. "At least the artifact room hasn't been breached." He was referring to the door on the right.

The companions cautiously opened the door and entered a great library. The doorway was up above the main body of the library and stairs led down into the numerous aisles of bookshelves. Tables were set up in specific study areas and books were piled on some of them. Across the room from them was an identical set of stairs leading up to another doorway. At the entrance to that doorway was a crowd of dark green robed figures. They turned to see the newcomers and a yell was heard. From below, a series of fireballs came up to greet them from different parts of the room.

Vera quickly put up a shield, but not before Kazin let two bolts of lightning loose at the elves on the far side of the room.

The shield reflected the incoming fireballs and the companions saw two of the enemy fall to Kazin's lightning bolts.

"Retreat!" cried Krendal.

Everyone listened even though it looked like they could have held their own.

When they were back in the safety of the hallway, Krendal explained his order to retreat. "We can't have fighting in the library! If any of those books are destroyed, it could mean hundreds of years of knowledge being lost!"

"Then what should we do?" asked Della.

"We'll have to go around," said the arch mage. He and Kazin collaborated and quickly came up with a plan of attack.

"We'll have to split into two groups," said Kazin. "Alric, Rebecca and Della, come with me and we'll cut across the artifact room. We have to check what lies beyond in the next room. Maybe there are allies who can help us. Vera, you and Cyril go with Krendal and take the left door." Kazin turned to the remainder of the group. "The rest of you stay here and use your trap related spells to detain anyone who comes through that door. Use the slow spell on the entryway and you'll have plenty of time to subdue everyone who comes back through here. Use force if necessary. Understand?"

The mages nodded grimly.

"Good." Kazin turned to Krendal. "Good luck."

The two groups split up and entered their respective doorways.

Kazin quickly led his group through the artifact room. Alric and Rebecca were awed by the vast array of weapons and unidentified artifacts. They were tempted to stop and look around, but their mission was too important to ignore.

At the far end of the artifact room was another doorway. Kazin led the group through and they wound up in a small room with two more exits. The room was barely big enough to hold all of them.

"Where do these doors go?" asked Alric.

"The left one goes to a room adjoining the library," said Kazin. "The right door goes to the meditation hall. It's full of thick mats where mages sit and work on their meditation skills." He spoke quietly because he didn't want to alert any would-be intruders to their presence. The doors in this part of the tower were magically enhanced to block out noises so the people in the library could study in peace, but he didn't want to take any chances.

"I'm all for the left door then," said Alric. He spoke with a quieter voice too.

"Let's try the meditation room first," said Kazin. "I don't want to walk into a fight without knowing my escape route is safe first."

Della nodded. "Good point."

"Why don't you use your invisibility cloak to check the rooms beyond, Alric?" asked Rebecca.

Alric reddened and gave Della an anxious look. He had hidden his secret so well he was beginning to think he was going to get away with it. Now the dwarf had unwittingly put him in a bad position. He couldn't deny he had the invisibility cloak any longer. His only hope was that Della wouldn't recognize or remember her old cloak. But in such close quarters it was unlikely she wouldn't notice.

"I - uh - I suppose -," began Alric.

Della was staring at the elf with a strange look on her face.

"It wouldn't make any difference," said Kazin suddenly. "Once I open the door, any element of surprise will be lost."

"My sentiments exactly," said Alric, relieved. He avoided Della's stare.

"The only way we could spy on the rooms next to us would be to go through the door without opening it," continued Kazin, "and that's a spell I don't have at my disposal."

Alric snapped to attention. He mentioned the spell scroll he remembered seeing in the mountains that was used by some lizardmen trying to summon Tyris. They had escaped using a 'pass through rock' spell scroll. "I vaguely remember it," added Alric. "But even if I did, I doubt I could cast it. It's a spell beyond my capabilities. If I had a spell scroll, I could do it. Anyone could, even a non-spell caster."

Kazin nodded. "It's a complicated spell that requires earth and air magic. Few mages can cast it without a spell scroll." Then Kazin remembered something. He turned to Alric. "I almost forgot! The air elemental wanted me to give you something." He held out his staff and gently touched Alric's hand with the orb.

Alric flinched when the orb made contact with him. "What did you do?" he asked, alarmed.

Kazin winked. "You've just received increased skill in air-based magic. It might help you remember the spell."

Alric closed his eyes and concentrated. Then he opened his eyes wide. "Yes! I've got it!" He turned to the door and chanted the spell. Then he slowly moved his hand toward the door. When his fingers touched the door, they seemed to melt right through it. Alric pulled his hand back and looked at the others excitedly. "It works!" he whispered excitedly.

"Now all you need to do is put on your cloak," said Rebecca.

Alric grimaced. He wasn't going to get out of it this time. He reluctantly pulled the cloak from his pack.

"Hey!" exclaimed Della. "That looks like my cloak!" She grabbed it from Alric and held it up to examine it. She nodded. "It's definitely mine! It has the same little tear in it like I remember." She turned to Alric. "Where did you get this?"

"I - bought it from a merchant," lied Alric.

Della narrowed her eyes. "You stole it, didn't you? Just like you stole that ring from that elf who was injured!"

"Della -," began Kazin.

Della turned to her husband. "He stole my cloak, Kazin! He's a thief!"

Kazin looked between the two elves helplessly. He suspected Alric had something to hide from the moment they had met. But the elf had proven himself on more than one occasion. This was not the time to confront him with this issue. He slowly took the cloak from Della and handed it back to Alric.

"Kazin!" objected Della.

Kazin turned to his wife. When he spoke, he spoke gently and deliberately. "If it weren't for Alric, I would have been dead several times over. He has saved my life a number of times and has earned my trust. I need him to help us right now. Then we'll discuss the theft and get to the bottom of it."

Della wasn't impressed. "Fine." She gave Alric a mean stare.

Kazin nodded at Alric. "Proceed."

Alric nodded and donned his cloak. He was glad to make himself invisible to avoid the other elf's gaze. Then he chanted the 'pass through rock' spell again. A moment later, he stepped through the door and entered the meditation room. The experience of moving through a sold object made Alric feel queasy, but it was only momentary.

He returned a moment later and spoke while still cloaked. "It's empty. I'm going into the other room now."

"O.K.," said Kazin. "Just gather information. Find out how many elves there are. We need to know what we're up against."

"O.K.," said Alric. He went through the next door.

The room he entered had several tables along one side. A long table sat across from them. There was a door situated behind the tables that Alric guessed led to the library. A door on the far side of the room led elsewhere. The door behind the long table was the most interesting one, because a number of dark elves were gathered around it, chanting to overcome the magical warding. Several human mages were lying on the floor in the corner. They had put up a reasonable amount of resistance judging by the broken chairs and charred walls. Three more dark elves were also dead. Their bodies were leaned up against the wall next to the dead mages.

A guard was positioned next to the doorway across the room. Movement next to Alric made him jump. A guard was next to the doorway Alric had come through as well. Altogether there were twenty-two dark elves in the room.

Alric had seen enough. He hoped his spell was still holding as he held his breath and walked back through the door.

"So, what does it look like?" asked Kazin.

"There are twenty-two dark elves in the room," reported Alric, "not including the ones that are dead." He added the fact that they were trying to get past the door.

"Those are difficult odds," commented Rebecca.

"Especially if they can all cast spells," added Della.

"We've faced tougher odds," said Kazin.

Then Alric remembered what Sawtooth had said about the green ring he possessed. He decided to bring it up. Alric explained what Sawtooth had said to him regarding the ring and the elite guard.

"Let me see it," said Kazin.

Alric removed his cloak and then passed the ring to Kazin. The arch mage examined it and passed it to Della. "Does this look familiar?"

Della took the ring and studied it. She had been in the king's court a number of times before. After a while, she nodded. "It sure looks like the rings the king's elite guard always wear. My guess is it's authentic."

"Should we take a chance that it works the way this - Sawtooth, you call her - claims it does?" asked Rebecca.

"She seemed unusually adamant it would stop the dark elves," said Kazin. "I think we should try it."

"We can't do it in here," objected Della. "It's too cramped. Someone could get hurt."

Kazin had an idea. "Alric, can you memorize the inscription on the back of the ring?"

"I already have. Why?"

"Because I want you to create a diversion so we can enter the room without being singled out," said Kazin. "If you can cast the spell and rub the ring while you are invisible, the dark elves will have no time to react. By the time they see you, the elite guard will be present. Then the rest of us will jump into the fray and overwhelm them."

"Some plan," muttered Alric.

"You stole my cloak, so you get the honours," said Della uncompassionately.

Alric gave Della a sour look and donned the cloak.

"You might need this," added Della. But the ring was already gone. "Whaa -? Where -?"

Alric was already chanting the 'pass through rock' spell. "Give me about fifteen seconds," he said. "And watch out for the guard on the other side of the door." Then he was gone.

Alric moved to a spot as far from the group of dark elves as he could get before performing the magic on the ring. Then he spoke the words inscribed in the ring and rubbed its surface. Some of the elves in the room looked around at the sound of Alric's voice but weren't prepared for the blinding flash. In an instant, the room was swarming with a dozen of the king's elite guard.

Most of the dark elves turned to do battle, expecting a bunch of untrained human mages. Then they discovered how ineffective their magic was against the elite guard. Ice bolts, magical arrows, and fireballs filled the room. Everything was a total mayhem when Kazin's lightning bolt added to the party.

Alric saw Rebecca take out the guard by the door with her dagger while Della fired arrows into the dark elves. On the other side of the room, Krendal appeared, casting spells with decisiveness. Cyril did combat with the elf sentry while Vera paralyzed some of the dark elves so the elite guard could round them up.

While all this was happening, Alric saw something he could scarcely believe. Ignoring the chaos around him, one of the dark elves continued to weaken the door's magic. Suddenly the magical ward dropped away with a shower of tiny stars. The dark elf turned to look behind him for a split second while opening the door. His face was visible in the bright flashes of magic, but it wasn't the face of an elf. It was the face of a lizardmage. Alric's heart leaped. At last! At long last! Alric paid no heed to his safety as he dodged through the crossfire of magic in pursuit of his nemesis. This was what he had been waiting for!

Meanwhile, Ice Blade saw that they were outmatched, so he cast a spell and escaped in a flash. Sparky followed suit. Ropeburn was not so lucky. She was slain by one of Della's arrows. Multibolt was subdued by one of the elite guard and Cleaver would have escaped had it not been for Vera's 'paralyze' spell. Longspike fought against Kazin using magic, but the arch mage dissolved any oncoming magic with his lightning bolt. With the magic removed, Kazin's lightning bolt continued unchecked toward the leader of the Dark Magic Society, killing him instantly. Kazin had his mind on other things as he simultaneously sent fireballs, ice bolts, and magic arrows in several directions at once.

The battle was winding down quickly with the last few dark elves being rounded up, so Kazin ran for the open door behind the long table. There was no doubt in his mind that was where the sick arch mages were hidden. He burst into the room, and stopped dead in his tracks.

Standing in the corner with his back to the wall was a lizardmage dressed in the robe of a dark elf. His hood was down. He glared across the room at Frosty. The unicorn stood guard in front of a number of cots which contained the prone figures of the dying arch mages and some master mages. A handful of clerics wearing robes which indicated their higher level of training stood next to their patients. Fear was in their eyes but they did not run.

Frosty looked at Kazin disdainfully. "It's about time you got here, Kazin."

"Kazin?" hissed Graf in surprise. "I thought you were poisoned and dead!"

"So did I," said Kazin. "I guess you underestimated me."

Graf growled. "It doesn't matter. Your people and land have been destroyed. As we speak, my minions march this way to lay waste to your villages, towns, and your precious tower." He nodded his head toward the patients. "Your mages won't stand a chance. They can't even stop a small group of dark elves from penetrating the tower. The armies that are coming are much more powerful. We have elementals at our disposal -."

"You mean had," interrupted Kazin.

"What?"

Vera, Della, Rebecca and Cyril appeared behind Kazin and observed the proceedings while Kazin spoke.

"You had elementals, and ogres, orcs, goblins, cyclops, and lizardmen at your disposal," said Kazin. "But they are no more. You are alone."

"Impossible!" shrieked Graf. "You are bluffing!"

Kazin shook his head. "No. But you won't live to find out for yourself."

Graf growled. "Unhand me!" He struggled with an unseen force and managed to yank the cloak from Alric's shoulders. Then Alric and Graf held each other immobile, neither willing to let the other go. They stared into each other's faces with undisguised hatred.

"You!" exclaimed Graf. "Have you come to clear your conscience?"

"I've come to rid the world of the likes of you!" growled Alric.

Graf laughed. "Nothing you do will ease your conscience of your involvement in my plan, elf! With the help of the cloak you stole, you poisoned the tower and set my plan in motion! I was able to test the poison and prove we were ready to begin preparations for our attack! I should thank you for helping me!"

Alric could hear no more. He struggled with the lizardmage, but Graf had a better grip. The lizardmage broke the elf's grip and threw him down. He grabbed his right hand with his left and looked down in surprise. "My ring! It's gone!"

"Are you looking for this?" asked Alric, holding the lizardmage's special ring. "You didn't think I'd let you get away with that trick twice, did you?" With his other hand, Alric threw his dagger at the surprised lizardmage.

The blade struck Graf in the chest. Graf hissed and then gurgled as his body sagged to the floor. He raised his hand to do one last spell but it never materialized. Then his hands relaxed and he dropped his staff to the floor. The top of the staff shimmered slightly and everyone recognized it right away. Protruding from the top of the staff was an orb.

Arch Mage Krendal suddenly pushed everyone aside. He reached down to remove the orb and held it aloft using a handkerchief. "An orb!" he exclaimed. "It's not a dragon orb, but it appears to be a powerful one nonetheless." He nodded his head. "That explains why he had the magical power to overcome our warding on the inner levels of the tower. The orb gave him that strength. I wonder how he obtained it."

Alric got to his feet unsteadily.

"You stole my cloak!" burst out Della in an accusing tone. "And you poisoned the mages in the tower! How could you?! You're an elf, not an assassin!"

"I thought you were our friend!" exclaimed Rebecca. She had tears in her eyes. "I trusted you! You betrayed us!"

Alric's shoulders sagged. All life seemed to drain from his body. His eyes were moist too, now that everyone he cared for knew he had betrayed them. His secret was out and no matter what he said they would hate him. If the mages in the tower wanted to put him to death for his involvement in the crime, yesterday wasn't soon enough.

"Why did you do it?" asked Kazin.

Alric shook his head sadly. His voice was barely audible when he spoke. "I didn't know." He sighed and pointed at Graf. "He knew my secret, and threatened to turn me in. At the time, I had no choice. I didn't know his plans. I didn't know. I'm sorry." He sagged back to the floor and wept.

While all this was going on, Vera was busy healing the arch mages, to the astonishment of the more experienced clerics in the room. All of the remaining arch mages began to awaken from their long slumber.

Arch Mage Fildamir yawned. "What's going on here?" he asked when he saw the strange group of people in the room.

"Fildamir!" exclaimed Krendal happily. He ran over to the old arch mage and pumped his hand joyfully. "It's good to have you back!"

Fildamir blinked. "I thought you were dead!" He shook his head. "Or am I dead now too?"

"You're quite alive," said a cleric near him, "although I'm not quite sure how." He looked at Vera and shrugged.

"Is that dwarven ale I smell?" asked Fildamir.

"It's the cure for what 'ales' ya," said Frosty.

The old arch mage raised his eyebrow at the unicorn's remark.

The captain of the guard of the elven king entered the room. He saw Alric's ring and approached the stricken elf. "The dark elves are in custody. We need you to go back to the king with us to explain the charges."

Alric looked up at the captain and blinked. "Huh? Oh!" He looked at Kazin. "We'll have to get Sawtooth. She'll know what to do next."

Kazin nodded. "Very well."

As Alric was led from the room by Kazin and the captain of the guard, Alric could feel the companions staring at him in hatred. He dared not look at Cyril. He was sure one glance at the cyclops' eye would result in permanent paralysis.

When they had passed, the others stayed behind.

Then Rebecca stomped her foot. "Aw, heck!" She turned and marched off after the disowned elf.

Vera, who was finished healing the arch mages, came up to Cyril and Della. She looked into Cyril's eye. "Coming?"

Cyril blinked but Vera was already on her way. Then he shrugged and followed the cleric.

Della retrieved her cloak, which still lay where the lizardmage had thrown it. She shook of the dust. Then she looked at the arch mages who were still groggy from their ordeal. Sighing impatiently, she followed the others.

Frosty whinnied. It was time for him to go outside for some fresh air. In a flash, he was gone.

Sawtooth was overwhelmed by the number of visitors she was receiving at her bedside. Alric had given back her ring and explained what had happened during the apprehension of the dark elves. He also mentioned the lizardmage who was dressed as one of them. At this Sawtooth was shocked.

"A lizardmage! But, how?"

Alric shrugged. "I'd say he was impersonating one of the high-ranking dark elves. He used the dark elves' hatred of human mages to advance his own agenda. He fooled me too." Then Alric mentioned how Graf had fooled him into poisoning the tower.

Sawtooth looked up at Alric with admiration. "But you fought back."

Alric shook his head sadly. "But not until it was too late. Do you know how many people have died because of me? Or how many could have died? Everyone who knows what I did would never forgive what I have done!"

"I would," said a voice behind the elf.

Alric turned to look at Rebecca. "You're just saying that to -."

"I mean it," interrupted Rebecca. She brushed her hand through the silver streak in her hair. "We've been through too much together for me to simply write you off. We've been traveling together long enough that I feel I'm qualified to be a good judge of your character. You stood up for what is right. You never took advantage of us, and, more importantly, you stuck with us until the end. That, in my opinion - or the opinion of any dwarf for that matter - is honourable. Many dwarves could learn from one such as you." The dwarf held out her hand.

Alric didn't know what to say. He shook the dwarf's hand and nodded in gratitude.

Then Cyril stepped forward. He looked at Alric's hand as he spoke. "Once, I did something terrible to someone who hated me. They somehow managed to forgive me despite what I had done. I thought I was better than him. Now I'm not so sure." He held out his hand. "You're alright, Alric."

Alric placed his tiny hand in the cyclops' large one. Cyril grasped it firmly and shook it.

"Stay on the true path, my friend," said Cyril.

Vera was tearful by now. She stepped forward and embraced the elf. "Oh, Alric!" She cried.

When Alric released the cleric, he was surprised to see Della standing in front of him. She held up the invisibility cloak.

"Here," she said. "Take it."

Alric stepped back and shook his head. "No! I can't do that. It's yours."

"Take it," insisted Della. She held it closer to Alric. "What you did was awful, but I think you will have to live with it for the rest of your life. That will be punishment enough. Maybe now you will learn to accept humans for what they are. We are all different, but we all want to live together in peace. Anyway, you saved my husband's life. I owe you for that. Take the cloak. You earned it."

Alric couldn't believe his ears. He let Della place the cloak in his arms.

Before she let go of the cloak, Della added, "But promise you won't use it to steal."

Alric flinched at this request but nodded. "O.K."

"Well," said Kazin, "It looks like your friends won't abandon you." He stepped forward and shook the stunned elf's hand. "I owe you my life. If you hadn't stolen the cloak, things would be different. Don't blame yourself too harshly. The lizardmage would have found others to do what he made you do. And even if he didn't, he would have poisoned the water despite your actions. People would have died regardless. In fact, your involvement in the defeat of the lizardmen may have been critical to our success. If you hadn't been in the right places in the right times, we could have lost the war. I could have died a number of times, and anything I have done to make a difference would not have taken place, from the creation of a cure to winning a war. Somehow things worked out better this way, even if you may not see it that way right now. If you are ever in need, you can find us - well - you know where we live." He winked.

Alric nodded.

Sawtooth got up out of bed. "In that case, we'll be going. There are a lot of loose ends to tie up back home. We have to restructure the Dark Magic Society so that it won't get out of hand again." She stuck her arm through Alric's. "You coming with us, Windoor?" Sawtooth waited while the captain of the guard and some of his elves led the injured dark elves from the room. They were all going back to the elven realm using the same magic that had transported them here. As they left, Sawtooth was heard saying, "So, Windoor, what do you think about becoming one of the new heads of the Dark Magic Society?"

"I love happy endings, don't you, Cyril?" asked Vera.

Cyril looked down into Vera's brown eyes. Suddenly he remembered to avoid his gaze. He looked away and groaned in despair. He had waited too long. He looked back down at the cleric expecting the worst.

Vera smiled up at him. "I've been working on my mental discipline. I can look you in the eye now, Cyril."

Cyril smiled.

× × × × ×

Lynch and Lyrr sat on the shore of Skull Island and examined the orb as it lay on the unfolded piece of cloth.

"I wonder how hard it is to control?" asked Lynch. "I'll wager you have to be good with magic."

"Graf's nephews and niece were too young to control it," agreed Lyrr.

"They say cracked dragon orbs have a different effect each time they are used," said Lynch.

"That's what I heard, too," said Lyrr.

Lynch looked at Lyrr. "Should I try?"

Lyrr shook his head. "I wouldn't. We should concentrate on selling it instead. Some merchants would give a fortune for one of these."

"Bah!" said Lynch. "I'll bet the thing isn't even any good anymore." He reached for it but Lyrr tried to stop him.

"No! Don't do it!"

But it was too late. The impulsive lizardmage had his hand on the orb. Lyrr tried to let go of Lynch's arm at the last second but it was too late.

A transformation took place then. The two lizardmages blurred into one. Their skin changed from the usual green hue to a drab grey. Leathery wings sprouted on their back and their feet became longer and grew claws. Their muscles bulged and their arms lengthened. Their hands became elongated and razor sharp claws protruded from their fingertips. The only thing that maintained their individuality was their separate heads.

Lynch's head grew stubbier, and his teeth hung out of the sides of his mouth in a kind of scowl. His ears became pointed and his eyes glared through slits.

Lyrr's head became longer and his teeth stuck out in a kind of grin. His ears became pointed like Lynch's but his eyes looked through narrower slits. He appeared to have laughing eyes rather than angry ones.

Their expressions were completely opposite one another. Lynch had the evil expression, while Lyrr had the happy one.

With a heinous shriek, followed by a horrendous laugh, the gargoyle took flight, heading north to the safety of the mountains.

x x x x x

Brind was almost on the opposite shore. He had given up hope that Graf would return. Undoubtedly something had gone wrong. He didn't care. Graf deserved what he got. If he didn't return within a week, it was time to seize power for himself. He was one of the most powerful lizardmages, and his fire magic was unequaled. He needed to carefully plan his coup.

Brind's planning didn't get very far. For no apparent reason, he found himself in the water. Somehow his raft had disappeared. It didn't sink - it shouldn't have because it was made of wood. It simply vanished! It was as if it had simply ceased to exist!

Brind had no time to concentrate on how it vanished. He had a more immediate problem. He couldn't swim.

Inherently, lizardmen couldn't swim like their cousins the skink warriors. Lizardmen preferred their homes deep within the safety of the mountains, while skink warriors - former lizardmen who were banished from the lizardmen's realm for not accepting magic - were confined to lives within the water. That way the two factions wouldn't clash.

All of Brind's spells were fire based, and none of them helped him stay afloat. Helplessly, he slid beneath the waves and disappeared from sight forever.

The disappearance of random things or parts of things stopped for a time, but a few months later, they resumed. Most of them went unnoticed - a rock here, a tree or shrub there. Nothing spectacular. But as things began to vanish more frequently, people started to notice them. When they tried to tell others about it, no one believed them because those things that vanished had never existed in the first place. Even those who had experienced the disappearance began to doubt themselves.

Years passed.

In time, even animals started to vanish. They ceased to exist, along with any descendants they would normally have produced. Then, people also began to vanish. No one seemed to notice or think about it. But some with magical ability started to sense something was amiss. The world was moving toward an uncertain future - a future that was being erased before it had a chance to happen . . .

Don't miss the other books in
The Dragon Mage Trilogy,

BOOK I:
RAZIN'S QUEST

BOOK III:
SPIRIT BLADE

Check out www.dragonmagetrilogy.com

About the Author

arey Scheppner is a first generation Canadian who grew up in a remote Ontario community. He was an avid reader of novels since he could read, and his favourite of these was fantasy novels. As an Electronics Engineering Technician graduate, he excelled in the  art of electronics. He tutored English and mathematics in college. Carey also went on to become a director of a board at a credit union and the treasurer of a church. Despite this, he still held a strong interest in fantasy novels and games. After reading a number of predictable novels, he decided to embark on writing his own fantasy novels. He wanted to ensure plenty of action and interesting characters to leave the reader thrilled with the unlimited possibilities of a fantasy world.

Carey enjoys the country lifestyle and enjoys fishing and hunting. It is a means of leaving the civilized world behind to breathe in the freshness of the country air. This leads to an unleashing of the imagination and the creation of strange new worlds...